HAWKE
MC SHIFTER ROMANCE
VERA FOXX

FOXX FANTASY PUBLISHING

No portion of this book may be reproduced in any form without written permission from the publisher or author, except as permitted by U.S. copyright law. This is a work of fiction. Names, characters, places, and incidents either are the product of the author's imagination or are used fictitiously. Any resemblance to actual persons, living or dead, events, or locales is entirely coincidental.

Copyright © 2023 by Vera Foxx

All rights reserved. No part of this book may be reproduced or used in any manner without written permission of the copyright owner except for the use of quotations in a book review. For more information, address: authorverafoxx.com

First paperback edition: Aug 2023

Book design by: Etheric Designs

Model: Golden Czermak

Publisher: **Foxx Fantasy Publishing LLC**

Editing by: Cissell Ink

CONTENTS

DEAR READERS

Please read the following trigger warnings and other important information regarding this book.

This book contains:

Dominate male.

Submissive female: This does not mean she is weak and fragile.

Sex Trafficking.

PTSD.

Blood, gore, torture.

Detailed consensual sex scenes.

Knotting.

Stalking.

Breeding Kink.

Primal Kinks.

Obsessive MMC.

Strong Language.

Memories of past rape, but written in passing. No details.

CHAPTER ONE

Delilah

The fabric of my slightly worn coat rustled as I tightened it around my neck. The weather was quickly turning from fall to winter. The wind surged around me, and my hair streamed out behind me, leaving my ears feeling exposed and cold.

The hair band squeezed my wrist tightly, but I wasn't about to take my hands from underneath the scarf to pull my hair away.

No, I would deal with the wind. It was only a four-block walk, anyway.

The bitter wind nipped at my ears as I looked into the darkness. The street lamps on this side of town didn't work so well, and the only light came from the bar across the street. A bar full of bikers I owed my life to.

I hopped over a slowly freezing puddle and laughed as I almost lost my balance. I was readying myself by finding the cheerful mindset of the person everyone perceived me to be.

Of course, I was happy. Why wouldn't I be? I was happy to be alive, to have a job, a home. I had two wonderful roommates, food in my belly, and a warm bed. There was nothing to be sad about.

No, not one thing.

But I was a greedy woman, and I knew exactly why I was having difficulty smiling all the time.

Once I gained my footing, I looked over my shoulder; I felt eyes on my back. My heart thumped in my chest, excitement filling my veins. His warmth seemed to radiate off his stare, and my cheeks heated as my lip curled.

But I bit my cheek, knowing what I needed to accomplish today. So, I continued on, passing rows upon rows of Harleys and speeders that sat in a perfect line. Their helmets, all displaying their names and ranks, sat on the back of the bikes.

My finger traced the grooves of the worn metal door handle. This was once an old, rundown tavern, but over the years, they had slowly renovated it. Locke and his crew had kept a lot of the original structure and character, such as the original thick wooden door and handle. The one thing that was different, however, was that it was expanded, making it large enough for their purposes.

But there were some things that Locke couldn't get rid of. It still had hanging moss in late summer that fell from the gutters. It gave the place a more welcoming look. Locke hated it, saying it wasn't a great look for a biker bar.

He didn't want it to look old and worn down like the rest of this side of town. There were still plenty of office fronts that were old, boarded up, and devoid of any life. But those few offices that were still in business, typically run by a club member, Locke made sure they lived up to *his* standards.

He wanted the buildings to look professional. To look like respectable businesses.

And moss did not make it look like a respectful business, apparently.

The Iron Fang bar stood tall at several stories high. They'd added the extra floors when they renovated it years ago. I remember going through my training and being told about the history of the place. It was only one story way back when, but since, it had exploded, and you could see the difference between the old and new structure. Large stones were cut and laid out in awkward positions, then when Locke added the building, he stuck with brick.

It had a rustic feel. The open, unfinished wood beams that held the place together made it that way. It was like inviting the past into the present with the fancy bar and lighting on one side while the band played on the other.

The bottom floor was meant for customers. The rest—who really knew what went on with the rest of the place—was for members only. I was just a server.

I was pushed forward by the icy wind, and the air was filled with the sounds of people laughing and talking. The wind wrapped around me, my hair blowing into my face until the door shut with a bang. I stepped to the right, seeing the extensive line of hooks for coats, jackets, bags, and a spare helmet or two.

The place was warm with all the bodies in the room. The way the bar and the tables were filled with customers, I knew I was in for a busy night and would warm up just fine.

"Hey there, Delilah," Anaki sang from far across the bar. He held a worn-out Guinness glass by the base.

The lettering on the etched glass was faded and scratched. He twirled it in his hand, his grip settling on the base, and tilted it to a perfect forty-five-degree angle. Anaki pulled the tap forward, letting the dark beer fill the glass. As the liquid rose, he straightened the dark liquid and left just a half inch of space at the top.

Once he set it down on the tray, I watched the surge settle and waited until the foamy froth rose to the top. "What's it like in New York City?" Anaki propped himself up on the bar, resting his chin on his fist.

His bright green eyes with flecks of gold glittered in the glow of the band's lights in the corner. His eyebrows rose, red flushing his cheeks as he took notice of others looking our way. "Because I'm a thousand miles away, but girl, tonight you look so…"

A large hand swatted Anaki on the head. Hawke glared at Anaki, but Hawke's eyes softened when they landed on me. He came out of nowhere from behind the bar.

Anaki tossed his strawberry blonde hair to the side, moving his body in a way more aggressive jerk than the smack could have created. He placed his hand over his heart, pushing his shirt tight up against his chest. He mock glared at Hawke with innocent eyes.

"I was just singin' to 'er. I must express mah love somehow!" Anaki cried in his thick Irish accent and put a cold bottle of water on the tray.

I snickered, knowing that Anaki was only flirting with me to get a rise out of Hawke. He did so every night, and I maybe flirted back just a little.

Hawke grunted and left the bar only to go sit with his *prez*, Locke. Hawke's eyes stayed pinned on me, but I wasn't about to give him the satisfaction of looking back.

"Hey, make me one of these." I pointed to the drink menu.

Anaki cocked his head in confusion, and I shooed him to make it.

It was made in a shot glass with a whirl of whipped cream on top. I stacked it on my tray next to the pint of beer. Anaki shook his head, throwing a towel over his shoulder.

I hoisted the tray on my shoulder, sashaying around the hordes of bikers to get to the middle of the room. I could waitress blindfolded. I knew exactly where every biker sat, how close they sat to the table, down to what their individual orders were. This drink, since it was just after nine, was due to be in someone's possession, just like every other night.

Bear lounged in his chair, contentedly rubbing his stomach after polishing off the three-pound burger. The grease from the overly fatty meat still lingered in several pools on his plate. There were no fillers in our burgers; everything was full of meat and fat. It made the fries taste even more delicious if they sat in the juices for a while.

"Your drink, Mr. Bear?" I winked and sat his large Guinness on the table, along with his water.

"I didn't order any water," he grumbled and took the cool glass of beer, opening up his throat.

He downed it in less than five seconds. My stomach lurched, thinking how heavy all that food must be sitting on his stomach.

I could barely eat a quarter pounder.

But he was a large man, and I guess he needed to keep up his strength. He was a brick wall, completely unmovable. He truly was a bear, the trunk of his body large yet firm. And hairy, so very *hairy.*

Once he finished, I pulled the shot glass from my tray and set it down on the table. The dark drink with the fluffy whipped cream sat there a long while as Bear stared at it.

"What's this?" He pointed, jutting his chin toward me.

"It's a bit of sweet dessert. You should try it. Maybe knock off some of that bitterness in that sweet teddy bear face I know you have under that beard."

Bear grumbled, pulling it toward him. I nodded, urging him to drink it.

"Is it poisoned?" he asked.

"If you think sugar is poison, then yes." I smiled. "Now go on."

Bear gripped the shot glass with two fingers and threw it back. He licked his lips, then ran his large hand over his beard. "Not bad. What is this called?"

I giggled. "Do you really want to know?"

The rest of the table leaned in and sat silently, waiting for Bear to finish his drink. Sizzle didn't look my way, but that wasn't unusual. Women made him nervous, or he hated me, one of the two.

"Yeah, what is it?"

"A blow job!" I chirped.

Bear began choking, the table broke out in a roar of laughter, slapping their hands on the table.

Bear grabbed the bottle of water, uncapped it, and began drinking right away. I laughed, picking up his glass and now empty plate so I could return them to the kitchen.

I'd been here almost exactly two years. I'd come to love these men like they were my own brothers. I'd figured out their favorite foods and drinks and knew their personalities like the back of my hand. They were stand-offish at first, but once they realized I meant no harm and wanted to see them smile at least once, they settled down.

They all needed a mother figure in their life, and I was happy to be it. I'd fuss over clothes, how they didn't clean up their feet before they walked in the door when it rained. If I was the one cleaning it up, then by golly, I was going to make sure they cleaned up their mess.

The door opened and a cold breeze followed it. Karma, who was always late to every party, strutted inside without wiping his feet. I glared in his direction, holding the tray in my hand. His face paled, and he stepped backwards to wipe his feet vigorously on the mat.

I nodded, smiling, and he waved back happily before he set off to his usual table.

What surprised these men the most was that I wasn't afraid of them. Most of the women that worked here were still jumpy, considering their backgrounds. Heck, I should be, but I wasn't. They save men and women from unfortunate situations. The Iron Fang weren't bad people at all, but how they rescued a lot of us wasn't necessarily legal.

The tattoos, the piercings, the playful banter, shoving, and the occasional punches to each other's faces—they were just big kids trying to work out their aggression.

"Hey there, Delilah!" Anaki sang from the bar again. He waved me over with his white rag, signaling that he needed some help. I took the tray, balancing it on one hand, and pushed it far above my head as I headed back through the crowd.

The club was bustling with not just MC members but other patrons, too. They come in here, trying to act like they were part of something great, but when in actuality, they were just supplying the club with more money.

They were charged a little more, not that they noticed. Club members ate for free as did those who they'd helped and who now worked here. That's how Locke designed it.

I could feel the heat of someone's gaze as I continued to battle through the crowd.

I set the tray at the end of the bar, still feeling the overwhelming uneasiness that bubbled in my stomach. Tonight was going to be different. I just had to be brave enough to let it happen.

"Did yah hear?" Anaki leaned over the table as if to tell me a big secret.

I briefly scanned the room, seeing if anyone needed me. But let's be honest, I was looking for *him.* But he wasn't anywhere.

"Hear what?" I playfully set my elbow on the bar and batted my lashes.

Anaki smirked, his bright white teeth glittering against the lights. "Grim has claimed Journey as his old lady, or mate, as they say in this club."

My bright smile didn't falter, nor did my eyes fog with unshed tears. Jealousy bubbled inside me. How dare me! How dare I envy what Grim and Journey had? I had it all. I was healthy, I had a job, I had...myself.

"That's amazing!" I almost cried, slapping my hand on the bar. "Journey is fine with this, right?" I quickly tempered my excitement.

Anaki smirked and nodded. "Yeah, she is. They're coming in tomorrow night to make the big announcement. You're working tomorrow, right?"

"Of course, I wouldn't miss it! It's so wonderful for them. Grim was having a hard time. Having a woman in his life will raise his spirits."

Grim was a rough soul. If there was anyone that rattled me, it was Grim. He had a feral look in his eyes at times. Like he was on the edge of something dangerous. I don't think he would ever purposely hurt someone he cared about, but his strength outmatched almost everyone else's in this bar.

"Hey, it's like marriage, you know. Calling someone your mate. I wonder if they'll have a ceremony or something? Or maybe they get matching tattoos?"

I hummed thoughtfully, putting the beer glass in the tub under the bar. Anaki fiddled with a few more glasses, organizing them in the order he liked. He was a particular fellow, a bit of OCDness if anything. He liked things in order, his rags, his glasses, and his cleaning supplies.

"Do you have anything for me to do?" I asked, changing the subject. Anaki was still going on about Grim and how the entire club was excited for the guy. And who wouldn't be? Grim was losing himself, and the few times I saw him since Journey came into his life, he was... Well, he looked alive. Not like he was going to kill someone.

"You're quiet, girl," Anaki said, loading more dirty dishes into the cart I pulled out from under the bar. Some servers were too lazy to take twenty steps back to the kitchen and would leave a mess on Anaki's bar.

He was not a fan of that.

"Just mentally checking some things off my list." I poked my temple with my index finger. "The girl on the last shift didn't clean up like you like."

Anaki growled, almost hissing.

I snorted, holding back a laugh, and he wagged his finger at me. "I'm not stupid, girly, you're changing the subject."

I smiled and hummed in agreement.

Yeah, I was changing the subject. But it was too embarrassing to speak out loud.

"But they left such a mess! Let's get this taken back." I pulled the cart, filled with dirty dishes, and backed away from Anaki. I pushed the swinging door open to the bar and backed my way into the next swinging door.

Other men who'd been rescued in similar situations and didn't have the heart to leave this place were flipping burgers, steaks, and making salads. I nodded, and they responded by waving their spatulas in acknowledgement.

"Delilah came to save the day!" one of them said, and I let out a bolt of laughter.

They hated doing dishes.

I wheeled the cart until I hit the back of the kitchen. The lights weren't the best back here, despite everywhere else in the kitchen. Maybe that was why everyone hated doing the dishes so much. They were just afraid of the dark.

But aren't we all really afraid of the dark?

I let out a huff, taking plate after plate and dumping the food scraps in the trash. Then I deposited them in the sink for a quick rinse before they went into the sanitizer.

My hands dipped into the sink, taking the sponge to scrape off the extra debris. The warmth soothed my cold hands, and I let out a small hum at how good it felt.

The same heat I'd felt many times tonight filled the side of my face. It grew more intense. My entire body was reacting to how powerful the heat was becoming. I let out slow breaths until someone behind me reached around and pulled my sudsy hands from the sink.

I was quickly turned and pushed up against one of the many metal shelves. Their hips pushed into my lower body, their erection settling on my stomach. My hands were pushed over my head while their other hand cupped my lower back to pull me into their body.

My eyes instantly closed, feeling the warmth, the longing of what I'd wanted for so long but could never have. The heat of their breath tickled down my neck while their nose followed quickly after it until it rested on my collarbone.

A low growl escaped their throat and my legs pressed together tightly as I waited to open my eyes once again.

"You've been ignoring me..."

CHAPTER TWO

Delilah

His smile broadened, revealing a set of brilliantly white teeth. His smile was so wide, the wrinkles around his eyes grew more pronounced. The radiance that emanated from his eyes was enough to make me smile again.

I could never stay angry at the biker who had somehow stolen my heart. He made life seem so much brighter than the shadows that he usually hid in. He was a man who rarely let anyone in, and I was happy to say I was slowly chipping away the cold, outer exterior he clung to so firmly.

But how long would it take? It's been almost two years of knowing the man, and I felt like I barely knew him. He didn't know me very well either, if I thought about it, but the attraction between us was undeniable.

Since the first time he'd put his arm around my wrist and led me away from a potential job and brought me to the Iron Fang, I knew I was in trouble. His warmth wiggled its way through my body and straight to my heart.

He put my brain into a fog. I couldn't think straight. Hawke was a walking red flag—everything your family and friends would have warned you to stay away from.

I was stupid, foolish. I knew that very well. I used to think I was a woman that could change a man just like in one of those silly romance stories that thought a bright smile could cure all.

At least I knew now that wasn't true. A smile doesn't cure anyone.

I should have known from the start. The way these men had seen darkness, not even the brightest light could penetrate the darkest of ashes covering them.

Why I thought I could be his light while his darkness hid me from my own demons, I would never know.

But that's just how life was. I broke the rules, I fell for the bad one, and now I was going to face the consequences because I was done. Hawke was the shady biker who'd given me no commitment to belong to each other. For all I knew, he could have slept with a woman every night after I returned to my apartment and went to sleep.

But I didn't want to think about that. While he was with me, I wanted to think he was mine, and I was his. I was weak in that regard. The taste of sin that I couldn't say no to. I couldn't help but long for his touch and crave his words of affirmation, claiming he cared for only me.

"Me? Ignore you? You're kinda big. You're hard to ignore." I playfully swatted Hawke's hard chest, feeling his nipple piercings beneath his shirt.

He wore his cut, his vest that had the MC's club logo on its back. On the front, his name was patched on the right side with wings spread over the name.

I stepped away from him, ignoring the urge to place my lips on his, and put my hands back in the water to finish my task. He trapped me though, and placed his body right behind me, his tanned arms resting on the sink. When I tried to move, he moved his nose near my neck, tracing it downward until he took in one large whiff at the nape.

"You always smell so good," he murmured into my shoulder.

I set the dish down; it splashed in the water before I twirled around with my wet hands. I tried not to smile, feigning annoyance, and wiped my hands on his shirt. "I didn't put on perfume," I said, my nose mere inches from his. I smirked at him. "You just smell the sweat of a hard-working woman."

"I know, and I like it that way. Never put any of that girly shit on. It messes up my nose." Hawke's thick fingers wrapped around my waist, and I giggled like a schoolgirl, wrapping my arms around his waist, too.

Despite being of average height, I felt so small compared to him. Hawke engulfed me, towered over me, and I didn't feel in the slightest bit scared about it. He was my protector, well, all our protectors of those who worked in the bar.

That was his primary job when he wasn't working for the MC; he was the bouncer for the bar.

"I really need you," Hawke muttered, his nose tracing my check. "I need to taste those lips."

His broken, raspy voice turned me into butter. The urgency to speak with him about concerns that had plagued me over the month faded away. My selfish side, my needy side wanted to give into this, but was that really being fair? To me?

Did I need another kiss? Another night of endless flirting and kissing? I hadn't even slept with the man, but I wanted him more than air.

"I need to talk to you," I whispered until he pushed his lips onto me. They were chapped from the cold, probably from taking too long of a bike ride in the blustery wind. He didn't seem to care because once he kissed me, letting out his whimper of a moan, I gave into his ministrations.

This was when I felt like he wanted me. Not just when he kissed me but when his voice cracked, and he spoke to me like no one else. Whispers of promises he had never kept, whimpers and purrs from his chest when he held me.

I felt my arms instinctively rise, and I tightly embraced him around his neck before passionately kissing him back. I took what he gave me because I was too far gone. I loved this broken man when I shouldn't. I was broken, too, and two broken pieces didn't make a whole. Especially if one piece doesn't want to fit.

After this kiss, he would go back to ignoring me. He would fall back into the shadows of his life, watching me from afar. He would go weeks without saying a word to me. Just watch me from either a darkened corner, across a lonely street or from the window outside my bedroom.

This was it, I told myself.

Hawke cupped the back of my head, making the kiss even harder to bear. His fingers found the hairband I had thrown my hair into and pulled it away. The band fell to the floor. His fingers tugged at the roots of my blonde hair. The sting was softened by his tongue entering my mouth, and a delighted whimper escaped me.

He pulled away, his eyes blazing with a hunger far brighter than I'd ever seen. My lips parted, waiting for him to speak, but instead he cleared his throat. The foggy haze that kept us both entranced with each other faded fast.

"I'm—" he began as he let go of me. I leaned back onto the large basin and touched my bruised lips. I could still feel the bristles of his beard on my upper lip, and the fresh peppermint schnapps still lingered on my tongue.

Before he could spout out *sorry*, like he normally did after such a kiss, I grabbed his shirt. I couldn't let him get away. He would not run from me ever again. He wasn't allowed. I was worth more than that.

I wasn't some woman he could kiss and leave, acting like nothing had happened, not anymore. He would not go weeks without speaking to me, only to come back and say he missed our friendship. To hell with friendship.

Friends don't kiss.

My heart couldn't take it.

"I need to talk to you," I said with more confidence than I felt. "Now."

The demand startled him. He tried to pull away again, but I gripped his shirt to the point of tearing. "What are we?" I hissed, feeling the venom leave my tongue. "And you can't run, Hawke. Not now, never again, until we have this conversation."

Hawke's stoic face returned; it was the usual demeanor he gave to everyone else. He was no longer playful after the sweet tango of flirting, followed by a regretful kiss.

"What are you talking about?" He pulled my hand away from his shirt.

I rolled my eyes. He cocked a brow in response.

I wasn't bratty, I wasn't mean, I was *little miss sunshine* to everyone. No one could hurt Delilah; Delilah was always happy.

Newsflash, *Delilah wasn't always happy.*

"What are we?" I softened my tone. "You talk to me, we flirt, you threaten people, we kiss, you run away. You always come back, and I let you." I bit back the tears. I would not cry in front of him. He wasn't worth it. No man was worth it.

But I was falling apart before he even answered because I knew what he was going to say. I could see it in my head. Hawke rehearsed it every day when he looked in the mirror to shave. He'd integrated it into every part of his being.

"We can't be more than friends." He gritted his teeth. "You know that, this job—"

"Friends don't kiss, not the way we do," I countered. "Not the way you hold–"

"Enough Delilah," he snapped. "We can't–" The vein in his neck pulsed.

His temper was rising, and he had never raised his voice to me.

"Can't what?" I said disappointedly. "Can't be together because of your job, your situation with the club?" I threw my hand out to show him the massive kitchen like he'd never seen it before. "I watched Journey and Grim. There can be more. Grim found happiness with that woman who was nearly a shell. Journey has grown in just a few weeks because they found happiness together!"

"Dede, stop," he hissed.

"Don't you see? We can have what they have. We can be a couple, be together, not be afraid—"

"Delilah!"

"No, you listen to me!" I stood into him, chest to chest. "I am not some toy; I am not someone to play around with. I've stayed far longer than any woman would have. I have devoted myself to you for almost two years. Wait, I take that back." I turned my back to him. "You have made sure no other man has come near me. Not that I would have accepted their advances."

Hawke's fingers balled up into a slow, tight fist. His veins protruded from his forearms. He growled at me, taking steps forward.

"I have stayed around, thinking, hoping..." I paused, touching the door frame. "Praying you would feel something more for me. Feel what I feel for you."

Hawke gritted his teeth, his perfectly chiseled jaw hid beneath his beard. "What's wrong with kissing every once in a while when we both enjoy it? Isn't that enough?"

"No," I snapped. "It isn't enough. None of it is enough. I need more, Hawke!"

"I'm not sleeping with you." Hawke stepped closer to me, but I took a few steps back.

God, why did that hurt so much? Not that I wasn't asking for it, that was beside the point. He didn't want to sleep with me, just fuck my mouth with his tongue. He was emotionally toying with me, and he didn't even know it.

"I want an *us*, Hawke," I murmured, fiddling with my dirty dishwater hands. "I want what Journey and Grim have." I was begging; I wanted him to take the bait. I wasn't supposed to be weak. I had come so far to be an independent person. I worked, I lived, I survived. But he made me want to fall to my knees and beg him to keep me.

Which I shouldn't. No woman should. Yet here I was, because of some unexplained pull.

These bikers didn't keep women. I've never seen the guys with their arms around any women's shoulders, their waists, or seen them kiss their lips. I thought it was a brother code to stay unattached because of the dangerous things they did behind closed doors. To keep loved ones away, to keep them safe.

But I was willing to take that chance. I needed to know if we would ever be anything.

When I saw Journey, I warned her what these men were like. They would never keep you, only make sure you were safe. They wouldn't give you any emotional support; they wouldn't claim you as theirs.

But Grim did. He surprised us all.

Grim was officially claiming Journey tomorrow, in front of the whole club, while I was the hidden dirty secret Hawke would never claim. As I came to that realization, I became more confident about what I needed to do, and what I needed to say, to push to get my answer.

Right now, Hawke was seething. If smoke could come out of his ears, I think it would. I had him trapped in a corner. He couldn't leave. He couldn't run away until I stepped aside.

I knew he wanted me. His erection strained against his pants, his heart raced, and his heavy breathing that would scare most of the people in the bar was stifling. But not to me, because I knew he wouldn't hurt me physically.

Emotionally?

"I need to leave," Hawke grunted, trying to push by me.

I did the unthinkable and pulled on his arm until my nails were embedded in his skin. I could hear the proverbial knives cutting his skin as he tried to slip by me. He growled, glancing at his arm and looking at me.

Good, he was in pain. Maybe he would know what it was like to feel something.

"Do you even care about me? Like at all? Do you not want to have what they have?" I pointed to the front of the bar. The kitchen was empty now; I could no longer hear anyone's presence.

"I care for your safety," he growled.

"And?" I prodded, coming closer. I put my hand on his forearm, and he pulled away like I'd burned him.

My heart burst into tiny pieces of tissue paper. Pieces that would never be able to be put back together again without seeing the tiny rips and crinkles on the surface.

"No, I do not care for you. Not like that," he said so low I barely heard.

"Not at all?" I whispered, still looking him in the eye. I would not break in front of him, not when he didn't care.

I wouldn't give him that last piece of me.

"You're too broken. You can't give me what I need, De. And this"—he waved his finger back and forth to us—"is officially over. Friends only. No more."

I pinched my lips together, watching his muscular heaving back head to the back door. He opened it, and a cold wind pushed inside.

"Hawke?" I yelled out before he stepped into the darkness.

He turned, but only so he could hear me.

"Are you seeing someone else?"

The thought that I was some side piece made me grip the counter. It barely held me up. My legs were weak, my heart was broken, and now I prayed he wouldn't piss on the mess of me.

Hawke refrained from responding; he rotated his head and ventured out into the pitch-black night.

CHAPTER THREE

Delilah

"Delilah?" My attention was suddenly pulled toward the cook, who was gripping a spatula in his hand.

He walked closer, eyeing the door that had just slammed shut. The sound echoed through the kitchen, reminding me where I was. There wasn't time for emotion or to process right now. The hollowness I felt in my chest had to wait.

"Everything okay?"

I cleared my throat and felt the tightness of my fake smile as I tried to appear happy. I smiled, bearing all my teeth, my hands shoved back into the water. "Of course, I was just finishing these up." I quickly threw the last of the plates in the dishwasher, not fumbling or being clumsy, which I could be when flustered.

Don't let your emotions show.

I slammed the dishwasher shut with one foot, pressing the button to start and swatted my hands to knock off the proverbial dirt. "There, all done. Do I have some food to serve? What time is it?" I glanced down at my watch. It was about time for Locke's dinner to be brought to his office. "Oh, Locke's dinner, I'll grab it."

Greg, or Gregory as I liked to call him, looked at me warily, but I patted his shoulder to pick up the plate of steak and potatoes, but lacking any vegetables. "Yup, for Locke, right?" I stared down at the plate, sniffing once more to hold back the tears.

Greg came up behind me, his height almost the same as mine. I could feel the heat of his breath on my neck. "Are you sure you're okay? You don't have to be okay all the time."

I chuckled, grabbing the plate. "Oh, Gregory, you are a sweet thing, aren't you?" I patted his cheek, not wanting any pity.

Because I had done this to myself, I knew what I was getting myself into when I fell into his trap. I was just the other girl, the one he toyed with for far too long.

Greg nodded, going back to flip a steak. He only seared the outside. These men liked their steaks almost completely raw. Remnants of blood seeped onto the grill as I gripped the plate full of food.

"Hey Delilah?"

I turned from the door way, raising a brow.

"You deserve better."

I bit my cheek to keep the corners of my lips from wobbling.

The night went on as if nothing had happened. I smiled, delivered food, drinks, and even got to request a song from the band, Moonlight Outcast. They groaned when I requested one of those upbeat pop songs from the early 2000s, but the leader gave me a wink and a gentle nudge as they played my favorite.

Of course, I brought them a few rounds of the best beer to soften them up a bit.

That made the night more bearable, putting a sway in my hips to forget *him*, just for a little while. Dancing through the crowd, watching the bikers roll their eyes as I pranced through the tables, but they secretly loved it.

I saw the smirks, the sparkle in their eyes that hadn't been there before. They were all changing, no longer the grumpy bikers. They were actually *feeling something*. It might be the rhythm of the ridiculous songs I liked to listen to or just that they were tired of being angry and grumpy all the time. But I could see it. I wanted to see more of this from the bikers who referred to themselves as a "family," giving me and countless others the feeling of security and warmth with their big smiles.

Just for a little while.

Anaki leapt over the bar, and his grip on my hand was firm as we spun around the dance floor. Any other night, it would get the bikers groaning, maybe even looking away. Not today. They were laughing and pointing, their bellies filled with not just alcohol but maybe hope?

Maybe some of them were happy for Grim. I heard his name echo several times through the tables. They were all...different. I couldn't put my finger on it, but I was happy for them.

Just too bad it hadn't changed Hawke. Or maybe I was never meant to be his.

By three a.m. the bar was closed. I swept, mopped, and cleaned for the next day. I waved my goodbyes to Anaki, the knot tying tighter in my stomach. He seemed extra close to me tonight, and it made me wonder if he knew. Did Greg say something? Did they all know? Was our conversation that loud?

I hooked arms with one lady I worked with. Savannah continued to banter about how one biker she has had a crush on for ages finally took notice of her. He had a lisp. He was a shy one—I believed his name was Surkash. Not many of the rescued knew about him, and I wanted to listen, but my ears had gone numb, like the rest of my body.

My autopilot was still working strong, but being able to concentrate on anything but work was difficult.

"And then he touched my hand. It was like warmth engulfed me," she muttered. "It's like love at first sight but by touching. His skin was cold, but when he lifted his hand off my arm I was warm, like all over." She leaned on my shoulder, sighing swoonfully.

"Yeah, is that right?" I tried to listen, but I couldn't. It was all too familiar.

I pulled out my keys and rattled them, opening the building so we could step inside. Our apartment building was a fortress. I was surprised Switch didn't put fingerprint locks on the doors as well.

"This is my stop," Savannah said. "I'm going to go have some spicy dreams now." She wiggled her fingers at me and opened the door, shutting it quickly. I heard the click and then I was left alone with my thoughts.

Which wasn't a good thing.

I trailed up two more flights of stairs, opening the door to my three-bedroom apartment which I shared with two other roommates. They didn't work at the bar. They worked in a cleaning business owned by Iron Fang. Locke made sure all the homes they cleaned were safe, which I think was another perk of working for the Iron Fang.

Locke was all about protection. He protected the survivors, the weak, the physically broken. But obviously, he couldn't protect us from everything, even his own men.

I let out a deep sigh as I carelessly tossed my keys on the counter.

Once I entered my room, I took the thick, heavy blackout curtains and closed them. An unusual thing to do, because I liked to leave them open and unlocked. Because I was a hopeless romantic, waiting for someone to come in and take me away from the nightmares.

And sometimes it happened. Hawke could get in anywhere. He would climb through that window and snuggle up next to me while I was supposed to be sleeping. I didn't know if he knew I was awake or not. I'd like to think he knew I loved his touch and wanted him there always.

But by morning, all I could hear was the sound of the wind blowing through the window, the coldness seeping into my skin because he was gone. No more warmth.

The only evidence of him ever being there was the faint scent of his peppermint schnapps and his musk.

My smile dropped, my finger fisting the curtain.

It wasn't time to cry, not just yet.

I reached under the bed, pulling out a large duffle bag. Inside was a burner phone I'd kept hidden, filled with the names of people from the bar that I could call if I got in a bind, such as Anaki or Bones. They didn't know I had their numbers, let alone my own phone, and it was better that way.

After staring at it for a long time, I shoved it back in the bag, then grabbed clothes I'd bought over the year. Some had never been worn, like those purchased from lightly used consignment stores. The clothes that I would often find hanging in my closet I had never bought; they just appeared out of nowhere with the change of the seasons.

I knew where they came from, and what I had once thought was a sweet gesture was now dirty to me. They were payment for stolen kisses. His apology for stringing me along.

I pulled them off the hangers, throwing them into the trash bin. Just like what he'd done to me.

Out with the old.

I stuffed the bag with the last bit of clothing, preferring to wait to pack toiletries and last-minute items, and zipped up the bag. As I threw it under the bed, I heard a thump at the window.

My heart raced, my blood rushing to my ears like turbulent, raging rapids.

My hands shook as I stepped quietly to the window. The last bit of hope of seeing Hawke on the other side fueled my curiosity. I gripped the thick curtain, ready to pull it open only to pause.

If I opened this window, I would be weak. I would let him in my heart once again, and I couldn't do that. I would not allow him to do that to me again.

So, I let go of the curtain, shaking my head, and backed away.

Not this time.

I turned on my heel, grabbing the diner apron that hung right beside the door. I was the pastry chef at a diner downtown that had nothing to do with the Iron Fang. And as far as I knew, no one knew about it.

I pulled it over my head, tying it around my waist, and I heard the tap at the window again.

I rolled my lips together, pushing the door to my bedroom open and left without another glance.

I stepped quietly down the stairs, my heart racing as I unlocked the door and peered outside. My window was on the other side of the building, but my feet betrayed me and carried me to the corner of the building nearest my window.

I laid my cheek on the cool brick, trying to calm my breath so I wouldn't be heard but also so as not to push out my hot breath into the night air.

Just one peek to see if he'd come for me, that's what I wanted to see. My heart was going to explode if I didn't find out, but what if he saw me? Would it give him hope that I would forgive him all over again?

I pushed my nails into my palm, feeling it almost pierce the skin.

No.

He gave me his answer.

I helped Anaki roll the last keg under the bar. There were six, and he was expecting a lot of drinking tonight. Grim and Journey were the guests of honors. I was more excited to see Journey. She had been the only woman I'd felt a connection to, to have a friendship with.

I mean sure, I was friends with the guys at the bar, but a female friendship was different.

Journey had been through more than any other person I knew, though. She had been used by sex traffickers, drugged, cut, and bruised. I couldn't imagine what she'd been through, so she very much deserved a man like Grim.

Despite his intimidating biker appearance, he had a kind and generous heart. I always knew he did; it was just hard to see beneath his own scars.

"Thanks, Delilah, that really helped." Anaki pulled a rag from his back pocket, wiping it over his face. Anaki was lean, but he was really strong. Lately, though, I'd noticed he'd been tired, maybe even weak. He couldn't pull as many kegs in as he used to, and that bothered me.

"Have you seen Bones lately?" I asked offhandedly, wiping the tops of the kegs.

He shook his head. "No, why would I need to?"

Anaki pulled glasses out from under the bar and set them on the worn tabletop. The door opened and more bikers came piling in. They were slapping each other on the back, shoving each other while Anaki filled their glasses.

"You don't seem yourself. I've noticed the past few weeks. You are...tired?"

Anaki and I finished filling the glasses, and we handed them out one by one. He sighed, leaning on the bar with his arms crossed.

"I'm more worried about you, Dede."

I scoffed. "What do you mean? I'm fine." I grabbed my tray, ready to make my rounds.

Bikes rumbled in the distance, and the band was already warming up. I stepped down off the step of the bar, rounding it until Anaki whistled to get my attention. It was so loud others around us looked up to see the commotion.

I chuckled, waving my head in his direction. "Come on, Anaki, we're celebrating Journey and Grim. I'm working with my best friends tonight. I've got nothing to complain about." I gave him a wink and pranced away, taking orders like I always did.

An hour later, Grim and Journey arrived. Once they settled, I picked up an empty pint and trotted over. If there was one person I was going to talk to before I left, it was her. No offense to my male friends, especially Anaki, but I knew he would be on Hawke's side. He was a member, a guy, and you know, bros before hoes and all that.

"So, how did you do it?" I asked. "All the women are dying to know how you bewitched the scariest one of them all!" I nudged her with my shoulder.

She blushed, heat rising up her neck. Her brown hair looked healthier, her once pale and gaunt face finally filling in. Journey was a beautiful woman, inside and out.

I glanced across the bar, my fingers wrapping around the tray. Three more pints of beer that I needed to deliver were set in front of me.

"It just sort of happened," Journey replied. "Grim knew what he wanted, and I guess he fought for it."

I gave her a warm smile. It was genuine for the first time in a long time. I'd worried that she would become a plaything like I'd been turned into, and I was happy it wasn't the case.

That big scary biker fought for her and didn't give a crap what anyone else thought. I admired that.

"I'm thrilled for you, Journey, I really am." I patted her hand. "And I'm sorry to tell you this, but I'll be leaving at the end of the night."

Journey frowned. "What? why?"

"I came into some money. You see, I've been working at a diner early in the mornings across town as a pastry chef and server. I've scrimped up enough to leave, and I'm going to do it."

Seven days a week, every morning from three a.m. to eight a.m. I made pastries, pies, and homemade bread. I didn't get tips, but the owner was so impressed with my work he paid me a bonus, and I had just enough for a one-way ticket out of here.

"But why? You said you were going to stay longer," Journey asked, visibly upset.

I shook my head. "I can't stay here anymore. Hurts too much. I'm gonna miss you, though. I think you are the first girlfriend I've had that felt real, even if it was for a short time. But I promise I'll write to you," I blurted.

"I'll write to you as soon as I settle down, but I need you to promise me something."

"Anything." Journey's eyes widened, leaning forward.

I was telling her too much about my departure, but I felt like she should know. She didn't have any close friends, just like me. But I felt a connection to her I'd never felt. It was like she was, *on my side.*

"Don't tell Hawke." I narrowed my eyes at her. "He can't know, or he'll stop me. I'm not even doing this as a game anymore to get him to come after me. I'm really done." My eyes pricked with tears, but I blinked to push them away.

Not yet.

"He'll come find you," Journey retorted. "I know he will."

"I doubt that. He made it very clear last night that nothing would happen between us."

She scowled.

"And I'm not wasting my life any longer. I deserve better, want more, and if he isn't willing to give it, then it's time I leave. Otherwise, I'll be stuck here and never get out." I could feel my lashes dampen.

But Journey didn't judge. She just laid her hand on mine, and I gave the best smile I could. With each passing moment it was getting harder and harder. And it only made it worse when I would see *him* peering at me in the corner.

I pulled the tray away from the bar, taking the last three pints of beer to the far end of the room. I set them down, feeling the cool condensation on my hand when Locke banged on the bar to get everyone's attention. The bar went quiet while me and several other servers finished picking up random glasses to bring back to the kitchen.

"Members to the church, we've got business to attend to," Locke shouted. Chairs scraped against the concrete floor. The harshness of the noise made me wince.

My perfectly neat hair bun was falling, the strings of hair irritating my eyes. At least, that was what I was telling myself instead of letting the tears fall.

"You alright, Delilah?"

I jumped, putting my hand over my chest. These guys could be sneaky, and normally I was prepared, but my mind was elsewhere.

"Delilah?" I wiped the sweat from my brow and saw Bone's eyes soften. "Are you okay?"

I nodded, giving him a wide smile. "Of course! Just a long night. You all know how to party." I wiped the table down with the now dirty rag from my apron and tossed it over my shoulder. "Shouldn't you be heading to the meeting?"

Bones eyed me up and down skeptically, then stepped forward to put a hand on my shoulder. "You know you can talk to me, right?" He lowered his voice. "That I'm here not just for the club, but for your well-being, too?"

As sentimental and doctorly as he was, we both knew who he really worked for. Locke and Hawke were both his best friends. I couldn't tell him anything because I needed to get away from his friend.

Hawke may have spat out those words of indifference like I didn't matter, but I knew he cared about my safety. Running off to another town, he would have thrown a fit saying my safety couldn't be guaranteed there, and that I needed to stay.

But I was running from my protector now.

"I'm fine," I said, pulling the tray up on my shoulder. "More than fine, actually. Tips have been pretty good this week. Might go shopping downtown for a new dress." Bones eyed me suspiciously. "Go on, now. You'll be late for your meeting. I'm sure Locke gets grumpy when you're late."

Bones looked carefully at the door and then back at me with a questioning look. My overwhelming urge to hug him was too strong to ignore, so I wrapped my arms around his waist, and he stumbled.

"Thank you." I took in his scent. At first, he didn't know what to do. His arms were wide as he stared down at me. "You can hug me, you know. You are like the dad I never had." Bones let out a bark of laughter and wrapped his arms around me.

"You've really made this place a lot happier since working here. Some of the stuff you do and say to get these guys to smile is comical. I just want to know you're happy, too."

I moved so the side of my face rested on his chest. His hand rubbed up and down my back, like he had done it all his life. But that's what he was, a comforter. The doctor with no degree to his name.

"I am," I lied. "Now that I've got my hug, you're set for a while. Now get out and don't make a mess on your way." I flicked the towel at his butt, leaving a sharp sting. He yelped, rubbing his butt and strode out the door, laughing.

I was going to pick up the tray once again, but a hand whipped out of nowhere and slapped the tray upwards. The glasses went airborne and smashed to the floor with a loud shatter. My head jerked to the offender. His eyes were dark, and his face was gaunt.

"What the hell was that?" He pointed to the door that was left slightly ajar. I could feel the cold trying to sweep into the bar, but thankfully the now absent bodies had left their warmth.

"What was what?" I defended, holding the towel in my hand.

"Don't claim innocence, Dede. Why the hell did you hug him?" Hawke growled.

He continued to walk toward me, his breath heaving with the smell of peppermint schnapps and whisky. He's been drinking, and a lot from the smell of it. It was not a good combination when he started drinking multiple liqueurs.

"Because he's my friend. He was asking how I was," I stated, lowering myself to the floor to pick up the glass. But I didn't get very far because Hawke grabbed my arm and pulled me back to standing. "What–?"

"You are going to hurt yourself. Don't pick that up," he snapped.

"Well, if you didn't knock it over, I wouldn't have this problem." I narrowed my eyes at him, and he let my arm go.

The warmth from his touch didn't fade, and I contemplated cutting off my arm, so I didn't have to feel it linger on my skin.

Hawke's face changed to an intense scowl as his dark eyebrows drew downward. His usual neat mohawk was in disarray, his cut not clean like it typically was. "I worry about your safety."

"Ha!" I grabbed the tray, shielding myself. "If you cared about my safety, you wouldn't have led me on for the past two years. But men are usually only thinking about the physical, right? Not the mentality of a person."

"Dede," he growled.

"It's fine, Hawke. I get it. Take what you want, don't think about the consequences. And you are damn right. I am glad I never slept with you. Otherwise, I'd go pop the tires on your precious bike or maybe leave a snake in your bed. But nope, just a kiss. Kisses mean nothing, you know?" I winked and put my tray on the bar.

The rest of those cleaning had scattered when the beer glasses fell. But I could feel their heated bodies on the other side of the kitchen door, listening, waiting. They would all see that whatever this was between Hawke and me was over. They would all draw their own conclusions about why I left, but by the fates of the universe, it wouldn't be because I was weak or a coward. It was because I would not put up with being trampled on.

"What do you want, Hawke? I've got to clean up."

Hawke followed me to the bar. I waited, leaning up against it. The heavy scent that still lingered on my pillow at night appeared. It almost brought me back into the fog, but my heart no longer beat for him. Not when he rejected me.

"I wanted to make sure you were alright," he whispered. "I didn't mean... It's just that things are complicated, Dede. Shit about me, that you don't know about it prevents me–"

From ever being happy?

"I'm great." I turned to him, giving him the brightest smile. "If friendship is what you want, you've got it. I just need a little space, you know? Just to do a bit of a reset on my end, alright?"

Hawke's eyes softened, and he stuffed his hands in his pockets. "Alright, if you need anything–"

"I'll let you know." I nodded and pushed the door to the kitchen open, leaving Hawke where he needed to be.

Away from me and my heart.

CHAPTER FOUR

Hawke

Delilah rotated her head in amusement, her smirk becoming more visible as she pushed the kitchen door open. The leering eyes on the other side quickly darted away from the door. The servers were washing damned imaginary dirt from the walls.

Letting out a growl, I swung my arm across the bar and the sound of shattering glass filled the air as I watched the clean glasses break on the floor. My breathing was heavy, my fucking wolf trying to press through the window of my mind.

I had no reason to continue behaving in this way, as I had already achieved what I wanted.

To keep her safe.

Delilah was just a *friend*. But that was not how everyone saw us as. They saw us as *complicated*. And whose fault was that? When drunk, my wolf seemed to have a mind of his own and dousing his cock in the slick heat of this female was his goal.

The reason she stood out was because she possessed qualities and traits that we did not have—a forgiving spirit, faithful beyond measure, and a heart made of the purest gold.

I was not worthy of Delilah, and I now understood that I was not the one she deserved. She deserved something much more than what this place had to offer.

I could feel my wolf scratching, eager to be released from within me. I could almost feel the blood drip down the walls on the side of my head. He had become more vocal, along with the rest of the clubs' animals. Either it all meant we were going to be dead and buried soon, or there was fucking shifter flu going around.

When the kitchen door opened again, I felt a rush of anticipation as I waited to see if it was Delilah. To see her pitiful face, to look into her blue eyes once more. My heart leaped forward, ready for her to yell, to scream at me. Show an emotion that was truer than the lies she spread on her face each day.

I wanted her to call me an idiot, a beast of the heart, but it never came from her.

Instead of seeing Delilah, it was Anaki. The slender dragon cautiously flicked his tongue out of his thin lips, taking in the faint smell of smoke in the air from cigarettes and cigars. "Smells like shit out here." He narrowed his eyes. They flashed a brilliant yellow before fading once again. "Oh, it's just you."

With a snarl I stomped closer to the bar, but Anaki stood his ground by crossing his arms and lifting his shoulders to make himself look bigger than me. And he was. He was a fucking dragon, but he didn't scare me. I wasn't fucking scared of anything. Bring me death, bring me peace, bring me the fucking river Stix. I was ready to swim.

Free me from this fucking pain in my heart.

"You want to go?" I nodded my head to the door, the glass beneath my feet crunched beneath the rubber sole of my boot, the high-pitched clinking making my ears twitch.

Anaki rolled his eyes. "I could lower myself to your level, but I don't enjoy being on my knees as much as you do."

This fucker.

I jumped on top of the bar, but he was already out the door, flipping the bird. "Stop being an ass to her. Everyone hates you!" Anaki sang in that stupid sing-song voice he liked to sing to Delilah in.

And she fucking liked it. She smiled at him. He smiled back. He didn't hide his affection toward her, and yet she ignored his sweet advances and came to me. She let me kiss her, let me be around her despite being an asshole.

Mine.

I pulled out my gun and felt the familiar ridges of the grip against my palm. It calmed me enough to jump down from the bar as I fiddled with it. I ran my calloused fingers over the rough grooves. I could barely feel the roughness, but despite all that, having the power in my hand calmed me.

Delilah wasn't mine and could never be.

And I was too big of a bastard to let anyone else have her, either.

The world looked so black and white to an outsider. They saw me as an asshole. They saw me using her, taking what she gave me so willingly because she was a selfless soul. And hell, she was selfless. And then I took it like the evil villain I'd become.

I took every stolen moment I could and pretended we met somewhere else, another time, another place, another realm. A time when the Goddess should have given Delilah to me, so that we could be together instead of living in an alternate reality where Delilah dangled in front of me, her soul hanging on a string, standing on the other side of a veil where she was too far from reach.

The Goddess was torturing me. *You can't have her. You already lost your chance.*

The club could only see the surface of what Delilah and I had. What they didn't know was how much I fucking loved her. How I would die for her, give up my soul for her, protect her with my last breath.

She wanted me as much as I wanted her, but I couldn't. I could not let that happen. How could I create a life with her when I wasn't sure how long I would live for? Not with a wolf going feral, rabid. It could be days from now or years. I would not put her through that. I would not get her hopes up for a happily ever after because there was none.

I was dealt the wrong hand. My cards weren't a royal flush. I was the joker, the reject, I was just surprised a woman like her looked my way.

A life with me wasn't fair to her. Delilah needed to find someone else to love and care for. Someone she deserved, some damned human that could take her away from the dangers of this world I'd brought her into.

But I had to go and spit with venom that she was too broken to have. Whatever she was running from in her past was too much for me to handle. She was too much to handle. The mask of indifference I gave to her last night when I said I didn't want her...

It broke her.

I broke the sun.

She fucking hates me now, but I do things with the best intentions.

I nodded to myself. This was how it had to be.

This had to happen and now that we were just *friends,* I was going to have to let her go. No more drinking, no more letting my wolf take over to steal her.

No matter how good she tasted, or felt in my arms, or how right every-thing seemed. Because it could never be.

She ran around the bar like some kind of magical sprite, and I'd never deserved such a bright and beautiful ball of sunshine. She talked to the roughest looking fuckers trying to get them to laugh or smile like it was her damned mission.

I had a strange mixture of loving and loathing for that trait of hers.

She saw no fear; she saw the good in everyone, and that was where she'd messed up. Because she had her sights set on me, and I had nothing to give her. I had nothing good about me. None of the members at this club did.

But she was broken, too. I could see it. She had secrets as deep as mine she had yet to spill. And yeah, I was an ass. I used it against her, telling her I didn't need any of her drama when she clearly kept it hidden.

I snatched my leather jacket from the hook and left the havoc of my actions in my wake. I rolled my eyes, feeling the phone buzz in my pocket and I turned it on to see Anaki had already sent a message to the crew in the back that I had left the building, and it was safe to come out.

Asshole.

Along with those words, Delilah was given strict orders not to pick up the glass.

Anaki was walking a thin line. Hell, they all were. Why the hell would Delilah give Bones a hug? She didn't give hugs willingly. She was only allowed to give me hugs.

Only me.

Was she going after another male? So quickly?

I felt a rumble in my throat, but I suppressed it by biting down on my tongue, as I made my way into the church. The upside down cross creaked in the wind as I entered, and before I could reach the sanctuary, men were already filing out.

Short ass meeting.

I watched as they all left, grumbling to themselves about the Goddess and second chances. Some seemed happy, rubbing their hands together and smiling at one another.

"A second chance. You really think that's what Grim and Journey have?"

a young pup asked.

"Don't see why not," another said. "She's got a mark on her shoulder, doesn't she?"

Ah, this was the meeting about Grim and Journey's theories as to why they believed they were second-chance mates. Locke had already spoken to me about it. He was completely against the idea since we didn't know if it was true.

You can't get the club's hopes up when there was no hope to be had. Miracles didn't happen for us; they didn't happen to anyone that had been cast out of their pack, their pride, and their families. We had done all that we could do, our graves were prepared, all that remained was when we would fill them.

This could all be black magic that some fae placed on Journey. No offense to her, but her memory of her time spent with the fae was fading. She could have had a spell cast on her, making it seem like she was a second-chance mate.

"Bullshit," Bear grumbled as he walked past me, handing me a full cup of coffee. "Sober up," he ordered gruffly.

I was taken aback as the big bear gave me a long, hard stare before stomping out the door and bellowing that he was going to take a shower. I couldn't help but smirk when I heard the collective groans from the members.

No one wanted to wash while Bear was using the communal shower. He made everyone utterly uncomfortable about his size. He wasn't just tall and built like a damn thick magical tree, but he was well larger than your average bear shifter.

I shivered, walking toward the front of the church.

Bones was inspecting Journey, listening for any signs of pain in her breathing. Her ears were dripping with blood. I furrowed my brows as I rubbed my hand over my beard, the sound of her symptoms muffled in my head. Loud noises? Heightened smell?

We both had a moment when our eyes met, however, we both decided to move on. There can't possibly be a connection between a human and a shifter. It was unheard of, damn near blasphemous in our world. Hell, if the council found out that there was a shifter and human pairing, our entire operation could be shut down.

We would all have to split up and hide, instead of being with each other in our broken pack.

We'd go rabid sooner rather than later.

But Grim didn't seem to care about any of that, disregarding everyone in the club. Sure, he wanted his female; he wanted a mate to save himself, but what about the rest of us? The brothers and sisters that just wanted to live in peace and try to find some sort of retribution before we turned to ashes?

Didn't matter, not where Grim was concerned.

His mannerisms and attitude were certainly not the norm. He'd fucking smiled earlier; he didn't glare at anyone for looking at him funny. No, he only glared when someone looked at his *mate* for too long.

My whole body tensed, and my fingers trembled, wishing desperately to take hold of my gun. All of this was wrong. Something was different, and I couldn't put my finger on it.

It could be Delilah and the raging guilt stirring inside me. She didn't even leave her window unlocked last night, and she always left it unlocked.

But why would she? You told her she wasn't worth anything to you.

Then I didn't answer her question about if there was another woman. Dammit, I was cruel.

But it was for her to forget me. And it was working. She'd shut me out so I couldn't get in. Delilah was being a good girl as she should be. She wasn't putting up with my shit anymore, and I needed that. I needed her to never forgive me.

I ground my teeth together as my fingers moved up the length of the exposed holster. The room was becoming smaller; the darkness closing in. My wolf was howling, my body restless as I waited for whatever the hell these men were doing, crowded around the helpless human.

I eyed the door. My mind was a fucking mess. I needed to make sure Delilah got home okay. That would settle my wolf; it would settle me. I would just be in the shadows. She would never see me.

A vibration buzzed in my pocket. It was Beretta. She'd sent a group text message alerting everyone at the front of the church. We all pulled out our phones to check.

They are ready to talk.

I tightly pressed my lips together before taking a deep sip of coffee. The black, bitter taste settled me just enough to announce it was time for Grim to take care of our intruder problem from a week ago.

The mayor and his band of goons from the next town over had a death wish, walking into our club. He actually thought he would get away with his idle threats, but he didn't know what type of animals we were.

Once it was announced, Journey looked up at Grim who relayed the message to her, her brown eyes blinking happily as she hugged his arm. "Go kick their ass, Grim."

I had to smirk at that. The tiny thing may have tamed the out-of-control enforcer, but after she let him loose, there was going to be blood.

Grim eyed her. His unease was strong enough for the entire room to feel it. I coughed lightly to gain the attention of those around me, signaling my readiness to provide my services to protect his mate so I could keep my mind off what would never be mine.

"I can walk her home." I stepped up, holding the coffee in my hand. With one final swirl, I guzzled it, savoring the sensation of the burning liquid as it slid down my throat. "I'll stand outside her door."

Sure, I'll be the babysitter so you can go have your fun. Gut the bastards while everyone else watches.

Locke shook his head. He knew what I was thinking. Same as him, most likely, that this supposed mate bond was too good to be true. Grim's gaze was so intense that it felt like it was being held together by an unseen force.

And it made me fucking jealous, but not jealous enough to hurt my Delilah.

CHAPTER FIVE

Hawke

I quickly disposed of my cup in a nearby trash can, and Journey separated herself from the rest of the group. They had their own shit to deal with, and watching Grim dismember a bunch of assholes wasn't on my agenda. My mind was on Delilah and getting this female home.

Once Journey was inside, I could check the security cameras, see if Delilah made it home and stayed there. Otherwise, I was going to have to climb the fire exit and– No. I can't do that anymore. I have to stay away from her.

The icy wind brushed over us. Journey was wearing Grim's jacket; she was so tiny, it swallowed her whole. But hell, all the females were tiny. They were physically weak, but some of the shit they'd gone through before we found them strengthened them in their own ways.

I was genuinely surprised to see how quickly Journey could progress on her own journey to healing. She was raped and put on computer screens forcibly to sell her body. Yet here she was, staring a bunch of ugly bastards in the face, not showing a care in the world.

She damn near glowed when she was near Grim, and an ugly knot of jealousy formed in my gut. I wanted that, but did I want it enough to hurt who I cared about?

"Do you think Delilah is your mate?" Journey blurted out of nowhere.

I stopped in my tracks, backing away like she'd burned me. How fucking dare she ask me such a thing? Mates were sacred, but I guess she wouldn't understand that.

She was human.

Journey shouldn't know anything about mates, the bond and shit. But Grim had already ingrained in Journey that she was his mate, just like he told everyone else tonight.

But I didn't believe it.

"Why would you ask such a thing?" I pushed by her with my shoulder, causing her to stumble.

I knew I was being an ass, but I was already in a shit mood. I wanted Delilah to be my mate, but there was no way. So, I stomped like a petulant child down the sidewalk while I waited for Journey to follow.

"Hawke!" Journey yelled. She slipped at the same time and fell on her ass.

I rolled my eyes, both finding it humorous, yet worrisome, because Grim would kick my ass if he found a bruise on his woman. I stalked over, eyeing her darkly and pulling her up by her biceps.

"Considering all you guys are big, bulky men, you sure act like a bunch of pussies," Journey snapped.

"Excuse me?" I asked, surprised.

"Yeah, you heard me!" Journey puffed out her chest. "You act like a bunch of pussies. You guys hold grudges worse than a woman. You don't believe in anything Grim told everyone in that meeting, do you?"

The way the woman glared at me like I was to be moved by such an announcement made me chuckle darkly.

"Of course I don't. Why would the goddess listen to a human? It was just a coincidence that you guys are mates, that you *prayed.*" I put my fingers up in air quotes. "Trust me, we are all thrilled for you both. Grim's my brother." I paused, realizing the light had turned green so we could cross the street.

Was I beginning to accept the idea that Grim and Journey were mates? Maybe, possibly, but it was only through sheer luck it was true. If they were mates, it was by coincidence, if they even were.

Journey claimed she prayed years ago to the moon to find someone to love her, to save and protect her. She didn't pray to the goddess; she prayed for something imaginary she didn't believe in.

"Why don't you think so? Why is it so unbelievable that the Goddess wouldn't come to help me?" Journey asked.

I stopped again once we reached the other side of the street. "Because the goddess doesn't come a runnin' when one of her children is hurt. She leaves them and lets them rot. Her children can only depend on themselves to climb out of the hole they find themselves in."

I pulled on her arm and tugged her along the street. We went to the back of Sizzle and Grim's tattoo shop, and I unlocked the door so we could climb the stairs to the apartments.

As I approached their apartment, I found the door heavily scented. I knew Grim could scent, that he had control over the ability since the first day Journey came to us. But hell, it was pungent. It was a mating smell, one that I quickly recognized from when I lived with my parents all those years ago.

It held Grim's musk, but it was also tainted with another smell. A smell that reminded me of a small pup before their transition. It was so faint, I nearly didn't smell it.

My nose was my strongest ability—a guard and a tracker was what I'd been in my past life—and being able to smell... This scent meant that my own abilities were breaking through.

What the hell was going on with me?

And what was up with the pup smell?

"He's scented the entire door and everything inside. I won't be able to follow you in. I'll remain here and wait for his return." I gripped the handle of my gun.

Journey stood by the door, pausing before going in. I lifted a brow, ready for another blunt question, and it wasn't long before she replied.

"You didn't answer my question," she said, crossing her arms.

I scoffed. "Little human, you shouldn't put your nose in another shifter's business. Now prance on in there and wait for your *mate* before he has my head, because I didn't follow through with my orders."

Because now, I was starting to believe it. That they really were mated.

"No, I will not." She stuck her finger out at me. "From what I gathered, you both are mates, whether or not you tell me. You look at each other, you secretly sniff her hair, and god knows how many times I've seen you look at her ass when she walks by you."

I felt heat rise to my cheeks.

"She looks at you like you hung the moon each time you walk into the bar. And shit, you do the same when she hands you a pint of beer. There's something there, I see it. And I would bet my left tit you're both mates, but you don't have the balls to pray to the goddess for your second chance. And when I bet my left tit, that means a lot because Grim likes that one!"

I was taken aback, and my mouth hung open in disbelief.

Despite her size, it was clear that this petite human and her voice should not be underestimated. She was an observer, a quiet observer, and I had to give her credit. She was smarter than she looked. Sneaky little shit.

"Do you kiss him with that mouth?" I smirked.

"It does a lot more than kissin'. Now spit it out, or you'll be making a grave mistake that'll haunt you for the rest of your days."

I didn't know if she was my mate. Or just a powerful attraction or yearning for what I'd always wanted.

I rolled my eyes. "I'll tell Grim to keep you out of the bar. Your language is atrocious."

Her expression was filled with intense hostility as she glared.

I pinched the bridge of my nose, my back hitting the wall. "I don't know if she's my mate or not, Journey. I care about her, but the life I live, what we all live, is complicated."

What if she wasn't my mate? What if I claimed her, and she died? What if I went rabid before then?

"I'm in more danger than most. I'm on the front line. Grim may be the tormentor, the punisher, the bringer of death, but I'm there first. I've always been that way, taking preventative actions before my brothers and sisters go into the fire. A life with me is not a happy one. What if I died?"

"But what if you live?" she asked.

My heart ached, and my head moved side to side in sorrow, unable to process my feelings. I didn't need to talk to her about this, not to anyone.

"What if you live once you have her, Hawke? You're breaking her heart by not being a part of her life. Isn't that what a bond is about? Being together? Trusting it?"

Yeah, look where that got me. Made me a rogue, lost my pack, my family.

"I lost my trust in the bond a long time ago. No matter the status I have, no matter what I can offer, I'm not enough. I'm not enough to give her what she wants."

"Then give her what she needs!" Journey shouted. "It isn't about wanting; it's about needing. You will die without her, and whether or not you think so, she will die without you. For humans, the bond thingy, it isn't strong at first, but once you are connected, it's...euphoric."

I gripped the handle of my gun. Journey talked like she knew this bond, and she described it so perfectly, but Grim could have told her all that. That this was what she should be feeling, and she got sucked into his words.

"She will find another human, one that isn't involved in this world." I gritted my teeth.

Her eyes glistened with tears. "You know, you're right."

"I am?" I asked, pushing off against the wall.

"Yeah, let her go find someone else to take care of her. Love her, cherish her, kiss her. Have endless nights of passionate love with her, touch her in ways you're too scared to."

A growl of rage ripped from my throat as I punched the wall beside the door, the sound echoing through the room.

How dare she.

Did she not know how painful it was to lose a mate? To feel a bond break?

Your soul breaks into pieces, then tries to heal itself. And when it does, it tries to fix itself, but a soul is a delicate thing to fix. The pieces don't fit back correctly; the parts don't match up. Then your soul has missing parts, holes need to be filled and there is no way you will ever fill whole again because your bonded mate has ruined you for anyone else.

Your body rejected you, and your animal has now settled with the idea we will be alone—forever. There was nothing that could be done to save us now. Animals go crazy, mad with fear, panic, and rage that our soulmate, which was destined to be ours by the Moon Goddess's pairing, rejected us.

They wanted someone else, not you.

Because you weren't perfect enough. You weren't strong, fast, handsome, or capable enough to take care of them. To put them in your nest, to have them scream in pleasure beneath you, to keep them safe from all forms of danger was not what they wanted from you.

No, instead they laid with another, bonded themselves to another animal while you were left to rot.

Your ex-mate would live on, connected to another soul. They wouldn't feel the pain in their body every day from an incomplete bond.

Mine and everyone in the club's souls were shattered. Broken because there was not another soul that could fix it unless a fucking miracle happened.

Journey snickered, not able to feel the emotions rushing through me like a torrent of wind and fire.

"I know you're mates. The goddess needs one of you to believe in her. Do you think Delilah will pray to a big rock in the sky when humans have their own gods to worship? It's time to eat crow, Hawke. The goddess is trying to make it right."

Journey shut the door with a click.

I curled my fingers into a fist in my pocket, pulling out my phone, only for it to drop to the floor. I swore, banging my fist into the brick wall until cuts appeared. Blood dripped down my hand, and I lowered myself to retrieve the goddamn piece of shit phone.

I tapped it, revealing the screen and immediately went to the security system app Switch had installed. I fingered over the app, only to find my claws elongated. It scratched the screen and I let out a loud, "FUCK!"

I gazed at them in amazement. It had been a while since I could pull them out of my body. They were sharp, black, and in good working condition.

"Shifter flu, must be some shifter flu?" I whispered to myself as I strategically pushed my finger over the screen.

There she was—Delilah's face solemn as she entered the building.

She was just as miserable as me.

My claws retracted from my fingertips, and I leaned up against the brick wall. I felt my cut snag against the tough surface and fall to the floor.

"What the fuck am I going to do?"

CHAPTER SIX

Delilah

Two Years Ago

I walked along the sidewalk, softly humming a song as I went. It was just past midday, and the day couldn't get any brighter. Even though this town was located further north than I had planned on traveling, I expected the clouds to block the sun. I was still taken aback by the beauty of the cloudless day.

As I reached the edge of the new town, I didn't realize how tired I was. I only had ten dollars to my name along with only a few sets of clothes and other personal items in my bag, but that wouldn't stop me. It wasn't going to stop this fantastic feeling of freedom and new life ahead of me. A new place, a fresh start, a place to call home.

Despite the sharp rocks that dug into the sole of my feet, I continued walking on the pavement, which should have felt hot and rough beneath me. My endorphins were running high, and the physical pain was dull. My newfound determination fueled me, and with the first few stores in town having *help wanted* signs, I knew I was in the right place.

I glanced around town, it was smaller than the last city I was in. This was more of a suburb, a smaller town feel, but the right size to keep the street streaming with people. They were going about their business, stopping in shops, and even laughing with each other, walking side by side.

Yup, this was the right place.

Instead of stopping in front of the first store I saw with a help wanted sign, I trotted down the sidewalk. I was looking for a sign, not just any help wanted sign but some unworldly push where I needed to go. And that was what I was following, that push, that lured feeling to come *here*.

Besides my bare feet, I was fairly clean. My hair was pulled back into a rather fashionable bun. My jeans weren't ripped, and my shirt was clean. As much as I wanted to dress up more, this would have to do.

As I ventured further into town, the buildings seemed to get more decrepit and worn. Large trees hung over a lot of the empty buildings. Moss grew in alleyways, and stray animals even rummaged through the trash.

Any sane person would have turned their butt right back around, but of course, I was following my gut. I took pride in my gut because it hadn't steered me wrong, yet. I was surrendering to this fate, destiny if you will, and I was going to continue on until I was in blatant danger.

And like a beaming light glowing over one lone building stood a book-shop on the corner.

Bingo.

The bookshop was small, with large potted flowers on either side of the door and a handmade decorative welcome sign made on a two by four and written in a beautiful script. I rubbed my hands together in excitement. I peered inside to see one lonely old man flipping through a giant book that might be a ledger, and I stood up straight.

How was I going to present myself accordingly with no shoes? I rubbed my forehead, listening to the street sounds behind me, but the voices of the patrons walking by grew quiet. Instead, I heard the roar of a motorcycle and the quick kill of its engine. I paid no mind though. I was on a mission. I was going to get this job, first time, first go around and, on top of it all, get to read books all day.

What could be better than that?

As I intently focused on the name of the bookstore, trying to remember when it had been established, I gradually became aware that the warmth of the sun on my back had faded. Instead, an enormous shadow appeared over me, and I heard the stretch of leather boots.

I leaned my head back into the darkness and noticed two deep, dark eyes fixed on me. His face was covered in scruffy facial hair, with his eyebrow raised, leading up to the top of his bald head.

"You have no shoes, woman," he grumbled.

I straightened myself and turned around. He was the source of the noise. His bike, or hog I guess bikers called them, was large, and I didn't think I could hold that thing up to ride it if I tried.

Now this guy may look rough and was lacking manners, but hell, he was eye-catching. For the first time in years, I squeezed my thighs together.

Hubba, hubba!

Tattoos raced up his arms as they stayed folded over his chest. The guy was massive, hovering over me like I was some doll, and I wasn't the shortest woman, but yet I still came up to just below his chest.

"Really? I haven't noticed." I wiggled my toes as I stared down at them.

They weren't particularly dirty, but they weren't clean either. They were well used, maybe a little scuffed up around the bottom, but they weren't in awful shape after walking twenty-five miles.

The biker cleared his throat, leaning down closer to my ear. I should have backed away from the stranger, but he smelled of peppermint and a hint of cologne that was trying to hide the lingering alcohol from the day before.

I would know, I've lived around plenty of people that drank before.

"Are you on drugs?" he asked, raising an eyebrow.

I squeaked, backing away. "No, are you? I'm not interested in buying any either. That stuff is bad for you. That's what my mama always told me. Mess you right up, and then you get arrested and go to jail, and she said you do not want to go to that place, you can *catch stuff* there."

The biker just looked at me, a scowl on his face I'm sure was meant to be intimidating, but I found it charming. I wanted to pinch his cheeks and see if he would smile if I did it, but I refrained.

Some people don't want to be touched, Delilah.

"Sorry, I haven't talked to anyone in a while. Guess, I got carried away. Now, if you will excuse me." I turned away from him and marched closer to the door handle of the bookshop until I came to a halt. My bag was being pulled away from me, and I turned to slap the leather glove that covered his hand.

The brute was dang near offended. His eyes widened in surprise, and he looked at his hand.

"You slapped me," he said.

"Well, duh, you were going to take my stuff. Not that there isn't much in there, but it's the principle of the thing."

He shook his head. "Listen, why are you going in there?"

I pointed to the help wanted sign, and he let out a heavy, annoyed breath.

"You don't have any shoes."

I pinched my lips together. "Yes, we have established that. Now, if you are done pointing out the obvious, I'm going in. Wish me luck!" I waved my hand, and he grabbed it, and a spark shot through my body.

Owie, what the heck?

He let go, an expression of shock on his face until he shook it away. "You can't interview for a job with no shoes."

"Yeah, I am, just watch me!" I turned, but he pulled on my bag again to turn me.

"No, you can't because you won't get the job." He ran his hand over his bald head.

He would look better with a mohawk.

"You should grow your hair into a mohawk," I blurted.

He stopped rubbing his head and looked at me.

"Unless you are naturally bald. Then that was pretty inconsiderate of me to say," I said, trying to retract my statement. "But if you can grow some hair, make sure it's in a mohawk style. It would make you look badass."

The biker's mouth hung open.

"Oh, you look badass now." I patted his arm. "Just saying more badassiness."

I tried to turn again, but he pulled me back around.

"You know, that's getting really annoy—"

He put his finger to my lip to silence me, but I licked it.

"Woman," he growled.

"Delilah," I chirped. "Name is Delilah, and you are?"

"Fuck."

"That's not a nice name," I snorted. "I bet kids can't call you that."

He growled again, making him sound like a dog, but a really badass looking dog.

"Why do you not have any shoes?" he asked, exhausted.

I wiggled from side to side, feeling a bit sheepish. Now I didn't want to look him in the eye because I knew he was going to call me crazy, but I *was* about to try to get a job without shoes.

I mean, really, what was I thinking?

"There was a homeless woman in the town I came from. She didn't have any shoes, and she looked like she needed them more than I did."

The biker's eyes softened, then he swore again.

"Is that the only word you know? The 'f' word and woman? Oh, and shoes?"

Then he smirked, showing off his pearly white teeth, and I swore my heart skipped a beat. To any other person, this guy would be terrifying, maybe a bit disturbing and rude with an odd fascination about shoes.

He might have a foot fetish.

Yuck.

He had scars on his fingers. The leather that covered his palms and the tops of his hands were worn and had holes riddled through them.

The leather vest he wore proclaimed his name as Hawke, and I blinked in realization.

"Hawke?" I whispered, and his eyes snapped to mine. Those dark eyes held something powerful that I didn't understand, but I felt the need to trust this man. "That's your name, right?"

He nodded, the stoic face softened, and a wistful breath left him.

"Where are you from?" he asked.

I shook my head, turning from him and putting my hand on the glass. "I don't know you. I don't need to throw all my problems on you." I would not share my burdens with someone else. That wasn't fair. I was a burden for most of my life, and I wasn't going to do that to someone I just met.

"You're running from something? Did you break the law?" His jaw ticked when I looked back at him.

"No, the law failed me," I whispered. "I don't concentrate on my past anymore. I look to the sun now." I smiled. "I look at what's in front of me, and I'm not going back."

Hawke stared at me for a long moment, then turned to walk back to his bike. He opened a leather side bag and pulled out a helmet.

"You need a job? I'll get you one," he said.

I tilted my head slightly and raised an eyebrow in curiosity. "What makes you think I can't get one on my own?" I put my hands on my hips. "I could walk into that bookstore and get that job." I pointed.

Hawke ran his hands over the black, shiny helmet. "I don't doubt you could with that attitude. But I can offer you room and board and protection from whatever you're running from."

I kept an eye on him, apprehensively taking a few steps away.

"As a waitress!" he shouted. "Nothing, bad, gods, no. Just a server, a waitress. The MC I'm in, we get people back on their feet. They can stay as long as they want, work for us, leave when they're ready, or not at all. We have a server position open."

I glanced around the sidewalks. The town was empty now. I could see people peering out their windows, but the police stood idly by, not paying any attention to Hawke.

My instincts weren't telling me to run; they were telling me to follow. *Go.*

I took a deep breath, my hands already missing that jolt of electricity I'd been given earlier. My gut was screaming at me to just *go with him.*

Please don't let me get chopped up into little pieces, I told the voice in my head.

So, I reached out and took the helmet. Hawke smiled when I did, and my stomach filled with butterflies.

I've never kissed a man with a beard before. Wait, I've never kissed a *real* man before, but I could see myself falling for this one.

It could be the air of mystery about him, the way he tried to look so angry with me when I saw the faintest of smiles on his lips. But I already knew I was going to have a lot of fun trying to make him unravel. An impossible task, but one I would not stop trying.

So, I took the helmet.

He tsked.

"You have no sense of self-preservation, do you?" He motioned me to the bike.

"What's the fun in being safe all the time?" I countered.

He sat on his bike, turning on the engine and revving it several times. He jerked his head for me to follow, and I hopped on the back.

"Where are the handles?" I asked.

He chuckled deeply and grabbed my wrists to put around his waist.

Oh, oh! This is nice.

Hawke's back was muscular, and he was harder than stone. My body tensed at how close we were; I hadn't been this close to a guy since—"

He revved the bike again, and my head snapped up. "Hey, you aren't wearing a helmet!"

He pushed the gas, yelling over the roar, "What's the fun being safe all the time?"

CHAPTER SEVEN

Hawke

Delilah was safe in her apartment. I'd watched on the cameras, but my wolf stirred.

I couldn't forget what Journey had said. She was marked. Obviously, there was something going on there. Maybe a bond, a real one.

I reached into my vest pocket, grasping the flask and taking a quick sip of the vile concoction. I can't recall what I put in there, but it was inexpensive and the heat of it was enough to ease the discomfort in my stomach. I took more, walking down the street back to the bar. I needed to rest; I needed to think and damnit, I needed more to drink.

I unlocked the front door to the bar. It was quiet. The members were already upstairs and in their own dorm-like rooms. I thumped up the stairs, not seeing Locke. He usually walked the halls until the early hours of the morning, feeling like he should take care of this broken pack.

But we had Switch, the cameras in this place were ridiculous. No one could break in without us knowing about it. And stumbling into a bunch of sleeping shifters was a damned bad idea.

As I approached my room, I saw Sizzle coming out of the shower. He'd officially been kicked out of his upstairs apartment over the tattoo shop he shared with Grim because Journey and Grim were too damn loud. I chuckled at that, happy that Grim was at least getting some. Because no one else was.

We all went into ruts, sure, and for a while, the males and females were all too willing to help each other, but as time went on, the ruts and heats faded, and no one got any satisfaction. That was where we were now. No one could get an erection, well, except for me.

And I hid that. I didn't want my brothers and sisters to be jealous, but it was only recently since Journey and Grim had gotten together that it had become worse. Almost unmanageable.

It was like a damned avalanche happening around here. The dynamic of the club was changing. Hope filled some of the members' souls, but I couldn't believe it, not yet.

Could Delilah be my mate?

I haven't even talked to Grim privately to find out how he knew Journey was his. The jolt of electricity we felt years ago. Could that have been a sign?

I remembered that moment like it was yesterday, smelling her from across the street. She was stunning, though a bit on the small side. She had no meat or muscle, but she held her back straight and was the proudest little human, even though she was at her lowest.

Those feet, gods, I remember those feet. They were battered and bruised, but she didn't pay any mind to them. I knew I had to help her, for the greater good of the club, for a woman who was in need. But I needed her far more than she needed me.

She would have survived without the club, without me. Delilah had a light and cheerful spirit, always looking for the silver lining in any situation, yet I knew dark and turbulent thoughts were hidden deep inside her.

To this day, I didn't know what the darkness was, but hell, I was going to find out.

I jutted my chin toward Sizzle. He nodded, going into the spare room he'd taken. He hated women and being around them, but he had a small soft spot for Journey if he was giving up his apartment to eventually live in the basement of his tattoo parlor.

I pushed the door into my room, slinging the gun on the bed. With a quick tug, I pulled the belt off and then proceeded to take my clothes off. I'd go to her apartment as soon as the sun rose over the horizon and talk to her.

I was not sure if there was a real soul connection between us, but I felt something, and I could not ignore it.

I couldn't just be her friend.

My wolf snarled.

I missed her touch, her lips, and I'd always been hot and cold toward her.

Despite my efforts to push Delilah away, it only resulted in further hurting her. And she didn't deserve that. I was making things worse for the both of us.

Delilah wasn't *her*—that bitch that threw me away like I was worthless. Why should I punish Delilah when I knew she would never...

Shit, all this started with the barefooted woman trying to apply for a job at a damned bookshop.

I growled, laying back in bed. I felt my cock stirring, remembering her sweet face. Her face was round, her eyes a beautiful sea blue and a soul so deep I damn near drowned in it.

She didn't think of me as an asshole, but a male that couldn't get this head out of his ass. Delilah thought she could fix me, raining attention on me. Fuck, she was giving me fucking love I didn't deserve. And then I cracked, stealing kisses, then feeling so damned guilty because I couldn't have her. I pushed her away, only to come crawling back because my wolf needed her.

Hell, I needed her.

I didn't want to hurt her, but I was hurting both of us by doing this shit.

Now I ached, and my cock throbbed. My cock and wolf seemed to know what to do. They wanted to claim her, and my wolf had become so overwhelmingly adamant about staying near her, it was painful.

I squeezed my shaft, my come already dripping down the head. All I could think of was Delilah kneeling before me, her bright blue eyes dilated with desire as she put her mouth on it.

I hissed, leaning my head back and imagining her hot, pouty lips engulfing me. How many times had I dreamed of this? To let her have her way with me like she had always wanted but had always been denied. Let her lick from the base of my dick, over my knot until she engulfed me whole.

I pushed my fist up and down the length of my erection, my cock angry, the head already straining purple. To be buried into her hot cunt, to shoot my seed inside her, to knot her, to claim her.

I grunted, cursing as I came all over my hand. It was so quick, I barely pumped twice before I came, but my wolf was howling for more. If I wasn't careful, I'd go into a rut and then where would I be?

I needed her.

I felt like I could not go on without her; the need was so intense it was agonizing.

She'd slowly melted the calluses on my heart with the tenderness she gave me.

A few hours later, I banged on the door to Delilah's shared apartment. I kept pounding my fists against the door that had been reinforced for extra security. However, there was no response from the other side. The outside of the apartment building looked worn, but it was a fortress to protect those the club had rescued.

I bashed on the door again, a small sliding door opened and a woman that lived with Delilah sneered. "What do you want? It's early," she snapped.

"Get Delilah," I retorted.

The woman smirked.

"No, she doesn't want to see you. Besides, you didn't say please."

I gritted my teeth. "Please, let me come in and talk to her."

"Why? So you can be all 'I want you, baby,' then leave her to cry about it for a few days until you come crawling back?"

I snarled fiercely, and she stepped back, her face whitening in fear. "Easy, Hawke," she said, whispering. "She really doesn't want to see you right now. You should give her a few days. She'll come out when she's ready."

I didn't want to wait for days. I didn't want to wait another minute. But didn't I deserve it? I'd told her I didn't want her how many times? Yet she always took me back? What I'd said was unforgivable. She wanted space.

"Fine," I spat. "I'll be outside until she comes out." I huffed and sat outside their apartment door.

I had all fucking day.

And I waited all day into the night and into the next day, but she never came out. I struggled to listen to her on the other side. It drove me mad, and it felt like a living death. How many times had I told her to get a cell phone, to take the ones I'd given to her all for her to push them back in my face?

She didn't want to owe me anything.

Or maybe you made her feel like a slut.

I was so taken aback by the loud snarl coming from my wolf that my body reacted by toppling over from my sitting position.

The fuck was going on?

Using gifts as an apology was a dick move. My wolf paced, moving more and more inside me. He was clawing and howling, and the only way to sate him was to see Delilah. This had been the longest I'd gone without seeing her.

Because I'm a stalking bastard.

Hell, enough was enough.

I rose to my feet, grabbed my boot, and delivered a powerful kick that opened the door. It slammed to the other wall, leaving a door handle imprint in the plaster. I strode across the room, following Delilah's sweet summer scent and wiggled the door handle.

"Open up, Dede, or I'll break it down," I yelled.

No answer, not even the sound of her squeak when she was startled. I let out an angry hiss as I stepped back, then proceeded to violently kick the locked door open to find the room in complete disarray.

Clothes I'd bought her were piled in the corner. Her bed wasn't made. Pictures of us that hung on the wall were now on the floor. My fist tightened, picking up the most recent one of us. It was when I'd finally agreed to grow a mohawk. She was smiling, trying to spike my hair with some gods awful blue hair gel. I looked like a damn Smurf.

Where the fuck was SHE!?

I roared a mighty battle cry and flipped over the bed. The iron rod bed bent as it hit the floor. My claws elongated, ripping through the pillows, the blankets, and the stuffed animal I gave her when she first arrived. I paused, holding up the brown bear with a cheesy ass heart on it.

She was gone.

The wolf inside my head was becoming more and more persistent in its snarls, pushing forward until I stumbled. Whispers came from the door, my hearing becoming too much to bear. My senses heightened, my strength increasing; the blood running through my veins was filled with adrenaline so strong I feared I might lose control.

"Get out!" I roared, throwing her desk chair toward the door. The women and men who'd seen me as the calm enforcer of the bar stood back in terror. The men hurried the women out of the way as I glanced at the window I had climbed in and out of too many times to count.

It was open, the curtains swaying, letting in the chilly night air.

Instead of going through the building, I rushed to the window, climbing down the fire escape, and ran to the bar. If there is one person who would know where my Delilah was, it was *that* human that told me to get my balls in order.

With a swift kick, I opened the door, the sound of my boot connecting with the weathered wooden planks echoing through the room. "Where is she?!" I yelled into the bar. Some flinched, but Anaki didn't. He continued to wipe down the bar with the same dirty rag.

As I gazed over the bar, my eyes landed on Grim's female. I tightened my fists, directing my anger toward her when I knew I shouldn't. She had some damned crescent moon on her head which stirred questions, but I didn't care about that right now. I needed my Delilah.

"You were the last to talk to her," I mumbled.

As the thumping in my head intensified, I could feel my wolf's mouth dripping with venom.

Grim stepped up, blocking his mate. He said something threatening, but all I could hear was my own beating, bloody heart. "Where is she?" I asked more desperately and turned to the rest of the bar. "Where is Delilah?"

Everyone stared, shrugging. Even Anaki shook his head when I glanced at him. "She hasn't been in, man," he said. "She's always here, and I didn't get two-weeks' notice or nothing. Her roommates say her room is empty though." Anaki's voice wasn't condescending or laced with malice toward me. He was sad, hell, everyone was.

Even Bear's usual scowl had softened, and his shoulders slumped.

I slammed my fist on the bar. "Her roommates wouldn't even let me in the apartment. What else did they say?"

Anaki scowled. "Well, they said she was fed up with the men around here. No one was able to commit, tired of having her heart broken. You wouldn't have anything to do with that now, would you?"

"No, I wouldn't," I snapped, shaking my head.

It was a lie. It rolled right off the tongue so effortlessly, just like any other time I'd lied about my feelings toward her.

Journey began to cough, and "liar" escaped her lips.

The bar patrons chuckled and turned to their own devices. Meanwhile, I looked like an idiot, but that was all I knew. For so long, I'd kept her away, and now I didn't know how to show her I wanted to keep her.

"Sorry, I'm allergic to denial," Journey said.

"Excuse me?" I scoffed.

"You heard me," Journey said, taking a sip of her milkshake. "You love her, and she loves you. If you'd just open yourself up to the goddess, she would be your mate. But you, as well as everyone else in this damned club," she said it loud enough for all to hear, "are just scared."

"Me, scared? Are you serious?" I said incredulously.

Journey nodded. "Scared of your own feelings. You may not fear death, but you are scared to open your heart again. You are scared to have it broken. Can you see Delilah rejecting you? Seriously? She's the happiest person in this bar, and the way she looks at you..." Journey tsked.

The way she looked at me? She looked at me like I was the only man in the universe. She made me feel things only a mate would feel. I had more of a connection with Delilah than I ever did with my mate.

But I had to protect her! What if the council came? What if she found out what I am? I couldn't put her life in danger for my own selfish desires! Unlike what Grim had done to Journey.

I swirled the glass Anaki'd left for me. I let the amber liquid coat around the cylinder.

"I've been hurt." I gripped the glass, speaking to Grim. He was trying to console me, trying to make me see what he could see.

Journey and Grim were in their own little world, happy, but what would become of it? She had a mark on her shoulder and her ears were bleeding. Who was to say that she wouldn't die in time? She was sick from the bite, the goddess had cursed her with that damn thing on her head because she was not his.

Like Delilah wasn't mine.

"You don't know how long—" I stared at Grim and glanced behind him. Journey was eating her burger again, oblivious to what we were saying.

But Grim knew what I was talking about, because he didn't know what would become of his *mate* either.

I shook my head. "I don't want to put her through that," I gulped. "I don't want to get her, only to lose her. If we are even mates."

Grim leaned closer to me, his mouth near my ear. "To have her as my mate for any amount of time is worth it."

I instantly sobered.

Maybe I could have Delilah. I could have her, not have my wolf claim her, and just be with her until my death. I could get her to understand I wouldn't be around for much longer. Tell her she needed to keep this secret after I pass. Surely the council wouldn't find out if she accepted who we were, which I think she could.

She could still live freely if she chose. Still have a life without me once I was gone. I had plenty of money for her to live off of. She would be taken care of; the Iron Fang would make sure of it.

After conversing with Journey and Grim once more and knowing Journey had no clue where Delilah had gone, I rose from my seat.

I was going to find her, tell her how I felt. That I wanted to be with her for as long as I lived, but I didn't know how much longer that would be. To have her, even for the briefest of moments before my death, would be enough.

CHAPTER EIGHT

Delilah

I was startled by the sound of the wind pushing the nearby branch up against my window. A loud screech joined the scratching down the side of the glass. I winced as the lightning flashed into the darkened room, ready for the thunderous roar to follow.

I held my blanket close, feeling the warmth of the fabric. The window creaked, and I shut my eyes tight as I braced for the rain to trickle inside. I hated storms as much as I hated smelling cooking Brussels sprouts.

Violent storms always reminded me of the horrific memories, which seemed to be permanently locked away in my mind. The storms brought them back so strongly, and it was then I realized how alone I was.

While I was in bed, it dipped down, and I was suddenly embraced by a warm hand around my middle. The heat of his wet body engulfed me, and instead of retracting in fear of the familiar peppermint schnapps scent I leaned into him.

"I could hear you crying from the streets."

Hawke.

"I'm sorry. I wasn't that loud," I tried to argue, but he kept his body against mine. I didn't pull away in disgust at his wet shirt plastered against me, I

was just happy he was here. "What are you doing? You can't be in here."

I should've pushed him away. I didn't know him. I didn't know what his intentions were, even though he'd given me a place to live, food, and a job. He could have done it just to get in my pants.

Yet, the gut feeling of running never surfaced. I just laid there in his arms, and he gently rocked me back and forth.

When was the last time I was hugged without instigating it?

"Your window was cracked, you really have no sense of self-preservation do you?"

I giggled, but another lightning bolt ripped across the sky, lighting up the entire room. The shadows on the wall moved in a mesmerizing dance, and the small sob that escaped me caused me to break down.

Hawke moved me onto my side and held me close to his chest, and the deep, almost purring sound in his chest soothed me. I let out slow steady breaths as he shushed me, cooed at me, and petted my hair like I was a small child.

"Why are you here?" I asked once the fear faded.

"I'm in charge of you. It's my job to see to your safety and health."

I shook my head. "You do this with all the women here?" A spark of jealousy hit me, jealousy I shouldn't have.

He was the protector, he was the guard of the bar and the apartments, he was the watchman.

He paused for what seemed like an eternity, almost as if he was considering not responding to me. "No, just you."

I felt my lips tug up into a smile, though I was uneasy with the way he had hopped into my bed without a second thought.

"Are you afraid of storms or is it something else?" he asked.

Both, I wanted to say. But that would just open up for a conversation I wasn't ready to have with this new acquaintance. Yet, here he was, cuddling me in bed.

"*The storm,*" *I sniffed.*

He didn't like the answer. His throat hummed out a growl, and he tightened his arms around me. "*Yeah, I don't like them either.*"

We laid there a long time, listening to the thunder roll slowly into the distance. I knew once the storm was over, he would leave, but I didn't want him to. It was the first time I felt... I don't know...safe. That I didn't have to put on a face for everyone to know I was fine. Hawke had now seen the vulnerability in me, and it didn't hurt my ego as much. He'd seen me at my lowest, and now I was connected to him in some strange way.

"*I tell you what,*" *he whispered, pulling away from me.* "*Each time there is a storm, I'll come visit. We will stay with each other until it's over?*"

Hawke coming back just to make sure I was okay was thoughtful, kind, more than I thought he would ever give. I guess the whole badassedness was just a front, too.

"*I'd really like that.*" *I snuggled deeper into his chest. The storm was gone now, but even he seemed reluctant to let go.*

"*I'll just stay until you fall asleep,*" *he said.*

"*Can you just stay the rest of the night?*" *I looked up at him. He was already looking down at me, and a flash of darkness swept through his eyes.*

"*It's best I go. I have others to watch over, too.*"

Right.

"*Listen, Dede–*"

"*Dede? Where did you get that?*" *I laughed. His face flushed red, and he rubbed his hand down his face.*

"*I dunno, wanted to give you a nickname. Doesn't matter,*" *he grumbled.* "*Anyway, listen, we can't be anything more than friends, do you hear me? I have jobs, responsibilities; it's against the brother code.*"

My mood faltered, but I kept the smile on my face. "*I understand. You have a big job to do. Protecting all those people. But it's probably best if you stay away then, because even if you're a big grumpy biker, I might fall for your charm."*

Hawke rolled onto his back, rubbing his bald head. "Ha, right, okay. I get it. I can't help it I'm fucking sexy as hell." He ran his hands over his wet t-shirt.

And yum, he looked good.

I cleared my throat, stopping myself from ogling. Hawke was unobtainable, but having him here in my bed was too good to pass up. What would it be like to feel those lips?

The urge was so strong, and I've never had a high sex drive. But lord have mercy on me, he was everything I liked. A grumpy exterior with a soft side. He proved that by cuddling up in bed with me when he could have left me to fend for myself.

"Since we can't be more than friends, and you won't be visiting anymore, can I ask you something a little personal?"

Hawke raised his eyebrow, a smirk forming on his lips. "Anything, Sunshine."

"Oh, two nicknames." I raised my fingers. "I must be really special then!" I snorted.

He smiled, brushing a strand of hair from my face.

I licked my lips, my legs pressing together. "Can I have just one kiss? To know what it's like?"

Because I'd never had a kiss that wasn't forced, and with how sweet Hawke was being right now, I wanted to know what it was like. To get a taste of the forbidden fruit before throwing it away and never looking back.

Hawke's eyes darkened, his breath shallow. "Just one," he said huskily. "Because this can't happen again, I can't have feelings for you, not in my line of work."

I nodded, and he sat up quickly. He stared at my lips, licking his own before gripping the back of my head and tightly gripping my hair. Hawke pulled me forward, his lips softly touching mine.

An explosion of light broke behind my eyes, and I knew it wasn't from the lightning outside. This was inside me, sparking an event that would forever change us. I knew this man could only be my friend. I could only see him from afar, but deep down in my soul, I felt we should be more.

His tongue slid into my mouth. The beautiful massage between us became heated. My arms wrapped around him as the kiss deepened. I moaned, and the rumble in his chest intensified.

I gasped for air and his face softened. I felt a wave of sadness as we both parted.

"Wow," I said, touching his face.

He didn't reply, just tracing my lips with his finger.

The loud alarm startled me and, I sit up straight in bed. My first instinct was to battle the clock by swatting it. I rubbed my eyes, the puffiness in my cheeks was still there despite the exorbitant amount of natural sleep aids I took.

There wasn't a storm last night, but the bustling lights of the city only reminded me of the lightning piercing the sky. The sirens that wailed, the horns that honked, it all blended together to bring in the perfect blend of nightmares.

I laid awake for I don't know how long, replaying the first time Hawke came to me during my first week living at the Iron Fang apartments. Now I was regretting leaving, because seeing him calmed me.

How could that be possible to be so angry with someone yet want them at the same time? I hated what he'd done to me, how he'd made me rely on him. It was some sort of game to him. Take a kiss, leave me wanting, and then go back to his life like he didn't care.

I acted quickly and yanked the covers away from myself and then immediately reached for the bottle of water on the bed.

I'd arrived two days ago, and with great luck, found a job at an upscale breakfast, brunch, and lunch restaurant called The Atlas. The only reason I was hired was because they were short staffed. They didn't even ask for references, which was a good thing because I couldn't give them any.

I wasn't about to have my cover blown by them calling the Iron Fang, and leaving the diner without notice would not fare well with me.

I showered and dressed. It was nearly five a.m., and I was due to be there soon. Luckily, it wasn't a terribly long walk. Luck was on my side when I arrived a few days ago. I was ready to stay busy and forget everything about the tattoo and pierced biker.

The more time ticked by, the angrier I became, not because of what he had done to me, but because the aching hole in my heart was no longer filled. I was certain that we shared something special, and that was why I'd stayed for so long. That he would retire, and we could eventually be together.

I never had a desire to have kids, not after what I went through. I wouldn't put a child through that. I could have waited for him. But then I saw Grim and Journey, and I snapped.

I wanted what they had.

To stop hiding, to live, to be normal.

I angrily tied the laces of my recently polished and shined shoes. Straight black was the uniform, along with hair in a neat bun. I was made for this, made to serve, help, and bring a smile to others' faces.

I quickly glanced in the mirror, making sure my smile was as bright as it could be. It was fake, not that anyone would notice.

Except Hawke.

"Dang it! Stop!" I groaned. "Listen here." I pointed to myself in the mirror. "All day today, you will not think about him. Not even wonder if he notices if you're gone." I pursed my lips.

He was drunk, of course he may not notice. He could be still sleeping off the regretted kiss as we speak, and it'd been days.

"And you are going to have a great day. Serve some people happy little coffee with happy little bacon and whipped cream faces on their pancakes." I nodded, satisfied with myself, and grabbed my bag from the table next to the door.

The extended stay hotel was more than I wanted to pay, but until I found an apartment, it would have to do. Besides, they do the sheets, and I hated washing sheets.

I sighed, opening the door, and looking back at the bed. I hadn't even made it. What was the point? I didn't even have the cute stuffed bear anymore, so it didn't remind me of *him*. But the absence of it clarified that I was emotionally fucked.

CHAPTER NINE

Delilah

I set down a plate of eggs benedict in front of the last customer, checking if they needed anything before I went back to the server's station. I surveyed my tables to see if anyone needed any additional coffee or drinks, resting my hip comfortably against the counter.

This job wasn't so bad. In fact, it was great to keep busy. When I was off the clock, my mind wandered back to the dark eyes and overly grumpy biker that stole more than kisses from me.

Dang, I was doing so well not thinking about him this morning.

Screwed that one up.

I slapped my hand on my forehead, earning a look from several other servers.

"Great," one server groaned. She set a pitcher of ice water on the table. "Colonel Sanders just sat down."

I squinted, focusing on the Colonel Sanders impersonator grumpily sitting in the restaurant's corner. He had pepper colored curly hair on the top of his head and a white handlebar mustache that he probably spent way too much time on to make it look halfway decent. He'd worn a plaid shirt with dark jeans every day since I'd worked here, and no one had ever said a word to him about the dress code.

He must think he is hot stuff or something around here.

This place was dress pants or dresses, not jeans and plaids. But not even the manager, Simon, who could be a real thorn in my side, dared to look him in the eye.

I couldn't see why no one had approached him. He was of average size, much smaller compared to the bikers I typically interacted with. His face was in a permanent scowl though, wrinkles lining his frown. His fingers were covered in gold and silver rings with various deep colored stones on them.

Who was he?

"I'll take him again." I rubbed my hands excitedly. Madison gave a grateful smile, but also a look of "what the fudge is wrong with you?"

For the week I'd been here, Colonel Sanders complained about everything. He sent food back to the kitchen several times and also requested multiple different servers in one sitting.

He had yet to get rid of me when I served him, though.

I tapped the counter, waiting for him to take a sip of the coffee the hostess poured for him as she spouted out the specials. She was shaking with nervousness, her hands trembling and her voice shaking uncontrollably. I waited for him to go off about whether it had too much sugar, or that the beans were burnt, or even, dare I say, made with tap water instead of filtered.

Because that had been brought up several times.

I'd tried being polite. I'd made sure his table was set up the way he liked it, only to be shunned, talked down to, or yelled at because his pancake didn't sit right on the plate.

This man had gotten under my skin, but it didn't scare me. I was determined to figure this jerk face out. The other servers were glad about that, because they wanted nothing to do with him.

"Delilah, your order's up." Charlie gave an apologetic smile and rested his hands on the counter. I made it a point to have Colonel Sanders's meal ready for him the moment he walked through the door, since it was the same order every day. "I made it just like you wrote it. Hope it works out." He shook his head. "But knowing him–"

"Hey." I held my hand out. "He's just being a jerk face. Give me that can of whipped cream over there." I pointed to the stainless steel whipped cream dispenser. Charlie eyed me curiously and slowly handed it over.

My hands were clean, so I rearranged his pancakes, stacking one on top of the other. I took two of the eggs and placed them on top of the pancake, one beside another, and used the bacon to make a smiling face, and then took the whipped cream and went to town.

Charlie was astonished, his eyes widening as he instinctively brought his fist to his lips in an attempt to hold back his laughter. "What the hell, Delilah? You are going to get reamed for this."

I giggled, finishing my masterpiece, and handed back the whipped cream. "Ah, it will be worth it." I placed the food on my tray and strutted over to Colonel Sanders's table. I smiled wildly, and he rolled his eyes and leaned back in his chair, ready for his food to be delivered.

"Here is your usual, three pancakes, side of two sunny side up eggs, bacon, and something a little extra for you today..." I sat the plate down, and he stared at the fluffy whipped cream for hair, the handlebar mustache, and bacon smile.

The vertically cut strawberry was a nice touch because it resembled his large alcoholic nose.

Instead of getting yelled at, he barked out a laugh so loud the entire restaurant drew to a standstill. Forks clinked on plates. The customers all stared in our direction at the noise in the corner and my flushed-red face.

I'd been bold back at the Iron Fang, but being so in a ritzier place like The Atlas was probably not wise. Yet, I waited for him to yell at me.

"Did you come up with this yourself or was it that lousy cook?" He took out a handkerchief and wiped his tears.

"I did it, sir," I said warily. If he was going to get someone fired, it should be me since I started this mess.

The manager, Simon, walked up to both of us, dread in his face as he stared down at the slowly disintegrating whipped cream and the eggs running down the pancakes.

"What's the meaning of this?" The manager hissed, grabbing my arm. "You are to respect our customers and look what you have–"

"That's enough," Colonel Sanders barked, eyeing the tight grip on my arm. "That was the best laugh I've had in a while. She's got some spunk. I like that. I want her every day from now on."

The manager let go of my arm, his eyes flip-flopping from the old man to me. "A-are you sure? This isn't the normal behavior our waitstaff has–"

"It's a damn shame, then. She's worked hard all week to get me to crack a smile and succeeded." He winked at me.

Colonel Sanders acknowledged me with a nod and doused his pancakes in syrup, not fazed by the sticky mess he was making in his eggs and fruit. "It is weird. She's the first one that hasn't been afraid of me. Strange that one." He pointed to me. "She hasn't shaken my coffee while pouring it, and she smiles like the devil is after her. That's my kind of woman."

Simon nodded, side eyeing the man, and walked off. He gave me one last look as he backed away, his eyes lingering on me.

"You got some fire in you." Colonel Sanders pointed his fork at me and to the chair across from him. I obeyed and made my way to the unoccupied seat, somewhat dazed.

Normally, I'll get a smile from a grumpy customer, but then that was that. I left them alone. I didn't have a full-blown conversation.

"Now, what is a pretty girl like you doing in a place like this?" The epic mustache man began sawing his pancakes into pieces, the sound of his knife scraping against the plate filling the air between us.

I gazed around the room. The white tablecloths, the expensive furniture, and the highly decorated brunch tables had me confused. This was a good job, one that had fallen into my lap easily. I'd say I was lucky to have it.

"I don't know if I understand what you are saying?" I asked. "This is more upscale than my last job." I tilted my head.

The old man patted his mouth, dabbing syrup from his mustache. "What I mean to say was, why are you here? This is a stuffy restaurant, the servers are nothing but spit shined pieces of shit. Everyone hates their job, but you make it your mission to make me, the bastard everyone hates, laugh."

I blinked, stunned.

"I'm here for a job, to make eating out enjoyable. I don't like to see people sad or upset." I sat on my hands to keep myself from fidgeting.

I felt like he could see right through me, which made me uneasy. I didn't get any warning flags from my gut to run away from him, so I stayed.

He hummed disapprovingly. "So, you make everyone else happy while you hide behind that smile, eh?"

My wandering eyes jerked back to him.

"You may smile on the outside, but on the inside, you are anything but," he said smugly, shoving a piece of food in his mouth.

Who the heck was this guy?

"I'm sorry, I didn't catch your name. I'm Delilah," I said. I reached for his hand. His mustache twitched, and he reached his hand out as well.

"I'm Bram, Bram Talbot."

I held back a snicker. *This dude thought he was James Bond.*

He let out another laugh, wiping off his face again with a napkin. He shook his head, trying to contain his laughter.

Great, I got a crazy one. The heck is he laughing at now?

"And Mr. Talbot, what are you getting at here? You don't know me."

"You are running," he murmured.

My stomach dropped, and my fingers gripped the tray, but I smiled. "I don't know what you're talking about."

He hummed, wiping his mouth one more time and pulling a few bills from his wallet to pay for his meal. It was more than enough, because he left almost fifty dollars in tip.

"I've been around these parts for a while. It's hard to get a job here, yet somehow the manager seemed to take you in without question. Now why do you think that is?"

My lips parted, my mind racing. What could it mean?

My past wasn't coming to get me was it? Did someone know me? I didn't hide my name; I didn't want to take the last bit of my identity and throw it away.

"Some awesome luck. Maybe it was destiny?" I shrugged, trying not to show agitation.

He gazed at me intently, his finger tapping the white tablecloth. "It was nice chatting with you, Delilah. I'm looking forward to our new friendship."

Woah, woah, woah.

We stood up from the table and heard the scrape of our chairs against the wooden floor as we both left the table. "Who are you? How do you know about me, Mr. Talbot? Why are you being so nice to me?"

A wave of unease settled inside me, the stress from years ago resurfacing. Did he know who I was? Did he know about the Iron Fang? Either way, it wasn't good, because I didn't need anyone bringing up the lives I no longer lived.

"Please, Delilah, call me Bram," he replied. "Nothing to stress over. I'm just happy to be served by a waitress that doesn't take my shit." He winked, his green eye peering over his shoulder. He took his jean coat and pulled it over his plaid shirt. "I'll see you tomorrow."

And with that, he left me with more questions than answers.

I felt a hand on my shoulder and jolted away with a squeak. Simon widened his eyes in apology. "I'm so sorry, are you alright?"

The sudden sympathy from the manager caught me off guard, but I shrugged it off as just nerves. Bram was intimidating, not by size but by some other powerful aura he exuded.

I nodded, clearing my throat. As I looked at my watch, I realized it was time for my shift to be over. "Yes, fine, is it alright if I go?" I hooked my thumb to the door.

"Of course, uh..." Simon rubbed his cheek with his hand and stuck it in his pocket. "Did he, uh, give you a name?"

"You don't know his name?" I asked incredulously.

"He always pays in cash. And the few times he's been in, I've forgotten. It would be quite rude of me if I asked his name again now, wouldn't it?" he said condescendingly, rubbing his head.

I opened my mouth to tell him the name but then my mind drew a blank. "I don't remember either." I rubbed my forehead. "He told me, I just...don't remember."

How do I forget a name? I never forget a name or face! Nor a favorite food or drink.

Simon pursed his lips and nodded. "Right, well, let me know next time he comes in. He's strange, but he tips well. If he plans on coming in more often, then I'll be sure you're his server."

I watched silently as Simon abruptly turned away, and I glanced out the window to see where he went. But he had gone, leaving only a wisp of his cologne lingering in the air.

As soon as I left the restaurant and returned to my extended stay hotel, I sat in front of the small desk with the mirror facing back at me. My dinner was in front of me, but my mind was full of Bram's voice.

Yes, I remembered his name as soon as my manager left, but I found it odd I would forget his name when someone asked for it. So, I left it. My stomach churned with unease when I was near the manager, so staying away from him was for the best.

Maybe there was something about Simon that wasn't right.

This Bram character, though, I didn't get the red flags to stay away from him, but I didn't get a good feeling either. He was peculiar, and his way of reading me, knowing who I was, was unsettling.

So, what if the manager hired me without a second thought during their brunch rush? He was desperate, waiting tables himself when he gave me a trial run, and I excelled with flying colors. But what if it all fell into my lap way too easily?

I pursed my lips, the sensation of my chapped skin sticking together overwhelming my senses.

Unless, Simon was working for *him*.

I hadn't thought about *him* in so long. I had forgotten the hold he had on me. Since the Iron Fang, since Hawke, all my worries had slipped away. I'd become happier, worry free. I wasn't being chased; I wasn't being tortured with nightmares.

My hands went to my neck, rubbing it softly. Only Hawke could make me feel completely at ease, and I'd left him. But he'd ruined it all. He caught me in a web of emotions and tearing through those was hard enough. I couldn't go back to look for protection now. Not even from the Iron Fang.

Because he would ruin me all over again. I couldn't help but love him, he was a magnet too strong to ignore—the further away from him, the better.

At least, that is what I was telling myself.

He didn't love me like I loved him.

Idiot.

I'd made my bed by leaving, now I must lie in it.

I desperately rubbed my temples to drive away my aching memories, yet the exhaustion of being deprived of sleep and the pain of unrequited love was unbearable. This past week was the perfect storm to relive memories long forgotten when I was with Hawke.

I was being sucked into the past; I could feel the cool air just as I was sitting in the county jail cell on the opposite side of the wall all those years ago.

The noises were loud, but not unbearable. The clinking of uniformed guards' freshly shined shoes echoed through the hallway. I sat on the "visitor" side of the glass, my hands folded neatly against each other as I waited.

Others were already talking to their significant others, husbands, children, friends. All of whom were arrested and awaiting trial. I rubbed my thumbs together, waiting for the one man I shouldn't see. But I needed closure. I needed to see he was on the other side of the glass, waiting to be transported to a high security prison.

There was a tap at the glass. The plastic phone rapped three more times before I looked up. He smiled, those white, blunt teeth shining despite the surrounding darkness. To an ordinary person, he looked like an outstanding citizen. But my stepbrother was the devil beneath those boyish charms.

"Dear sister, what do I owe the pleasure?" he mumbled into the phone.

I didn't know what it was. Everyone saw him as such a saint. It could be the enormous amount of money he donated to charities, his volunteer work, his outstanding reputation for being a wonderful religious man. But I saw him for who he really was.

"It makes it worse when you call me that," I tutted. "You know they listen to these calls, right?"

He wasn't my blood brother. Not by a long shot, but my stepbrother. He just got off on calling me sister.

Shane smiled, the wicked smile the wolf gave before he tried to eat Little Red Riding Hood. "I know they listen in, and they should. That is part of their job, to protect the public from criminals. Once they realize they have the wrong man, I'll be free."

I gritted my teeth, trying not to lose my temper. I had become quite good at hiding my emotions from Shane. He thrived off pain and suffering. The only way I could make him angry was smiling and acting as if nothing was wrong.

With a demure flutter of my lashes, I propped my cheek up with my hand. "You are certainly right, Shane. I do hope they catch the criminal and lock him away a real long time."

Shane's fake smile fell.

"And once the prison realizes that they committed crimes against an underage person, I'm sure he will get what he deserves. I heard even in prison such a crime is frowned upon. Death often coming to them."

Shane's hand gripped the phone, his breathing deepened.

"I certainly hope they catch the right man," he said. "We wouldn't want the innocent to suffer, otherwise the accusing party will suffer dearly. And trust me, there are friends on the other side of the glass that are making sure the innocent are set free, dear sister."

I kept my ticking jaw from being seen, but Shane just chuckled. "I can't wait to get out of here, Delilah. We have much to catch up on. I hope you wait for me at the mansion. I would hate to have to find you. It would break my heart to send out our guards to find you. I need to protect you."

I stared at him, seeing the evil in his eyes. My stomach turned into knots, my consciousness telling me loud and clear.

Run.

CHAPTER TEN

Hawke

When I felt the engine rumble between my legs, I was whisked away to a destination far from my current reality. A place where I didn't suffer from the absence of shifting into my wolf.

Since losing my wolf and the ability to transform into the animal that I shared this body with, it'd broken me. Hell, it had broken all of us in the Iron Fang.

That's why we took up riding. To feel the wind in our hair, the power beneath our legs. We wanted to ride all day to feel...alive.

I rode for hours, and the loud engine, the wind in my hair, and my wolf's snarls kept me company. It wasn't a pleasant experience; the longer we rode, the more my wolf became frantic. His panting was labored and loud, like he was trying to break through the windows of my mind.

I hadn't felt this sort of power from him in a long while. He had become docile when our mate rejected us. It was like he was in a drug-induced coma, only sniffing or huffing when he approved or disapproved of what I did.

That all changed when Delilah came around. He would stand, pace, and nudge me to get closer. Sometimes he won, other times he didn't. I was in the driver's seat; I was the one in control. I'd always had excellent control over him. But there would be a day he finally snapped and took over my body for one last time.

When I go rabid, it's over. There was no going back, there wasn't changing back into my human form and going about my day. When I went rabid, I would be an angry beast, and there would be no stopping it.

That was why the rogues had banded together. The good ones anyway. We wanted to make sure we didn't harm any innocent beings and to be put out of our misery.

So, when my wolf woke, when Delilah was around, it scared the shit out of me.

Was this when he took over? Was Delilah truly safe around me?

My hand trembled as I rubbed it down my face, overwhelmed with frustration.

I cared enough about her to push her away. But she didn't understand that, and I knew when I found her, I would have to grovel. I would sit on my knees at her front step until my skin bled and my body ached from the cold. I would get her back.

Somehow.

I'd have to tell her what I was. Why I pushed her away. And how all of this was fucking dangerous.

I'd gone back and forth between telling her who I was or just coming up with a lie. That I had an incurable disease, and I couldn't have sex with her, but I'd give her everything she wanted, so she didn't have to know my secret.

That I was a wolf, I had a knot, and her knowing about all things supernatural was against the law of the Royal Council.

But she knew I got hard for her. My cock ached when she was even in ear shot, and I heard her sweet voice. I felt the shape of it through my jeans as I grew closer. My wolf could sense her, feel her inner turmoil as we approached.

I was such an ass. I'd been so blind before. All this time, I was trying to protect her physically; I hadn't thought of the mental.

I straightened my back, taking a deep breath as I looked in through her window.

Delilah was asleep, barely though. She was tossing and turning like she had for the past five days I'd been here. Dede wasn't sleeping; she woke with dark circles under her eyes, and she cried randomly in the night.

I wanted to break down the door, wrap her in my arms and whisper promises until her tears were all gone.

But I could no longer do that because I had broken what we had. The trust she had in me to take care of her not just physically, but emotionally as well, was gone.

Delilah had come from a past so terrible she said she never wanted to speak of it. I didn't know what she was running from, but she said being a part of the Iron Fang was the closest thing she'd ever had to a family. She felt safe with them, with me.

I pulled out my switchblade, waving it back and forth as I stood on the top floor of the extended stay hotel. This place was a shit hole. No one even dared to call the cops on me. I had to set up my own cameras to make sure no one broke into her room.

As I stepped away from the window, I could feel the worry radiating from Delilah. She wasn't sleeping, she wasn't eating right, and delaying this much longer was going to be the death of the both of us.

Stop being a dumb shit, my wolf snarled. *Go in and claim her. You stand out here like a pup with his tail between his legs.*

That was the other annoying part of my day. My wolf had resurfaced and had become chatty on the way down here. I worried he would go rabid, but he assured me he was very much in control of his actions. He had mentioned several times he would take control to claim what was rightfully ours.

I was still not convinced. *A second chance, mate? Really?*

"Mine," my wolf snarled.

"Yeah, I get it, buddy." I sighed, pulling out the empty flask. No more alcohol to numb the pain, no more wrong decisions. I was going to do this right and by doing the right thing, I was going to woo the shit out of her.

Be the man she deserved and then some.

And give her the knot. My wolf snorted. *Knot her real good, breed her so she will never leave.*

Knotting was done with mates only. It brought souls closer together before using a biting mark to complete the bond. But Delilah couldn't be.

"She is!" my wolf argued. *"You are just too dumb to see. I feel her, I smell her, her soul is ours. Second chances are here, now."*

I wanted to believe it, but luck had never been on our side.

"Just hurry up and piss on her doorstep so no other shifter will come near. At least stay true to your roots."

I rolled my eyes, undoing my zipper to sate the fucker. If I didn't do it, he'd hound me all night long that I wasn't a wolf anymore and had become too much of a human.

Once I'd finished, I took one last look in the window. She'd settled now. She did that when I was close. I'd managed to get a room beside hers today, and we had both slept better. I could feel her, which was the strangest thing. The strength of her emotions were so profound that it almost frightened me.

Delilah may never forgive me, but I wouldn't ever give up. It was already proven I was feeling better; my wolf felt better. It was best we explore what we had, especially now. When she left, my heart broke, and I couldn't imagine how she felt after I spat out nonsense to her.

I laid my hand on the glass, watching her still body breathe. "Tomorrow," I muttered to myself. "We are taking her back tomorrow."

My wolf's joyful yips were in stark contrast to my own nerves and apprehension.

I was taking her, like it or not, and I didn't know how she would react to that.

I followed her to work like I had the last few days. I watched her get on the bus today rather than walk to the other side of town. The richer side of town had flowers growing in large planters beside each door of the stores. There were name brand stores filled with useless bags and shoes. Women and men dressed in linens, dresses, and slacks.

With a roll of my eyes, I chose to take the back alley way instead of the main path. I took out the chair I had stuffed behind the dumpster. I already had the restaurant rigged with plenty of cameras. I could see inside the kitchen, the restaurant—no corner was spared to make sure my Sunshine was safe.

I cracked my knuckles, opening up the app on my phone, and watched her help prepare the tables for the early morning. I fucking hated that she was doing this, getting up at the crack ass of dawn to work.

But she was used to it, and I had no say in what she did or didn't do. She'd told me that many times, but she thought her early morning diner jobs were secret from me.

They weren't. What kind of protector would I be if I didn't know where she was at all times?

"You don't do that for the rest of the females."

"Shut up," I muttered.

He snorted, the heat of his nose running down my spine. *"You don't place trackers in anyone else's shoes."* I narrowed my eyes, my fingers ticking. *"You don't watch the other females sleep; you don't cuddle them in bed; you don't take them to the fair; you don't—"*

"Shut the fuck up," I growled.

"See, she is ours. Even if you do not want to admit she is our mate. We will claim her."

"If she forgives us."

"You mean, if she forgives you. She will love me. I'm a damned dog to her. She will give me all the pets," he said proudly.

"We don't even know if she can survive a claiming bite!" I threw my hand out into the air.

"She will. Journey did. And Grim's bite was deep. I could feel it. Journey is going to change into one of us."

I sat up straight.

"Yeah, she is. And she will survive. I felt the Moon Goddess's presence in Journey's body. Grim's wolf could not feel it, but I can."

My wolf always had great intuition, except for the mate who rejected us. He could sense magical power, if a being had a spell cast upon them, or if a darkness was hiding within their body such as a demon or dark magic.

"Will she survive if she shifts?" I asked him, curiously.

"I cannot answer that." He bowed his head. *"Only she and her wolf can*

decide that.”

"Just like any other shifter." I pinched my nose.

Sometimes a born shifter did not want their animal because if you were gifted with your animal, you must find your fated mate, and there was a fear of rejection. If you refused your animal when you had come of age to shift, you could fight them internally and reject them and live as a human. You could be free to mate and fall in love with anyone you wished and leave the realm of Elysian.

There had been many that tried, but only a few survived fighting off their animals. Shifters didn't want to feel the bond break. It was the most painful feeling in all the realms. I would know, many of us knew. It did something to you—made you numb to falling in love with anyone.

But now I felt again, and it scared the hell out of me.

My wolf and I listened intently as we watched the hidden cameras. As always, Delilah acted as if nothing as wrong and pranced from table to table to pass out orders. She received a smile from all of them. Of course they would. She was the sun, even the male who had given her a hard time all week was finally smiling.

I wanted to slit his throat the other day when he yelled and berated her over the smallest things. Her heart would break every time, but yesterday, she made him laugh and now he expected to be served by her every day.

I despised him.

But my wolf was intrigued.

"He has magic," my wolf said. *"But I am not sure of his intent."*

We weren't close enough for my wolf to feel his aura, and we weren't about to step in today, because we had another mission. And that was to get my Delilah back.

"Mate," my wolf said. *"You mean, get our mate back?"*

I cleared my throat, and the clattering of dishes and the hum of conversation slowly died away as the servers and cooks left for the day. There was only one left—my Delilah doing the rest of the dishes in the kitchen.

Swiftly, I shoved my phone into my back pocket and extracted a pin to unlock the back door. It was quick, barely took me three seconds, and I was in the back of the kitchen. Delilah was rustling with the dishwater, music playing on a radio in the distance.

She was on the low end of the hierarchy. They must be forcing her to stay late and do dishes.

My wolf growled lowly.

Cautiously, we crept closer, and we couldn't help but take in the view of her backside as she leaned over the sink to get a plate from the bottom. My cock roared to life, my wolf prancing excitedly as we approached.

She was so goddamn beautiful, and not just her body, but her soul, too. And I'd pushed her away. Delilah was my complete opposite, and we were both meant to be together. How could I not see that? How could I have been so blind?

"Because you are an idiot." My wolf huffed.

I stood right behind her. Her movements were slow as she felt the heat of my body. Her heart raced, blood rushing to various parts of her body. She knew I was behind her. I knew she could smell me. She's often told me if she was blindfolded she could pick me out of a lineup of the guys because of the peppermint schnapps I drank and just the heat of my body.

I held my breath, and her body trembled as she put the plate down. A strand of her hair fell from her messy bun, and my finger longed to put it behind her delicate ear.

"You're here," she said breathlessly, still facing away from me.

Gods, her voice sounded so good.

"She doesn't sound mad, maybe she forgave us already!"

Fat chance.

Delilah turned around, and shit, was she a sight for sore eyes. Her face was paler than normal, her eyes puffy, but hell, it was so good to see her. I knew I didn't look so good myself.

I reached out to touch her cheek, and her hand raised too, but it wasn't to tenderly touch me.

CHAPTER ELEVEN

Delilah

Before I had the chance to realize what was going on, I found my hand swaying in a wide arc. The slap across his beard muffled the sound, but just above his cheekbone I could hear my wet hand slapping across the skin. He was surprised when his head suddenly shifted, but instead of stepping back, he remained in place.

"I deserved that," he said, licking his lip where it bled from hitting his teeth.

How dare he come here!

But he came.

Neither of us uttered a word, and I felt my breath coming out in large, uneven breaths.

Hawke was here, so close I could smell the leather of his jacket, and I couldn't say a word. I felt a chaotic mix of fear and happiness coursing through me.

Happy that he'd found me, happy that he would go to such lengths to find me, but also, anger.

Hawke wouldn't let me go. He would not let me live in peace. I would never get over him if he continued to pursue whatever this was. Every time

I laid eyes on him, my breath hitched in my throat, and my heart ached. I couldn't be his friend.

I leaned back against the sink, feeling the cold metal against my palms. I glanced to the ground, still feeling the heat of his gaze. "You should go," I muttered. "You aren't wanted here."

His throat made a funny growl sound, the one that could make my pussy wet within seconds.

"Is that what you want?" he stepped forward.

I was pinned to the sink. I had nowhere to go. I would not run though. I had to face this. Hawke was the runner, not me.

I straightened my back, crossing my arms over my chest. "Yes, I want you to go. There isn't anything between us anymore. You made that perfectly clear. And I can't be friends with you." I bit my cheek, trying to forget the sting in my eyes.

No way. I would not let him break me.

But something about his scent. That peppermint smell, it smelled like home, it reminded me of the good times we shared. It reminded me how happy I was when I as with him, how much I cared and wanted him.

I swear I didn't remember it being this strong to want to be near him. Maybe it was the days away from him that had strengthened it, but I couldn't ignore the power he had over me.

"I don't want to be your friend, Delilah," he muttered.

My heart felt like it had sunk even lower and so, without hesitation, I lifted my hand to strike him again. Was he now attempting to put me in my grave after he had so cruelly stabbed my heart? Was he trying to twist the knife to make sure I bleed every drop for him?

"I want you," he purred, "to be mine."

His teeth looked longer. Dare I say he had fangs? My knees trembled over the obscene amount of power radiating from him.

"Delilah?" Simon's voice rang out from the front of the restaurant, breaking the trance.

Simon's footsteps came closer. I turned to find Hawke was gone, and my body shuddered in relief.

He was so dang sneaky.

Simon had my driver's license in hand, tapping it against his fingertips. "Here is your ID. Congratulations, you are officially a server."

"Thanks." I grabbed it and put it in my pocket to put in my bag later.

Simon eyed me up and down, shoving his hands in his pocket. "I'm glad you came in that day. It was a real blessing. Keep up the good work." He nodded and turned his back to leave.

As he did, a hand covered my mouth, and a shockwave of warmth settled over my body. I felt a scorching heat within me, a fire that seemed to reach down to the depths of my being and spread out between my legs. I'd fallen into a lust filled fog, my body settling up against the one man I would almost do anything for.

"I'm here to take you home." Hawke let me go, and I turned to give him a scowl.

"No." I walked away from him to finish the dishes, which were almost done anyway. He waited silently in the corner, leaning against a rack filled with dry goods.

"A home is where the heart is; ever heard of that? My heart has no home," I spat.

I continued washing the dishes, waiting for Hawke to say something more, but he was always a man of few words. I was the one that kept the conversation going, doing silly things to make him laugh or make him talk.

I let out the water, drying my hands with my apron, and reached for my bag in the corner.

"You're still here?" I eyed him and stepped past him to grab my tips at the front.

He raised an eyebrow, amused at my careless attitude toward him. It wasn't my style to ignore him. I usually gave him a pretty little smile and told him everything was ok when it wasn't.

But nothing was okay anymore.

"I'm so sorry." Hawke reached for my hand, but I pulled away, walking to the front to grab my tips.

Once I grabbed my tips, Simon gave a silent wave, and I went out the front door. Usually I went out the back, but Hawke was still there, and I wasn't about to deal with him in the back alley. I'd been pinned too many times in the dark corners of alleyways, closets, and lampposts with his secret kisses, and I wouldn't let that happen again.

No sir, he ain't gettin' any of this.

Because I'm worth it.

I pulled my bag over my shoulder, tightening my grip.

How in the heck did he find me? Sure, I dreamed he would come and look for me, but that was beside the point.

He shouldn't be here.

I knew the Iron Fang had connections. They could find anyone if they wanted, but I was careful. It took three different buses to get here over two days to get to this town. Yet, here he is.

I could feel my teeth clench involuntarily as the sound of his engine grew louder and closer. I swear I could hear him chuckling, being a complete butthole and smiling like nothing was wrong.

"Get on the bike, Delilah," he barked.

I shook my head and kept walking. We had an audience now, all the rich fancy people staring at the tattooed biker and the waitress walking down the middle of Main Street. They were pointing, gasping at his appearance like he was a freak show. Then, of course, one of them had to pull out a cell phone to take pictures.

"Leave, Hawke, you're making a scene," I said, keeping my back straight. "They'll call the cops on you, and you don't have any jurisdiction down here." Because we both knew the Iron Fang had the cops in their back pocket because they took care of criminals in unconventional ways.

He revved the engine again, the loud noise echoing off the buildings. I stopped, stomping my foot.

"Leave, isn't that what you wanted? You wanted to die alone and miserable? You got it! I left. I have released myself from the protection of the Iron Fang and from you. Now get out of here!" I waved my hand for him to go, but he pushed his kickstand out and killed the engine.

He trotted up beside me, grabbing my arm, but I pulled it away.

"I know I hurt you," Hawke began, "and I can't tell you how sorry–"

"No, you can't tell me how sorry you are because you always say you're sorry. Then you try to act best buds, maybe a little more. Kiss me, make me fall deeper–" I bit my tongue. "It will not work out between us. I should have cut you off a long time ago for my sanity."

I turned away from him, but the grip on my arm was too great. He ripped me around, placing his lips on mine. At first, I fought him, pushing against his chest. Hawke deepened the kiss, his lips massaging me until he slipped his tongue in.

I tried to understand why his kiss felt so intense, stronger, and more passionate, but I could not explain why it felt so good.

I can't let this happen.

So, I raised my knee and hit him where it hurt.

He groaned, grabbing his balls, and fell to the concrete.

"Take that, you piece of crap." I stomped off on my way to the bus stop, completely satisfied with myself. Yet my heart still yearned for him, unfortunately. And if he continued to pursue me, I'd make sure he paid for it.

I ran the vibrator over my clit. The vibrations were pulsing through the water as I played with it between my folds. It had always taken me a long time to get *in the mood* or the right *mindset.* I needed stimulation, like a rock hard body holding me at night while I slept. Then when he slipped out, I went to town, and I got my needed release.

My back arched as I teased myself. I ran it over my clit and pushed it inside my body. My body shook, almost coming to climax until I pulled it away, teasing myself. It was my own punishment. I shouldn't be thinking of *him.*

Each time his face flashed in my mind when I was about to climax, I ripped it away, trying to tell my body we didn't need him. We could think of some other man. Maybe one from one of those romance novels, but none of them compared to him.

Dang it.

After I arrived back at my room, I could hear his bike—a bike I should have been listening for, but maybe my muddled mind pushed it away. Lots of people owned bikes, but somehow I knew it was his. Had I really ignored the signs?

But now I could hear it loud and clear, knowing it was him. I could almost feel him, like he was in the next room.

That was impossible, right?

But he found me here in a large city hours and hours from our small town.

I rolled my eyes, not caring about the logistics of it all. I needed to concentrate on my vibrator while I was in the tub, tingling my clit which I'd come to really know over the past two years with Hawke in my life.

I'd never been such a sexual person until Hawke. Not with my past. I found sex gross, humiliating, but it was the company that was the problem.

With Hawke, I imagined nights of sweet love making our first time. Filling me with the head of his ruddy cock, pushing and pulling it against my walls until my pussy tightened around him. Milking him until he spilled into me.

To see those rippling abs, pull on those pierced nipples with my mouth. I groaned, imagining running my tongue down his body as he squeezed my ass.

My nipples puckered as I curved my back, feeling the vibrations between my legs. My nipples were hard as stone, and I took one and pinched it harshly, enjoying the pain as my clit throbbed with need. Again, I pulled the vibrator away.

I couldn't think about him anymore. I couldn't give my heart away to him. Not when he would crush it all over again, not when he would use me and run away.

I may have given him that kiss earlier, but he caught me by surprise. He'd chased me because he wanted me. Now he might be miles down the road because that was what he did.

Kisses and leaves.

But in my mind, in the far corner in the filing cabinet that had Hawke's Dirty Desires written on the folder, I pulled from that. Thinking of when one day, when my hopes were high, he would break and make love to me. He would pin me to the crisp sheets and watch himself stretch me wide enough to make me bleed.

So many hours, I imagined what his cock looked like. He was a tall man, large, and his cock wouldn't be any different. Not after feeling it against my backside, I knew he was at least eight inches. But it wasn't the inches I wanted, it was the girth. I wanted to feel so damn full.

I rubbed the vibrator against my clit, pushing it inside, tweaking my nipple. My leg jerked, spilling water on the tiled floor, and a moan escaped my lips.

As I prayed for the walls to be soundproof, I let out a whine of satisfaction, feeling my walls clench around the overly used vibrator. My sounds continued as I pulled it out, rubbing my thighs against my swollen clit.

Breathless, I put it on the side of the tub, my body aching from unused muscles spasming. What I wouldn't give for a massage right now, but I guess the hot water caressing my body would have to do.

A pounding at the door roused me from the tub, however. I let out a growl of frustration and smacked my hand on the side of the tub. If it was Hawke, I was going to kill him.

Or mount him.

Dang it.

Do it.

"Stupid voice, I'm not listening to you anymore!"

I exited the tub, the steam following me as I towel-dried my hair. I kept my robe tightly closed, ready to yell at the scum bag.

Nope. He wasn't there.

And yet, I was slightly disappointed.

Yeah, knew you would be.

Oh my god, save me from myself.

Even though Hawke wasn't there, there were a dozen red roses with a card placed beside them. I bit my lip, my walls trying to crumble, but I put that concrete back into those cracks because I would not let them fall.

I yanked the card from the floor, ripping it open with a gruff. And when I opened it, it had the cheesiest card you could imagine—a beagle puppy with big droopy eyes with a stuffed heart in his paws. My lip twitched, trying not to smile.

When I opened it, it read, "I've been pawfully lonesome without you."

CHAPTER TWELVE

Delilah

I frowned, deeply. The kind of frown you had to push down really hard to try not to smile. Because dang it, that was a cute card.

It was completely cliche and cheesy. The exact card I would pick up and give to Hawke, which I had done many times before. One time, he was really under the weather, growling and mumbling incoherent things. He stayed at his apartment for days, and the guys were really worried about him.

Bones mentioned taking him to the forest to get him some fresh air, to be out in nature. That didn't settle with the rest of the guys. They were all upset. Grim was tapping his forehead on the side of the wall when drinks were being passed around the bar, and they raised a toast to Hawke, hoping he would get better.

I don't think anyone believed he would because they all remained somber that night.

So once the bar was closed, I reached in my bag and pulled out one of the many cards I had in there for such an occasion. People got sick and sometimes they didn't want you hugging on them or whatever, so a card was always nice.

I hid under the bar until all the lights were out. Even Switch went to bed that night, which was rare. I tiptoed to the spiraling metal stairs at the back of the bar and climbed up the shaky thing and went down the long corridor where the members stayed.

Not even the cleaning crew could go back there. Members had to clean up after themselves. One lone light hung in the hallway, and each door I passed had a name on the door. Despite it being apartments for bikers, the hallway was pretty clean, and I could even smell scented candles as I went by each door.

As I drew closer to Hawke's, my heart raced, and my chest pounded with anticipation. I could get fired for being back there. It was one of the first rules of working for the Iron Fang. Don't go into the members' apartments.

I couldn't shake the feeling of dread that consumed me, and I knew I had to make sure that Hawke was safe. Three days was a long time without seeing each other back then, and it ate me up.

Instead of knocking, making anyone aware of my presence, I pulled down on the handle, hearing a tiny click. The door opened to a darkened room with a lighted salt rock in the corner. There was a haze of light and a rumpled body on the bed that tossed and turned.

I could smell the sweat from his body, the restlessness in his sleep. I stepped inside, shutting the door and locking it so no one would surprise me.

"Hawke?" I whispered, coming closer.

He didn't reply, and I saw a basin of water beside the bed with a towel, the fabric still damp from its recent use. So, I dipped it inside, catching the cool water, and placed it on his forehead.

Hawke's eyes flew open, his heavy, ragged pants his only movement. He grabbed my hand that laid on top of his head and whispered my name like a silent prayer. "Delilah?"

I chuckled, rubbing the cool cloth on his head. "Hey, big guy, I wanted to check on you."

"You can't be back here." His voice was rough, like he hadn't spoken in days. "You need to leave. I might hurt you." He went to sit up, but I pushed him back on the bed.

"The only way you are hurting me is by not letting me see my bestie. I've been worried. Wish you would have let me visit."

Hawke groaned in pain. His shirt was soaked with sweat, his body aching.

"What can I do to help?" I asked, rubbing the wet cloth over his forehead.

"You shouldn't be here," he said, "but you make me feel better."

I squeezed his hand, pulling the card from my bag.

"Good, and I have something else that will really make you feel better!" I opened the bright yellow envelope, and it showed a picture of a puppy dog on the front. Despite the mattress being soaked with his sweat, I curled up next to him, holding it out so we could both see.

The puppy on the card was wearing a cone around its head, looking so pitiful. Then on the inside it said, "At least you don't have to wear a cone."

Hawke barked out a laugh. It rumbled through the room. I didn't think it was that funny, but he obviously loved it.

And that started my thing of giving him cheesy cards.

But I had never received one. Instead, I was gifted with teddy bears from the fair and clothes and shoes that I didn't need. All I wanted was for him to tell me he cared.

"You can smile, you know," Hawke said, coming out from next door.

And he ruined the moment.

"What the heck are you doing in that room?" I glared, holding the card to my chest.

Hawke sheepishly stepped out, his black shirt stretched tight across his chest.

Not fair at all, showing all those big muscles.

"It's the room I rented when I found you. I can't stay away from you," he said desperately.

"I thought you would be long gone by now. You got your kiss. I'm surprised to see you around."

I picked up the roses. I shouldn't keep them, but they were so beautiful, and I had never been given something so grown up.

"Dede, I never wanted to hurt you–"

"But you did, and look where we're at now? You have hurt me for years. This is over. Whatever we were. I gave you a chance, and you blew it." I took the roses and went inside my apartment. I wasn't quick enough to lock the door, and Hawke stood in the doorway, letting himself in.

"Get out!" I snapped. "You are such a walking red flag, you know! Stalking me, watching me, following me states away to come to find me after you said we would be nothing more. I could call the cops on you, you psycho!"

Hawke shook his head, approaching me and taking the flowers and putting them on the table. "Yeah, but you liked it. You like how I look after you, even when I pushed you away."

And I did. I did like that he still looked out for me. It was sick and wrong, especially with my past. I was used to always being watched. But with Hawke, it was different. He did it out of duty for my protection, and I had hoped because he had deeper feelings for me.

I wanted to be the woman to fix him, but I was obviously not that woman.

"But you want nothing more from me. It's best if you stop," I whispered.

Hawke stepped forward as I stepped back. This continued until I landed on the other side of the room, pinned to the wall. Both of his arms pushed against the wall on either side of my head, his face so close to mine. "You and I both know we can't stay away from each other, Dede. Not in a million years. The only reason I kept pushing you away was because I'm no good for you."

I scoffed, crossing my arms.

"Yeah, you also said I was no good either. You said I was broken, and you couldn't deal with it." My lip quivered, recalling his harsh words.

As I ran my hand up and down my arm, the rush of embarrassment returned, and I felt as though I was experiencing those emotions all over again, my heart hurt.

"Dede, you are killing me." Hawke's voice sounded pained. He tried to come closer, but I slid from under his arms and walked away from him.

His closeness was stifling. I wanted to forgive him, like all the other times, just so I could hold on to one more moment of what we had.

I'd relive those kisses all my life, but this couldn't continue. It was un-healthy.

"Why are you here?" I whispered.

"Dede–" he pleaded.

"Why are you trying to torment me?" I whined. "I am not going to continue this cycle of pain you have put me through over the years. You knew my feelings had grown deep, only a fool wouldn't have noticed. And what did you do? You took it from me, you took advantage. Do you remember that night where you took advantage of me?"

Hawke scoffed, stepping away to give me breathing room. He ran his hand over his hair. It was a mess now. It was no longer gelled back and filled with hairspray, so the wind wouldn't be too brutal on it.

"Yeah, I remember. You were the last one at the bar, like you always were, and I was drunk off my ass." Hawke sat on the bed, resting his forearms on his legs. "But little did you know why I was so damn drunk, Dede. You just don't know."

I stepped forward, my fingers fidgeting and interlacing with one another. I was still in my robe, my hair almost dry, and I knew coming closer to him was going to ruin me. But I couldn't help but inch toward him. I hated it when he was in pain, and maybe that was why I took the pain I had.

Because I wanted that little piece of him. If I couldn't get love out of him, I wanted...the pain.

Wish I could afford therapy.

Hawke spread his legs. He pulled me in by my waist to have me stand in front of him.

"I was thinking about you; every time I drank, I thought of you."

"That's not very healthy," I mumbled, fiddling with my fingers.

He chuckled. "No, it isn't. But it dulled my emotions for you, for a while anyway. Then you had to sit across from me with such a determined look on your face and tell me you liked me." He grinned up at me.

I blushed. It was such a twelve-year-old move, but after being around the guys for six months, I realized I couldn't beat around the bush with them. You had to be straightforward and just spit out your intentions.

"You didn't say anything back. I thought you were going to laugh at me."

Hawke brushed away a drying lock of hair from my face, chuckling deeply. "No, I just didn't know what to say back because I didn't like you."

My heart sank.

"I fucking loved you, Dede."

My lips parted, my heart stopping. "You're lying."

He shook his head. "No, I'm pretty sure I fell for you as soon as I saw your messy bare feet trying to walk into a bookshop for an interview, but I was too damned stubborn to realize it until then."

"So, then you hide your feelings?" I hissed at him, trying to push him away. "You loved me, and you couldn't respond?"

I tugged at him, trying to get away, but he growled deeply and wrapped his arms around my waist, and his knees hit the floor.

What was this powerful man doing on the floor? Kneeling before me?

"There is something wrong with you, Hawke! Let me go!"

"And do you remember what I did after? After you told me you liked me?" His voice was muffled by my stomach. Tears formed in my eyes.

I squealed. "I don't want to hear it! I don't want to!" I covered my ears, and he pulled my arms down as I cried.

Hawke stood up, his hand gripping the back of my neck. "I wrapped my hand around your neck and kissed you like I've never kissed anyone in my life. I poured my soul into that kiss and every kiss after."

I sniffed, tears messily dripping down my cheeks. "No." I shook my head. His grip tightened around my neck. "No, you didn't. If you did, you would have...would have..."

"Don't you see, Delilah? I was trying to be the good guy. I was trying to be the knight in shining armor you deserved. You deserve the world, you see. You deserve a man dropping to his knees and worshiping the ground you walk on. A man with good morals that doesn't have blood on his hands, who isn't a darkened soul, and who doesn't lead a life full of danger. You deserve the white picket fence. A man that will live a good life."

I whimpered, his lips grazing my cheek and nestling up right next to my ear.

"But when you ran, I realized something." He nipped my earlobe. "I'm too selfish to let you go. If I can't be the perfect man for you, I'll be the villain. I'll be the dark one that hides in the shadows so you can dance in the sun. I'll be your silent protector, the guard that will kill a man or woman that dares look at with you with lust." He chuckled. "Because let's be honest. I've come close to killing my own brothers who looked upon you with a wandering eye."

He swallowed.

"And even though I can't promise you I'll be alive tomorrow, I'll make sure you know every second that I am alive that I want you, love you, and I will be selfish enough to keep you until I can no longer breathe."

And instead of feeling salty tears run down my face, I felt tears of arousal begin to run down my leg.

CHAPTER THIRTEEN

Hawke

"*I smell her,*" I heard my wolf say. "*She wants us. I can taste her.*"

He licked his maw. I could see him so clearly in my mind now. He wasn't covered in mange, his hair was growing thicker, and his muscle mass was growing by the minute. There was a pull, no doubt about it, and damn, I was kicking myself for being so damned stubborn.

She had to be my mate.

"*No shit, Sherlock,*" my wolf snorted.

I took a deep breath of her; it was a comforting, familiar smell. Her summer scent was now tinted with a citrus that I had smelled far too often before, but it was amplified tenfold.

"*Our mate likes what you have said.*" My wolf purred. "*Say more seductive shit.*"

I ran my large hands up and down her body, feeling her, touching her smooth skin beneath her robe. How I missed her the past week, not having my hands on her. It was so hard to stay away, to watch her talking and laughing at her job to keep customers happy day in and day out.

I just wanted her to myself, and now I was going to get that chance. But

I would have to do it slowly.

"Fuck that, take her now," my wolf howled.

"We should get you to bed." I cupped her jaw and leaned in to kiss her forehead. "We have a long ride tomorrow." I stepped away, pulling back the covers on her bed, but she stood there dazed.

"Why don't you act like your hairline and back the hell up?" Delilah pointed her finger at me.

Do what?

"I-I am not going back with you!" Delilah tightened her fists and put them on her hips. "I have a job here. I'm going to work tomorrow!"

I growled, stepping toward her while feeling the top of my head. I wasn't going bald. As I reached to pull her to me, she slapped my hand.

I grunted, barely feeling a thing.

"I don't mean to be so violent, but you aren't giving me much choice." She rolled her eyes and went to her suitcase, pulling out her nightclothes. "You have done nothing to prove you are going to stay. We could head back and start this nonsense all over again. Your words mean nothing." She spat in anger.

"Fix this, fix this!" my wolf urged.

"Dede, now wait." I tried to touch her again, but she backed away.

She must feel the bond, this connection we have. My mate dissolved at my touch, and she was more pliable to work with, but since she wouldn't touch me, she wouldn't see reason.

"She's smart," my wolf purred. *"Perfect for us. I like her sass. If only you'd pulled your head out of your ass sooner."*

"You have a family back home, Delilah," I said. "Everyone was really upset that you left. Anaki and Bear in particular." I remembered their crestfallen faces. They were devastated. But I knew why Delilah hadn't told them. They would have told me. The bonds of the brotherhood bound them to do so.

"They did?" she whispered, holding her nightclothes to her chest. "I didn't mean to hurt them."

"Yeah, you didn't just hurt me." I ran my fingers through my hair, as I felt for a bald spot. "You were trying to get away from me and, in turn, you left your family."

"They see me as family?" Delilah perked up.

My little mate really had no one, and I seemed to forget that far too much. She was as alone as the rest of us.

"Of course they did, Sunshine. You are the joy of that bar. Even the band was playing somber music when I went in and yelled at everyone to tell me where you were."

She held back a smile, bowing her head.

Fuck, I was an idiot. Delilah saw everyone at that bar as family. Where the hell did she come from to take in a bunch of rowdy idiots and consider them family?

"Come to bed Delilah. You haven't been sleeping," I ordered her.

She narrowed her eyes to me. "Just exactly how did you find me, Hawke?"

"Oh shit," my wolf snorted.

I tried to change the subject. "Delilah, you're exhausted. Get to bed. I'll watch over you so you can sleep. We can talk in the morning."

"No." She crossed her arms.

No one tells me no. Well, except for her.

"I want to know how you got here. How do you know I haven't been sleeping? I went to great lengths to get here without being discovered!"

I sighed, sitting on the bed. Delilah could be as stubborn as me sometimes, and it was irritating. She was also smart as a bullwhip. The club kept a lot of its unlawful hunting of traffickers and enemies silent from the humans, but Delilah was always watching, noticing things.

I opened my mouth, but she gasped. "You put a GPS tracker somewhere in my stuff!" Delilah ran around the room, pulling out her clothes, making a mess in the process. She ran to the bathroom, throwing her toiletry bag on the floor, emptying its contents.

I pinched the bridge of my nose and went to find her. She was pulling clothes out of the hamper, checking each tag for a little device.

It wasn't unheard of for the Iron Fang to use trackers. Switch was skilled, and we had put trackers on our own people to make sure we always knew where everyone was. We were a broken pack, but we protected each other. Delilah knew that and knew about Switch pulling up members on the computer when we couldn't find someone.

"Is that why you didn't take your bear?" I put my hand on her shoulder. She sniffed, turning around.

"Yeah, thought you would stuff one in there." She rubbed her eyes with the back of her hand. "It hurt to leave him, but I couldn't have you follow me. Not after what you said."

My wolf howled.

Yeah, I was a dick.

I pulled Delilah to my body, hugging her. "I was an ass," I mumbled in her hair. "I said it to hurt you, to keep you away, and look what it did."

She sniffed again, and she let me pick her up. Delilah wrapped her legs around me. Her pussy was bare, and it was taking every ounce of me not to wiggle her up and down on my growing cock.

"Where did you put the tracker?" she mumbled in my chest.

I chuckled, petting her head, then kissing it. "Your shoes."

"Which ones?" she asked, defeated.

"All of them?" I winced.

Delilah groaned, tilting her head back to look at me. "You are impossible, you know that? If it was any other person doing that, I'd be throwing you out."

"But it's me." I smiled. The only smile I would give was to her because she made me happy more than anyone. "And you knew I would do such a thing."

Delilah shook her head, then tapped her chin on my shoulder.

"I'm still mad at you, Hawke. I'm not giving you my heart." Wetness covered my shoulder, and I wanted to cry myself.

I had royally messed up, and I hated myself. "I know Sunshine." I continued to run my hand over her head, stroking the softness of her hair. "I'm going to prove to you I won't run anymore. I'm not breaking us apart. I want you; I want you more than anything."

"I hope you mean that," she said. "Because let me tell you, the last relationship I had, well, it was a lesbian relationship."

I pulled her back, raising a brow. "What?"

"Yeah, it was with a man, but he was a complete bitch."

"Oh, she burned you good," my wolf snorted.

Delilah threw her head back and laughed, her hair tumbling down her back in beautiful ringlets. I loved that laugh. I loved how she could be so carefree, but right now, she was forcing it. Trying to show she wasn't hurt, but I knew she was.

She ached so far down in her soul, I could feel it in mine.

I didn't laugh. I acted annoyed, which I knew she liked. It gave her great satisfaction to see me miserable right now because I couldn't have her.

My *mate*, yes, my mate could do what she wanted with me as long as I could get her back.

As her laughter quieted, I felt her exhaustion. We both were. We had been away from one another, and it took her to run away from me to realize she was the one keeping my wolf from going rabid too soon.

What if I never came to my senses? What would have happened?

"I would have gone rabid," my wolf said. *"But it seems another couple has taken on accepting a human as a mate. The goddess is working miracles."*

I guessed if I had accepted Delilah sooner, it would have been Delilah and I trying to explain to everyone that second chance mates could happen.

What an idiot.

"Let's get you to bed." I kissed Delilah's forehead. "I want you well rested if you want to work tomorrow."

I pulled out the covers. Her robe was still on, but I would not let her get back up to get dressed. She could wear what she had.

"You are going to let me?" she asked, yawning.

I nodded silently, tucking her in. I stripped off the laces of my boots as I sat on the bed, and she rubbed her eyes again.

"I'm not *letting* you do anything. You decide what you want to do, Delilah. I will do anything you ask, anything to prove that I will not run from you, not any longer. I want you and if that means you working in this crummy town for a while, I will support you. Just know once you are mine, I won't let you go."

Delilah bit her lip, contemplating my words. After my shoes were off, I kept on my pants and climbed into bed with her. I couldn't let my cock out, my damned wolf would probably dry hump her in the night.

"You aren't wrong," he said.

Delilah cleared her throat. "What are you doing?" She eyed me as I held her.

"Going to sleep."

She shook her head. "No, I'm going to sleep. You have a bed next door." She hooked her thumb behind her head, meaning for me to get out.

"No," I growled, tightening my hold on her. "You ran from me. I'm going to stay right here and make sure you don't run again."

"Oh, like you don't have more GPS trackers all over my stuff. I'm not leaving again; I've got a job. Besides, you need to be groveling and listening to everything I say." She stuck out her tongue.

I pulled her face toward me, my fingers pinching her cheeks. "I'm not leaving this room."

My wolf wholeheartedly agreed. He would not give that up.

Delilah took the pillow that was under me and threw it to the floor beside her. "Down boy." She pointed to the floor, and my jaw dropped.

"On the floor?"

She nodded, pulling the blankets over her. "You can go get the blankets from your room. I need these to stay warm."

My wolf cried, whimpering, because he wasn't getting his way. *"But you let her kick us in the nuts,"* he whined. *"I wanna sleep in her bed."*

I sighed, rolling out of bed. Delilah was right. I was going to have to work for it, and she was going to let me sleep on the floor and not in the next room. I should be grateful for that.

So, I left, and when I returned I didn't just bring blankets, I brought her the teddy bear. It still had a rip in it where my claws pierced through it when I was angry, but it was better than nothing.

I knelt down beside her bed. She was already asleep. Her eyes were puffy, and tears were still glistening in her lashes. I caressed her face, just thinking how lucky I was to have her still. She could have kicked me out, not that I would let her, but she was willing and even trusting to let me stay in the room with her.

I took the bear, opening her arm so she could cuddle it. And she did, holding it close, and she instantly relaxed.

With blankets I brought from next door, I made myself a small bed. I could sleep on the floor without the padding, but my wolf was insistent we make a make-shift nest. Not that we would use it anytime soon, but he was hopeful. And hell, I was too.

She was our mate; I was almost sure of it. If she wasn't, it didn't matter. She was the other half of my soul, and I would keep her and have her until my dying days.

My wolf took over my body, moving the blankets that satisfied him. It made me wonder if he could shift, if he could run in the forest again, but he was too insistent to make this nest. To have it prepared in case we needed it.

"You should pray to the goddess," my wolf said. *"You should ask her what to do next."*

I shuffled into the blankets, my leg wrapping around a pillow to act as if it was Delilah's body. It was cold; it was nothing like her warm body. "I don't know if I could do that," I whispered back to him. "I'm still so angry."

My wolf curled inside me, his restlessness settling once he saw Delilah's arm hanging over the bed. The sight of her body just a few feet above us was enough to let us close our eyes.

My hand reached up, caressing her fingers. She hummed and wrapped her hand around ours.

Soon, I'll pray to her soon.

As soon as my Delilah forgave me.

CHAPTER FOURTEEN

Hawke

One Year Ago

"I had so much fun, thanks for taking me riding!" Delilah unzipped her lightweight jacket.

It was summer, but the warmth of the sun hid behind the clouds. So, the wind brought a chill to her human skin.

As much as I tried to get her to gain some weight, she was just naturally slim. She ate almost as much as I did some days and still didn't gain an ounce. Which meant with no meat, she was cold, often.

Not that I complained. I enjoyed being around her. Her presence had been good for my wolf ever since she'd revived me from my deathbed. But I wasn't around her just because of my wolf. I was around her because I liked her, maybe too much.

"Now, remember, Dede–"

"I know, I know." She waved her hand back at me. "Don't tell the others that I rode on your bike. Some brother code and me not being your old lady." She winked. "But I loved it and if you ever want to take me again..." She

fluttered her lashes.

"You'll be the first I ask," I murmured, opening the door to the bar.

It was her day off, but everyone hung out at the bar on their day off. It had excellent beer, food, and company, a bunch of broken humans and shifters alike.

Once we entered, though, it was a sight to behold. The bar was turned upside down. Yellow and turquoise streamers hung from the overhanging lights over the booths, twisting and twirling up to the middle of the room. Balloons were scattered around the room, and there even was a big sign that said, "Happy Birthday Dede."

The bar was empty, not a note playing from the band as she took in the scene. Her mouth dropped, and I placed my hand on her lower back to nudge her go in further.

"What—"

And then my brothers rose from under tables, and humans walked out of the kitchen. The humans were filled with enthusiasm and excitement. They ran around the tables and straight toward Delilah.

"Happy birthday!" They all screamed at her, pulling her deeper into the crowd of humans. My brothers and I just watched. Anaki was the only one showing much enthusiasm, pouring shots for Delilah and the other humans.

I sat at the end of the bar, but Delilah kept looking back at me with a bright smile until the women showed her all the decorations of yellow flowers and girly shit.

I took one shot from Anaki and threw it back really quick.

"You gonna tell her it was all you?" He took a shot himself, and we both put our glasses back on the bar for another fill.

One woman with flaming red hair picked up the tray full of shots and brought them over to Delilah, forcing each one at her.

I shook my head. "Don't know what you're talking about." I let the burn flow down my throat and set the glass down for another.

The itch under my skin continued. Delilah was being passed around not just from human to human, but shifter to shifter. They wished her a happy birthday, touching her, hugging her.

I felt my blunt nails scratch the bar, my head throbbing.

"You sure about that, man? I got our messages screen shot so I can show it to Dede later. She would love to know that the wolf she's been crushing on pulled off the unthinkable all by himself."

I growled to myself. I had woken up early Sunday morning and forced Anaki to put up decorations with me, not that I would ever admit it. I made him swear he would say he did it because I knew the little human would take it the wrong way.

We just weren't compatible. A human? A shifter? It would never work, not to mention I would go rabid, eventually. Her calming effect wouldn't last long.

"You say one word to her and I'll–"

"Yeah, yeah, choke me in my sleep. I got it." Anaki chugged back another shot and brought some fruity drinks to the women. She was laughing, thanking everyone for coming.

What I wouldn't give to have her in my bed every night. Hold her, love her, fuck the hell out of her. Imagining the way my name rolls off her tongue in a scream after I eat her pussy gives me shudders every time. I wanted to see that smile when I railed her up against the bed. If only I could, if only my knot wasn't so prominent and, oh yeah, the rules.

"Treading dangerous waters." Locke, our acting club alpha or president, grabbed my shoulder and squeezed it, nursing his own beer. He sat down, staring at Delilah.

"Don't know what you're talking about." I watched the condensation drip down the bottle of beer Anaki left me.

"It's hard, I get it." He cleared his throat. "I think it's fine to have a friendship with them." He rolled his lips between his teeth. "I feel like she saved you from your sickness. If it weren't for that, I'd tell you to stay away from her."

I whipped my head to stare at him.

He knew?

Locke tutted. "Hawke, I know everything that happens in this bar and the apartments. She snuck into your room the day we all thought was your last and the next morning you were fine. Can't say I know what it is. Maybe you just needed a little sunshine around to keep your wolf wanting to live a little longer. I'd stay around her too if she was keeping me alive." He pulled out a cigarette and lit it.

"Wish we could find that for Grim," Locke said and jutted his chin at Grim, who sat in the corner. He had a beer in hand and wore a deep scowl. He was mute now. Bones, the club doc, said he'd lasted a long while longer than he ever thought he would.

"Just keep a good head on your shoulders, Hawke. Don't endanger the rest of us for some ass." He nudged me in the arm, but I snapped. My hand went around his wrist to pin him to his seat so he couldn't leave.

The bar stopped their chatting, looking in our direction. Locke let out a manic laugh and wrestled his arm away from me. He pulled my arm around, pinned it to my back, and shoved my cheek to the bar.

He continued his maniacal laugh, a shrill cackle that seemed to come from nowhere and made everyone feel uneasy. If he didn't get his way, his face would become contorted with rage.

He bent low, whispering in my ear.

"I will protect this MC, Hawke. She isn't to know, none of them are."

He let go of my wrist, and he slapped me on the shoulder again and walked away.

He was right; I had to keep my affection for her under control, for her safety and mine.

"Another, another!" Delilah slapped her hand on the table, demanding another margarita. The group of girls around her all broke out into a fit of laughter. They had long finished their drinks. They were just watching Delilah squeal and giggle.

Most of them had to work in a few hours. Luckily, Delilah did not.

"That's enough, Dede, I think you're done." I grabbed her hand and pulled her away from the table. The women surrounding her watched me, their smirks indicating they knew there was something between Delilah and me, but they said nothing. Humans, well, human women, just knew when there was an attraction to anyone in this bar.

It was damned annoying.

I let out a sigh of disapproval as I took Delilah's arm and pulled her away from the gathering. The decorations were being taken down for the Sunday evening crowd.

"But one more! It's my birthday!" Delilah giggled and fell into my chest. "Whoopsies! Fell right into that. You are like a brick wall." She poked my chest until she felt the hard piece of metal through my nipple.

"Oh...you got a piercing there. I forgot. Can I see?" Delilah batted her

lashes. She pulled on my shirt, trying to lift it. "Abs, wow, look at those." She ran her hand up my bare skin. I gritted my teeth, forcing myself to push the fabric down.

"Dede," I hissed and tried to stand her up, but she fell right on top of me again.

"The floor is moving! When did it start doing that?"

I rolled my eyes, picking her up behind her legs with one arm and the other around her back.

"Lookie! I get a ride! Wee!"

The girls who were tidying up the room had a good chuckle, smiling and waving at her. "Go get some Hawke tushie!" one woman yelled.

Delilah snorted, wrapping one arm around my neck while the other poked at my piercing. This woman was going to be the death of me.

As I got to the door, I was stopped by Bones, Bear, and Sizzle. They stared at my woman in my arms, who was babbling about wanting to pierce her own nipples, and my cock was growing hard by the second. I shuffled her to hide my growing problem; I didn't need the rest of the club becoming jealous I could still sport an erection.

"Maybe we should take her back to her room," Sizzle offered. I glared at him. He didn't like women, and he certainly stayed away from Delilah when she came near. Was it because he liked her? Didn't know how to handle her?

I growled low, and Delilah settled in my arms. "That was hot. Do it again," she said breathlessly. "All you bikers and growling, it's super hot, gets the juices flowing, if you know what I mean?" She tried to wink but closed both her eyes. "Too bad you guys don't like women. Let me ask you though, are bikers normally gay?"

All three shifters gasped and stepped back. "You think we're gay?" Bones asked, appalled. "Nothing against gays, just, you think we are?"

Delilah shrugged. "Well, we have a bunch of pretty ladies at the bar and none of you hit on them. Hawke won't even kiss me." She pouted.

Sizzle rolled his eyes and left, mumbling, "Just let him take her. Apparently, we are all gay now."

Bones scratched the side of his face. "I don't know. Anaki might swing both ways. Like I said, nothing wrong with that," Bones said quickly.

"You mean you aren't gay, Sizzle? You hate women," she shouted to Sizzle. He flipped her off.

"That's so weird. If you aren't gay then, do you just wank off in private? Do you only find yourselves sexy then? That's a bit vain. Don't you think that's a bit vain, Hawke?"

My face flushed red, and I shook my head. "Let's get you to bed."

Bones and Bear stared at each other, their flustered expressions still plastered on their faces as we left. Once I got to Delilah's spotless apartment, I laid her down on the bed.

"Thanks for not ratting me out," I mumbled, tucking her into her warm bedding. She loved to be covered in an enormous amount of blankets, no matter how warm she kept her room. She curled right up into them, like her own little nest.

The longing to have her curled up in my nest with me was strong. But we just couldn't be that way, not when I had my brothers to think about. If the council found out we were having relationships with humans, telling them what we were, it would be death for both species. They couldn't give humans a memory erasing spell, it would be too harsh on their minds.

"I'd never," Delilah said, snuggling deeper into the pillow. When I went to pull away, she grabbed me and pulled me closer. "But I do think you should give me a reward for that."

Her eyes were hazy, her breath still smelling like sweet strawberries from her drink. I couldn't think of anything better than to kiss those red-stained lips, but I promised myself that I wouldn't let this happen again.

Locke's warning was enough. I couldn't put the rest of the club in danger because of my fascination with a human.

"We shouldn't," I told her. Her smile faded, and she pulled on my hand and rested it against her cheek.

"But it's my birfday!" She said childishly. "If I want a kiss, then I should get–"

I covered her mouth with my hand, too worried that someone could walk past her window. But then she licked my hand. I pulled it away, and then she tried to nip at my finger.

"Woman, what is it with you and licking my hand?" I rubbed it down on my dark jeans, and she giggled.

"I'd bite you, but I'm trying to be nice. Now kiss." She pointed to her lips.

Delilah had wanted nothing, always working hard to please the club and her friends. She never asked for anything, and the one thing she wanted... Would I deny her? So being the selfish fucker I was, I leaned in and pressed my lips to hers.

Her hands roamed up my chest, feeling my pierced nipples and tugging them. My erection grew, our kissing becoming an entangled mess of passion as I pressed her into the pillows. She tasted so damned good, and my body pressed her into the mattress as I laid on top of her. The blankets kept us apart, but I could still feel the outline of her body.

My hips gyrated into her; a breathy moan escaped her lips, and a loud bang on her door broke our trance. I jumped from the bed. Delilah was still hazy with arousal, and a small smile formed on her lips.

Her fucking roommates.

"That was amazing, thank you." Her eyes began to close, and my heart leaped from my chest.

I wanted more of that. I wanted it all. But I couldn't give it to her. I couldn't put her or the club in danger.

Delilah rustled in the covers to get comfortable. I laid out medicine and a glass of water for her to take when she woke up the next day.

She mumbled under her breath, whispering my name. I lifted the covers to hear her, to make sure she didn't need anything else.

"I wished on my birthday candles for you to love me, like I love you."

My breath, hell, my heart stopped. "What?" I asked, leaning closer to her.

But it was already too late. She was fast asleep, dreaming of happy endings that could never happen.

CHAPTER FIFTEEN

Delilah

He shifted uncomfortably on the hardwood floor.

I stared over at the bed, tapping my fingers on the pillow. I had initially fallen asleep quickly, but now it was two a.m., and I was wide awake. It was the deepest sleep I'd had in a while, and I was very grateful for that.

When I rolled over, trying to get into a better position, I immediately remembered the biker on the floor. He had pillows, blankets, and clothes all around him. He was sprawled out, laying on his side.

Hotel room floors were disgusting, and even worse was the bare side of the mattress. I mean, he was touching it, almost reaching? Or was I playing that in my head like he really wanted me?

I'd drilled it into my head for such a long time that we could never be, and now Hawke walked into my life saying he wanted me. I was just supposed to accept it and savor it? Were we going to walk off to our happily ever after?

I knew Hawke, and he was one fickle person.

One minute he was kissing me, the next he was running off into the night, avoiding me for days. He probably used those dang GPS trackers to make sure I wasn't coming near him.

Gah, what an idiot.

The whole GPS tracking thing should have bothered me, but it didn't. Not with my past. In fact, it comforted me that someone I trusted was watching me so closely. I always wondered if the past would catch up with me and steal me away. If I was taken, now I knew for sure they would have found me.

It was nice to know they would have rescued me.

The rushing lights of the traffic flew by the window. The honks of the cars created the constant echo in my head. Now I would never be able to get to sleep, not with the familiar sounds plaguing me.

I stared back down at Hawke, only to see him staring right back at me. But instead of the intensity that usually oozed from him, I found a more vulnerable side. His eyes were round, innocent looking. It was the epitome of puppy dog eyes.

And then he whimpered.

He whimpered like a guilty puppy stuck in the corner.

As I saw his vulnerability, I couldn't help but bite my lip. Hawke had confessed he loved me, cared for me, but they were just words. I needed action. I needed to know why he really stayed away for so long.

I mean, look at Grim and Journey. Grim said he was going to have Journey, and he did. Hawke didn't do that for me.

I clamped my jaw shut, trying to hold on to my anger.

The rough-looking biker, sleeping on the floor below me, as close as he could be without being on the bed, was whimpering. I exhaled heavily, battling with the thoughts in my head.

I wanted him to suffer, but in turn, I was making myself suffer as well. I wanted him, even though I shouldn't because of the two years of emotional turmoil. I should make him lay there on the cold ground until he was completely broken like my heart felt.

But I wasn't that person, now was I?

How could I make us both suffer like that when we both wanted each other? There had to be some other reason why he'd stayed away. Was I not pretty enough? Was there really another woman on the side that could fulfill his desires? The reason had better be good, and if it was another woman, I really would cut off his balls and hang them around my neck.

I just wish I didn't have to take such drastic measures to get him to see his feelings for me. But men were different, sometimes it took a good hit to the balls for a man to realize he'd lost something.

Hawke did finally wake up, but at what cost? Why do I have to be so forgiving? He was going to have to really work to get me to go back to our friends and family.

As much as I cared for all of them, my heart had to be mended first. Hawke was the one that would have to fix it.

Hawke had stayed here far longer than any of the other times he'd slept over. That was one brownie point so far, but the night wasn't over.

I lightly tapped my hand on the mattress, feeling the gentle bounce beneath my fingertips. He raised his head, his face illuminated with a glimmer of hope. "I might regret this, but come on up."

No, you won't.

Shut up, stupid voice.

Hawke didn't just scramble into the bed. He picked up all his blankets and his pillows and began making a pillow and blanket fort around us. He threw pillows in opposing directions and set up blankets that nearly covered all sides of the perimeter of the mattress.

He folded and refolded blankets, meticulously smelling them, coming over to me and rubbing it on my body. I sat there stunned, watching him rub the blankets and pillows on his body as well. Then he shoved it right up to my nose.

I blinked as he continued to nudge it toward my nose, and I finally sniffed like he was doing. He nodded, urging me on.

So, I sniffed. It smelled like my shampoo and his peppermint smell I loved so much. "Smells like you," I said in more of a question. He nodded and continued to shape the queen size bed into a giant nest of blankets.

"What are you doing?" I choked out a laugh. He turned back to look at me, and his eyebrows wiggled.

What the heck?

His face had transformed from its stern demeanor, his smile now radiating joy. Once he settled the last blanket and pillow in the right place, shoving it in the right corner of the bed, he flipped around on both his hands and knees and gazed at me.

I felt a chill run down my spine as I nervously laughed, taking in his chiseled features.

"Are you drunk?" I covered my hand with my mouth to hide a smile. Because this new side of Hawke was, dare I say, fun to be around? He wasn't all business, which I really liked, but this version of him was so much easier to read.

He shook his head, grabbing me by the waist, causing me to squeal, and tucked me under him like the little spoon. He wrapped his arm around me and snuggled his head between my shoulder and my neck, and I heard his contented sigh.

No words were exchanged, just his constant purr like humming escaping his throat and chest.

"Hawke, are you okay?"

He nuzzled into me deeper, his arms tightening more. "Mine," he muttered, kissing the nape of my neck.

I wanted it to be true. I really did, but I still had my reservations.

Hawke purred again, I shivered, and I could feel the fire inside me burning. He darted his tongue between his lips, licking the spot he kissed, and my leg jerked back in surprise.

"Woah there! None of that!" As much as I wanted more kissing and more cuddles, we couldn't let it go too far. Not until I knew he wouldn't leave. It had only been half a night after all, and I wasn't about to give in that easily.

Liar.

Ugh, shut up.

He grumbled under his breath, muttering a curse, and kept his body wrapped around me. The noises from the outside faded away, as did the flashing of the car lights driving by my window.

I felt safe, truly safe, after a long while without having Hawke right beside me. And we both were lulled into a peaceful sleep.

I heard a husky, gentle whisper, "Delilah," from between my thighs. Humming vibrated between them, and I clamped them shut.

Something hot, thick, and really satisfying settled between my legs. I'd had some wonderful dreams before, but this one took the cake.

The warmth of his breath tickled across my legs, the heat heading straight to my core. Gentle laps of a tongue soothed the sting of the heat, only for the hot air to come in waves yet again. He was breathing faster than his tongue could keep up with.

I could feel my pussy throb, my body becoming needy. I just wanted his tongue. Right there, he was so close. He was going around the very spot I wanted, and I was dying of frustration.

"Ugh, more!" I groaned, my arm slinging over my eyes.

I was startled awake by a low, reverberating growl, and my eyes opened in alarm.

This was not a dream.

I dared to look down, and Hawke's big puppy dog eye stared back at me in horror. He was blinking uncontrollably, his lips parting in shock.

Shock that I caught him or shock he was down *there*, I wasn't sure.

"What are you doing?" I whispered.

I mean yeah, kissing Hawke was hot. Having feverish dreams from time to time was freaking amazing, but he'd never touched such an intimate part of me with his mouth.

Oh, and I liked it too much.

His nostrils flared, his eyes closed, and he took deep breaths near my core. I could feel my arousal dripping out of my body, and even though I was completely mortified, begging him while I was half asleep, I wanted him to get started.

The selfish part of me wanted to take everything he would give me right now. I'd waited two years for him to put his hands on me. But he never did because he knew he couldn't give me the relationship I wanted. He knew I wasn't a woman that took a one-night stand. But right now, I was a horny woman that hadn't had enough time with her vibrator, and he was *right there.*

Was I going to do this?

Do it, the voice whispered to me. And guess what? I didn't push her away; I wanted to listen.

I lifted my leg, putting my foot flat on the mattress, exposing myself. My robe was loosely bound around my waist, causing the purple robe to fall away from my leg. My pussy was now exposed, and Hawke, who sat so close to it, breathed hot breaths onto my skin.

"You tempt me," he said. His voice was playful, like another person, but it was the same Hawke I'd always known.

Could it be he was just happy that we were here, away from the Iron

Fang? Was he finally accepting me? I wasn't sure, but my raging hormones wanted to find out.

"Is it not tempting enough what I'm offering?" I whispered.

His fingers dug into my thighs, his growl turning into a moan as he kissed up my thighs. My heart quickened, my body shaking with anticipation.

"I've waited years," he purred, his beard rubbing against my leg.

Ha, yeah, me too, big guy. Ever since the day you found me barefoot and homeless.

But was the wait worth it? Should I let him continue? He may not have run out on me last night, but what about in the future? Would he still be there after he gets a taste? Or would this be the final act?

"Then don't wait any longer." I grabbed his hair, thankful he'd grown out a mohawk just for me and I tried to guide him lower. He pulled back, grabbing my wrist.

His lips descended on my wrist, taking a long, low kiss. Then he suckled, nipped, and bit until he took his long tongue and licked all the way up to my little finger, inserting it into his mouth. Letting it go with a pop, he bit down on his bottom lip.

"And I want to savor it."

Cheese on a cracker.

He lowered his face between my thighs, his thick beard rubbing against the tender skin. His nose drifted to my core, settling on my clit. "Fuck, you smell so good."

I whimpered, enjoying the praise. I wanted nothing more than to get rid of the anticipation and have him lick me, kiss me there. My breath grew rapid, my heart pounded in my ears, and his tongue took several swipes to my engorged clit, sending me right over the edge.

My back arched, and his fingers dug into my hips to keep me still. He groaned, his tongue lapping up the juices of my quick climax. He continued to part my folds with his tongue sucking them, cleaning my body until he roamed back to my most sensitive parts.

"I want you to come again," he mumbled inside me. "All over my tongue."

I whined while he licked me everywhere but *there.* He was teasing me, chuckling while I gripped the sheets in frustration.

Before I could shout at him, tell him to eat me out like a real man, my alarm blared, bringing whatever we had going to an abrupt stop.

CHAPTER SIXTEEN

Hawke

I was rudely awoken from my peaceful sleep by the shrill sound of the alarm blaring into my ear. I shook my head and covered one of my ears. As I steadied myself, I smelled the most wonderful scent I could have ever imagined.

It was Delilah, amplified to an extent that my cock would stir if I continued to breathe it in. Except, I was already hard, my come dripping onto the sheets.

I smiled to myself, only to realize that I was face to face with the most beautiful pussy I had ever seen. Her sweet pussy dripping with her arousal, her nub swollen and pulsating beneath the bundle of nerves. I focused on the beautiful puffy lips, and my cock involuntarily pushed into the mattress.

The alarm stopped, my heart stopped as well, and I gazed up to see a flushed face. Sweat beaded her brow, her lips red with indentions from her teeth.

Did she?

"Hawke?" she said in the meekest voice I'd ever heard her speak.

"Beast," I muttered inside me. My wolf whimpered, his head bowed in

shame like a puppy who had pissed on the carpet.

"She liked it. She. She begged for more," he tried to defend himself.

I rolled my lips over my tongue, tasting the sweet nectar from between her thighs. Delilah liked it. She. She came all over my tongue, my beard and even now, it dripped onto the sheets.

What was I to do? I couldn't blame my wolf. I couldn't tell her my animal took things into his own paws and tried to seduce her. Which he did an excellent job with because now that I looked around the bed, he'd also made a nest.

Damnit.

My wolf was hellbent on trying to mark her when I wasn't sure if this was the right route to go. I could die. Delilah could die after the bite. A human with a bite mark was still uncertain.

Was Journey still alive? I rubbed my hand down my beard, letting her arousal coat my hand.

I had cut all contact from the Iron Fang, from home. I dismantled my GPS, not even Switch could find me. I was excellent at covering my tracks, and I wasn't about to call them. I didn't need them hounding me, telling me to return.

I needed this time to win Delilah back.

"I'm sorry," I murmured, sitting back on my knees.

Delilah covered herself, tightening the strap on her robe.

"You're sorry?" she asked again, so meekly. "You are sorry you stopped? Or sorry you ever touched me?"

Oh hell. This was fucking dangerous.

"Once I can feel we can shift, I am never letting you out!" I internally yelled at my wolf.

He snorted. *"I'd do it again. Now don't fuck this up."*

I cleared my throat, trying not to look at the fine mesh of the robe she was wearing. I crawled up toward her head, pulling her into my lap, letting part of my animal instincts take over because I was shit at being a human. I hated everyone. I trusted only a few, but with this woman, I couldn't act like a normal asshole.

Delilah gave my wolf part of her body, and I was jealous as hell. I wasn't there to experience her first orgasm. With my anger lingering for my wolf, I breathed in her scent deeply and sighed.

"I am sorry I pushed you," I said. "I wasn't in control of my actions at the moment I–"

Delilah crossed her arms. "So, you do regret it?" She pushed away from me, hopping off the bed. "Figures you would regret it. You regret every kiss we have ever had, and now you are going to regret this and run off somewhere."

"Delilah, wait." I reached for her, but she'd already grabbed her work clothes from the dresser. She stomped into the bathroom and slammed the door.

Damnit.

"Yup, already fucked it up," my wolf howled in laughter.

"This is all your fault," I whispered, only to see Delilah standing in the bathroom doorway with the toothbrush in her mouth.

She scowled, grabbing the hairbrush that was on the dresser and stomped back inside.

"Goddess, why do you torment me!" I growled, pulling at my hair. "For once, can you make things easy on me, for the rest of us?!" I stormed to the window. Darkness still loomed over the city, the moon slowly disappearing.

"Can you make this easy? For once?" I cursed at the blasted rock. "I'm trying to protect her, protect my brothers, yet you mock me. Am I going to go insane once I finally start believing that she could be my fated?"

I punched the wall to the side of the window, leaving a large indentation. I pressed my forehead against the window. I didn't know if I was mad at my wolf for tasting her before I had, at myself for pushing Delilah away for all those years, or at the Moon Goddess. It could have been all three.

Shit.

"Alright," I whispered, my breath leaving fog on the window. "Please help me." I swallowed. "If Delilah is to be mine–"

The door to the bathroom swung open. Her hair was in a messy bun, and her black shirt was tucked into her black pants which showed off her tiny waist. "I'll be back after my shift." Delilah grabbed her bag and went to open the door.

"I'm taking you," I growled, stepping in front of her.

Delilah ripped her arm away from me before I could even touch her. "I think you have done enough for the day."

She opened the door, but I slammed it shut with my hand, making it shake against the thin walls of the hotel. "No, Delilah." I pinned her against the wall.

My hand grazed her skin, and an electrifying shock ran through my body. My wolf purred, and Delilah relaxed despite the lightning sparking between us. Her body didn't shake and tremble with fear at the venom laced through my voice. "You will ride with me to and from work. I will make sure you are safe, and you will not leave my sight."

She rolled her eyes. "Yeah, you gonna sit in the restaurant looking like that?" She eyed me up and down. I was still in my gray sweatpants with a thin, loose white shirt.

"I will sit in that restaurant bare ass naked if it means keeping you safe. I'd fight off the cops in this corrupt town if I had to, just so I can watch you sway your hips and bend over to pick up a stray fork from the floor. But if you give me a minute..." I winked. "I'll get dressed in something more suitable."

Delilah swallowed, clutching her bag.

As I smirked, I leaned away from the door, but before I left, I kissed her.

"I want to do this right, and I took advantage of you. I'll make sure it doesn't happen again, and we will discuss our limits after your shift." My nose traced along her neck. "Do not run away from me, Delilah. We both know I'll track you down. The next time you run from me, I'll redden your ass."

Delilah

"You smell different," Bram said. I'd just delivered his breakfast—pancakes with two eggs for eyes, a bacon happy face, and I even put a little of whipped cream in his coffee, which he loved.

I think the old man just needed some good-old-fashion loving and a belly full of food. Maybe no one babied him in his life and that was why he could be such a grouch.

"I bathed with the same shampoo last night?" I shrugged, taking a napkin and wiping his chin.

He smiled, digging into his pancakes.

"No, it isn't the shampoo. You smell more like a–" He paused, looking at me. He stared at me up and down and squinted his eyes. "Like a dog."

I blinked. "A dog? I don't have a dog. And why are you telling me I smell like a dog? Do I stink?" I raised my arms to smell my armpits, but no dice. I didn't smell like anything.

Just that peppermint smell Hawke seemed to have left on me.

I left Bram's table to go to the adjacent one to pick up the dirty dishes so I could put them away, but Bram continued to watch me.

"Do you have a friend that has a dog?" He slurped the syrup from the corner of his mouth.

Hawke was the only other person I'd been around, and he didn't have a dog. Not unless he randomly petted a few before he saw me yesterday.

Hawke sat in a secluded corner of the restaurant. He was only wearing dark-colored jeans and a plain black t-shirt. He ordered a big breakfast for himself and tried to feed me while I worked. He had stayed there all morning until I got questions from Simon. He didn't seem thrilled that my friend was here and wouldn't leave.

It wasn't like we were packed. There were plenty of tables, but the vibes most people got from Hawke were overwhelmingly dark and uncomfortable. I was just used to his demeanor and that of those in the Iron Fang.

Every time I thought of them, I felt a wave of sadness wash over me. But I couldn't return until I knew Hawke was going to be true to his word.

Hawke didn't like me talking to Bram, though. Hawke scowled each time I passed by Bram's table. That heated gaze never left me for long, but it seemed to burn holes in my back when I talked to the handle-bar-mustache man.

"No, my friend doesn't have a dog," I said distractedly, then Bram perked up his head and stared into the back corner of the restaurant where I was staring.

Bram's mouth opened, closed, then he resumed cutting into his pancakes like he wasn't bothered. "Is that your friend?" He stuffed another piece of bacon in his mouth.

Damn, he's hungry.

"Yes, he's my friend. Why?"

Hawke dropped his fork on the table, loudly, causing others to stare.

"He stares at you a lot, like he's going to gobble you up." Bram chuckled, until his laughter grew, and he started coughing on his pancake. I went to pat him on the back, but he scooted away from me.

Bram waved his hands in front of him. "Oh, no, I'm fine." He wiped his face with his napkin. "I don't want to start any trouble."

"Trouble?" I raised my eyebrows. "What do you mean?"

I mean, yeah, Hawke was trouble. He didn't like me serving customers, and I'd been paying a little more attention to Bram than I should have. He was just interesting, and I was trying to figure him out. Besides, not even the lower level wait staff would come and refill Bram's drinks when I was busy, so I had to attend to him.

"Delilah," Simon barked.

Great Balls of Fire, what now?!

I carefully carried the empty plates over to another dirty table. I wiped my hands on my apron as I walked over to Simon. His appearance was quite disheveled, his shirt was not tucked in, and his hair was messier than usual.

"Is there something I can help you with?"

I knew my tables were taken care of and lunch was about over. If he was asking me to stay late again, I think I was going to have an aneurysm. I had too much to think about with Hawke and doing dishes wasn't something I was ready for.

"Despite being relatively new, you have done an exceptional job, and I rarely permit inexperienced servers to take care of the special clients and businessmen who visit our restaurant. But I'm going to need you to work for me because these are very important clients and your qualifications are exactly what they're looking for—" His eye twitched and sweat beaded on his brow. "Can I trust you to handle these customers, Delilah? You cannot let me down."

I smiled, nodding enthusiastically. I was excited that he trusted me, even in my short time working here.

During my tour of the restaurant, they'd shown me a special conference room. It was overly ornate with a beautiful chandelier, bust statues of famous people, and greenery throughout. Only the most experienced were allowed back there to serve, and the tips were astronomical.

"I'm going to need you next Friday morning. They should arrive by ten a.m., and you are strictly to serve the men in that room. I need your best behavior and no taking care of"—he nodded to Bram's table—"or your friend that day." Simon looked at the back of the restaurant where Hawke was sitting. Hawke was glaring back at him, his hand in a fist. "He isn't going to be here every day, is he?" He slumped his shoulders.

"I mean, he is a paying customer?" I said. "He's tipped well, too."

Simon pinched the bridge of his nose. Food here wasn't cheap, but Simon seemed awfully annoyed.

"Just don't have him here the day our special guests arrive, and you are no longer to serve him. Have one of the other servers do it."

I nodded in understanding, about to return to clear tables.

"Delilah?" Simon asked again, his face softening. "Did you happen to catch..." He nodded again at mustache-man's table.

I just knew it!

"Um, no sir."

Simon sighed again and turned to leave. This was a business, Simon's business, and I had to listen to what he said about not having Hawke here. Besides, Hawke would be a distraction. He already was. I was glancing back at him every few minutes to see if he was still there, ready for him to run like he always had before. But he didn't. He stayed, sipping on coffee and drinking a mimosa here or there.

I was still mad about this morning. When the alarm went off, it was like he was shaken from a trance that had settled over him during the night. Did he think he was dreaming?

Because if he dreamed like that, I couldn't wait until he was in full control.

But right now, I had to wait and see if he ran after our conversation later today. Because he needed to show me how serious all this was.

CHAPTER SEVENTEEN

Hawke

Delilah left the restaurant from the back entrance, and I had taken up a position there in order to meet her. I saw the rest of the humans she worked with when they exited, and they all looked at me warily. I didn't give them a second glance. They all oozed with fear, even the cooks took a wide berth around me.

I knew it was hard to wait on tables, deal with customers, and being a server was a thankless job. Any sort of service industry was tough. I was glad I never grew up in the human world, because some humans thought they were gods and deserved everything on a silver platter.

But wasn't I born that way? I was given a lot during my childhood; I didn't have it tough like most of my brothers. I received the best training, best food, best everything. And at one point, I thought I had it all, and I let it get to my head.

My pride was quickly shaken when *she* stepped into my life, though.

Most customers didn't care about the people who worked in the service industry. They saw servers as lower social status, as if they were just there to take their food and be done with it, but not my Delilah. She fucking shined at what she did. She took into consideration every customer's needs. If there was a child, she made sure they were taken care of so a parent could eat in peace. If there was an unhappy customer, she made sure they were happy when they left.

Which brought me to a certain person I was getting really pissed off with.

The man with the plaid shirt and fucking overly grown mustache. Whenever he wanted something extra, like jam or butter, he would always wave my Delilah down to get it for him. He enjoyed talking to her, and I fucking hated it.

She smiled at him like any other customer, but there was a wall she had cracked after a few days trying to get him to laugh. I wanted to kill him when I watched their interactions. He was having a tantrum, but Delilah didn't let it get to her. She tried again the next day to make him laugh.

With a camera in every corner of this restaurant, you didn't get a true feel of the room unless you were standing inside of it. And it was fucking eerie with him in it.

There was no doubt in my mind that this wasn't his genuine form. Although I was uncertain of the magnitude of this magical being, I was aware of its magical properties. He had one hell of a cloaking spell, and the glamour spell he had placed on himself was top-notch. If my wolf hadn't surfaced, I wouldn't have smelled it.

It wasn't dark magic; it was laced with light and a bit of earth, which I knew nothing about since I hadn't talked to any natural born earth witches and warlocks, which were few and far between.

Delilah hoisted the bag onto her shoulder and confirmed that she was all set. With a stern look, she watched me as I took it away from her.

"I can carry it. I've carried it plenty of times," she argued.

Not saying a thing, I tossed her bag over my shoulder and took her hand in mine to lead her to my bike.

"You don't carry your burdens anymore, Dede. I'm here to lighten the load." I put her bag in one of the compartments on my bike and pulled out her brightly colored helmet. She stood on the curb, waiting, and I stood up to check our surroundings.

Across the street, I noticed the male who'd demanded my mate's attention at the restaurant with a large cigar in his hand, twirling it as he inhaled the smoke deeply.

"What's his name?" I jerked my head in the direction of the old man with the mustache. He rubbed out the ashes on the side of the brick wall, and the smell of smoke clung to the air as he walked down the street with his hands in his pockets.

"Oh, that's um." She patted her finger on her lips. "Dang it, I always forget his name when people ask me. He's super nice, though, now. He was one of Simon's grumpiest customers, but I got him to smile one day, and now I'm the only one he talks to." She beamed.

Delilah had an air of optimism about her that it natural for people to smile in her presence. But the name forgetting was intriguing.

I replayed the morning in my head and not once did I hear her say his name. "Did you say his name when you were serving him?"

"Yup, loads of times. I just draw a blank when people ask for his name. Weird, huh?" Delilah took the helmet I held out for her and put it on.

I reached out to clasp the buckle under her chin, trying to find any excuse to touch her. I fastened it until it was on snuggly.

"Did you mean what you said?" Delilah asked as I hopped on the bike, revving the engine. She wrapped her arms around my waist and pressed her helmet against my back.

"What?"

"That my burdens are yours to help carry now?"

It was so soft I barely heard it over the idling of the engine. I grabbed her arm and pulled her in front of me, so we could have this conversation face-to-face. She wiggled as I set her down, so she straddled my waist.

It was bright outside, the mid-afternoon sun blaring down on us. The noise of my bike was louder than anything else in the vicinity. There were onlookers, eyeing the outward display of affection, but I didn't give a fuck. Those rich twats could suck my dick.

"No, only Delilah can do that. This dick is for Delilah only," my wolf grumbled.

"Fine, my asshole. They can tongue my asshole," I said back.

"Ehhhh," my wolf started, but I blocked him out.

I'm not into asshole licking.

"Sunshine, I will take on anything. Physical or emotional, you are my priority, and I am here to keep you safe. I'm yours now, and no one will hurt you, not when you're with me."

Her lip twitched. "What if you're the one causing the pain?"

"Dude, she got you." My wolf snorted.

"I'm never fucking leaving you, Dede. You're mine now." I revved the engine and had her wrap her legs around my waist.

"You can't drive like this!" she shouted.

"Like fuck I can't. Now be still," I growled.

The vibration between my legs from the bike and Delilah's sweet pussy in front of me brought memories of this morning. *Beautifully pink, dripping, her scent encompassing me like a warm blanket. Her body was limp in my arms, gorgeously sated,* Those thoughts from waking this morning with my arms around her made me grow hard in my seat.

I took in the fresh air, the wind in my beard as we flew down Main Street. I couldn't floor it like back home. I had no jurisdiction here, but I'm sure I could fucking scare a cop out of a ticket.

My palms rubbed the handlebars, the tips of my fingers begging to touch Delilah's glorious tits. Would they be pale pink? Or a darker dusky color, just like her neatly trimmed cunt?

My wolf purred, growling too loudly, and could be easily heard by Delilah. She didn't speak, however, as she tried to nuzzle under my neck despite the bulbous helmet.

I was stupid, so utterly stupid to think that I could live without her. My wolf was doing funny things inside me, things he'd never done before I was rejected from my first mate. My wolf wanted this so badly, he was whimpering. He wanted to mark her.

But marking her? What would happen?

The urge to call Journey and Grim was strong, but I also didn't want Locke to know where I was. I didn't want to be called home and forced back to the Iron Fang. I needed to let Delilah feel like she had a choice, even when she didn't.

Because I wasn't letting her go. And there was no trail even for Grim to find with his nose. It was what I did—the guard that hides in the shadows. The darkness that looks over the light.

I drove her back to the hotel. The extended stay hotel was a shit hole, and I had plans to move her to something nicer, but then my wolf had made a damned nest. He wouldn't like it if I moved rooms now because he had put our scents all over it. Messing up a male's nest before a female could inspect it properly was bad luck, and I needed all the luck I could get.

I killed the engine, keeping Delila's legs wrapped around me. I knew she had some major separation anxiety going on with us right now, but I had to see what this old man was about. I had to protect her.

Her safety was at risk, and I damn well knew he knew what I was. His shifty gaze continually looking back at me when Delilah was distracted meant he knew something was up. If he was on the wrong side of the fence, he could squeal to someone who could get in touch with the council, and that would fuck everything up.

"Dede, I have to run an errand." I unbuckled her helmet.

Her nose wrinkled, her brows furrowing.

"What kind of errand? Couldn't you have done it while I was at work? I thought we were going to talk now?" Her words weren't demanding or accusing, just on the curious side.

I was in a new town, my brothers weren't here, and I didn't really want to leave her. But I had to.

"Remember when I said I was protecting you? That I'd do it with my life?"

Delilah nodded.

"That's what I'm doing. I need to check on a few things, and I'll be back. If I'm not back by dinner, I want you to order some pizza. Do not come out of your room, lock the door, and when I get back we will talk, okay?" I pulled my wallet out, handing her a hundred.

Taking care of her physically wasn't the only way I would protect her. She would have everything she ever wanted—a house with a picket fence, a place to live when I'm gone, clothes, and food on the table. She would live like the queen I saw her as.

Delilah looked at the money and back at me. Her face, now solemn, shifted to a smile that didn't reach her eyes.

"Okay, fine."

The hair on my wolf's back rose. *"Danger, danger, Will Robinson."*

"Who the fuck is Will?"

"Doesn't matter, he's dead now, and you will be too if you leave her."

"She said it was fine," I replied to my wolf.

"When a woman says fine, she is in fact, not fine. Do you even know how to take care of our mate? Maybe you should let me take over. She sure loved

me this morning."

I gritted my teeth, looking Delilah in the eye. "I'll be back. I promise." I traced my thumb over her cheek, giving her a kiss on the forehead. "And we will talk, figure things out between us, okay?"

Delilah nodded, and I patted her ass as she got off the bike. I waited until she unlocked the door and stepped inside. She shut the curtains quickly and an unsettling feeling settled in my stomach.

She only shut the curtains when she was pissed.

"Oh, you fucked up."

"I told her I was coming back," I replied, revving the engine. "First, we need to find out about this mystery magic mustache fucker. If he puts too many pieces of the puzzle together, we could be fucked."

I might spill blood today to keep my Delilah safe.

My wolf stayed silent, knowing exactly what I said to be true.

CHAPTER EIGHTEEN

Delilah

That stupid douchenoggin.

He left. He left after he knew how I felt about that. I thought he would change, that he would stay. And yeah, I'm childish, thinking he would stay with me after that orgasm wake-up call this morning, but he could have run his "errand" while I was working.

He said we would *talk* later.

Now I'm stuck with my own thoughts, and that could be a dangerous thing. Especially when my body and my mind were out of sorts.

Because a switch flew on in the bathroom this morning, and I'm not talking about the light switch. I felt myself being connected to Hawke, like a live electrical wire that had sparked to life. It was dead before, still connected to us but now, someone turned up the juice, and the generator was running.

I craved him more than pumpkin pie at Thanksgiving.

The feeling of animosity and admiration mixed together and over-whelmed me. Because I was supposed to be mad and make him work for me. But at this moment, all I wanted was for him to stay close to me. It was like my body felt it was absolutely wrong to be leaving him the moment he stepped away from me. Nausea rose in my throat because I didn't know where he was.

Panic, pure panic.

Why was I feeling this?

I locked the door, pushing the curtains closed. As the room plunged into darkness, I turned on the light. It illuminated the room and then my eyes darted to the bed.

Although I'm not sure how, a familiar scent lingered in the air, and I somehow knew it was him. It wasn't just the peppermint, but more of an earthy, musky smell, and it decorated the bed so beautifully.

I wanted to roll in it and be engulfed by our combined smells. We hadn't even made the bed this morning. In the past, I was well known for always making my bed. It was a routine instilled in me at an early age. But for the first time in ages, I didn't make it.

When walking out of the bathroom after that electrical wire switched on inside me, I fell in love with how it looked. The rumpled sheets, blankets, and pillows all spread out in a random pattern, but yet, they were all meticulously placed by him. Disturbing it seemed so wrong, so vile, but with the anger rising in me I couldn't help but stomp over.

I hated myself for wanting to bury myself in it.

I hated that Hawke had left.

I hated being left alone once again.

But what I couldn't stand most of all were these emotions erupting inside me, pouring out of crevices I'd hidden so deep.

Hawke had given me pleasure on this mattress, and immediately I could feel dampness weeping between my thighs. If I wasn't careful, it would leak down my leg, and then I'd have to go take care of myself in those sheets that we'd desecrated.

Oh. My. God. Why the hell had he left?

"It's for a good reason." She whispered.

That stupid voice echoed in my head. I was starting to think I had schizophrenia, and I was blaming the disorder all on Hawke. He'd broken my head, and now my heart was a jumbled mess.

He'd left.

"But for a good reason, don't give up on him, yet."

My forgiving heart could only go so far, and the idea of kicking him in the nards again was sounding better and better. But what if I could get him back? That would be even better.

I picked up the vase of flowers, my anger rising higher by the minute. They were beautiful, romantic, lovely. They were the symbol of love and affection. I should be angry, not fawning over these flowers. So, with all my strength, I flung them to the far side of the room.

The faux crystal glass shattered against the wall in an instant. The tightly closed roses burst into a rain of petals, falling to the carpet.

He'd been here for a while, but I hadn't seen him. He'd followed me, found me, and stayed with me. But then after the orgasm he gave me, he ran away again.

It felt so good to lose control and take out my anger on an inanimate object, so I continued. I took the giant mess of a bed and threw all the blankets and pillows to the floor. Cursing his name over and over in my head.

I had reached my breaking point, and there was no desire to keep it hidden any longer. Deep, dark fears surfaced, and I couldn't stop the roaring rapids of emotions bubbling closer to the surface.

I'd been alone for so long, and then when I met Hawke, I knew I couldn't fall for him. But my body and heart had betrayed me.

I felt like these feelings, this longing to be close to Hawke had grown tenfold since this morning. I ached to be with him, and I didn't know why.

I had a mission when I came here. I was doing so well in the short time I was on my own. Then he had to mess it up.

With blankets and pillows on the floor and the room looking like an utter mess, I stomped to the bathroom and picked up all my toiletries and dirty clothes. I stuffed them hastily into my bag with no regard for organization.

If he wanted me, he could chase me.

As I rushed outside the bathroom door, I saw the two pairs of shoes sitting beside the mirror. He said he'd put GPS in those shoes. That's why he knew where I was. And I was too emotional to hunt through the shoes to find the GPS, so barefoot it is.

I left the key in the door, my feet hitting the warm cement of the walkway leading to more rooms. I glanced back at the closed doorway next door, just waiting to see if Hawke would come from it, begging me to stay. But that was all false hope because he wasn't here.

Shane's confident voice sounded in my head, *"No one wants a sour puss, Delilah."*

I adjusted the shoulder of my bag, climbing down the stairs with angry steps. My soft feet hit rocks and debris, but it didn't compare to the emotions flooding through me.

I wasn't thinking straight. I was in a panic, I knew this, yet I couldn't control my actions. I wanted Hawke. I wanted to be angry, but I felt this over whelming feeling telling me to stay.

I felt like I was on drugs, my thoughts running through my head faster than I could comprehend.

As I stepped on the asphalt, ready to find the bus station, to leave this all behind and start over somewhere else, that stupid voice did it again.

"Stay."

My gut was a mess. It lurched with disapproval when I tried to take another step away from the hotel. Maybe I could stay for a day. Take time to really think about leaving again.

Am I thinking irrationally? Or am I finally seeing things for the first time?

"You're worthless without me, Delilah. You and your mother are worthless without my father and me." Shane's voice came into play, the deepest part of my nightmares resurfacing.

I couldn't leave, not when *his* voice was coming back.

I clamped my hands over my ears in an effort to muffle his words.

"You owe me. We kept you fed, clothed. My dad did your mom a fucking favor. I kept you safe..."

I gritted my teeth, ready to punch my head into a nearby brick wall. It would feel better than the harsh whispers, the gaslighting, the humiliating words bouncing around in my head.

And my heart was about to explode from not being near Hawke.

I'm supposed to be mad!

So, I did the next best thing I could do—the only somewhat rational thing I could. I went to the front office and asked for another room, one on the other side of the hotel. I'd still be near Hawke and know he was close. When I was ready to see him, I would go to him.

But I hadn't needed him in a long time. I'd done fine on my own.

"You need each other."

"He's such a blunderbuss though," I spoke back to the voice.

That seemed to satisfy her, she didn't respond, and I took my key from the confused receptionist. She watched me leave, and I went to my new room and settled on the crisp clean sheets.

They didn't smell like him. They smelt of bleach and detergent, but at this point I didn't care. Because the emotions flashed in front of me every time I closed my eyes, and like hell was I going to close my eyes again. Not until I figured out what the hell was wrong with me.

Hawke

I revved my bike once the door to her room was shut. I sped off, letting the tires rip through rocks that had once been solid concrete. This place was a dump. The more I looked at it, the more I hated it.

Delilah deserved better, and once I figured out this unknown supernatural, I would take her somewhere safer. It would take time for my wolf to reconsider, however. He was constantly bantering about the perfectly good nest he'd built. He could build another, an even better one. But first, we had to make sure we didn't have a spy who reported to the council. We didn't need that mess. Not just for Delilah and me but also the club.

The vibrations from the bike radiated through my hands as I traveled back toward the town center. The main street was alive with people making their way to the upscale stores. When my bike came closer to the sidewalk, the humans that were leisurely walking there glared at me intently.

My wolf's ears suddenly rose to attention, and the fur on his neck rose in response. *"He's close,"* he said, warning me to silently park and get off the bike.

As we parked, I sniffed the air. This supernatural's smell was covered and with an untrained nose it would be untraceable, but not for me, not for my wolf. It smelled similar to ozone, that odd smell you got when you tried to purify the air. I could feel this scent in the back of my throat like it was coating it with a dry, metallic powder.

Whatever the supernatural used, he knew how to use it well.

My boots tapped on the cement. The gun hidden beneath my cut in the back of my pants was a constant reminder I couldn't use my claws; I couldn't show my true form—an act almost impossible because my wolf was screaming to be released.

My claws lengthened, longer than they had been in quite some time. I shoved them in my pockets, letting the sharp daggers pierce my thighs. My wolf howled, his patience wearing thin.

Now that he understood our mission, to protect Delilah and our brothers, he was more on board with finding this male. But unfortunately, we were both antsy, our soul stretching and yearning to be with Delilah again.

"She's unsettled." My wolf panted, his head weaving back and forth between my eyes. *"Make this quick."*

Hastening my pace, I intended not to stay away from Delilah any longer than was necessary, when I stumbled upon a smoke shop on the corner. It reeked of expensive tobacco, incense, and that terrible scent coated the entire store.

As I pushed against the door, the sound of the entry bell rang as if it was a gong and set my senses on edge. I felt myself becoming stronger, feeling my wolf's body taking over. We needed to be near Delilah. The bond was stretched as it was.

As I entered, our boots echoed into the heavily decorated wooden decor. It was straight out of a saloon you would find in a western movie. I would know. For some damn reason, I had been stuck watching too many westerns when I couldn't sleep at night.

This room was more elaborate, however. Tall, round tables for playing cards, a pool table on one side of the room, and shelves upon shelves of various tobacco from all over the world, a golden plaque naming each one, filled the space. Every shelf was polished until it gleamed.

Located at the back of the store was a bar setup, complete with barstools and a wall adorned with beer glasses to give it a more traditional bar atmosphere. On three shelves, there were a small selection of beers and whiskeys available to choose from. It was a smaller bar than back at the Iron Fang, but it was enough to serve a few customers.

It was a full service store, maybe even inviting men in for poker nights, beer, and smokes. Hell, I was impressed with the setup.

The saloon doors pushed open as the scent of ozone became more apparent and thicker. The air became electrified, and there, standing in front of me, was the male I needed to see, holding a wooden box in his hand.

My wolf's ears were standing at attention with excitement. His growl made the air feel thicker and pushed the ozone back toward the male. The male stepped back in surprise, but overall seemed unafraid.

"Was waitin' to see when you would show up." He carried the box to the bar and set it down with a click. "Nice to meet you, Hawke, or should I say, Gunnar?"

CHAPTER NINETEEN

Hawke

My eyes widened. "How the hell do you know that name?" I gritted my teeth, my tattooed hands pressed flat on the table.

The fucker had the audacity to smirk, brushing off the wooden box as if there was dust still left on the pristine surface.

"Didn't think you would recognize me under this illusion. It is one of my better ones." He winked.

I felt a deep, aching pain and an overwhelming rush of emotion erupting from within us, prompting a whimper from my wolf. A chill ran down our spine, and we felt a cold, eerie presence in the room, as if the Reaper himself had come to take us away.

Anger at this male and memories that had been buried deep roared to life. Flashes of my past—being rejected, broken—fluttered behind my eyes. My wolf howled with sadness, recalling the pitiable expression on her face as she held onto the mate she thought would be a better fit for her than the one the goddess had chosen for her.

I gripped the bar with one claw to keep from falling. The other hand clawed at my chest, ripping my shirt to shreds before I fell to the floor in excruciating pain.

The male came around the corner, the box in hand as I sat there vulnerable as the day I felt the bond break from my previous mate. He could kill me now and put me out of this misery that could be my wolf going rabid. He was shaking and howling for the enormous pain in our heart to stop.

"Get away," I yelled, slapping the male's hand away.

But he tsked, putting his hand on my shoulder. A dim, low light radiated from his hand as he touched me. As I tried to put the pieces of the puzzle together about who he was, he opened the box, shuffling through its contents.

"Don't be so damned stubborn, and a stubborn one you are. How the hell did you live this long?" He swiped a match over the top of the box and grabbed several strands of hair that had fallen on my shoulder. He pulled them closer, letting the flames engulf the hair. As the flame shifted to a pink color and the hair on the match had completely disappeared, he sniffed it curiously.

He eyed me, his eyebrows raising until he gripped me by the shoulders. "You have found another?" he asked, panicked. "How did you activate it? How did this come to pass?" His voice cracked, the old male's voice falling away, and a younger one replacing it.

"Who the hell are you?" I rasped, gripping my heart.

"Doesn't matter, not now anyway." He shook his head. "But right now, you have a big problem. Your mate, which I am certain is that waitress, is going through bond sickness."

"How the hell do you know?" I gripped my chest, feeling another stab of pain.

Bond sickness was very real and very dangerous. Once a couple found each other and recognized each other as mates through smell or touch, the timer began. A bonded pair had a few short weeks before the bond sickness would sink in. Bodies became dependent on each other, and souls would shatter and become weak the further apart they were. If they didn't come together to complete the bond, both of them could become sick and die.

Bond sickness could bring about intense, almost uncontrollable emotions, so you were forced to depend on the person who was the other half of your soul. With all I had endured mentally in my past, and whatever Delilah had gone through before, we were a recipe for disaster.

"I just did the test. Did you not see it? It flashed pink, and it smelled of roses." He snorted like it was the most oblivious thing. "I don't do fucking magic tricks; that is so cliche." He stood, stepping away from me, taking the box along with him. "Now tell me, how did you know she was yours? What did you do? How did you meet her?"

I growled, my claws lengthening once more. They swiped across the lower part of the bar, leaving five deep scratches.

"Damnit, get a hold of yourself!" he snapped.

"I have to go." I stood with barely any energy left. I was draining fast, and if the bond sickness this warlock was speaking of was truly happening, I didn't have long before Delilah would be overcome with it.

But I still had a mission. I had to know this warlock wouldn't report us to the council.

"Who the hell are you?" I gritted my teeth again, my fist banging on the bar.

The male cocked his head, rubbing his fingers through his mustache. "That is a story for another day, Gunnar. Just know I am a friend and not your foe. You have little time now." He looked at his watch and glanced back up at me. "A human will not fare well with bond sickness."

"What do you mean? How do you know?"

The male rounded the bar once again, pulling out keys from his pocket and dangling them in front of me. "There is an apartment above this store. You can bring her here and make your nest." He reached for my hand when

I didn't take them and forced them into my palm. "You need to mark her or, at the very least, do not leave each other's side."

"I won't force her," I yelled. "I would never, I can't believe–" I tugged at my hair. "I can't believe this is happening," I choked out a growl.

"Please don't cry here. I find it very uncomfortable." The male took me by the arm and led me out the door.

"How do I know you won't report us to the council? How do I know you're helping us?" Because my damn wolf was all out of sorts. I could pick up a lie, an inkling of betrayal. But right now, my body was out of sorts with sickness. I came up with nothing but static when I tried to read this male.

The male sighed. "You don't, but know I hate the council as much as you." He rolled his lips between his teeth. "I've also been rejected, and if a blubbering idiot wolf can have a second chance, I better damn well get one, too." He pushed me out the door, following me to my bike.

"I'll be here until you return. I'll go out and retrieve unscented blankets and pillows for preparation." He fiddled with the door handle until we both found the sidewalk.

I looked at him in disbelief. *Why the hell was he helping me?*

"I have little time left, and let's just say this warlock doesn't need his soul darkened any further." He glanced around us, his nervousness now radiating to my wolf more clearly. He weakened his cloaking spell, which enabled me to detect his objectives more readily by smell and feel.

He wasn't lying, and I suddenly felt more at ease. He needed me. That's why he was helping. But if he found out I'd prayed to the Goddess for guidance and answers, would he leave Delilah and I high and dry?

Not having the ability to argue back, I threw my leg over the bike. "We'll return once we're both stable," I said.

"She will be once you return to her," he added. "If she is affecting you from this far away, she is suffering more than you are. I've got herbs to help her. Just go," he said urgently.

I wanted to take Delilah back to the Iron Fang, but if she truly had bonding sickness, then it was imperative we stayed close together. She would be weak for several days afterward, not just in the physical sense but the emotional one, too.

What I could not understand was why we both came down with the sickness so fast.

"You prayed, the goddess answered," my wolf snipped. *"We have been around her so long, and once you asked for* help, *the bond snapped. Of course, we would both get sick so quickly. You've held off taking her for years."*

Shit.

"Stubborn ass human." My wolf rolled his eyes.

And instead of beating the shit out of the warlock and interrogating him further, I revved the engine, leaving black marks on the concrete in my wake. Because if I could feel the pain, my mate must be feeling it more. And as much as I wanted to know who this warlock was, Delilah needed me more.

****

I sprinted up the stairs. My mind raced a mile a minute, trying to figure out what the hell to say to her.

"I'm a wolf. You're my soul mate. Since I've waited so long to claim you, you are sick. But if I claim you, you may shift and not survive. All this pain you are going through is because of my indecisiveness." Great, that sounded absolutely fucking fantastic for a wolf trying to regain a second chance with his *second chance.*

Fuck, fuck, fuck.

"I'm a wolf, a shifter. That's why I haven't been completely honest with you," I said over and over until I reached the door. With my hand clutching

the handle, I could feel my pulse pounding in my ears as my breath came in short, shallow pants.

What if she rejected it? Rejected what I was telling her? What then? Was she going to feel trapped? Because the only way for us to survive now was by mating with each other or staying with each other, always.

Not unless she mated with another. Could a human do that?

"NO!" my wolf howled. *"She will not reject us!"*

I shook my head, my chest throbbing with pain. My heart pushed me to the direction to the door and as it fell open, I tripped, falling onto the dirty carpet. "Delilah?" I scoured the room, but I could not find any traces of a heartbeat or her fresh sunshine smell.

The bed was torn to pieces. Pillows and blankets were scattered across the floor. The roses I bought her were smashed to pieces, possibly even stepped on in anger.

"Told you not to leave her." My wolf scowled. *"She has ruined our nest, she has destroyed it!"* His body had gone stiff, his hair stood up on his neck. His maw leaked venom, and his eyes glowed red.

Delilah didn't know that destroying a nest could be hurtful. I couldn't blame her, but damn it hurt like hell to see the first nest I'd ever created torn to shreds. My wolf was deeply wounded. Hell, I felt disappointed myself that it wasn't good enough for her to want to stay. She could have wrapped herself up in the nest, our smell dulling the pain enough until our return.

But she rejected it.

My wolf howled, both in anger and humiliation.

"She didn't know," I tried to soothe.

But it was like a slap in the face.

Hell, I deserved it. I'd ignored all the signs for years, and this was payback. But the thought of her being gone, running away from me again, gave me a new mission. To find her, take care of her, and spank her ass so she would never do it again.

I let out a snarl of frustration before stomping off toward the bathroom. All of her things were gone, her clothing, her toiletries, but the sweet smell of sunshine lingered in the air. Everything was gone except one item that she knew I could trace—her shoes with the GPS tracking system.

She didn't want me to find her.

A lightning bolt of pain ripped into my chest, my breath leaving my lungs as I crumpled to the floor. I had to get to Delilah, and fast. How the hell could she leave when she was in so much pain?

I grunted, pushing myself back onto my knees and using the bed to lean on. "Delilah!" I roared, grunting until I was fully standing.

I continued to scream her name, like she was hiding somewhere in the room, but my wolf and I knew she wasn't here.

My wolf wrestled with me, trying to take control of my body. His efforts did not go in vain, and another wretched shock went from head to toe. He snarled, fangs elongating and his claws scratching through the walls as he used them to hold himself up. Once we stumbled out of the hotel room, we saw the sun was setting. It was too bright for our enhanced eyes, and it took time to adjust.

His nose went into the air, like he was smelling for the blood of his enemies. He was on his own mission while I tried to contain the pain that we were both feeling.

"She's close," he grumbled, stomping down the stairs.

He took every noise and scent into consideration. He sniffed down the hand rails leading to the front office. A female sat inside, checking other humans into their rooms.

But our nose caught another scent. It was sunshine twisted with shadows of darkness. A whimper that damn near broke my already bleeding heart was heard to the right of us.

"Close," my wolf murmured.

I knew he was angry, I knew he was still hurt by Delilah ripping apart our nest. I wasn't sure what he would do when he found her, so I continued to push, trying to retake control of my body.

"Let me out," I pleaded, able to take control of my lips. *"She doesn't know, we can't hurt her. She was upset we left."* That much I knew. If she left, it was because she felt like I had betrayed her.

If only my wolf didn't fucking eat her out, we wouldn't be like this.

"She wanted it; she wants us!"

"But we had to leave!" I argued back. *"We had to make sure—"*

"Fuck off, it's all your fault! You are too much of a damned pussy!"

I huffed in annoyance. *"I had to think of the future, not the here and now!"*

"She's mine!" he roared, finally coming to a door that smelled of her. Not just her, but pain, suffering. My soul reached out to latch onto hers and never let her go.

Before I could fully take over, my wolf kicked in the door. It slammed open, the handle now lodged into the wall. He yelled her name again, causing me to wince at his thunderous voice. "Delilah!"

The room was dark, but our eyes quickly adjusted. We didn't find her anywhere on the bed. It didn't smell like our room at all, just the sterile sheets and bleach.

"Delilah!" my wolf roared again, not bothering to shut the door.

We stomped to the bathroom, the little light that radiated from the crack in the door catching our eye. Once we opened it, it blinded us with a bright light that should have been heaven's gates. But unfortunately, we found Delilah laying on the cold tile, whimpering as she clutched the bear we'd given her.

Delilah clutched the bear like it was her lifeline. Her nose was buried in its head, her body coiled into a fetal position. She was sweating, her skin clammy, and worst of all was her coloring. Instead of it being slightly tanned, it was grey and white.

"Oh, Dede." My wolf relinquished control, and I went to pick her up. Her body shook as if she was freezing.

"No, go away. Don't need you," she cried.

My heart broke further.

"But Sunshine, I need you," I pleaded. "Please let me help, please let me take care of you, I'm so sorry for leaving, I shouldn't have."

Delilah clutched her bear tighter, her eyes squeezed shut.

"N-no." She shook again, and then let out a strangled cry.

Fuck, I had to take her. It was hurting me too much.

I pulled off my cut and my ripped shirt, leaving me in nothing but my jeans. The more skin-to-skin contact we had, the quicker she would get better. She wouldn't feel the pain as much while she recovered. And like hell did I want her to feel this pain anymore.

She still had her eyes shut, and I gently picked her up off the floor. She cried out again, as if my touch hurt her.

"Shh, sunshine, it's okay. I've got you now. I'm never leaving you. I came back, see? I found you."

Delilah wrapped one arm around my neck, her face buried in my chest as I took her to the bed. I sat up by the headboard, slowly rocking back and forth. I didn't know what else to do. Treating her like a baby seemed the only way that made me feel better.

"Dede, talk to me." I sniffed, my own tears beginning to run down my cheeks. "It's going to get better now, I promise."

"I feel so much," she cried. "I feel everything."

"I know, Dede, I know. And when you feel better, I'll tell you what's happening, okay? But I need you to trust me. Just one more time. When I left earlier, I had to make sure we were safe, and we are. We are going to be just fine. Just trust me."

"Don't want to." Her pouty voice was muffled by my shoulder.

I chuckled, the pain finally subsiding.

"I know you don't, but if I promise to let you kick me in the nuts, will you?"

Delilah was silent for a long time, then she nodded.

CHAPTER TWENTY

Delilah

Hawke's embrace suggested that I was more delicate than a newborn. His fingers moved gently through my hair as his lips lingered on my forehead, the warmth of his breath calming my nerves. He rocked me slowly, the sound of his humming and gentle purring creating a soothing atmosphere that lulled me into a relaxed state.

I loved the feeling. I felt my emotions—the overwhelming feeling of drowning, falling down a rabbit hole and then being sucked into the vortex of a black hole—subside.

Before he arrived, I thought I was dying. Breathing was nearly impossible, my chest constricted, and the only bit of comfort I found was the teddy bear that had the faintest scent of Hawke. It was both a blessing and a curse because it made me want him more when part of me wanted to stay angry.

Hawke didn't act without a good reason. It's how he protected every server at the bar. He watched, he prepared, he took calculated precision when he had to escort or throw customers out of the bar so no one else got hurt. We were all protected. I felt safer with him than at any other time in my life.

So why did I have to get emotional about it? It was the ultimate spaz moment, bringing back old feelings buried so deep I never thought I would have to deal with them again.

And now it was all a distant memory. I felt so much better.

I sighed heavily into his chest. His bare chest, mind you. He had a sprinkling of dark hair over tattoos, along with his nipple piercings. I'd never seen him without a shirt, and I cursed myself for not making him take me to a pool, so I could check out all this hotness.

I ran my hand over his chest, feeling the muscles so large that I swore I could feel the sinews between each fibrous thread. His purr-like rumble radiated deeper, making my muscles to feel like puddy. As I pressed my cheek against his skin, I felt the warmth radiating off him, a tangible reminder of the affection he continued to give me.

How long had I wanted this? For him to hold me? To not worry when he would run away?

For a long time, I felt worthless. That I was never quite good enough for him.

"I'm so sorry I said those awful things to you that night," he said.

I sniffed, not bothering to reply.

"There is no other woman, there never was, it has always been you," he whispered.

More encouraging words spilled from his mouth. More words of affirmation that I craved. How strong I was, how brave I was, how amazing it was that I'd left and decided not to be taken advantage of by his fucked up head.

Leaving had been worth it all along. It kicked him in the pants.

And secretly, I hoped he would come for me. Because I saw him as worth fighting for, but I needed him to realize I was worth fighting for, too.

No one else saw him for who he was, and even if I didn't know his history well, I knew who he was today. Maybe he led a wicked life before me, but it must have molded him into the man he was now.

I was still going to bring it up until the day I died that I had to wait for him to man up and grow some balls, though.

Going against all better judgment and giving him another chance because my gut was hell bent on me accepting him, I soaked in his words. His words were beautiful and everything a woman would want to hear from a man. If I wasn't still weak from my anxiety attack, I bet he would be on his knees in front of me kissing my feet.

It wasn't just his words that felt so good, but also the touch of his skin. I couldn't explain why it felt so good to have his body touching me, but I wanted more. It was fire and ice at the same time—it tingled, it sparked. It did everything in between.

I huffed, wiggling in his lap.

"Sunshine," his voice rumbled down to my core, "what's wrong?"

"I don't know." I shook my head. Everything was so much better, and yet it wasn't. "I need more of something." I wiggled again, my body not feeling completely sated even when Hawke was right here.

Hawke was right where I needed him. He was in this room, he was with me, and he wasn't going anywhere. I honestly believed that.

I rubbed my cheek over his chest again, like a cat searching for the perfect spot. My hand roamed over him, touching him everywhere. He didn't say a word, letting me do what I wanted until I got the great idea to just pull my sweaty shirt off.

His eyes widened, his arms opening so I had enough room. I kept my bra on, but then I straddled his lap and plastered my body to his.

Oh, so damn good.

That's the stuff.

I relaxed further, melting into him. He moved his body, so he was lying on the bed. Laying on top of him, I completely covered him and felt better than I could have ever imagined.

I'd gone insane. What the heck was going on?

Hawke's hands ran up and down my back, his finger fiddling with the bra strap until he flicked it off and groaned. "Sorry, it was in the way."

I grinned and grabbed ahold of the bra and pulled it out from under me. It landed on the floor with a thump, and my breasts laid right on top of his cold nipple piercings.

"Why does touching you feel so good?" I moaned, rubbing my cheek next to his neck. "I thought I was dying an hour ago, and here I am, feeling so much better."

I felt a wave of darkness wash over me, but I pushed it away and kept it buried deep within my heart. I did not want to reenact that slap, not again, not now.

I wasn't sure how long those dark memories would stay hidden, so I concentrated on the sweet paradise I now had.

Was I so weird and broken I had emotionally attached myself to Hawke and talked myself into thinking he was the only medicine that would keep me from breaking down?

The sound of Hawke clearing his throat was accompanied by the delicate sensation of his fingers tracing up and down my back. "There's a reason for that, and I'm afraid it's my fault you felt all that pain. And why you feel so much better after my touch."

I lifted my head, cocking it to the side. "What do you mean, it was your fault? You didn't have anything to do with it." I laid my head back down on his chest, soaking up more of his steady heartbeat. "I was having a panic attack. I've never had one so bad before. I used to get them—a long time ago."

Nope, not going there.

Hawke growled, sitting up and gripping me tightly. He moved my head to the crook of his neck, where I could take in his scent. "You are not messed up or broken. It is my fault, and I need to explain why."

"It can't be your fault," I said, my voice muffled in his shoulder. "I'm tired and fed up with fighting my feelings if I should let you into my heart or not, plus you leaving gave me some sort of PTSD. I can't expect you to be around me all the time. I'm just a little broken—"

Hawke gripped the back of my neck, pulling my hair in the process. He looked down into my eyes, and a fire erupted in my belly. His grip tightened, and a moan left my lips. Damn, he was hot, and the sexual frustration we'd both felt over the years was stifling.

Hawke tightened his grip in my hair, driving me wild in the worst moment.

He was trying to be serious, and I'd become a horny woman after a panic attack. He could tell me he was going to eat me out right now, and I'd let him. My body had decided Hawke was the only one we wanted. My heart still questioned.

"Sunshine," he murmured. "You are not broken. You have every right to question everything I say. I didn't have time to explain who I really am when I left earlier. I left you at the worst time, and I knew it was wrong, but your physical safety was at risk, so I had to choose. Obviously, I chose wrong and hurt you more."

"What does having to know who you are change any of that? And why do we need to check our safety? No one knows us here."

"We both were in danger, and I'm going to explain it to you. But first, you are weak, and I need to get you fed."

Hawke had a weird fascination with food. Anytime I was upset, he would get me food. He liked to stuff me full of the most random and fattening things, trying to get me to bulk up, but I had a fast metabolism. I couldn't sit still for a minute if I tried.

Hawke shuffled his hips and reached into his pocket, pulling out his phone. He opened a food app, tapping the screen with his thumb several times.

I stared as he tapped at the screen and ordered food to be delivered. He didn't ask, because he didn't have to. He knew my favorite foods, and he also knew I hated deciding.

That was one thing I loved, I never had to decide. I hated deciding, and he made it so easy to just be and not worry about anything when I was in his presence.

His thick eyebrows furrowed, his lips even puckered as he tried to decide for the both of us. The usual deep lines that accompanied his scowl had lessened dramatically, like he had got some serious Botox or visited a spa at some fancy resort.

I silently giggled, albeit weakly, thinking of a muscular biker with cucumbers on his eyes. He just looked so much younger, not as growly, scowly, and unapproachable as some might say.

That made me smile widely and made me realize he was happy with me. He was less conflicted, and part of his burden had been lifted. I tilted my head, watching him, hoping I had something to do with it. The overly optimistic attitude that filled my heart was a curse sometimes. But who wanted to concentrate on the bad times, it was utterly depressing.

And with that optimism, I didn't want to fight anymore. Hawke came back, and he said he'd left for us, to keep us safe. Safe from what? I wasn't sure, but my answers were coming soon and that was all I could ask for.

Hawke put the phone down and immediately ran his fingers through my sweaty hair. His dark eyes had lightened considerably, showing hints of gold instead of dark blue.

"You know," I said, keeping my naked body pinned to him.

Nothing felt more right than being in his arms. He didn't grab my breast, didn't try to rub my lady bits all over the enormous erection he was sporting. He was just here, holding me, loving on me like an animal would with his nose in my now messy hair, his hands on my back keeping me plastered to his chest.

"Mmmhmm," Hawke hummed, running his nose down my hair to my forehead. He placed a kiss on the apple of my cheek, and my faced flushed red.

"You can't tell me you have a secret to tell and then not tell it."

Hawke chuckled, his beard tickling my bare shoulder. "I can't, can I?"

"Nope," I popped the p. "Because it's going to make me sick with worry all over again."

Hawke pulled away, his eyes searching mine for either truth or pain. I smiled guiltily, shrugging, and laid my head back down on his chest. He sighed, his hand running over his face and pulling at his beard.

"I'd rather you be fed first," he mumbled.

"Why? Is it going to shock me so much that my stomach will flip inside out?" I quipped.

He shook his head, pulling me away. This time, he got an eye full of my breasts.

"Goddess, you're gorgeous."

I covered my face in embarrassment, but he pulled at my wrists to look at me. "I mean that, Dede, you are the most beautiful woman I've ever laid eyes on."

"You've seen them before." I couldn't look at him, so I bit my lip and stared everywhere but him.

He took my chin, grabbing my attention, and gave a wolfish grin. "That I have, and they were beautiful then, and they are beautiful now."

My heart dropped into my stomach. "You really saw!?" I squealed.

It had been a rough day a few months ago. The entire Iron Fang was in an uproar about finding a sex trafficking ring that was traveling up and down the west coast. Rumors of these parties fading in and out of Switch's radar were both frustrating and intriguing. They were hell bent on finding the ringleader, and they soon did because they found Journey months later.

But at the time, Hawke had to travel three days away from the club, which was a long time for any of the bikers to be away from home base. They worked together as a team, became so closely bonded, they worried for each other's safety and didn't leave overnight unless there was a pack of them.

Hawke had traveled alone, and I was expecting him back the next day, so I didn't bother covering myself with a towel when I walked back into my room. I never imagined there would be a greedy, attention seeking tattooed male sitting on my bed with wide eyes.

I hid in the bathroom for nearly ten minutes while he tried to coax me out, saying he saw nothing. *"I was looking at your heart, not your boobs!"* he kept saying.

"I think we both know I saw." He wiggled his eyebrows. "I was trying to get you to come out. I missed you and didn't want you upset, so yes, I did fib. A little." He held up his index finger and thumb, showing me how little he meant.

I bit my lip, pulling on the chapped skin of my lips. He took his thumb and softly tugged my lip away, sending shivers down my spine as he caressed it.

"I think you're stalling," I whispered.

He licked his lips. "Yeah, but I really want to taste those lips."

Before I could playfully ask, "Which ones?" he crushed his lips on me, savoring every bit I gave him. His hand roamed my back, pulling me closer to his erection.

I moaned, leaning my head back as he kissed down my neck, to my shoulder until he sucked the skin so hard the pain mixed with pleasure.

"Hawke!" I whined, rubbing myself on his dick like a feral cat. I wrapped my arms around him, as I went to my knees. He let go of my shoulder to put his mouth on my breasts, and I hissed as he sucked violently on one while he palmed the other.

My fingers tangled in his hair, pulling his scalp and thus pulling him away from me. His grip broke with a loud pop, and his eyes were filled with a passionate black.

I wanted more.

"You want more?" he read my mind. "You want me to finger fuck you? He was already beginning to unbutton my pants but then became frustrated and ended up ripping them past the zipper to give himself more space.

A growl spread through him, vibrating his body all over. He sighed, and his fingers parted my lips. "You wanna know what I did after I saw your breasts that night?"

I mumbled incoherently, and he pinched my nipple. "Pay attention, Sunshine, you don't want to miss this." He pushed his thick digit into my pussy. My back arched, trying to get more of him inside me.

He chuckled, almost evilly. "I thought about them for months, what I would do to them, to you with that flimsy bath towel you had around your waist."

My heat engulfed him as he pushed in another finger. I was stretched as he pushed his fingers in and out of my body. He was using his strength to thrust deeply, and another finger tickled my entrance.

He licked my nipple, watching it harden beneath his gaze. "How I would kiss you senseless, touch every inch of this glorious body, show you how a real male can worship a queen." He took his free hand and rubbed against my clit.

I cried out, feeling my orgasm build. Three thick fingers, thrusting inside me with wild abandon. The bed was shaking. Hawke moved every bit of his body as he pushed me farther into oblivion.

"And then I would fill all your holes with my cock. Fill you with my seed, my scent, so no other male would ever approach you, let alone touch you," he growled.

I whimpered, biting my lip to hold in my screams.

"No, no, Sunshine, I wanna hear you. Let me hear those pretty little whimpers as your greedy little cunt milks my fingers."

Oh, the dirty talk will be the end of me.

As I grew closer, my arousal seeping down his fingers, I felt his fourth finger.

No, he wouldn't.

"Not today, but soon," he panted, as he had me bounce on his fingers. "Every inch of me is going to stretch every inch of you."

I cried out, my forehead landing on his shoulder as I felt the waves of my orgasm crash into the shore. He continued to finger fuck me, his mouth finding my neck and sucking on it violently.

He was marking his territory, and I loved every minute.

He nibbled my skin but nipped it too hard, piercing the skin, and I yipped in surprise.

"Shit, shit, I'm sorry, I'm sorry!" he panted, pulling away. "I-I oh shit."

I reached up to my shoulder. It was only a drop of blood; he'd barely pierced the skin. I laughed hazily, wiping the blood on the sheet. "It's okay, just went a little too hard. It was actually kind of hot. You can do that again–" And when I looked up to see his face, his teeth had taken another shape. They didn't look human anymore.

"Hawke?"

CHAPTER TWENTY-ONE

Hawke

Delilah blinked, her skin becoming ashen.

Shit.

"Dede, it's okay." I raised my hands away from her, but that seemed to upset her further.

The contact we both shared was shattered, except for her bare pussy rubbing on my tight jeans.

My cock strained against the thick fabric. I wanted nothing more than to rip them off to get some breathing room, to unleash the beast becoming wetter by the second while her essence continued to drip.

I kept making mistakes, resulting in more poor decisions, which was detrimental to my mate's wellbeing. I took a deep breath. My wolf purred with delight as more of her sweet smelling cunt dove deeper into our lungs.

Now wasn't the time to savor what we just shared, however. As fucking amazing as it was... How soft the inside of her cunt felt. How tight she was. She took three of my damned fingers, letting me stretch her wide; I could smell the sweet tinge of metallic as her body accepted me.

My knot... It will fit.

I will make it fit.

It was all I could do not to stick my fingers in my mouth and lick up the remnants. But I'd nicked her shoulder. And based on the look on her face, my elongated teeth had come out. Of course, she would be shocked.

Dede was going to think I'm crazy or worse, a vampire. I had a limited amount of time to try and get her to focus on the present and hopefully, hopefully, not think of me as a monster.

"Gods, you are dramatic," my wolf huffed. *"By the way, great job. This time I wasn't the one to fuck up first."*

I inwardly rolled my eyes and cleared my throat. I did the best I could to pull my elongated teeth back inside my mouth. Not that it mattered, it was too late. She stared at them with parted lips and pale skin that seemed to become even more gray.

"I'm a werewolf," I told her, worried that my mate would somehow draw conclusions that were far worse than what they actually were. "Well, that's what humans call us, sometimes," I fumbled. "But we are actually shifters, I can shift my body into a wolf. I'm part animal. They are a part of me, almost like a separate entity."

Delilah continued to stare, unphased.

"I think you broke her," my wolf snorted.

But her heart continued to beat, and it didn't palpitate. Delilah held onto that stare, unwavering.

"Sunshine, say something," I pleaded, grabbing both of her arms and clinging to her.

That statement roused her from her trance, and she had to face reality again.

"Really?" She fluttered her eyelashes, her head tilting to the side. "Journey really was right?"

"What?"

"I'm tired," she closed her eyes. "I need to sleep." Her eyes closed suddenly, her head tipping forward and landing on my shoulder.

"You really broke her!" my wolf screamed, panicking and running around doing zoomies in my head.

"Cut that out!" I yelled, trying to hold on to my mate as well as bring peace to my animal. "She's breathing. She is just exhausted and in shock." I told myself rather than to my wolf. I rubbed my hands up and down her body. My mate was still warm, but slightly above her normal body temperature.

"You suck at talking. Next time, let me talk," my wolf huffed.

"Sure, so she can freak the fuck out when she realizes I have two different personalities? That sounds so much better."

"A schizophrenic wolf, I like it!" he yipped.

I went too far, once again. This time, I was the only one to blame. But her arousal had permeated the air so fiercely and quickly I couldn't help myself. Not only that, but her glorious tits had fallen free. Alright well, I ripped the blasted contraption off her chest to feel her on my skin.

And damn, it felt good, better than anything I could have imagined having my body pinned to hers. I continued to relax, no longer aching with bond sickness. We couldn't be separated any longer. We couldn't leave each other's side now. If I had any reservations about staying away from her, I'd thrown them out the window.

If we were separated, we would both die.

Not that I ever wanted to be separated from her again, but fear controlled me.

I had to decide if marking her as mine was worth it. If I bit her, she would change. My venom would seep into her body and slowly change her, just like Journey. Was Journey even still alive? Did I even want to find out?

I brushed my mate's hair, leaning her back into the bed. Her pants were ruined, her body was a jumbled mess of red handprints, and she had a very large hickey on her shoulder with a pinprick of a bite.

"Shit."

"Is that your new favorite word? Usually it's fuck."

I hissed in vexation. Why the hell had this wolf been paired with me? I would never know. We were complete opposites in every way.

"I ask myself the same thing," he mumbled. *"I try to keep you in line, and you completely ignore me. It's frustrating."*

I ran my hands up and down her bare skin. She was littered with red marks and bruises on her delicate skin from my tight hold. A sickening feeling formed in my gut. What if she wasn't strong enough to take my venom? To change?

Damn it, humans were so fragile. How the hell did Grim do it with Journey without killing her?

"Ew, that is a nasty picture I can never erase."

After rerouting the food to a new address, I dressed my mate, opting to put my shirt over her body to keep my scent surrounding her. I had never released my scent, but I found it easy to do. My wolf was more in control of that part of my body.

When my scent sunk into her skin and hair, I realized I was taking one more step to make her mine. No one, not even my brothers at the Iron Fang, would approach her until a mark could be placed on her shoulder. All shifters around the area would know that she was partially claimed, and a fight to the death would ensue if anyone tried to take her from me.

Not that my brothers would even dare think about touching what was mine. I made it perfectly clear over the years that Delilah was mine, and no one was to approach her. She was friends with everyone, and she made it damned difficult with her batting those lashes at all my brothers.

But scenting was part of the courting phase. It could last a few hours to a few days, depending on the pack, lineage, or royal line. For a warrior or guard, it was normally instantaneous to mark and claim their mate where they stood. It was in our blood; we were more ruthless and possessive. And with my terrible memories already trying to bubble over from my past, marking Delilah sooner rather than later seemed a more favorable option.

Or maybe I should wait, see what would happen?

I shook my head. Delilah wasn't *her*. Delilah was so much more.

And dare I say, I had felt more for Delilah than I ever had for the mate that rejected me.

I felt the bond growing stronger. My wolf's teeth were itching to pierce her skin to permanently mark her. Leaving bruises, although part of me was ashamed for marring her skin, gave me such delight to see our handy work, our hands and mouth making her ours.

But fear was holding me back.

She might not survive the shift.

The worn room she had chosen was worse than the one she originally rented. It was long overdue for new floors, furniture, and a television. I didn't even know they still had box televisions with rabbit ears, but this one certainly did.

My wolf and I made the conscious decision that we didn't need our mate here any longer. I had to prepare us a nest, a place where she would feel safe until I figured out what our plan of action was once we were both rested from our near brushes with death.

Traveling home seemed like the better option, but letting Delilah be part of that decision was vital. Ultimately, it would be her decision, but her passing out after revealing part of the truth was worrisome.

Would she accept what I was? What we were together? What we all were at the Iron Fang? The thought alone of her rejecting those who consider her as much part of the club just without the fancy lettered cut was almost absurd.

But one never knew.

I picked up the bag she had yet to open and stuffed the bear inside. Her work pants were ruined, so I gently slid them down her legs, doing my best not to stare at the wet spot on her bright pink panties.

Damn it, don't look.

Fuck it.

I looked and gazed in awe at how much I'd turned her on. I could replace her underwear, but with my wolf breathing heavily in my mind to take another quick lick of that glorious pussy, it would be far too tempting.

Then I realized my fingers were coated with her slick. I greedily sucked on them, groaning at her taste. Like fucking sunshine. She tasted like sunshine.

Once my fingers were licked cleaned, I threw out her pants. I knew damn well that she wouldn't be able to sew them back together. As optimistic and talented as she was in everything she did, she couldn't fix a hole to save her life.

Then I rifled through her bag, pulling out a pair of black joggers and slipped them up her legs. I took one long look at her underwear, so devilishly tempted to pull them down and lick her clean.

"I know you want to," my wolf sang. *"You haven't tasted the glory of those pink lips from the source. Aren't you jealous?"*

I groaned, palming my dick through my jeans. I was going to have major blue balls for a while. But it was well worth it after the two years of teasing.

I chuckled, throwing her bag over my back, and picked up her limp body. Her head rested against me, one hand resting on my chest while the other laid limp as I carried her like a child.

Before we could go, I needed to collect my things from my room. I trailed back up the stairs with a limp body in my arms, and no one seemed to care. I watched as humans passed by and never got a second glance.

Humans could be so cruel to their own kind.

I shuffled Delilah in my arms, moving her head to rest on my shoulder and her ass in the crook of my arm. She was light as a feather, but I had to awkwardly hold her while searching for the stupid key in my pocket.

As I pushed the door open, I froze, seeing the bare mattress where I had ripped the blankets in haste to make a bed in Delilah's room. A red-colored cloth laid on top of the sheets. It was the red bandana I used to wipe off dirt and mud from my boots. I stared at it longer than I should have, but hell, it made me see things I shouldn't. Like the moment that changed my life forever...

My excitement was palpable as I rushed up the cobble stone stairs, taking two or even three at a time. I'd prepared for this. I had excelled in every category to become the perfect guard for the Royal Council.

The years spent with the werewolf royal family had been plentiful, fruitful even. They helped me grow while I watched over their family, their children. They trusted in me more than any other. I was swift; I was lethal; and hell, my nose could track anything. Even the king himself said my nose surpassed his.

I was in good favor, and with the king's good recommendation, I would move on to the Royal Counsel's table as the head guard. I'd be their guard, their assassin, and their tracker. It was what my father had dreamed of for me ever since I was a pup, and I was happy that I could fulfill his dreams.

But another event happened that would surpass it all. I had found my mate after many years of waiting. I was older, thirty-five years old in fact, but the wait was worth it because I was to be mated to the king's youngest princess, who had just turned eighteen.

Ruby, being the ever thoughtful one, wanted to wait until after the interview, which was scheduled a few weeks away. Plus, it was common for royalty to hold off on their mating. Duties got in the way, parties needed to be held, but Ruby knew that our nesting, our bonding, would disrupt the interview process.

The parties that would ensue after our announcement would be great. Shifters from all the realms would want to be in attendance for the youngest daughter's congratulatory parties. It would be a royal affair, but she knew how important this interview was to me.

"Let's wait to tell my father. I want you to prove you got this position because of your own hard work and not because of my status," *she told me.*

Ruby had known all her life how much this position meant to me. I remembered smiling at her with such admiration that she would wait for me a little longer, no matter how hard it was to keep our hands off each other.

Our life was going to be fruitful, special, and we would build a family together. We would also hold noble titles, give our pups the best schooling and training—a prosperous life. All of which could be scarce in the realm.

We would both be recognized as part of The Council's inner circle. I would provide her a home nearly as beautiful as the Shifter Palace, along with all the material things she was accustomed to. Everything was perfect and going just to plan.

And to make things better, I got my interview a whole week early. A great surprise.

I went through the process of straightening my military uniform, ensuring that it was neat and presentable. The buttons shined, the black tailored suit hugging my body tightly. I straightened my collar again, ready to surprise my mate that we wouldn't have to wait a week longer. We could be together now. I could take her away to my den, and we would solidify our bond.

As I reached the overly decorated wooden door, my wolf shuddered, letting out a pitiful howl. A chill ran down my spine as I grasped the door handle, and my soul felt like it was slipping away.

Fear for my mate increased, I staggered and used the momentum to forcefully push the heavy door open. I fell to the floor, my face hitting the expensive, thick carpet. It broke my fall, but my mind was not ready to see what was before me.

My mate and another male laid tangled in the sheets. Her shoulder displayed a bite mark, blood spilling onto the pristine silk sheets.

Her eyes widened in shock, her fingers digging into the shoulders of the male that hovered over her. My eyes narrowed. I felt the rage building inside me as my wolf prowled to the surface. All I could see was the blood dripping from her shoulder, her marking spot. Who the male was did not matter.

"Kill," my wolf snarled. "Kill them both."

I choked, feeling my soul dwindle inside me. I clawed at my uniform, the buttons scattering across the pale pink carpet. I continued to scratch and claw my way through until I hit my bare chest, ripping the skin until it bled.

"Were you forced?" I heaved out a breath. "Did he force a mark on you?"

Forced marking was punishable by death. The opposing party would have their assets seized by a high-ranking warlock from the council in compensation to remove the mark. It could be done if the full bonding had not been completed.

This male that hovered over my mate's shoulder was unmarked. She could still be saved because a return marking must be done of her own free will.

My mate's normally braided hair was undone, messy and thrown over the pillows her eyes staring wide in horror as she stared back at me. The male's protective presence was palpable, surrounding her like a shield.

It was my job to protect her, not his!

I stepped up, my chest bleeding and dripping over the once immaculate room. My mate shook her head and then sunk her teeth into the male's chest.

My wolf let out a ferocious snarl that echoed through the room before he jumped onto the bed. He pushed the male to the floor, blood still dripping from his wound. His cock was wet, sprinkled with her innocence. My wolf curled his lip and spat on the princess we once called ours.

My wolf began his shift, fur falling from our once beautiful coat, and howled painfully. We were becoming rabid, mangey, and we would no longer be beautiful in this form again.

My wolf wanted blood spilt, he wanted to destroy both of them because now, I would suffer the price of being alone, dying alone, my soul disintegrating into the spirit world.

My wolf hovered over our mate, his fangs dripping with venom mere inches from her neck. He licked his lips, ready to end her. It was the ultimate betrayal, to reject a mate, to reject everything I was ever taught.

"Was she taught nothing?" *my wolf snarled.* "Did the king not teach his own daughter?"

The heat of my breath curled the small hairs surrounding her face. I once thought of her as beautiful, now I saw her as nothing but a hollow shell of lies. She held no ties to me, no commitment, no love. Was I that blind to not see the web of lies and betrayal she'd woven to cover my eyes?

I wanted to scream at her, chastise her for her ignorance while my wolf wanted to rip out her throat so she could experience the same sort of death that would befall my wolf and me.

But I pulled back. I maintained control of my wolf. I had trained my wolf to completely obey me, so I was utterly in control. I leapt off the bed. The code of a soldier and guard was too ingrained into my human mind; I couldn't take the life of a princess. I would be seen as a traitor and an enemy. That wasn't what my father, my family, would have wanted.

Instead of snarling, howling, letting my wolf take control of my body and killing the blasphemous couple, I stood tall. I puffed out my chest, ready to meet my death as a rogue.

I was now slowly dying.

Warm hands rubbed my cheek.

I blinked, bringing me back into the present to find my mate standing instead of cradled in my arms. I was sitting on the bed, and she was straddling me, holding my face in her hands.

"Are you okay?" she whispered.

I scoffed, rubbing the tops of her hands. "You passed out after I told you what I was, and you are asking me?" My eyes softened, and I pushed my face further into her hands.

I soaked in her warmth. She held me so gently while I was breaking. I had never known that feeling before.

My parents could be cruel, telling me I was not good enough. But to Delilah, I was everything to her. And she didn't give up on me when she should have so long ago.

She shook her head slowly and sighed, her breath ruffling her hair. "This might sound crazy, but..." She licked her lips. "There is a little voice in my head." She tapped her finger on her temple. "She's never steered me wrong, and she told me to trust you. I also get this feeling in my stomach, like when I know danger is near or something is a bad idea. Plus, long story short, Journey said that Grim had fangs a couple weeks ago, and I didn't believe her then." She laughed.

I cupped her hand as she rubbed my cheek.

"So, if you say you are a wolf and I say there is some creepy voice in my head, that means we are even. Right?" She giggled nervously.

I pulled her to my chest, both my smell and hers completely entangled with one another. "Yes, we are even, little human."

"That makes it sound like you are an alien. A wolf sounds cooler." She broke away to stare at me once again. "Wait, does that mean I can call you puppers?"

"Um, no."

CHAPTER TWENTY-TWO

Delilah

Hawke was hell bent on getting us away from the hotel. I was too tired to argue. I was too overwhelmed to question why he wanted us to leave.

My head pounded with the information about Hawke not being human, but part animal. Which, come to think about it, didn't sound all that crazy when you put the pieces together.

The entire club worked like a wolf pack. They were all insanely protective of one another, ate an enormous amount of red, bloody meat, and didn't date because those they rescued were human.

They were protecting us not just from our pasts but from themselves, too.

I should have listened to Journey. I should have believed her. But after all the trauma she went through, seeing her rapist and the club beating the crap out of everyone, I thought she was hallucinating.

Obviously not. They all really were animals.

But why hadn't I seen any wild animals running around the bar?

Again, my head pounded, a small voice whimpering inside me to chill out. She continued to speak to me like I was her best friend when I still felt like I was slowly losing my mind.

Hawke unbuckled his belt while I sat on his bike. I swayed, trying to keep my heavy eyelids open, but once I heard the loud slap of his belt coming out of the loops, I perked up.

"Not now, Sunshine," he smiled. "I'm just making sure you don't fall asleep and fall off. It's only a quick ride, but I'm not taking any chances."

Hawke sat on the bike, my front to his back and wrapped the belt around me. It was stifling and tight, and I could barely breathe.

"Is this necessary?" I asked uncomfortably.

Hawke remained silent, only the sound of the engine revving in response to the question. Lucky for me he wrapped us up tight, because I fell asleep as we rode down main street.

I exhaled, the sounds of Hawke's bike long gone. I wasn't painfully strapped to him with the wind blowing in my hair.

Ugh, I fell asleep.

I was prone to falling asleep so easily around Hawke before I was even sick. I'd find myself in my bed after falling asleep at the bar, talking to him, or at a movie or in the forest we often went hiking in. But now, knowing he wasn't human, I should have been more aware. I should have been worried that the man I'd known for two years held a secret so large it made my heart ache.

I couldn't hold it against him, though. Because he was trying to protect me all along, and he was here now. But what made him flip the switch to tell me this great secret?

I stretched, feeling the tension in my back slowly ease away with each crack. Hawke's body shifted, his breathing heavy and slow as he rolled onto his back, and his arm fell across his eyes.

The bed was decorated similarly to the night before. We nestled into the mattress, cushioned by the soft, fluffy pillows and blankets. Right, maybe a wolf thing. It made more sense now.

The small fan that was mounted on the wooden desk created a gentle breeze that caused the curtains to sway, thus providing the room with dim lighting. The entire room was decorated in a rustic theme, featuring bare beams, a wooden dresser, and wood flooring.

It smelled like the outdoors, of moist dirt, pine, and cedar, all intertwining their smells together, giving it a healthy and clean scent. It smelled nothing like the city, which was thick with smog, exhaust, and noise pollution.

This room was its own paradise away from the life outside these walls, and I realized I might not be in the city at all.

My bare feet hit the animal rug on the floor, and I crept to the window. As I looked outside, I sighed in relief that we weren't in the middle of nowhere. In fact, we were on the same street as the diner.

And then my eyes widened, tightening my hold on the curtain.

I was late.

The door creaked open, and Hawke jumped out of the bed like a bat out of hell. He rushed forward at amazing speed and grabbed Bram by his neck.

Bram was holding a sterling silver tray when it slipped from his grip and landed with a loud clatter on the ground. As each item, ranging from glasses of juice, to croissants, eggs, and sausage hit the ground, they shattered into pieces and spilled.

"Hawke!" I screamed and without hesitation, he looked at me, but didn't release his hold.

Bram choked, holding onto Hawke's wrists, but he didn't seem in the slightest bit worried. His face was turning purple and when I raced toward Hawke, he let go of Bram, who fell onto his knees.

"You almost killed him!" I slapped Hawke's bare chest.

His meaty, bulky chest. *Yum.*

Hawke kept my hand on his chest, holding me close to his body. His lips curved into a sneer, and he pulled me away from Bram, who was slowly getting to his feet.

"It's alright, girly." Bram pushed up onto his knees and brushed off his shoulders. "I'm older than I look."

I blinked, watching him move to a nearby chair and sit in it.

"It's, *I'm younger than I look*, right?" I asked.

Bram threw his head back, slapping his knee. "No, I meant what I said. I'm older than I look. And quite a bit stronger, too." He winked, but his face fell. "Ah, Delilah, how about we get you to sit back down?"

Hawke growled, pulling me closer to his body. A wave a dizziness hit me again, and he gently picked me up and laid me on the bed, wrapping me into a cocoon of blankets that smelled heavily of his scent. I relaxed instantly, but I tried to wiggle free.

"Be still," Hawke's deep voice didn't invoke fear but straight arousal. My heart skipped a beat, and my thighs clenched together in anticipation as his gaze met mine.

We'd experienced so much sexual tension over the years. The past two days were full of touching that I would love to repeat over and over, but I had a job to get to.

"I have work–"

"No. You don't," Hawke gruffed, wrapping me back in the blankets. "You are sick. I need to get you better."

"I don't want to give it up yet!" I argued. "I promised him I'd help him next week!"

Hawke growled again, his teeth growing larger, bigger that his mouth should be able to accommodate. I gazed up at him, growling back, and

Bram chuckled in the corner.

"Don't worry, Delilah. I've already taken care of your leave of absence." Bram used air quotations to get his point across. "It is highly advisable that you don't leave your mate's side." His voice became dark. "This sickness isn't to be taken lightly, and it could put you both in danger. You must remain close with one another until it's resolved."

I remained in my cocoon, and Hawke sighed heavily, brushing his messy hair with his claws. Yes, claws, they were black, long, and I shivered at what they would feel like if he decided to run them up and down my leg.

"You are killing me, Sunshine," Hawke whined.

I gazed at his crotch and Calamity Jane. It was thick.

His nose flared and turned away from me to look out the other window on his side of the bed.

The air was not only thick with tension but questions, too. They both knew things I didn't, and I was getting quite frustrated, but most of all, I felt tired and weak.

I hadn't felt this way in a long time, not since... *Shane.* And like gravy and meatballs, I felt like crap.

"Can someone please, kindly explain what is going on?" I asked. My head slumped back onto the pillow.

Hawke leaned against the window frame, his muscular chest breathing deep and heavy. The ripple of his side muscles made me lick my lips, and Bram chuckled as he riffled through the dresser.

Bram carefully pulled out a clump of weeds and then pulled a lighter from his pocket. He grabbed one end of the object and, as the flames flickered, he moved it around the room in a sweeping motion.

Hawke paused for a moment, taking in the atmosphere, rolled his eyes, and then joined me once more on the bed. He gently ran his claws through my hair while sitting beside me. The scraping of his claws was so delightful that I almost felt my eyes rolling back into my head.

"This is white sage," Bram began.

Bram looked like the stereotypical western man. The handlebar mustache, the plaid shirt, and the cowboy boots called him out on that. Now that he was burning a bundle a witch would use, I shifted my views on him into a whole new light.

"This burn is cleaning and purifying the room. I'm clearing out the negative energy, the doubts, the fears that would fill a human when it comes to the unknown."

Bram continued to walk around the room in a clockwise circle, hovering the burning bundle over the bed until he placed the remaining burning sage on a plate that was safe for fire to burn on. He brushed his hands off and put his hands on his hips.

"Are you a witch?" I blurted, before I had time to think.

Hawke's lip tilted in amusement.

"Not a witch, a warlock. Same thing except I am a male." He eyed me.

It made me smile, shaking my head and laying back into the comfortable pillow.

"Of course you are. There are shifters now, warlocks, anything else? Vampires? Unicorns?"

Their reaction to my rambling was a simultaneous snort of amusement.

"No unicorns, not that I know of," Hawke said. "But there are vampires, fae, fairies. Anything else you want to know about a species, I'll be glad to tell you. Right now, you need to rest."

"I have work," I argued. "I have things to do. I can't be stuck in bed all day."

Bram tutted, lowering himself to put the broken piece of glass and food back on the tray. "Yes, well, you don't have to worry about that job anymore. It was too dangerous. I've taken you out of the equation of that dreadful place."

"What?" Hawke asked lowly. "What do you mean, dangerous? You said we were safe here."

Hawke's hold on me tightened, and he pulled me up to his lap, putting my head on his shoulder.

"Can't breathe!" I mumbled, and he pushed me away.

I cleared my throat, the silence between them becoming deafening.

"Why are we in danger in the first place? Why the hell am I sick?"

"Language, Sunshine. I don't like hearing that shit come out of your mouth," Hawke whispered in my ear. The blunt part of his teeth grabbed my earlobe, giving a quick nip, then soothed it with his tongue.

Well, spread me over a piece of bread.

"I think Hawke should be the one to explain why you are sick, but as far as the danger, I will tell you what is amiss." Bram sat in the rocking chair in the corner, pulling out a pipe. He tried to light it several times until he chucked it to the floor.

"Sorry, I'm trying to get used to this male's mannerisms. Lighting a fucking pipe is the worst."

I stared at him like he'd grown another head.

"This isn't me, well, it isn't my body. Right, well, it is my body. I created a potion so I could look like the human male that owns this place. I needed a place to stay for a while, so I've been here about three weeks until I figured out where I need to go next. Luckily, my stay has been fruitful, and I met the both of you." He winked.

"But where is the other guy?" I panicked.

Bram smiled. "In a coffin out back."

"You killed him!" I shrieked.

Bram grinned, rubbing the tip of his mustache with his index finger and thumb. "He's partially dead, not dead dead."

What like The Princess Bride scenario!?

"Oh, my god!"

"Get to the point, warlock, I haven't got all day." Hawke's hold tightened, his nose diving into my shoulder. "I'll explain everything. Just hang on a little longer."

Easy for you to say, buddy.

"Right, right. Well, as I was trying to place a basic 'forget-me-not' spell, which is very hard to do by the way, only the most talented of warlocks could accomplish such a thing. I just erase your face and name from a mind, lasts about three weeks. Anyway, I asked your manager Simon a few questions as to why he needed you so much because the human was being really resistant to forgetting you. Meaning, his life was on the line. He wouldn't answer, saying it was none of my business, so of course, I had to apply a truth spell on him. And damn, it was too strong; he confessed things I didn't even need to know. Did you know he was cheating on his wife with one of the waitresses? He frequently gets blow jobs behind the potato sacks in the back pantry."

I gaped at him.

Hawke rolled his eyes, a growl escaping his throat.

"Anyway," Bram said disappointedly. "When you gave your driver's license to Simon, he ran a background check. Come to find out, you were reported missing, and immediately he called the police, who then got in touch with a private investigator in charge of your case. A man named Shane Cunningham has been looking for you and was going to collect you next week during this special guest meeting."

I felt the blood drain from my face.

"I'll find you, Delilah."

CHAPTER TWENTY-THREE

Delilah

I don't know how this could have happened.

I changed my last name, paid an exorbitant amount of money to hide myself, and gave myself a new identity. There was no way *he* could have found me. My background was humble; I was a teenage dropout. I never got my GED and worked at various diners under the table for a few weeks just to get across the country until I landed in Iron Fang territory.

My references were none, but the Iron Fang took me in after an extensive interview when they asked me if I was bringing ill intent to their club. I told them I didn't want to speak of my past, that I was no longer in danger of being found. I was the one that was wronged.

They didn't pry and respected my wishes. Locke's glare softened when my voice trembled when I told him I would rather die than go back. And thank god, he had a soft spot.

Locke, along with everyone else, believed I was telling the truth. They let me stay, trusted me, and I had been safely hidden ever since.

"H-how?" My voice trailed off, shaky as Hawke held onto me.

"You gave them your license, of course. If you had missing persons report out to find you, they would find you. Why give them that information?" Bram rolled his eyes like I was the stupid waitress he'd met for the first time.

"It's a fake name!" I countered. "My last name, anyway. I didn't want to give up my first. It was my grandmother's name. She–"

Hawke hushed me, pressing his lips to my temple. "That's enough. We will talk in private." Hawke's glare to Bram gave no room for a reply, and Bram rose from his seat.

"Very well," Bram cleared his throat. "I'll bring up another tray of food. In addition to that, a special tea needs to be consumed to help her restore her strength. Make sure she drinks it if you want her healthy." Bram eyed Hawke, who glared in return.

Bram swiftly opened the door and closed it behind him, and we listened as his steps continued down the stairs.

I relaxed further into Hawke's arms. I'd never felt so weak and vulnerable, not since I ran away. Since I'd known Hawke, he had seen me as the peppy person I'd always been when I was with him.

And it wasn't an act; I truly was happy with him. He made me feel things I'd wished for my entire life. A sense of belonging. It felt right to always be near him. I took what I could, even though he didn't give me enough.

After some contemplation, I understood he had acted out of love to protect me.

"Sunshine, we need to talk. I want to know every bit of what you're running from, but I think I need to get some shit off my chest first. I've hidden it from you for a long time, and it's only fair. But hell, none of this is going to be easy."

Hawke pulled me closer to him, and I could feel the heat radiating from his body as he embraced me. His embrace was like a shield, and in that moment, I felt nothing could tear me away from him.

"It was supposed to be easy until now?"

Dude, you are a shifter-wolf thing.

Hawke scoffed, his nose dipping into my shoulder. "I suppose not, but now I have to do something I'm not good at, and it's going to be hell for me."

"You mean talking?" I quipped. "You aren't very good at that or expressing your emotions."

Hawke wrapped us in a tight embrace, as if the bed couldn't contain us both, if that were possible. We were cocooned in a nest of pillows and blankets, feeling their softness around us. He continued to wrap me in blankets as if I was made of glass and huffed with satisfaction when I could no longer move.

"How about we start with this?" I nodded to the blanket wrapped around me tightly. "Because I feel like you are an icky spider about to eat me."

Hawke's smile grew as he petted my hair, the feeling was soothing against my head. "As you know, I am a wolf. Wolves have dens. My den is back at the Iron Fang, my apartment. It's my safe space, and it's near my brothers because we are a pack, a unit."

I nodded, silently encouraging him to keep talking.

"Our bed is our nest. Males create one for their females to entice them to stay. We release our scent. It is supposed to make our mates feel secure, loved, and ultimately protected."

I rolled my bottom lip into my mouth. "We? Why are you saying we?"

"My wolf," he stated. "My wolf is in my subconscious, well, more like on the surface. He talks to me. He is definitely more animal than human. In fact, he made the nest the other night and also woke you up with his tongue between your thighs." Hawke's eyes darkened, his large hand gripping my backside to pull me closer to him.

"T-that wasn't you? It was your wolf?"

He nodded, pressing a kiss to my cheek. If I weren't wrapped up like a burrito, almost unable to move, I would have been rubbing my thighs together.

"So, you didn't do that? He did?"

Hawke nodded.

"Have him do it again." The voice purred.

This voice was going to kill me.

As weird as it was, his inner animal licking me, touching me... It was still Hawke. And I suppose that since they were both one and the same, then it was okay?

Sheesh, I'll have to question that part later—

"And why did you say, mate? What is a mate?" I stared up at him. His dark eyes sparkled with a happiness I'd only seen a few times.

He beamed, cupping my cheek, and placed a sweet kiss on my lips.

"All supernaturals believe in the Moon Goddess. She is the matchmaker of souls, and with the help of Fate and Destiny, supernaturals are led to their supposedly one true love."

Hawke had a sorrowful voice when he spoke, a pain I couldn't describe. It wasn't toward me or didn't feel like it was. Instead, he stared at me like I was his light house, guiding him home.

"And you think we are soul mates?" I whispered.

"I know we are, Sunshine. From the very first time I saw you, when I touched you, I knew you were. But my stubborn ass didn't think the gods would grant me a second chance at finding my soulmate. I thought I was reaching for something I could never have."

"Wait, what?" I cocked my head. "Second chance? So, there was another that was yours?"

That did not sit well with me. Hawke was supposed to have another soulmate? How did that work? How did I know I wasn't just the second best replacement?

The voice in my head growled; she didn't like that either. A growl escaped my own lips, and Hawke raised an eyebrow in surprise.

"I'm not finished with my story," Hawke said sternly. "But I fucking love it when you get all possessive. It's hot as hell." He rolled his hips between the apex of my thighs. Even with the thick blankets, I could feel his raging erection.

I whimpered, wanting to escape the cocoon of blankets, but Hawke stilled, resting his hand on my lower back.

"The Moon Goddess may suggest a pairing for souls. They are instantly attracted to one another, but all supernaturals are given their agency. A choice. They can reject the bond, reject the soulmate. When that happens, they choose a chosen mate and seal their soul with the other person."

Hawke's eyes went cold, his grip on my waist like iron.

"W-what happens to the one that gets left alone?" My words were a mere whisper, my heart racing in my chest.

"They become a rogue." Hawke's voice went hard. "A broken soul. Without a complimenting soul, they slowly die with no chance for redemption. My wolf has not been out of my body for years, unable to shift because we've been too weak. His hair grew matted, his body becoming weaker by the day. Once I realized I needed you and couldn't live without you, he came back to me. Once I decided I wanted you and was going to keep you, he was there, ready to claim you."

My heart ached, seeing Hawke's face drop and his eyes fill with sorrow. But that didn't stop him from claiming my lips with fervor, and the kiss that ensued was electric. I felt a sudden surge of warmth, my hands desperately pushing away the heavy blankets.

Hawke was rejected by some bitch, but I was glad. I was glad that he was, so I could have him. As I thought about the Goddess throwing me at him as a second choice, it bothered me. But even without this bond, I would have been attracted to the big grump.

This bond that wove us together was strong, but what was stronger was my feelings, my heart that had been quickly enamored of the big grumpy biker. I still had a choice, he had a choice, and I was damned happy he was finally choosing me and not going off of some bond.

"He was always meant to be ours," the voice whispered.

Hawke reluctantly pulled away, and I felt the warmth of the kiss still lingering on my lips. His mouth was gentle and searching as I felt him on my cheeks, neck, and ears, and we both panted heavily. "I thank the gods now that I have you, Delilah. Because my first would have been a terrible mate for me. I was too blind to see that."

"Then why didn't you tell me sooner? Why didn't you tell me what you were?" I asked.

Hawke kept his face in my neck, his hand cupping the back of my head. "We have rules set in place to keep the club safe—"

"I would have been understanding, like I am now! You know I've always liked you! You shouldn't have gone through this alone. And your poor wolf," I cooed.

He chuckled, pushing the hair away from my face. "There has never been a second chance, mate. Becoming a rogue meant your life was over. You couldn't mark a chosen mate because your soul was too broken from the original bond breaking. We were cast out from our packs, our homes. We were shunned."

I frowned. "That's awful! What about your family?"

"It's the way things work where I'm from. That's why Locke and Grim created the Iron Fang. For all the rogues to come together. We live a little longer when we're around our own kind, and we can–"

"Go save others that need to be saved," I finished for him.

Hawke nodded. "Protect those that need it, a last chance at redemption before we die."

"It doesn't sound like you need redemption from anything," I said firmly.

"No, those that are a part of our club were rejected for dubious reasons. They were not evil, just had selfish mates who gave in to their own selfish desires."

"We were always meant to be his," the voice said. *"Don't make this complicated, just follow your heart."*

That was certainly easier said than done. I'd been thrown through the ringer here.

"Then why now? Why do you think I'm your mate now?" I asked.

"I've always known, but I didn't believe it. I didn't believe you could be mine, not after I'd been rejected and was dying. Like I said, there has never been such a thing!" he said exasperatedly. "Hell, I'm still dying, but when I saw Grim and Journey, how happy they are. How he swears up and down that she is his mate and has claimed her as his–"

"Then you started believing," I muttered.

Hawke nodded, and I slapped his shoulder. "We could have been the first-second chance mates, and you blew it!" I flung my head back in laughter. "You are a stubborn old wolf, aren't you?!"

I pulled away the blankets, and the sound of my movements was the only thing that could be heard as Hawke gaped at me.

"I think it is high time I'm in charge here. Obviously, you don't know how to control your feelings for me, so I'm just going to take things into my own hands."

I crisscrossed my legs on the bed, staring down at him. I crossed my arms, raising my breasts a little higher, and his eyes dropped to take a gander.

"Now, tell me why I am sick. You keep blaming yourself for that."

Hawke took his claws and ran them through his hair. After he did so, I pulled his hand into my lap to feel the sharpened points. He showed me how he could will them in and out of his body, how his body hair could be regulated as well, giving him a grizzly man's appearance.

We did this without saying a word as I examined his body, even pulling his chin down and looking inside his mouth. He had more rows of teeth than a human would. The molars in the back were few, but his carnivorous teeth were plentiful and sharp. Why I had never noticed before, I wasn't sure.

"Go on." I shooed him with my hand. I continued to rake my hands down his body. He was only wearing joggers, and I wanted to check his toes for claws as well. "Tell me about my sickness and why I got dizzy and had a panic attack all alone in my room yesterday when you went god knows where."

Hawke frowned, not taking my joking manner. He sat up from the bed and wrapped his arms around me. "I really didn't know, Sunshine, I'm so sorry."

I tsked, still trying to touch his toes.

"It isn't your fault. It's not a big deal. I feel much better. I'm probably PMSing plus the PTSD about you not coming back might have been a factor, but it's cool now." I smiled, ready to move on.

Life was too short to stay angry, to hold grudges. And now that I was receiving more answers, I felt much better about where we were going.

Hawke didn't huff with an agreement. Instead, he had me straddle his lap and cupped my face. "I'm so fucking sorry," he said again.

I sighed heavily, annoyed. "For what, puppy?"

"Don't call me that," he snapped.

I smiled cheekily. "I wish you had a tail. I bet it would be wagging. Does your dick wag instead when your tail isn't out?"

"Delilah, I'm trying to be serious!"

"And since when have you known me to be serious around you?" I poked his chest. "I can't be all serious when you make me happy."

Hawke's eyes softened. "You mean that, after all I put you through?"

I nodded, playing with my fingers. "Of course. You spent a lot of time with me. You tried to do what was best for me. Maybe at the time, I got mad at you." I smirked. "Now that I know why you did it, to protect your family, friends, even the other little humans like me." I batted my lashes flirtatiously. "I always knew you did it for a reason."

Hawke sighed, pulling me into a hug. "You're too good for me."

"I know." I patted his back. "Now tell me."

I could hear Hawke's steady breathing as he held me close, his arms not loosening. His hand went down to my lower back and a zing of arousal hit my core.

"As much as I want to start something—" I rolled my hips on his crotch. He groaned, grabbing my ass cheeks and letting his claws sink into the fabric. I moaned, my head rolling back. "I need to know why I got sick."

He grumbled and agreed. "Bond sickness. It happens when you wait too long to bond with your mate. Our bond was weak since I met you because I didn't believe in the goddess. But once I prayed to her again, once I asked for help and for my second chance, it snapped into place. It caused our two years apart to come rushing at once, and now we get sick if our souls are not close."

I pensively looked at him. It made sense. I didn't like being away from him, especially not since yesterday.

"When did you pray to her to ask for help?"

"Yesterday morning, and by yesterday afternoon when I left you, it was solidified, further making me believe you are my true mate. That was why you got so ill. For a human, you feel it ten times worse. I was still in pain, but your little body felt the brunt of it." Hawke's shoulders slumped, and his hand cupped my cheek.

"You are a stubborn butt." I crossed my arms. "You could have prayed to your goddess to find out for sure, and you didn't?"

How could he have waited two years, not praying to a deity? This shifter was like any other human male who would not ask for directions.

Hawke nodded sheepishly. "We both now have Bond Sickness. We cannot leave each other's side until we have completed our bond."

"What is a completed bond?" I asked.

"Like a marriage for humans, except this is deeper, Delilah. It's so much more. This is for eternity." Hawke leaned back against the headboard, his hands never leaving my body.

Hawke was touching me all over—my arms, my hips, my waist. His hands ran up and down my legs and even through the black leggings, I could feel the fire run up my inner thighs.

"And you want to complete that with me? Right?" I asked.

Because I was really curious how this would work if he didn't bond with me. We couldn't leave each other's sides without being sick; I can't imagine how his job and mine would even work out.

"Of course, I want to bond with you!" he snarled. "I want it more than anything!"

"Then act like it. You act like I'm going to be the ball and chain!" I snapped.

Hawke snarled, pushing me into the mattress. His fingers dug into the back of my hair, pulling my neck so it was bare to him. I could feel the heat of his breath trickle down my shirt, to my breasts. They hardened with each breath he took.

His nose traced down my neck until it tickled my shoulder. A zing of fire ran from my collar bone down between the apex of my thighs. I let out a helpless whimper, wanting nothing more than for him to bite me there.

I didn't know the reason, I just wanted it.

"I want you more than you will ever know. And that makes me question if I should bond with you. Because let me tell you something, when we bond, you will change. You won't be my little human anymore. Your body will change into something more feral, more animalistic. And with that change comes pain, pain I never want to see you experience."

I swallowed. Hawke's voice deepened further.

"Two things could happen. You finish your shift, and you become like me or—" The deathly silence was thick, the room becoming smaller by the second. "You die in the process, and my fucking heart can't take that."

CHAPTER TWENTY-FOUR

Hawke

"I can become just like you?" A look of intense excitement and delight twinkled in her eyes.

Had she not heard that she could die in the process?

My wolf snorted. His arousal was at the forefront of his mind. He didn't care about the repercussions that could put our mate in the cold dirt. No, he wanted to fuck her senseless and rut her into oblivion.

I wanted it too, but we had to think this through.

"Did you not hear what I just said?" I moved closer, my head tilted, and our lips connected in a loving kiss.

"Yeah!" Her body jolted, pushing me back harder than I thought her capable of. "I can be a wolf shifter, just like you! What color would I be? Would I get to run in the woods and prance around and hunt tiny defenseless animals and have them become my prey?" She rubbed her hands together excitedly.

"Damn, sexy as hell," my wolf whispered.

I shook my head. "No, Dede, do you realize what could happen? You may not survive your first shift! Some shifters can't even survive it. What about a human?" I looked up and down her body. She was petite in the weight department. She was taller than most human females, but she lacked muscle, she looked like she might be anemic. I'd never seen her eat much red meat. She was lacking the proper nutrition.

"And whose fault was that?" my wolf snipped.

While she rambled about how amazing it would be to be just like me, I jumped off the bed and opened the door. Bram had left a tray of food on the floor just outside.

I didn't like to have to rely on others for food, but like Grim, I had become helpless while taking care of my mate. I needed a pack. I needed the strength from my brothers, but Delilah and I were both weak from stretching the bond so thin.

And part of me didn't want to call them to ask for help. I hadn't asked Locke for permission to leave the club, and I also didn't want to know if Journey hadn't made her shift.

With great care, I lifted the tray and put it on the bed. Delilah was animatedly waving her hands around as she described what she would do if she could take on the form of a wolf. Running, frolicking, jumping over logs, the small things that I took for granted when I was a younger wolf. I did nothing but train to be worthy of my father's expectations.

All of it was for nothing because of his untimely death at the Royal Court, along with my mother, since their bond was strong. And on top of that, my former mate rejected me.

I pulled the plate of eggs, sausage, waffles, and hash browns from the tray and then held out my hand for Delilah to come closer to me. She prattled on as she sat on my lap. I picked up the fork and enticed her to eat. Her mouth opened in response, her eyes closing and moaning at the taste of the buttery eggs.

My wolf purred in happiness that my mate would eat the food we were feeding her. It was a great honor to feed your mate, and Delilah took it all so willingly. Between bites, she tried to speak, but I coaxed her to eat.

The tea he'd left smelled bitter. I smelled it once more to be sure there would be no poisons that would hurt my mate and then dumped a heavy helping of sugar into the liquid.

She smiled, knowing how she liked her tea. She couldn't stand anything bitter, or healthy for that matter. It had been hard over the years to get her to eat any sort of vegetables.

Delilah took it willingly, though. She was completely submissive, which caught me by surprise. She has always been strong, independent, and even more so with my rejection.

But with the bond and goddess helping me, I had a chance to win her over. If Journey's claims were true that the Goddess had spoken to her, then maybe she was speaking to my mate as well.

That could be the voice speaking to her.

My cock was stiff in my sweats. My balls felt heavy with the need to release the tension building inside. There was no question that she could feel it. She continued to move in different directions, her ass sweeping across the obvious bulge. Each movement caused a groan to leave my chest, but she continued to speak as if she couldn't feel it.

I wanted her to become like me. I wanted her to experience the fullness of the bond that I felt for her.

But to mark her, knot her, only for it to end up in disappointment would devastate me. She didn't deserve a short life. She deserved a long one.

As I fed my mate the last portion of food, I licked the side of her mouth where a small crumb lay. She smiled, and her hand rested on my cheek.

"Do you not think I am strong enough? Or do you not want me to be your forever?" she asked solemnly.

"Damn, I felt that stab my heart," my wolf whimpered.

I put the plate down on the side table. My fingers brushed through her hair so I could see the entirety of her face. She was hopeful, she always was. She looked for the good and was optimistic about everything in life. Yet here I was, the pessimistic one, looking for the bad in everything.

"I want you. I've wanted you despite my actions. I've only done what I've done because I wanted you protected. I don't want your life cut short because of me."

Delilah rubbed her lips together, her eyes straying to the window. The sun that shone brightly outside was darkening as the passing clouds of a storm rolled in. I could smell the wetness in the air, the electrical charges becoming more frantic as it came closer.

"What is it to have a long, miserable life compared to a short, beautiful one?" she asked.

My body warmed with a love I'd never felt before. It burned brighter as I stared at her, watching her in awe as she looked out the window.

"I know I'm not that old, but I'm not young either. I'm twenty-six, I've seen some shit and even though I haven't shared my past...with any-one"—she gave an apologetic smile—"I would like to think I would be stronger than I appear."

Shit.

"No Dede, I... Shit." I engulfed her with my body, giving in to the undeniable urge to connect us. To keep her safe from it all. I wanted to show her how much I cared for and loved her, but she didn't believe me, not yet.

It hadn't gone unnoticed that she hadn't told me she loved me, coher-ently anyway. Part of me knew she did, but I wanted the reassurance. To hear the words leave her lips, to have her call me hers would be a far greater gift than just to knot her.

But I had to prove myself.

I squeezed her tightly, and she squeaked in surprise. My wolf purred loudly, making sure she was aware of his presence. I could feel the upturn of a smile on my bare shoulder. Her fingers raked down my back in a soothing motion.

"Is that a purr, really? Not you being growly?" she giggled.

"Yes, it's my wolf. It's his way of communicating when he likes or enjoys something."

Delilah hummed into my shoulder. "He's done it before, all those nights you came in to check on me. I've always loved it."

I kissed her shoulder. Chills ran across her skin, and her fingers dug into my sides. "I don't think you're weak. I've never thought that. It's just humans. They don't heal the way shifters do. We can heal ten times as fast. We're physically stronger. Our genes are just very different. I'd be changing your DNA, it's painful, or at least I think it will be. I've never witnessed a full change."

Delilah sat up, her fingers running down my chest and stomach. "I think I can handle it," she whispered. "Besides, if you prayed to some goddess to keep me, I don't think she would stop it now, would she? Not unless she's cruel."

At one time, I thought the goddess to be cruel. Why pair me with a female that would eventually reject me? But then she wouldn't have her choice that we were all allowed. But why was I being saved now? Why were any of us?

I'd been given a second chance, and I wouldn't waste it.

"Whoever rejected you was a bitch," Delilah scoffed.

I eyed her, foul language not suiting her perky personality.

"But, I'm glad she did. Because now I have you, and I never want to give you up."

Delilah straddled me once again, a new position she seemed to adore because now she could face me. She grasped the sides of my face, her kiss more passionate than I had ever felt before.

She was confident; she was feral, her kissing becoming more frantic by the second.

I grabbed her hips, pulling her down to rub up against my erection. She moaned happily, fingers trailing along the elastic on my sweats.

I could still taste her breakfast on my tongue. The sweetness of the waffle syrup combined with her fresh taste of sunshine made me groan as her breasts rubbed against my chest. Her nipples were already hard, the pink peaks ready to be sucked.

My mouth descended, sucking on her tits, and she wrapped her body around my head to keep herself steady. Fireworks erupted as our skin touched, and her body writhed against me.

Her fingers traced every ridge on my muscular back. She drifted to my sides, slowly descending until she pushed me. I let go of her nipple with a pop, watching her try to pull on my joggers. She tried to push them down, ready to unleash my cock. I heard my heart pounding as I became filled with hesitation.

"What's wrong?" Her lips were puffy and swollen from our kiss. Her eyes were glazed with lust.

I puffed out my chest, preening that my mate would look at me with such want. I'd wanted her the first moment I met her and looking back, I'm not sure how I could withstand not having her.

"I'm different. I have a different anatomy than that of a human male," I confessed.

That didn't deter my mate. She seemed more determined than ever. "Why, is it extra-large?" She quirked a smile.

I bit my cheek, trying not to egg on her foolishness. "Much, and I have something extra, it's called a knot."

Delilah's smile widened instead of balking back in apprehension. "Really? And what does this knot do?"

My concerns faded the more excited she became. She wanted to see it? Know what it did? Where had this bravery come from?

"It's at the base of my cock." I cleared my throat. "It gets larger the more aroused I get and once I get close to, uh..."

"Exploding your seed all inside my body?" Delilah glittered with excitement.

"*Fuck, she's perfect,*" my wolf purred.

I swallowed, my hand running down my face. "Yes, when I get close, I lodge it into your body so none of my seed can escape."

"You want to breed me?" Delilah shuddered, her legs squeezing mine as she straddled them.

"*Holy fuck yes!*" my wolf howled.

"Where did you learn such terms?" I narrowed my eyes. "And why are you so excited? I thought you would be terrified!"

Delilah caressed my chest, then flicked the nipple piercings. Her body was a raging furnace, ready to explode from overheating. She was so damn sexy. A perfect package I was ready to ruin.

"I read books," she said sheepishly. "I have an e-reader I hide under a floorboard. I have an extensive collection of erotica books." She smirked. "Tell me more. How big is your knot?"

Goddess bless me.

My voice lowered, my grip on her waist tightening. "Big. I may hurt you."

Delilah's face flushed. She liked the idea of me stretching her, to fill her up with my seed, to mark her. My wolf prowled, licking his lips and pushing me to take her now.

"Do you like the idea of me stretching your pussy?" I growled, cupping her mound.

My mate was wet. She was dripping inside those leggings of hers. I could smell her arousal seeping into the cloth while her breath quickened. "You want me to stretch you like I did yesterday?"

At first I thought three fingers might have been too much, and four would be really stretching her. If I could stretch her to four fingers, my knot would have no problem.

Getting her wet enough wasn't much of a challenge, but I certainly welcomed it.

But then Delilah shook her head at the offering.

"I want you to stretch me with your knot."

CHAPTER TWENTY-FIVE

Hawke

Her breath was like a heated whisper as it hovered over my lips. The atmosphere was charged with our arousal.

I captured her mouth, my teeth nipping at her bottom lip. "You aren't ready for my knot yet, little human."

She shuddered, and her palms laid on my chest. "Then, at least, can I explore?" Her blue eyes sparkled with curiosity, her fingers fidgeting with the white string that held the sweats around my waist. I leaned back on the bed, giving my mate permission.

Once she saw my knot, she would back down, surely.

I'd seen the sticks human males had. My cock was far more enormous. But my mate surprised me again as she pulled down my sweats, my cock springing free, and giggled excitedly.

The silver ring that pierced the head of my dick reflected the sudden burst of lightning that lit the room. Her lips parted, staring at it with curiosity.

My dick slapped my stomach once I was free of my sweats. The shaft was already damp with my precum. My hand went right above my knot and stroked my shaft upward. My thumb lightly strummed over the piercing on the head.

Delilah was filled with wonder as she stared at my shaft and knot in all its glory. She licked her lips as I put pressure around the head. Come pearled at the tip until it ran over, dripping down my knuckles. I groaned, happy to feel the pressure. Too worried about my mate, I hadn't jacked off in days. The stimulation of her observing me was almost painful as she watched me stroke myself.

And she enjoyed seeing me touch myself. Her nipples were hard, ready to be bitten. I reached forward, palming one of them and pulling on it tightly with my fingers. "You enjoy studying my cock, Sunshine?"

Delilah's arousal seeped further into the room, her sweet scent filling my lungs with so much want. Her body was frozen in either fascination or fear as she gazed at it.

I jerked my hand, giving my cock a powerful tug, and the precum dribbling down the head knocked her out of her trance as she licked her lips. She then hastily pulled down her leggings. I bit my cheek to hide my amusement at her eagerness as she threw them off the nest.

She crawled toward me, her head right above my leaking cock. My mate darted her eyes to me and back to my shaft, licking her lips wantonly. She reached out, her fingers running over the bar of my Prince Albert piercing. Come dripped from the metal, and she traced her fingers over the silver and brought it to her lips.

She pushed it into her mouth, her tongue wrapping around the head as she seductively sucked.

Holy shit.

Maybe she wasn't so innocent.

My wolf growled in pleasure. Her eyes were dilated with desire, her body nearly shaking as she grasped my shaft. She stroked it, almost lovingly, feeling the thick veins that wrapped around the head.

In my moment of bliss, having my mate run her hands over my thigh and my cock, my wolf took my mouth and spoke, "Suck me off, my pretty ray of sunshine."

I was filled with sudden terror as my heart ceased to beat for a moment. I was concerned that she would be insulted and not prepared to accept such instructions. But instead, her eyes became hooded. Her thumb continued to stroke the bar of my piercing, which caused my dick to harden further.

My mate's tongue slipped from her lips, licking the bar, tasting my precum as she dipped the upper half of her body to the bed. Her ass was in the air, her knees spread as she took me down slowly until I was fully set into her throat.

My girth was large, but her mouth accommodated me well as she bobbed her head. She was careful of my piercing, rising and falling into a steady, beautiful rhythm.

My hand entangled into her hair, feeling the rise and fall of her head.

"Good, girl. Fuck, yes, Sunshine, just like that."

As she bobbed, she wrapped one hand around my knot. It was swelling, painfully so, but I greeted it with happiness. My knot had never felt so large, so swollen, and I knew it would be perfect to keep my seed inside my mate.

Delilah continued to suck, her gentle hums radiating into my balls. I fisted her hair, tightening my hold, and her free hand went between her legs.

"Are you going to play with yourself?" I growled. "You dare touch what belongs to me now?"

Delilah raised an eyebrow, her mouth releasing my cock.

"Please?" She let go gently. "Please, can I touch it?" she begged.

I hummed, trying to keep my stoic expression, and eventually nodded.

"You may." I tightened my hold around her hair, bringing her to my lips. "But keep sucking. I haven't filled your mouth with my come, yet."

She bit her lip, keeping herself from smiling.

I didn't let go of her hair but gave her enough slack so she could return to my cock. My mate sucked it down harder this time. There was a twinge of pain as she deep-throated me. I hissed when I felt the bar slid down the back of her throat.

Fuck!

"Stick your fingers inside yourself, Sunshine. I want to hear how wet you are," I ordered.

My mate forced her fingers inside, two from the sound of it, and I could hear her soaked pussy sucking her fingers. She was completely drenched just by sucking me off alone. "Now rub your clit, I want you to come before I do."

And she better do it fast, because I was so damned close.

I fisted the sheets, my claws ripping into the material. Her suction around my cock was so fucking tight. My mind went to places that it shouldn't. To be lodged into her hot cunt, have it milk me of my seed. To mark her, make her mine.

I wanted to tie her to the bed, fuck her, and have my way with her.

She moaned into my cock.

"That's it, give me everything." I gritted my teeth. "Those sounds are mine. No one else can hear those sweet little moans."

Once her orgasm subsided, and her mouth eagerly went back to pleasuring me, I snarled, ready to release. "Give me your fingers!" I grabbed her wrist. "Don't let go of my cock."

I sucked on her fingers while her other arm steadied herself. She flicked her tongue over my piercing, and I felt my load flowing through my shaft until it throbbed, pumping into the back of her throat.

"Swallow it all, don't waste a drop," I cried, sucking her fingers as more and more of my come spilled.

She continued to suck, choking on the exorbitant amount of come until she broke free so she could breathe. More spurted, landing on her cheek and breasts. And fuck, if it wasn't the hottest thing I'd ever seen.

It spilled onto my stomach and chest, my cock far too excited to have the woman of our dreams sucking it dry. And hell, it was a lot, and it would be. I was a damned wolf not some human.

"Lick me clean," I commanded. Her tiny tongue was already at work before I commanded her as she licked my thighs, my stomach and chest. Once she reached my nipples, licking the last bit, I pulled her against me.

I had her lay on my chest, our bodies in a mangled mess of my seed. My cock was still hard, my knot filled with heat and desperation to be lodged in her cunt.

As we panted, my hand ran through her hair until I took the back of her head in a firm grasp and pulled her head back so I could look at her. Her face was flushed, eyes still dilated, and her breasts looking delectably heavy.

"You didn't have to do that." I kissed her forehead.

"I didn't think I had a choice," she said cheekily. "You were so bossy; it was so hot." Her chest rubbed up against my sweaty body. "Besides, I wanted it, and I still do," she said hazily.

I took in her appearance once more; her dilated eyes still hadn't returned to normal until I saw a flicker of pink sparkle in the whites of her eyes.

The bond was a powerful gift. It gave you the desire to please, to fuck, to bond with your mate, to search for that deeper connection you were always supposed to have. But this, this flicker of pink I saw in the whites of her eyes, was not a human trait, not in the slightest.

The tea.

Motherfucker.

"I'm still, really–" Delilah took in a deep breath. "I want more. I've always wanted more, but I want more now, even though I am so tired."

Her eyes were barely open, her arousal still seeping down her leg.

My instincts were to go downstairs and beat the bastard's face in for what he had done. He had enhanced the tea with some sort of warlock concoction.

"I know, Dede, I know." I placed a loving kiss on her forehead. "Let's get you cleaned up so you can rest."

She didn't protest, laying limply on my body. I chuckled, pulling her into my arms and taking her to the small bathroom on the other side of the room.

The only light was a hanging lightbulb in the middle. I pulled on the string, making sure my mate was still secure in one arm, and filled the enormous bathtub that sat to the right of us.

We were both naked, and both sated in our sexual desires. For now, anyway. Her body was still producing the aromatic scent of her arousal, making me want to take her all the more. But she needed rest. She wasn't a shifter, and she would not heal like a typical female shifter.

What if I break her?

"You won't break her," my wolf chided. *"That warlock is trying to prepare her body for your knot, as assholish as it was."*

"He should have asked," I replied simply, turning off the water.

"That he should, but there is no denying he wants this to work between the both of you."

I hummed in agreement, still wary.

I lowered both Delilah and myself into the steaming bath. Shampoos, soaps, and even expensive oils covered the shelves of the small bathroom with the overly large tub. I kept my claws short, as much as I wanted to mar her skin with love bruises. We tenderly washed her.

I didn't like washing my seed off her. But until Delilah was fully immersed in my world, I couldn't force her to keep it on her body. Not yet anyway.

My scent, the one that mattered the most, was still prevalent, even after bathing her. I'd be sure to scent her again and the whole damn room.

I didn't think warlocks can smell as well as a shifter, but I would saturate the room so he would fucking smell it.

Delilah hummed as I massaged her shoulders, her head leaned back, and I got the perfect view of her breasts. They were perfect for me. I could barely cup one in my hand, but it was her tits that I loved the most. I loved sucking on them and rubbing them, and I wanted more time with her pussy, too.

My cock twitched next to her ass, but she didn't notice or didn't comment. Her eyes were closed, and she leaned her head on the other side of my shoulder. I got a perfect look at her neck, and it was a glorious sight. She was covered with my markings now, but what struck me as surprising was that she bared her neck.

Baring a neck was such a submissive, vulnerable position. It meant they trusted, adored, and gave their life to the person they were submitting to. Delilah wouldn't know, nor understand what this meant, but to me, it was the greatest compliment she could give without saying the three words I wanted to hear.

I wish I had trusted her from the beginning. Wish I had bared my neck to her.

As the steam of the bath dissipated, I carefully lifted her out and wrapped her in a soft, warm towel. "I can get dressed," she said and tried to take the towel as she stepped out of the tub.

I shook my head, struggling to comprehend the sight of her beautiful body. "Please, let me. I've wanted to do this for so long, and now I have the chance."

Delilah tilted her head in curiosity until she nodded gently. I dried her hair and lotioned her body with my calloused hands. She wasn't born a princess, entitled to carry on a noble line, but she was my queen, and I was going to treat her like she damn well deserved.

Once she was pampered, I settled her into the rocking chair, the wood creaking softly beneath her. As I changed the sheets of our bed, I watched her intently, making sure the fog of lust that continued to fade wouldn't bring on fear.

Yet, she looked at me as if I hung her moon as I made our nest.

My scent poured from my body, bringing comfort to the nest and our room. And as I did, Delilah's eyes grew heavier by the minute.

I chuckled, striding toward her, and lifted her with ease. Her thin body relaxed against me, and I laid her amongst the pillows and blankets. I removed the towel, taking one blanket and nudging it around her body so she was snug inside.

"I must talk to the warlock," I whispered.

Delilah's head perked up. "Yes, Bram." She smiled. "Oh, I remembered his name," she said sluggishly.

I brushed her hair away from her forehead, watching her eyes flutter in exhaustion. "He's a warlock. They don't like people knowing their names. A name is powerful. I wouldn't be surprised if Bram wasn't his real name, either." I pursed my lips. "But I must speak with him, find out his true intentions."

Delilah nodded, reaching her hand out to touch my bare chest. "Don't be long? I don't want to be alone."

"You aren't alone anymore, Delilah," I muttered as she fell asleep. "Never again will you be alone."

CHAPTER TWENTY-SIX

Hawke

I took one last look, savoring the sweet scent of her breath as she slumbered.

All I wanted was to take her in my arms and whisper the words *"I'll never let you go"* in her ear. We both still had trust to build with one another. Well, she had more of a journey than I did. I wanted her no matter the outcome, if I marked her or not.

I still couldn't stand the thought of her dying because of me. Not that I would have to hold that guilt for long because I would soon follow her into death.

My wolf mumbled curses at me. He was holding onto what Delilah wanted and that was to be happy in the smallest of moments rather than be miserable for a long life.

We shut the door, watching our mate's sleeping form until the door softly latched with a faint click. If there was no protection spell, then I wouldn't leave her. But I could feel, smell, and taste the magic that surrounded this cigar shop. There were holes, though, small and minute enough that a weak witch or warlock could not penetrate it.

But if there was stronger magical beings, then we could be in a heap of trouble. This Bram was not as strong of a warlock as he once was, that I knew. He had weaknesses in his glamor that I could now see, knowing what he was.

I stepped onto the metal stairs, feeling the vibrations as I descended the winding staircase. I could hear Bram's voice speaking with a customer. Bram immersed himself in the body he filled with a raspy, grumpy voice. His reasoning vague and argumentative as he tried to explain the unique properties of a special tobacco grown on some southern plantation.

The human male was skeptical about where the tobacco was grown based on how it smelled, but once I entered the room, his face fell. "Fine, I'll take it." The human flipped open a leather wallet holding several hundred-dollar bills. He took one out, taking the box of cigars from the counter, and strode out of the shop with a huff.

"Thank the gods you showed up. I did not know what I was talking about." Bram leaned against the counter, crossing his arms. "Apparently, the human that owns this place bought a new strain of tobacco and knew little about it. I tried peering into his memories of what was so damned special about it, but nothing came up."

I strode over behind the counter, my claws lengthening until I gripped Bram by the collar. I gave him a hard push against the wall, making the glasses of vintage scotch and rum rattle against each other. I pushed him one more time into the shelf, he grunted and grabbed my wrists with his old crooked fingers and smirked.

"Is there a problem...Gunnar?"

"Don't call me that, Bram," I hissed.

His eyebrows raised, and his eyes blinked with amusement.

"Looks like the bond is already growing, if you know my human name.

I'd like to hear more about it."

I bore my fangs, my body thrumming with adrenaline. My body had become stronger in just the one night of staying close to my mate, but I damn well knew it wasn't enough to overpower this warlock. I lowered the warlock until he could touch the ground. He rubbed his turkey neck and stepped away, pulling out the same box I saw him with during our first encounter.

"I know you're angry with me–"

"That's an understatement," I muttered.

Bram chuckled and opened the wooden box. He pulled out a small glass vile filled with tiny pink dust. "What I gave your female is strengthening her. Unfortunately, the side effects is heightened arousal. She is going to feel like she is in the early stages of heat. It's supposed to bring you both together. That is what you want, is it not?"

I scratched my claws on the wooden bar, watching the ribbons of wood curl beneath them. "Yes, but of her own accord. Not because her body is betraying her. I want her heart."

The warlock tutted. "And you don't think you have it?"

I tightened my jaw, feeling the grinding of teeth against my cheek. I knew she loved me, but I wanted her to say it. I wanted to earn what I had lost. The trust, the devotion, the fucking spark she always had.

I ran my hand over my sweaty forehead. "I fucked up. I'm trying to make things right."

Bram studied me, rummaged through his box again, and pulled out a small parchment of paper. It was rolled up like a tiny scroll, and he pulled it lower until he reached for a blank segment.

"Are there more like you and Delilah, then? More of these human mates?" He pulled out a quill that was too large for the box. It was appearing longer and longer right as he pulled it out. I looked at it in question. It was a magical device I had never seen before.

He pulled it closer to him so I couldn't look inside. He eyed me carefully in warning. "Well, is there?" He raised his quill and black ink flowed through the feathers until it landed on the tip of the sharpened quill.

"Why do I need to tell you anything?" I snapped. "I still don't know your intentions. I don't know who the hell you are. Warlocks don't just do shit out of the kindness of their heart. You either want something or you are working for someone."

Bram's face twisted into a frown as he shut the box securely.

"I have given you a safe haven, a place to put your nest. I have brought down my walls for you to see my true intentions. You can tell if I am lying, your wolf can read any ill will, and yet you still question my loyalty?"

My wolf didn't stir. He sat patiently, waiting for an order. He wagged his tail like an idiot, sniffing closer to the window of my mind where he could see.

"How do I know you do not have another spell covering anything up?" I asked. Because it was possible, some deep magic I wasn't aware of. Magic was endless, and I knew very little about it.

Bram stood still, his brow furrowing. "Because I am just like you. I've been rejected, and we both know what comes with rejection. Weakness. I am not strong like I once was. But that is no longer something that holds any importance to me."

Bram laid his quill down on the parchment. It rolled back into one piece so I could not see what he'd written. He hurried over and flipped the open sign to *closed* and shut off the front of the shop's lights.

"The reason I know your name is for two reasons." He turned to face me after pulling down the shades of the front windows. "One, I knew your father. I could sense his presence in you."

I swallowed heavily. He knew my father? My father never told me he knew any warlocks. How would I know if this was true?

"I was also there when they approved your status to become a Royal Council guard."

I narrowed my eyes as he walked back to the counter. "I had a premonition of what was to become of you after you left. You left so quickly, I didn't have time to stop you without looking suspicious."

I stood my ground, giving no hint of any agitation. My curiosity was piqued, but so was my wariness of his truths. My wolf could taste no lies on his tongue, but when in the presence of a warlock, and a powerful one at that, I still had to be careful.

"I cloaked my appearance, changing myself into a raven, and flew to the highest bedchamber, watching the miserable event unfold," he said with disgust.

My breathing stopped, and my heartbeat slowed. I could hear the thundering of its beats in my head.

"Once she rejected you, I was angry for you, Gunnar. Angry that this misfortune continued throughout Elysian. And know that it was happening to my rescuers' lineage, I knew I had to step in."

Bram's eyes darkened, a black cloak appearing over his body. It rained down like smoke, his mustache disappearing and leaving a pepper colored short beard. I didn't recognize him, didn't know his scent, and that put the fear into me.

He was a powerful warlock. A shifter at full strength could not fight this male. He was certainly older, wiser, and even with his broken soul, still stronger than any other broken-souled male I'd ever felt.

"Unfortunately, I wasn't able to help your father, so that repayment falls to you, Gunnar," his eyes softened for a brief moment.

I still did not want to believe him.

"In the words of our mate," my wolf interrupted, *"it is because you are a*

stubborn ass."

"What did you do?" I growled. "Why did you follow, to watch me be rejected?"

Bram threw his head back and laughed. "Really? You think I get off on humiliation? Gunnar, please." He licked his lips. "I waited to see if you could do what needed to be done."

My thoughts were in a jumble with a thousand different possibilities running through my head. What the hell was he talking about? Ruby rejected me, chose another. The only action I could have taken was to end her and her mate in vengeance, but I was not trained for that. I was a protector, a guard. To kill a member of the royal family was treason. I would have been killed on the spot, thus ending my life even quicker.

I had too much self-preservation to kill her.

"And when you strutted out of that bedchamber with your head held high, your fur already beginning to fall from your skin, I knew it was my turn to take care of my rescuers' son."

Oh shit.

"After your soul was shattered, and you were escorted off the royal premises, I knew then it was my time to shine." Bram closed the shades to the window next to the bar. Dust went flying into the air as streams of light reflected upon the dirt.

The room darkened further as the overhead lights flickered. The ominous tone of the room was palpable as his boots hit harshly against the dark, stained wood. If I didn't have my wolf with me, I may have backed away, but I stood with both feet planted firmly on the ground.

I didn't feel his anger directed toward me, but I felt the rising power of his magic filling the room. The ozone, the aromatic scent of nothingness, overpowered my nose while I watched his stature grow above my own.

"They had planned this!" Bram choked out a yell. "The royals already knew the princess was going to reject you. The king permitted it, relished it, planning for his daughter to marry a duke, instead of a guard."

My wolf snarled at the betrayal. How could we have not realized the lies of a king? Was I too love struck at the time?

I was blind, too prideful of my accomplishments.

"After the elaborate flaunting of wealth after their mating ceremony, which was when I took my place, Gunnar. I did it for your father, for you." He winked, but it wasn't playful in the slightest. "And for the future."

Bram rubbed his hands together, putting pressure on his palms. With his hands rolling together, he produced a sphere that was both translucent and blue with bright, electrical currents weaving through it.

Bram snapped his fingers and a close-up picture of Ruby's sleeping face appeared in the orb. "Ruby, the youngest princess of King Shapen and Queen Rachel, was found dead in her lover's arms by morning." The sphere grew larger, backing away from Ruby's body to show a blood bath. A hole was left in her chest, blood covering an elven-made, white silk dress.

"Both of their hearts were cut from their bodies," Bram laughed maniacally. "The princess's heart burned in the fire because of her lustful desires of the flesh. That fire still rages in the palace today in her former bed chamber. All while the selfish lover who married her for status was fed to pigeons on her balcony."

Instead of feeling pain or sorrow, I felt a burden had been lifted from my shoulders. I no longer had to think of her, because she was dead, along with that male. I was free; I could live as if they never existed.

Because to me, and especially now with Delilah in my life, there were no emotions remaining for the life I left behind.

"Their bodies may be buried together, but their hearts are separated, permanently," Bram said. "They will never find peace in the afterlife." Bram's eyes glowed red, his fists balled up in anger, until he released them.

A satisfied smirk fell on his face.

I didn't feel anger or sadness over the death of Ruby. There were many nights I thought about returning to the Elysian realm to finish them both. To tear that male apart while she watched, to watch the light leave her eyes as it had mine when she chose another.

To make her feel pain.

But this warlock had done it for me. He destroyed my greatest enemies. He avenged me so I did not have to. I didn't know if I should be grateful he had or upset I couldn't do it myself.

Bram was making his way toward me. His gait was slow, his hand falling while the sphere stayed in place hovering between us. As he came closer, the sphere faded, leaving the last picture as the eternal flames flickering in the fireplace.

His presence seemed to throw my wolf into a state of confusion between wanting to tear him apart and expressing gratitude.

Bram pulled a leather woven necklace from his cloak. It held a wolf's fang in the middle. He grabbed my hand, squeezing it so my balled fist would relax, and placed it into my palm.

"To show further proof, This is your father's." The whooshing of blood filled my ears. "He gave it to me when he was a boy. Said it would make me feel better." He chuckled.

I fiddled with the fang in my hand. It was indeed a wolf's fang, but one much smaller than that of a shifter.

A typical wolf.

I brought the tangled leather to my nose. The ozone smell was apparent, but leather was a funny fabric. It could retain scent for years, and with my trained nose and deep concentration I could smell hints of my father's scent. The same scent that was present in mine.

It was my father's.

This was all that I had left of him. After so many years of not being able to return to my home realm to gather my things, I had something of him. I put it over my neck, not intending to ask if I could keep it.

Bram stepped away, his cloak fading into black sand that slid beneath the wooden floorboards.

I wasn't a sentimental male. I didn't cry over shit, but this warlock didn't know me. He didn't know what I had done to Delilah over the past two years. And if he had, he would most likely strike me, just as my own parents would have.

A few minutes ago, I thought he was going to rip a black hole into the damned room, and now he wore the largest grin imaginable. The darkness cleared from his face, his fake appearance returning.

With that stupid mustache.

He was so pro-bond, so hell bent on finding a happily ever after, it was almost funny. And now he was left broken, just like I was. However, his seemed to be more recent with the power he still wielded. He wasn't close to dying, not yet anyway.

"I have renounced the Royal Council and their ways. They are in it for money and power, and I hope you understand that." His hand went to his wrist, unbuttoning the cuff.

He rolled up his sleeve and the once gold rune marking him as loyal to the Royal Council was now covered in black, jagged lines.

Bram had burned his rune off, or at least tried to remove it. The rune was a magical burn placed on all of those with the deepest loyalty to the council. Their duty was to uphold the peace and keep each race of supernaturals under control, so no one race overpowered the other.

To disfigure such an honor would be worthy of death.

"He speaks truth." My wolf bowed his head. *"And you know this to be true."*

"Please," Bram pleaded. "I need to know how you did it. How you obtained a second chance. I need to know if there is more to the life I now live; the oppressive air of hopelessness is smothering me. I need a mate to breathe life back into my lungs."

He was a dark, poetic, scary fucker.

I wanted to ask him about his story, how he lost his first mate. If he was so pro-bond, how the hell did he lose his? He didn't seem like one to wait and take no for an answer since he was so pro-Goddess. It wouldn't surprise me if he would have stolen her and forced her to be his or used some sort of spell.

However, each rejection was personal. We all felt like the rejection was our fault. We all felt inadequate, so why talk about it?

They were personal. I didn't know any of my brothers'. There were few who knew I was a royal guard, but none of them knew I was supposed to be mated to the princess of the wolf shifters.

And this warlock, this magical being that wielded enough power that could easily wipe out a city block, was begging me, wanting to know how I'd obtained Delilah. After this warlock took care of my past, as well as helped me and my mate, he was asking for such a trivial thing.

And since finding happiness again and beginning to feel emotions, I couldn't help but grow soft.

"I prayed to the goddess." I swallowed hard. "I prayed for her to help me."

Bram's eyebrows rose in surprise, accompanied by an exasperated huff. "That's it? You just prayed? Asked for help? I've been doing that for years."

"I've known Delilah for two. I felt she was my mate, but I thought I was being hopeful. It wasn't until I prayed this morning that the bond snapped into place."

"Lucky bastard." Bram twisted his mustache.

Words escaped me. I wanted to comfort the male who'd avenged me, who was continuing to take care of my mate and me. I felt like I owed him far more than he owed my family, but for now, I did not have much help. Not with the bond sickness that Delilah was suffering through.

I heard my own quiet breathing as I went to put my hand on his shoulder, the gesture intended to provide some comfort at the moment's awkwardness. I wasn't a male of many words.

Bram nodded in recognition and went back to his parchment next to his magical box and scribbled more notes down before tossing his items in the box.

"I guess I will continue to pray then," he gritted his jaw. "And I will continue to help you and your mate. Maybe the goddess will shine upon me once I make up for any transgressions I've committed."

I cleared my throat, unsure of what to say. "Thank you?" It came out more like a question.

He smiled, patting his box. He changed his emotions so quickly; it was giving me a whiplash. My own emotions were a mess, and now with my mate sleeping upstairs. And I still had lingering thoughts if I should claim her.

If this warlock knew I was fighting with that fateful decision, I'm sure he would cast a spell to bring on my rut. Then all my thinking would go out the window and be turned over to my wolf.

"What about this Shane guy?" I asked, breaking the silence. "What do we need to do about him?"

Bram crossed his arms, leaning on the bar. "Don't know, seems to strike fear into the human. Has Delilah told you about him? I'm assuming he is part of her past?"

I groaned, running my hands through my hair. "She hasn't told me anything about her past. No one knows except what's in her background.

High school dropout, no jobs–"

"And your hacker Switch didn't find that strange?"

"How do you– Never mind." I waved my hand. Warlocks had their ways of finding information. It was the old way, not with human technology, but it was still just as effective.

"She was honest about everything else. That she wanted to hide from someone bad. Locke can still sense truth by reading her heart beat better than the rest of us. He's the strongest, well, second strongest, if you count Grim since his mating."

"And now you," Bram added. "You will become stronger than Locke with your skills in tracking, and your wolf's ability to detect ill intent."

"He didn't see betrayal with Ruby."

My wolf snarled at me.

"As the humans say, love is blind," Bram chuckled, pulling down a glass of whisky.

He raised it to me as if to ask if I wanted some, and I shook my head. No more drinking, not for me.

"It's best you find out what your mate is hiding, then. I'll see if I can hop on one of these dang-fangled-doohickeys and check out his name." Bram threw back the drink and smacked his lips.

"Now please, tell me more about this Grim and his mate? I need their story."

CHAPTER TWENTY-SEVEN

Delilah

"M ate," a throat cleared. "Dede, can you wake up for me?"

I groaned, the sound muffled by the blankets as I rolled over, feeling the downy fabric beneath me. I took a deep breath in. That wonderful, peppermint and beautiful forest smell rested in my lungs, and I sank into the bed even more.

Wait, *nest*. That's what he called it.

"Come on, Sunshine, up you get."

I did not feel like sunshine, and I did not want to get up.

"But I don't want to go to school," I moaned. "I just wanna sleeeeep."

Hawke chuckled, that deep-throated laugh was becoming more frequent as the minutes went by. He sounded happy and looked livelier. Maybe his decision to let me into his life was settling him, and I was extremely happy about that.

"Why don't you come in with me?" I opened up the blankets for him to cuddle closer.

Hawke laid the tray of food on the dresser. It was complete with two sandwiches, a bowl of soup, and some of the nasty tea. I could smell the spiciness from here.

I kept the blankets open, ready for him to climb in, but his eyes darkened, his large hand landing on my thigh and that was when I realized I was as naked as a jaybird.

"Ope!" I wrapped my body back in the blankets, but his hand was already firmly planted, digging his fingertips into the skin.

He ripped the blankets off my body, his mouth tasting my neck, then my chest and finally down to my breasts. "If I get this view every time I wake you up, you better believe I will wake you up more often."

Hawke's hands ran up my body, his nose trailing down to my navel, then he paused. "But the reason I'm here to wake you up isn't because I need to be buried deep in your cunt."

He. Did. Not.

I could feel the heat of embarrassment rising in my face. Even though I was not familiar with this type of dirty talk, I was able to tell myself one thing about it—

I freaking loved it.

Hawke sat on the bed, pulling my hands away from my face, and kissed my knuckles. "You have started your period."

My jaw slacked, and an inaudible *what the fuck* slipped from my mouth. I pulled the blankets away to see that I had indeed started my period.

Perfect, just perfect. Just when we get intimate and do the nasty, this had to show up.

I groaned.

"Don't worry, a little blood won't stop me from claiming you," he purred.

Wait, what?!

"H-how did you know!?"

This is so embarrassing!

The morbid fear that someone could smell a dirty pad slammed against me. Did my blood stink!?

Hawke pulled me into his embrace. He loved touching, talking, soothing, almost petting me as much as he could. I relaxed into him, still mortified but enjoying how sweet he was being. He wasn't afraid of affection anymore.

"I could smell it from downstairs." He kissed my hair.

"Oh my god," I whined.

"Shh, now listen. I'm a wolf. I'm going to have stronger senses. Sight, strength, and even smell."

"You've known every single time I've been on my period?"

Just let me crawl up in a hole and die.

Hawke nodded. "Usually when I'm right next to you, now that my wolf is getting stronger because of our bond strengthening, I could smell you at a distance."

So gross.

"It's normal. I don't know why you find it embarrassing. All females have periods. Humans more so than she-wolves, but it is natural nonetheless."

Hawke placed his hand in mine and lifted me out of the bed. To my surprise, there wasn't that much blood on the sheets, which was a big plus.

I guess?

I looked between my legs, not so subtly, to check if I was dripping, and there was still nothing.

I felt the pull of his hand on mine as he pushed the door in, and his back flexed. He pulled a pair of comfortable underwear from the pile of clothes he laid in the bathroom and held them up. "I went through your clothes. I hope you don't mind." He winked.

"I guess not. You have seen me naked. Clothes in my bag aren't that much different. As long as you don't watch me pee, I think we are good."

Hawke frowned. "Why can't I?"

I snapped my head back at him as I approached the toilet. "What do you mean, why not? That's private!"

"I'm not leaving this room." He crossed his arms.

"What the heck are you talking about?" I crossed my arms mockingly. "You can't be in here when I put in a tampon, now shoo!"

And a pad, because I bleed like Aunt Flo is staying for a week.

"Did you shoo me?" He raised his brow.

"I did, now get." I stomped my foot.

He shook his head, the sound of his footsteps echoing as he walked toward me. "I'm gonna be here, with you, forever. Might as well pee in front of me, because I'm not leaving."

"You went downstairs," I pointed out. "I think you can handle a closed door."

He frowned. "And it fucking broke me as I left. The tea you drank helped you sleep and not feel the stretch of our bond, Dede. Not that I'm trying to belittle what you are feeling." His arms fell to his sides. "I've made a lot of mistakes in your care. Kissing you, leaving, ignoring you, then crawling back is giving you the ultimate emotional whiplash."

"You can say that again," I muttered.

Hawke stepped forward, carefully. His hand reached out to grab mine. "You know little about my kind, Sunshine. I'm going to be possessive, overprotective, and damn it, I want to take care of you. It's what we do. The males are supposed to cater to every one of their female's needs."

I stuck out my bottom lip, wrinkling my nose in disgust.

But secretly, I think I liked the idea.

"It's weird, though. Guys aren't supposed to want to help with that sort of thing. It isn't like I've had that much help before–"

Hawke winced, and I immediately regretted it.

"I'm sorry, I didn't mean–"

"Sunshine. I deserved it." His fingers ran through my hair. "I wasn't there because I'm a stubborn asshole. You can call me anything you want, but from now on, I'm not giving you any space. Especially since we haven't mated yet."

Mated, so sex? Well, that's a no go right now.

Once the period is over, then we better get to it then, so he isn't up my butt.

But I might like that.

"Yes, you would," the voice purred.

I shook my head. "No, you can't be here when I change—my stuff. I know you differ from me." *Like you are a dang wolf shifter.* "But that doesn't mean it gives you a free pass to do things I'm not comfortable with."

Hawke pursed his lips, and then let out a little whine.

I gasped, and he cleared his throat. "Was that the puppy!? Is he upset?" I petted his head as if he were a dog. He grabbed my wrist and placed a kiss on my pulse.

"He's not a puppy. He is a furious wolf that will fucking kill anything that thinks of looking or touching you," he growled.

Oh, this was hot.

If I wasn't on my period, I swear I'd jump his bones. He was being so cute. He was even blushing!

"Aw, puppy, are you sad that I'm being difficult?"

Hawke whined again through his throat but tried to stifle it with a cough.

I'm going to have so much fun with this.

"Right, right, you are so big and bad. I can't wait to see all those big bad teeth. But, I need to acclimate to this. I mean, spying on me while I'm sleeping in my apartment is one thing, but watching something super private for a human is not okay," I said. "Can you give me time to understand you?"

Hawke tilted his head, then nodded.

"If it makes you feel better, you can stand over there, turn on the faucet and turn around. And don't you look." I wagged my finger.

Hawke or his wolf, whoever I was talking to, reluctantly agreed, and I was grateful to be given this much privacy. But knowing Hawke, he would have never left the bathroom, so giving him a bit of what he wanted was the best choice.

"I will explain everything," Hawke spoke while I grabbed my underwear and my joggers. "I'll tell you everything I've wanted to say ever since I first met you."

"Oh, my god!" I squealed, then slapped my hand over my face.

Hawke had already turned around, snarling and grabbing me as if someone was coming through the window. He huffed in my ear, his heated breath racing down my bare back, and sighed when he realized I wasn't in danger.

"What's wrong? Are you hurt?" He put both hands on my shoulders, scanning me over until he reached my breasts. I didn't miss the heated look, but concern swept right back over his face.

"I just remembered. Did Bram kill that guy who really owns this place?"

Hawke's shoulders slumped, letting out a held breath. "No, he's just in a deep sleep. He's in the storage room. I checked on him."

I slumped in his arms as he scratched my back with his claws.

Oh yes, this was nice.

"Let me help you get dressed and feed you. I will explain everything about me and the club. Then maybe you'll be a little more willing to let me help you in all ways."

"Hmm, don't know about that."

Hawke didn't respond. He picked me up and set me on the counter like I was a doll. I wasn't that short of a woman, but he still towered over me as he brought out the hairbrush and gently brushed my hair like I was a child. Luckily, he let me brush my teeth while he brought in one of his t-shirts. I didn't mind it because it smelled better than a cologne coated sweatshirt, and I put it on eagerly.

He also took the lotion from the nearby corner and coated his hands. He rubbed my arms up and down and gave me a hand massage that made me melt like butter.

When we used to watch movies in my apartment, he would massage my hand. Squeezing, stretching, pulling every finger. I made overly dramatic moans just to egg him on, and it worked every time. He always went home with a raging boner, and I felt so evil for it, too.

It had never worked to get him to kiss me or to advance our physical relationship. His will was strong. But now I realized it was because he was trying to protect me, not to make me feel more worthless than I already did when he kissed me. Once the movie was over, he acted like he was going home, but in the middle of the night I would see him sitting out on the fire escape. Dirty, dirty thoughts entered my head.

Did he do the nasty while he watched me sleep?

But now he didn't have to do that anymore. He was standing in front of me, taking care of me, like he had been doing it all along. And now that we were taking a step forward, I was excited for new beginnings.

CHAPTER TWENTY-EIGHT

Delilah

The next six days blended together as one. There were times we were silent, times where we talked and laughed for hours and times we argued about what could have been and why he was such a stubborn butt.

But a lot of the time was spent touching each other and holding one another—almost mourning what could have been. But after hearing the sorrow of his past, I couldn't help but feel understanding for the way he thought.

My favorite times were the ones where we watched the city be decorated with Christmas lights. We people watched—how they went about their day, buying presents, or hauling trees. We even made up stories about what and who they were shopping for, and I don't think I'd laughed so much in a really long while. Who knew Hawke could have such a great sense of humor?

I had already received the greatest gift for Christmas, and he had held me all week, explaining who he was.

Hawke told me of his father and who his father wanted him to be. All the hard work Hawke had done, but his father couldn't see it since he was killed in a pack war over territory in the realm of Elysian.

Yes, another realm.

The voice inside me continued to be the gentle support I needed. She seemed to know how Hawke was feeling more than I did and with that, I better understood why Hawke treated me with such distance.

But Hawke was mated to a princess before me. She treated this man like trash. He was such a hard worker in just the time I knew him. He was constantly watching over all the humans, his brothers, as well as the territory that the Iron Fang claimed as their own.

He was loyal to a fault, and he trusted deeply in the precious gift a goddess was supposed to give him.

For a time, when he explained the bonding, I grew angry with her. I listened to the heartbreak of how supernaturals were raised to complete a bond, yet some decided to destroy their mates and choose another.

And Hawke had to walk in on his supposed mate having sex with some guy. It ended up breaking Hawke's heart and dissolved whatever bond he was supposed to have with the princess.

Hawke left out those gruesome details, thank heavens. I had some terrible jealousy when I found out he was mated to another. I could feel steam rolling out my ears, but the soothing voice inside my head continued to calm me, telling me it was never meant to be. This was the path that led me to him.

Because every soul faced a choice. The princess made hers, and she was soon met with death.

The old man downstairs was more powerful than he let on. He was a warlock, a powerful one, and he was indebted to Hawke for some promise he made to Hawke's father years ago.

Hawke brought me up to speed about his life, about the club, and Bram and then we'd stayed in this apartment getting to know each other all over again. It had become a safe place, and I didn't have the urge to leave it anytime soon. Because Shane was lurking in the back of my mind, and tomorrow was the day he was to come into town.

"And during my rut, I have to either take a special concoction that Bones prescribes or stay in my room and take care of it. Before you there were other ways, but I won't get into that."

My mouth dropped open, and then I covered it with my hand.

Hawke had not spared me the gruesome details of what it meant to be a wolf shifter. And this whole rutting and heat thing was both interesting and terrifying at the same time.

"During this rut, you have to take care of what?" I wasn't used to the terms, and there were a few times where I had to ask what they meant. This one looked more embarrassing to explain because Hawke blushed.

He reached behind his head, scratching it.

"A rut, kind of what male animals get into. The need to, ah, well, expel seed."

"So, you're horny. Like all the time?"

He swallowed. "Yes, very much. A hand can only do so much. It feels better when it's, uh, ah, shit." He rubbed his forehead, not able to look at me.

"I know you had a life before me, Hawke, and even though I'm jealous you were with other women, I understand." The taste was bitter on my tongue as I said it but what was I to do? Hold the guilt over his head?

He sighed, his shoulders releasing the tension. "I never knotted them," he quickly added. "My knot is only for my mate." He reached over the bed and caressed my thigh.

Hawke's touch on my skin, no matter where it was, heated me where it mattered most. Straight to my core, and I was grateful my period was almost over because I was ready for more of that intimacy.

Stupid irregular heavy flow.

"And knotted means, you force it into the–" and then I pointed between my legs.

He nodded, and his hand went up my thigh. "It is a special connection I did not want to share with anyone. You only knot your mate, and I've saved it for you."

That was damn hot. Being completely stretched, but it was also very intimidating.

I let out a shaky breath. The voice inside me told me to relax. I still couldn't believe he wanted me. I kept thinking this was a dream, and I would wake up at any moment and none of this would be real. Which was a genuine fear, because everything I've learned about the Iron Fang, another realm, shifters, warlocks, vampires, it was so overwhelmingly...fantastic.

And sometimes when he explained about the other realm, it seemed familiar. Flashes of a portal, tall blue-barked trees with deep red foliage, flittering bits of light raining down around us. It was like a long-lost dream as he explained it.

The past few days had been wonderful, getting to know him, understanding that the world was a far bigger place. But I hadn't told him my secrets.

It had only come up once, and that was to ask who this Shane was. But I froze, too scared to tell Hawke about my deepest and darkest nightmare.

Once I told him, I feared he would look at me differently. I felt ashamed. I enjoyed leaving my life in the past. And I certainly didn't want to receive pity from anyone for what happened to me.

I was private in that regard. I didn't want to be a burden.

"Tell him," she said. *"He will understand."*

I nibbled on my lip.

A mate, he was mine now. Even if he hadn't completed the bond yet, which he had yet to tell me about what that entailed, he was irrevocably mine.

He made it clear I was his. I mean, he followed me everywhere. There was no space between us even when I would go look out the window, shower, or simply rearrange the pillows on the bed–which he liked a lot. He purred constantly when he saw me rearranging things. His cock would stand at attention in his sweats, and his heated gaze bore into my skin when I fluffed a pillow.

If I had known fluffing pillows turned him on so much, then I would have done it a lot sooner.

"Hey, Sunshine?" he whispered, his lips tracing my bare shoulder.

Oh, I know that voice. It's when he wants something. And it was really adorable too when he did that because I could never say no.

"Yes?" I peered up at him from under my lashes.

I knew he was going to ask again. I could feel it.

"I've told you everything about me, and I know nothing about you–"

"He's not wrong."

"I just don't like to talk about myself." I chuckled nervously. "Seems selfish of me to do so. I mean, look what all you have been through, and the other club members. Who could reject Anaki like that?"

Hawke growled, pulling me onto his lap and playfully biting my shoulder. "Don't talk about him."

"Why? Are you jealous?" I fluttered my lashes.

"I told you I'm a possessive motherfucker, and I'm not going to have you talk about another unmated shifter." His nibbling became softer, now licking away the sting. "Your safety is important, Delilah. And tomorrow is the meeting. I need to know what I'm dealing with."

I gaped at him. "You will do nothing. We are going to hide in here and do nothing."

Hawke snarled. "Like fuck I will. If you are too scared to talk to him, I will fucking kill him for giving you nightmares. He is the reason for your nightmares, right?"

I scrunched my face in defiance. I just wanted to fade into the shadows and hide. It was cowardly, but I also didn't want anyone having to fight my battles. Not when I was becoming happy with Hawke.

"My wolf is getting stronger now. I can read you like a book, Dede. I can feel your fear. I can taste your arousal. You really think I haven't noticed how you tremble? You haven't even said his name since Bram brought him up."

I pursed my lips. "It isn't that big of a deal."

Liar.

Hawke took his hand and wrapped it around my neck. He didn't cut off my airway, his hand only squeezing each side of my neck to let me know he was in charge. Instead of shying away in fear, I relished the touch.

I felt safe there despite him being so much stronger than me. For two years, he'd kept me safe and watched over me. The command, the control. I felt like I didn't have to worry when he was near.

His lips grazed my cheek until they reached my ear. His hot breath fanned my neck, and goose bumps ran down my arm. "I will protect you from this human. Do you doubt me?"

"No," I whispered, my nipples hardening.

"You are mine in all ways, Delilah. In body, in heart and soul. I will protect you, and I will kill for you."

I licked my lips as he backed away. A shadow ran across his eyes that I swore was his wolf.

"Tell me, who is he?" Hawke commanded.

"Maybe if you give me one of those orgasms you like to gift me? I might be more compliant then." I giggled, to relieve the tension.

"You said you were bleeding. Not that it would deter me. I am an animal." He grinned wickedly.

Holy hotness. But that is just not my jam, not yet anyway.

"I guess that means we will have to wait until I'm finished. Darn, that means he will have come and gone by then." I smiled sweetly.

"Delilah," Hawke warned.

My smile faded and was replaced by a miserable frown. I ran my hand down my face as he let go of my neck. I could feel the darkness I'd kept away for so long creeping in.

"He's my stepbrother," I muttered, not offering any more information.

"What did he do?" Hawke's voice lowered. "Did he hit you?"

"Amongst other things." I couldn't look Hawke in the eye.

Shame bubbled inside me and the fear that both he and my friends at the Iron Fang would look at me in disgust rose to the surface. No one would ever look at me the same, would they?

Hawke pinched my chin, directing me to look into those deep pools of his eyes. His face softened considerably, his other hand rubbing against my cheek. I rubbed against it, trying to gain whatever warmth I could.

He waited patiently as I sighed heavily.

"I never knew my dad. All I ever knew was my mom and Grandma De," I smiled. "Grandma De would watch me at night while my mom worked. Mom was an exotic dancer, and despite the bad rep that comes with that job, she really enjoyed the dancing part."

Hawke cuddled me closer, his chin resting on my head. "One night, she came home and said she was engaged to some rich guy. She wouldn't have to work anymore and told us we were moving to his big house the next day. As a five-year-old, I thought it was great. We would move out of our crummy apartment and have an actual house."

"Did she not date the man? Why would your mother just agree?" He tried to remain calm, but I could feel his heart thrumming against my arm.

I shrugged my shoulders. "I was young. I don't remember. But Grandma De, who I saw as my second mother, was old. She couldn't take care of me for much longer, so she was happy for Mom. Grandma De died just a year later."

"Shit, I'm not liking this so far," Hawke muttered.

"Just wait," I chuckled. "It gets worse."

Hawke frowned.

"They got married, and then I got a new brother—Shane. We were introduced as siblings and really, he was the best big brother I could ask for." I sniffed and felt my eyes brimming with tears. "Shane was five years older, but we did everything together. We made forts so big we could watch movies in them. We would eat candy, laugh, and even sleep in there together when the movie was over." I gave a shaky smile. "He would drop everything when his friends were over and tuck me into bed. He'd read me stories, helped me with homework. I thought he was the best big brother ever."

Hawke tightened his grip around me. My tears now flowed freely.

"Then one night, it all changed."

A roaring purr settled in Hawke's chest. It poured into my body, vibrating until I could compose myself. I hadn't spoken to anyone about what had happened. And now, telling the one person I cared about the most, well, it was damned terrifying.

And so shameful.

"His bedroom was next to mine. I heard him yelling at his girlfriend, then his bedroom door slammed open, and I heard her leave. My door cracked open shortly after, and then Shane poked his head in. He looked like he'd been crying. His face was all red. I sat up in bed, and he asked me if he could stay with me that night."

"I thought nothing of it. I was twelve, and he was my big brother–I wanted to make him feel better." I gripped my fists together, feeling my nails pierce the skin. Hawke pried them open, shaking his head.

"We fell asleep. We stayed on two different sides of the bed. I fell asleep but sometime in the night, I felt him touching me." I sobbed, shaking my head.

Hawke let out a low growl. It wasn't just anger, it was made of pure fury. It rattled the bed, and the pictures on the wall fell to the floor. The shock shook the dark memories from my mind, and I redirected my attention to his face.

Dark. Murderous. Terrifying.

And kinda hot.

"What else?" He gripped my chin to meet his gaze.

I could tell he wanted to ask for more details. He continued to part his lips, shutting them, closing them tightly. His nose flared, and the thick veins that trailed up his neck continued to bulge.

"After that, I always gave excuses not to let him sleep with me anymore. I felt so dirty afterwards. He was my brother. I know we're not blood related, but he was a brother to me." I nibbled on my lip.

"Of course you would feel that way. You were young, and you saw him as such. He fucking took advantage of you, Dede."

I nodded, agreeing.

Just wait, it gets worse.

"At the time, I didn't fully understand what was going on, but looking back now that I am older, there were signs of his obsession growing."

"Obsession?"

"Yeah." I rubbed my hands together. "He told mom and my stepdad that I shouldn't go out with friends. That the friends I had at the academy were a rough crowd. Of course, they listened to him, they knew Shane cared a lot about me. So, little by little, year after year, more things were taken away from me." I swallowed.

"What hurt the most was when those friends automatically shut me out. But I knew why, it was because one of them reported my brother to the police. He stayed there maybe two months, and when he got out, he made sure the *anonymous caller* paid for it."

Hawke balled up his fists, his claws pierced his skin. Tears dropped into his palms, washing away the blood that stained his hands.

"I was homeschooled after that, but I never got my high school diploma. He had me go to an online college and take classes, but even then I didn't receive a diploma."

"Why the hell not?" Hawke growled. "Why couldn't you get any of those things? And where were your parents during all of this?"

"Because it would grant me freedom," I whispered. "I could get a job and leave. Shane didn't want that. He was keeping me from everyone. My friends, my mom, they forgot about me."

"What the fuck was your mother doing during this time?" Hawke snapped. "Didn't she find this odd?"

I huffed out a breath. "She was traveling a lot with my stepdad. Shane was next in line at his father's business. Shane was to be Don of the upstate New York Irish Mafia."

"Holy fuck."

"Potty mouth," I let out a forced laugh. "But yeah. Shane had a lot of power, even if he wasn't in the mansion. I was monitored constantly, hardly any privacy, and I never really knew why, until I reached my nineteenth birthday." I swallowed.

Hawke's growl continued. The tingles on my body grew hotter by the minute.

"Hawke, Shane just isn't my stepbrother. He's also my husband."

CHAPTER TWENTY-NINE

Hawke

She spoke hesitantly, and her head hung in embarrassment.

As I held her close, I could feel the intense shame and humiliation radiating from her through the connection we shared. I didn't let go, and I comforted her while she wept against my chest.

I understood the rationale behind her behavior, and I could comprehend the way she reasoned. Even though there was no blood relation between them, she viewed him as a brother. She felt no romantic love for him and now, after the disgusting, vile things he had done to her, there was no love at all for him.

He took advantage of my mate.

The mother fucking bastard.

I would skin him alive, mount his head in the basement of the Iron Fang. He wouldn't be the first head mounted on the wall. Usually, we just place the skulls of the damned in our torture chambers, but Grim wanted to create a new tradition.

One of Journey's rapists was being prepared by one of our very own taxidermists and fuck, it was going to be a hilarious sight. All our enemies would see the fear contorting the tortured faces when they entered the basement. It would be hilarious to see.

And soon, I would tear this Shane apart with my bare hands.

A snarl ripped through the room, my mate shuddered, and she buried a sob into my chest.

"You're scaring her, you fucking idiot," my wolf snapped. *"She thinks you are angry with her."*

My shoulders drooped, my hand caressing my mate's head. "Delilah, my Sunshine, I am not angry with you. Please don't think that."

"You are disgusted with me, aren't you?" her sobs continued.

I lifted her chin. She wiped away the tears that had caused her eyes to become red and swollen. Yet she was still beautiful to me, she always would be. "I am not disgusted with you. He is not related to you in blood, and even if he was, you did not want him. You did not want his advances. He forced you."

She nodded and hiccupped. "But I'm married to him!"

I shook my head. "You didn't want to marry him, did you?"

"I had to, or he would have killed my mom."

My grip tightened on her chin. "You were forced, Delilah. You were coerced. I do not believe in human marriages anyhow. It is only a fucking piece of paper. Humans have no authority to bind souls together. It means nothing."

Delilah wiped away her tears with the back of her hand. "Yeah? A priest was there, though?"

"For a god that does not exist," I said soothingly. "The only goddess that binds souls is Selene, the Moon Goddess."

"I don't understand." Delilah continued to wipe back her tears.

"Marriages between humans mean nothing in this life, Sunshine. They are only partnerships. They are not binding after death. Humans have not been granted soulmates. At least, not to each other yet."

I held Delilah, stroking her hair, sharing comforting words of how much I cared for her. That none of this was her fault and how strong she was, because she was strong, and so fierce.

But the more silence there was between us, and the more I comforted her, the more anger I felt rising inside me. I couldn't wait until I saw Shane tomorrow and ripped the bastard to pieces. I wanted to watch him slowly die by my hand for torching my precious woman.

"Sunshine, how did you ever survive for so long with this male? You were with him for five years before you found me. What made you run?" I ran my claws down her back and goosebumps appeared. She moaned softly, her face rubbing against my bare chest.

"Shane always had full control of me when my mom was alive. He threatened to kill her, if I ever did anything stupid or tried to run away. But I learned to *love him*, I guess." She shivered. "I became the perfect actress. He really thought I cared about him. And then one day, my mom and stepdad died by poisoning, and then Shane became the Don."

"Were you sad when your mother died?" I asked.

"At first." She swallowed. "But if she really cared about me, she would have seen I was miserable."

I held my mate a little tighter. Never again would she suffer. Never again would she have to act brave in front of anyone ever again.

"My acting paid off, though. Shane believed that I really cared about him. After our parent's death, he had to go away on business. He left me at the house, telling me he would only be gone for a few days. A maid approached me; she handed me a bag and pulled me down corridors I didn't even know about. I didn't even know who this maid was—never seen her before—but my gut told me to follow. She led me outside, and she pushed me off the property. It was like I had no say, she just shooed me to go."

She smiled, wiping away a tear. "She went back into the passage like she was never there, and then I hitchhiked across the country and got far away."

I closed my eyes and leaned my head back on the bed. She could have been raped, beaten, or murdered hitchhiking like that. But thank fuck she hadn't been, and I found her when I did.

"Never hitchhike again, Sunshine."

And thank the goddess for that maid.

She wiped the rest of her tears away. "I won't. I'm here now. If you still want me?" she asked hopefully.

"Of fucking course I still want you! I don't want you putting yourself in danger like that, ever again, damn it!" I grabbed the back of her head, pulling her toward me and pressing my lips against hers.

I bit at her lips, causing her pale pink lips to darken, abusing them until they parted, and I slipped my tongue into her mouth. We both moaned, our bodies pressing against each other. I raked my hands down her body, cupping her breasts until I flicked her nipples through her shirt.

"You are mine, Delilah." I pinched her tits.

Her moans echoed in the wood covered apartment as I pushed her down into the mattress. Her hair flared out onto the blankets, her lips parted, and her flushed cheeks looked so fucking sexy I was ready to fucking knot her right there.

"I want you so fucking bad, Delilah, and I don't want you to ever doubt it again."

"H-he touched me, though. My brother–"

"Don't care–" I took my claw and ripped my shirt off her body. She was left in nothing but her boy short, pink underwear with black trim. It was hot as hell, and my cock strained in my sweats, leaving drops of come on the front.

"You're mine, and I'm going to leave my marks all over your body. I will wash away any signs of his scent with mine. Do you understand?" I growled into her ear.

Her body shivered as I pulled down her underwear. There was barely any blood, and I didn't fucking care if she was bleeding a fucking river. I was going to claim her pussy with my cock today. She would know I would claim this pussy whenever I wanted.

"Do you want my cock, Delilah?" I asked, pulling down my sweats.

My cock bobbed, slapping my stomach with a smack.

She stared at the head. The piercing glinting in the light as she watched the come dripping from the head. There was more precum than a human, that was for sure. It continued to drip like a fucking faucet. I'd had blue balls for days, waiting for my mate to be finished with her damned cycle that went on forever, but I waited since she was so sensitive about it.

But no longer. I would take her no matter if she was bleeding or not from now on. I was going to knot her whenever I wanted.

"Y-yes, I want it." She licked her lips. My cock jumped at the way she stared at it hungerly.

I kneeled before her, grabbing it close to the knot and pumping it several times.

"Will you take this knot of your own free will?"

Her breath shuddered, and she backed away to take in the full sight of me. "It's huge," she whispered. "Will it fit?"

I smirked. Good, I'm bigger than that fucker Shane.

"Sunshine, it's my job to make it fit. I'm going to make you nice and wet, but from the looks of it, I won't have to do much."

Delilah blushed. Her legs tightened together, and she pulled them closer to her body. I crawled closer, spreading them, shaking my head.

"I don't like you hiding what's mine. You're perfect, everything about you, and now that you are accepting of me, I want to see all of it."

"I'm still bleeding," she whispered, slowly letting me pry her legs apart.

"Like I said, I'm an animal, Delilah. I would have licked you clean days ago, but I'm trying to ease you into this lifestyle."

"Cheesus," she panted.

My hand raked down her inner thigh, her beautiful butterfly folds parted, and I snaked two fingers into her pussy. She laid her head back as I curled my fingers, feeling her pussy already fluttering around them.

"That's it, relax for me. I want to feel your pussy pulse around my fingers. I want two orgasms from you before you suck on my cock with that pretty pussy you have."

She whimpered, and the precum that continued to leak dribbled over her leg, marking her further. Soon she would smell nothing but my scent. Shifters from miles around wouldn't be able to come near her. Hell, even the warlock downstairs wouldn't be able to come near her, she would reek so much.

I smiled at that. Maybe even the human that would be in town tomorrow could smell her. I should show her off, show him I had her. Take him into the woods, dangle her in front of him, show him she was mine and always would be.

I shook my head. I couldn't ever bring my Delilah in front of him, but my words, maybe a lock of her hair would be enough to piss him off. Show him that I had claimed her as my own, that she chose me instead of his nasty crusty ass.

I continued to thrust my fingers into her body, her pussy contracting around them. She screamed, her arousal coating my fingers as her body rose from the bed, giving in to her first orgasm. I rubbed her g-spot, spurring on another orgasm as quickly as the first one came, and sucked on her tit as she rode down her second high.

Sweat trickled down her brow, and a satisfied smirk laid upon my lips as she stared up at me with such awe.

My balls were heavy with need, my knot ached and was ready to be lodged deep into her cunt to keep my seed. I was ready to keep my body locked with hers. It had been a long time coming, and my wolf was eager to mark her as well.

But one step at a time. Let us knot her first.

"You know I fucking love you, right?" I asked.

Delilah nodded excitedly.

"Because I'm going to fuck you like I don't."

Delilah's eyes widened, and her nipples tightened into beautiful pebbles. They were already red with my teeth marks.

I rubbed the tip of my cock's head with her wetness, then upwards over her clit to soak my shaft. We both groaned as I coated my heat with her arousal. Her nails dug into my skin, and I lined up and thrust the tip of my cock into her entrance.

She screamed, and I groaned as I set myself deep inside her, leaving my knot at the base of her pussy. I pulled back and thrust inside her again until I had a steady rhythm going in and out of her. With each thrust I let out the animalistic noises of my pleasure. The primal part of me took over as my wolf came to the front. He stretched her further as more of my knot entered her and she opened her legs wider to accept me.

I'd wanted to do this since the first time I met her. Night after night, I'd taken my hand and dreamed about fucking her, making sweet slow love to her. Now I needed her more than I needed air. I need her hard and fast.

She whimpered, moaned, and panted, spurring me further into a frenzy. My mate dug her fingers into my shoulders, drawing blood, and my wolf howled in my head to take her deeper and harder.

"More!" she screamed, her hips tilting to take me deeper.

My knot grew harder. Her eyes turned dark. My curiosity at her eyes only lasted for a minute before she leaned forward and sank her teeth into my shoulder.

A euphoric feeling settled over me, my knot becoming extremely sensitive as it lodged inside her. I could no longer thrust. I was locked in place. I continued to roll my hips, pushing us gently back and forth along the mattress in rhythm with my heavy breathing. My clit thumped as I felt my heart racing inside her pussy as I gently rocked it inside her.

Her teeth stayed lodged in my shoulder. I could feel my blood running down the front of my chest, but I dared not tell her to let go. It fucking felt incredible, feeling my cock being milked by my mate, feeling the pain in my shoulder that radiated through my body. I felt my soul locking with hers.

My teeth elongated as well, my wolf urging me to bite her too. But that would complete the bond. It would make her change.

"*Bite her,*" he urged me. "*Do it, now.*"

I growled, arguing with myself until my wolf ripped control of my body from me and sank my teeth into her porcelain skin.

We both experienced another orgasm. I shot another load into her pussy. I could feel my come trying to leak out of her pussy, but it only pushed further into her womb. My lower back continued to tingle, pushing more and more of my arousal into her body as her body shuddered against mine.

Holy fuck.

"Ahhh, oh god!" Delilah moaned, her head falling backward.

Out of the corner of my eye, I could see the small canines forming on her teeth, along with blood dripping down the corner of her mouth.

My teeth sunk in further, my wolf staking the claim of her soul and fuck, it felt like fucking heaven taking her as my own. All thoughts of her dying, of not making the shift were thrown out the window because that wasn't a worry anymore.

Everything was going to be okay.

I thrust my hips forward, my knot burying deeper.

Delilah whimpered, her fingers digging into my back, her hips trying to force my knot further inside her. We held each other tightly as we let the bond take over, and I tried to figure out what the hell came over Delilah to spark her biting me.

CHAPTER THIRTY

Hawke

Before my knot retracted from her body, my mate's eyes closed, and she fell asleep. I hoped that she'd only dozed off and hadn't lost consciousness.

I gently laid her body onto the soft duvet, hovering over hers as I panted over her dampened skin. Our bodies were covered in a sheen of sweat, and drips of blood oozed from our bites.

Shit, we fucking bit each other.

I groaned, placing my forehead on hers while she slept. But instead of feeling the guilt I should have felt that my mate had taken my venom and would shift into a beast like me, I was...elated. I attached my soul to hers. She was mine, and it couldn't be undone.

My tongue slipped from my mouth, licking the blood that no longer oozed from her shoulder. I cleaned her like a suitable mate should, taking in every bit of the metallic taste into my mouth. I groaned, growing harder by the second as I tasted her sweet sweat, the smell of her arousal, already permeating the room again.

Her nipples hardened, her chest pushing outward, and I kissed down her chest to taste them again. How fucking sweet she tasted and how cool her skin felt on my burning lips.

I trailed my warm hands down her skin, cupping her breasts, giving them a gentle squeeze before I traced down between her thighs. Then I used two of my fingers to push the come trying to escape back into her pussy. I didn't want it to escape. I wanted to fucking breed my mate, further keeping her trapped with me.

What a sick fucker I would be if I were a human. But I wasn't, was I?

I was a damn wolf. The thought of breeding her, filling her womb with pups, to watch her swell and continue our genetic line made my balls ache with desire.

I continued to scoop my seed, pushing it further into her cavern until the thought of her not wanting this crossed my mind. I took her raw, and I would do it again, but what if she didn't want it?

What if she wasn't on any sort of birth control?

Would it even matter?

I snarled, still shoving my come back inside her. My cock was already leaking again. Never in my life had I grown so hard, so quickly, ready to penetrate any pussy.

But this was my mate, my one desire, the one love I'd always wanted.

My mate let out a needy moan, her head thrashing as I held her in my arms. Her arousal smelled sweeter, her nipples turning a darker pink. She couldn't be? Could she?

My wolf howled, elated at the prospect.

My cock burned, ached at the sight of her leaking cunt. I gripped my throbbing cock, pumping it several times, only to be greeted with no relief.

This couldn't be happening. It would be too soon, right?

Gently, I laid my mate in our nest. Wrapping her with the greatest care. I needed answers, and unfortunately, that meant leaving her in the nest alone.

I grabbed my shirt, covering my privates, and headed down the winding metal stairs. I left the door open so I could hear my mate's cries if she needed me. I jumped down the last five steps to be greeted by Bram, shooing a customer out the door.

He flipped the sign to closed and flipped off the lights. He turned, his eyes flickered red with the last remaining light. "You've mated with her. Congratulations. But I must ask why you are down here?" A smirk appeared on his lips as he passed me going behind the counter.

"She bit me first." I ran my hand through my hair.

Bram paused, his back facing away from me. "Delilah did what?" he asked, amused.

"She bit me first. I wasn't planning on completing the bond. Just knotting her, I wasn't sure–"

"You weren't sure if she would survive a shift, so you were just going to take the first step."

I nodded, gripping my cock. It was going to fucking explode if I didn't rub one out soon.

"And you bit her back?" Bram turned, raising an eyebrow in curiosity.

"My wolf wouldn't have it any other way. He took over and—"

"Of course, he wouldn't. Animals are selfish bastards." Bram picked up a glass of bourbon underneath the counter and swallowed the remnants from the glass in one go. "But that presents a new problem. You've gone into your rut."

"Shit." I gripped my cock through the shirt. My come was soaking the material, but I gained no relief.

"Hawke!" A cry from the corner of the room made me drop the now soaked shirt covering my dick.

Delilah stood on the stairs with her purple silk robe barely covering her breasts. Her hair was ruffled, covering half her face, the bite mark that was once red and angry was now a beautiful scar that held my mark making her mine.

Even though she looked in pain, disgruntled and worried, I was fucking proud of how my mate took my mark so well.

I rushed to her, dropping the dirty shirt, and I heard Bram groan as my ass hung out for him to see. I covered her body, holding her as she fell into my arms. "My mate, what is wrong? Why are you up?"

"I'm hot all over," she breathed. "My... Between my legs, it's so hot."

When I touched her, she felt cool to me. My cock brushed between her legs, and I felt instant relief. I bet I would feel more once I buried myself deep inside her. She must feel the same because she wrapped her arms around me, sighing deeply into my chest.

"She's in heat." Bram mentioned from the other side of the room. "Rather odd, since she was just bitten."

I turned to him, my mate not paying any attention to the warlock.

"What?" I snapped.

"I'm saying it should take longer for the venom to work for her heat to come in," he mused. "Venom doesn't work that quickly."

Delilah cried out again, her fingers digging into my skin.

"Take her," Bram ordered. "I'll leave you food and pregnancy preventives until it's over."

"But Shane," I countered. "Don't you have something to delay the rut and her heat? Do you have rutting root?"

Locke used to carry rutting root around in his vest, his cut, when new members who still had their rut joined the Iron Fang. It helped them control the rut, so they didn't need a female. I wanted to take care of Shane, make sure he would never bother my mate again.

Delilah let out a terrible cry, her knees giving way. I pulled her into my arms and kissed her forehead gently. "It's alright, Sunshine. I've got you."

"You will need to delay your fight for another day. Your mate is more important," Bram said sternly. "But your day for revenge will come."

I clenched my jaw but didn't argue. As I gripped my mate tighter, hearing her cries, I raced up the stairs and took her to our room to make sure my mate would no longer feel the pain of her heat.

Delilah

From the whisper of "*bite him*" to the raging heat and tingling in the lower parts of my body, I had a growing fury of want radiating from my body. I felt so close, yet so far from him. It was excruciating.

I wanted him near me; I wanted him inside me. I wanted to touch him, feel him physically, yet I already felt him inside my soul.

My fingers fumbled with the silk robe. I could barely tie it, and by the time I reached the bottom of the stairs, I don't know if it covered my body. Hawke stood in front of Bram, his muscular ass uncovered for all the world to see, and my pussy clenched, wanting his cock to enter me again.

Once his name left my lips, my eyes rolled back and the next time I opened them, he was hovering over me, his hand cupping my cheek.

"There you are, Sunshine. How are you doing?"

"Hot." I swallowed. "But better when you touch me," I whimpered.

To my dismay, Hawke took his hand away and pulled more pillows away from the bed. I didn't question him, too busy reaching for him to come back.

"Do you remember what I told you about rutting?"

"Uh huh." I reached between my legs, showing no care for modesty and cupped my mound, but pulled away when I felt how damp I was.

"I'm going into my rut, and you are going into heat. It is just like a rut, except it is for females."

I looked in his direction. His cock was leaking profusely, dripping onto my leg as he pushed my legs apart. He lowered his face to my mound, rubbing his cheek next to it.

"Humans don't go into heat," I squeaked.

"Let me ask you, why did you bite me?" Hawke licked my clit, and I moaned happily.

"The voice in my head told me to."

He hummed thoughtfully. "Well, that started a chain reaction, my dear mate."

Hawke gripped under my ass, pulling me closer to him. He raised me up, so I straddled his lap. He took my nipple in his mouth, sucking it roughly until he let it go with a pop.

Crap, it felt so nice.

As he brushed my hair away from my shoulder, his finger traced where he bit me earlier. It tingled, causing heated goosebumps to race down to my core.

"What was that?" I asked.

"When you bit me, my wolf bit you back, causing our bond to be woven together."

I felt a jolt of energy as my eyes widened. "What?"

"You're my soulmate, Sunshine. You started our bond, and I finished it. With our bites, my knot, we are bonded forever." His husky voice sent shivers through my body as he said, "And now our bodies will devour each other for days."

Hawke pulled my body forward, the slick of my pussy running over his knot. We both shuddered as he lifted my hips and placed me over his lap. "Now I want you to ride me, Delilah. I want you to fuck me how you like it."

I let out a soft whimper as I felt my body being lowered. I sat right above his knot while he held me in place. I gripped his shoulders, and he hissed as my fingers dug into the teeth marks I left behind on his right shoulder.

"That's it, good girl, now rise and show me how fast you like it."

I relished the praise, a sick part of me wanting more of it. I never needed it before, but when I was sitting here, riding my boyfriend's cock, no, my mate's cock, I wanted more of it.

Hawke must have seen a twinkle, a spark in my eye once the words left his lips because he smirked and jerked his hips upwards to meet my thrusts. "That's it, baby, gods, you take my cock so damn good."

I moaned, my breasts feeling heavier by the minute. Could it be possible they were growing? I wouldn't doubt it with this supernatural crap going on, but sensing my distress, Hawke cupped one of them while keeping a firm grip on my hip.

"Fuck yes, Dede, just like that. Ride me. Your pussy grips me like a vice."

I groaned, my head doing its best not to bounce around like a rag doll. Hawke snarled, his hip thrusts becoming more frantic. "Want me to take over?" He spoke in a hoarse, rumbling tone.

I couldn't speak, only a whimper escaped. I wasn't weak. I wanted to prove myself, but how could I convey that when I could feel so much?

Emotions, both his and mine, collided like one raging fire tornado and one winter hurricane. I felt his love, his desire, his fear, his excitement, his love, but most of all his lust. He wanted to be rough with me, but the fear he would scare or hurt me over rode it.

I wanted to give him everything, but my fear of not being adequate enough stood in the way. I wasn't being fast enough for his liking.

Hawke paused his thrusts, gently laying me on the sheets as his shaft twitched inside me. He stared into my eyes with a fire burning brightly inside them.

"You are my everything. You are more than adequate, my mate."

I gasped, the sound echoing in the room as I felt his heart beat against my chest.

"You are more than anything I could ever imagine, more than I ever deserve. I know you're overwhelmed. I only want to give you pleasure from now until the end of time if I have to."

"It's just so much right now, I want to be in charge—"

Hawke's laughter was like a thunderclap, resonating throughout the room. "The only time you will ever be in charge is when I let you, and even then, will you ever be in charge?" He nipped at my lip. "Now let me take your worries away, my sweet girl. Your body is changing. It was selfish of me to expect you to ride my cock as your body is experiencing its first heat."

Hawke tenderly rocked his hips, touching each part of me. His kisses ran down my neck, but the fire still burned in the pit of my stomach. I wanted more.

"More," I whispered. "I need more."

Hawke's teeth were bared in determination, his movements becoming more and more frenzied.

"Thank fuck, because I need to be rough."

Hawke pulled from my body, flipping me over. I raised to my knees, pushing my ass in the air. He growled in appreciation and pulled my hips toward his massive erection. It didn't take long for him to push into my weeping core, his knot continuing to slap into my ass.

"Yes! Oh, more!" I cried out, gripping the headboard.

Hawke gripped one of my hips while his other hand wrapped around my hair, pulling it until I leaned back and could stare into his eyes.

"My mate looks so beautifully taking my cock. Fuck, Delilah, you do not know how long I've wanted to fuck you like this. Those pouty lips, this perfect ass. Fuck."

I cried out as an orgasm washed over me. It dulled the searing fire of pain. Hawke shortly roared when his orgasm took over, and his grip tightened in my hair.

As I felt spurts of his come jetting inside me, I felt an emotion I had buried deep inside and had buried so deep I never thought it would see the light of day.

Hawke must have felt it, he had to, because he released himself from me. He didn't implant his knot this time, instead he fell to the side and pulled me into his embrace.

My sweet mate. He cupped my cheek, and my tears fell. "Are you still in pain? I'm ready to go again. I'm always ready," he chuckled. "I've got more seed, and I can go all day and night."

I shook my head, the salty taste of tears on my lips.

His eyes softened, and he kissed my forehead, my cheeks, and my lips until I composed myself. "I just love you. I didn't want to tell you because I was afraid—"

"I would leave," Hawke interrupted.

I nodded.

He pulled me to his chest, his shaft already hard against my thigh. I could already feel the burn between my legs, my nipples aching to be sucked.

"Sunshine, I've known you loved me. I've always loved you, but I was too stubborn to admit it. But I'm never letting you go. You understand me? Never. You're my mate and nothing is going to rip us apart. And while our heat and rut are going on, I will fuck you until you realize I'm not going anywhere."

I laughed loudly, quite un-lady like, and he rolled on top of me, planting kisses all over my cheeks, my chest, and down my body.

CHAPTER THIRTY-ONE

Delilah

After four days of never leaving the bedroom, our sex craze simmered. But that didn't stop the lust we still had for each other. I was ready to stretch my legs, to feel the sun on my face, but it took another two days to find the motivation.

Part of me worried Shane was lurking around the corner, and the other part didn't want to leave the bubble of paradise that we'd created for ourselves. I guess having food brought to us three times a day, being completely naked and screwing around was nice, but I missed the sunshine.

It wasn't until day seven when we emerged that my ears bled. My sensitivity to sound had heightened tenfold and Hawke rushed me down to the shop where Bram was burning a bundle of herbs and spices on the counter while flipping through a large book.

Hawke sat me on the counter next to the fire burning on the fire resistant plate and pointed to my ear, and Bram rolled his eyes.

"Yes, Hawke, it is normal." Bram closed the book. "But you already knew that. You have seen it before with Journey. Why are you bringing her down here now?"

"I-I needed a second opinion! What if I'm wrong? There isn't as much blood as when Journey's ears bled. What if she won't fully shift? What if she won't shift at all?"

Hawke's body shook, I could also feel his panic through the bond we now shared.

I cleared my throat, touching my ear. It was barely a drop, maybe comparable to someone getting their ears pierced. "I'm not in any pain."

I gently grabbed Hawke's forearm, which flexed under my touch. He wrapped his arm around my waist and laid his head on my chest.

Bram chuckled, pulling out a rolled up parchment from his robe. These past few days he had brought us food, his face was different. He didn't have the handle-bar mustache, but instead had a short salt and peppered beard. He also had kind eyes.

But even that wasn't his true form. Hawke mentioned that witches and warlocks would never show what they truly looked like or tell their true name, only to their mate.

"Because Delilah isn't like Journey. Journey was gifted a wolf. Delilah somehow had a wolf inside her all along, and it's laid dormant. Her fangs and the urge to bite you gave that away. Whether she inherited it from a relative, or it was buried in her soul, is the genuine question."

The voice inside me hummed contentedly. She wasn't saying anything or volunteering any information.

"Have you heard any strange voices?" Bram cocked his eyebrow.

I licked my lips, Hawke already nodding.

"Yes, she does. She said she's heard them before."

"I can speak, you know!" I snapped. "If I'm going to be talking about crazy things in my head, I should be the one to voice it."

Hawke's fear morphed into worry. "Dede, I didn't mean to upset you, I just—"

Bram waved him off. "It's quite adorable how sappy newly mated couples get. I can't wait to get mine." He gave a soft smile. "Anything else peculiar?"

I rubbed my stomach, which was getting weird butterflies in it. "I get a weird feeling in my stomach sometimes when I am about to make a wrong decision, or I'm going to be in danger."

Bram hummed, acknowledging what Delilah had said.

But that couldn't be right, because I was sitting inside the shop with Bram and Hawke. I was in the safest place I could be. Away from the town getting ready for Christmas, away from Shane.

Bram told us days ago, the black sedans had departed, and Shane was nowhere to be found. Even the restaurant owner was still in one piece, which was surprising. Shane had no patience for insolence.

"Hawke, your mate is fine. Let me see if any of my texts have any information about gaining their wolf's voice before their shift. Delilah, can you talk to her whenever you want?"

I shook my head. "No, she talks and answers me only when she wants to."

I sighed as Hawke continued to talk to Bram. I honestly wasn't worried. The voice in my head was normal to me now. Every once in a while, she would ask how I was doing, and when I would approach the subject and ask who she was, she would go silent again.

Maybe I wasn't meant to know who she was yet, but she hadn't steered me wrong so far.

Later that night, I was awoken by pangs of pain in my stomach. I felt a writhing sensation, like a mass of snakes coiling in my stomach. I rose from the bed, my limbs shaking, and Hawke sat up beside me, a low growl emanating from his throat.

"What's wrong?" He groggily pulled me to his lap, wrapping his strong arms around me.

"Danger, something is about to happen," I whispered.

In a flash, our peaceful paradise vacation was shattered by the sound of banging on the downstairs doors.

Hawke jumped from the bed, landing without a sound, and placed his ear to the floor. I held my breath, feeling the anticipation tingling through my body as I pulled the blankets up over me.

I normally couldn't hear anything outside of the room. Bram cast a spell to make our room completely soundproof, but his magic must be fading or he wanted us to hear.

"No, I've never seen her," Bram said in the raspy, grumpy voice I'd first heard when I met him at the upscale diner. "Why are you banging on my doors so late? I'm on vacation this week!"

More mumbling sounded, and Hawke's lips curled into a snarl. His fists gripped together tightly, and fur ran down his back. I had yet to see his wolf, but the patches of dark fur in the moonlight led me to believe it was black or dark brown.

"No, you can't come in. You aren't cops and don't have a warrant!" Bram yelled, and the sound of the door slamming open and glass shattering made me jump from the bed.

Hawke grabbed me before I could hit the floor and pulled me into the bathroom, our naked bodies colliding as he pulled a bag from the closet. He locked the door quickly and put his hand around my neck, his thumb tracing my lips. "Shh, don't talk, put this on," he whispered harshly and put on his pants.

Sounds of wood splintering, broken furniture breaking into pieces and being and thrown beneath us made me wince. More glass was thrown up against the walls and then large thuds of shoes climbing up the metal stairs made my heartbeat quicken. I could hear them yelling, shaking the round stairway on the other side of the bathroom walls. Their voices were familiar and distant all at the same time.

Was Bram okay?

How did they find us?

The only way to get out of this apartment was to go down those stairs, and we were trapped in this bathroom.

I shakily put on the leggings, almost falling, but Hawke pulled me by my waist, giving me an encouraging smile as he threw a prepped bag over his shoulder.

After hearing the stories of Hawke being a guard and a solider in the other realm, it was no surprise that there was a bag hidden in the bathroom for a quick escape.

But now I was worried as he pulled me over to the window that wasn't meant to be opened.

I gasped as he lifted his leather boot. "We are two stories up!" I whispered.

Hawke pushed his boot into the glass, and it fell like a trickling waterfall.

"In here!" a voice boomed. I could easily recognize it as one of Shane's men. Chad, the chief bodyguard was also in charge of the estate when Shane was away.

He was large, close to two hundred and eighty pounds of pure muscle. His eyes lingered longer than they should, and he partook of drugs during the many parties held at the mansion. Chad was not a good guy. I'd seen him kill our own men for minor mistakes too many times just because he could.

It was so beautiful on the outside, so glamorous and elegant, but on the inside, it was pure hell. The devil rounded every corner, and the sinners constantly congregated there with their drugs, weapons, and sex parties.

I hated feeling so weak, especially in Chad's presence. It made him feel so big and tough, and it filled his ego. But he was so much bigger and stronger. Hell, everyone was back where I grew up.

I was dragged back to the present when Hawke made me straddle his waist and jumped on the ledge of the window. I squeaked. Once he gained his footing, he leaned out and eventually let go of the wall.

I gripped hold of his muscular body, his muscles flexing, contorting like a cat as he made himself comfortable as we free-fell out the window. More glass flitted around us. He'd bent his knees, bracing himself for the fall and pushed my face into his chest.

I wanted to scream. I could feel the bile rising to my throat as the fall was coming to an end. But instead, Hawke's knees bent, and his stance widened as he landed with perfect precision; both feet and one hand on the ground to steady himself.

The bag was still on his back, and he turned to face upwards to see Chad staring back down at us with a scowl. Hawke huffed, taking off on foot, carrying me like I was nothing, and raced to the back of the long alley where his bike was covered in trash bags.

Hawke set me down quickly and gently and pulled out my helmet. He shoved it into my hands without looking at me as he pulled his keys out of his pocket. One large leg was thrown over the bike, and he straddled his seat, settling himself, and revved the bike several times.

Once my shaky fingers snapped the strap into place, Hawke snarled as he saw the men from the sedans coming out of their cars at the other end of the ally. I snaked my arms around him feeling the vibrations in his chest. Then I heard his deep, gravelly voice speak straight into my mind.

"Hang on."

Oh, that's new!

"What about Bram!?"

Hawke didn't answer. Instead, the tires skidded along the surface of the murky, stagnant water as he pushed the throttle. When the tires finally got traction on the cement, we saw more black sedans gathering near the exit, blocking our escape. Hawke rolled the throttle toward him with a tight grip. The veins in his hands looked blown, as if they would burst at any second. The roar of the engine echoed through the alley, but that didn't override my enhanced hearing. Guns were being pulled from holsters.

"You said you wanted some adventure in your life," his voice echoed in my head.

"Yeah, something a little more on the controlled side!" I yelled back.

He laughed maniacally as I squeezed his body tighter. When I glanced back up at the black sedans, I saw Shane emerge in slow motion from a limousine behind the barricade in a perfectly tailored gray suit that was offset by a glossy black tie.

His gelled blonde hair gleamed in the light, and the intensity of his stormy blue eyes made me feel like he was looking right through me. His gaze narrowed, and his lips pursed together tightly, a clear sign of disapproval.

I looked away, no longer afraid of what Hawke was going to do. I was ready to be away from the man who'd traumatized me for years.

Feeling my distress, Hawke growled and gripped the handles, driving straight toward a car covered with a tarp. I readied myself for the impact, but instead of smashing into it, we hit a ramp, launching us onto the car and over Shane's vehicles.

Hawke lifted his hand off the handlebar to flip him the bird. I bit back a giggle, watching Hawke's fanged smile. Shane showed no emotion and watched us land perfectly on the road away from him.

Despite that smile, I could feel the tension in Hawke's back as we rode. We rode out of town and continued on with no sedans behind us. No one followed, and that worried me, but I was relieved at the same time. It was an odd feeling, but the pit of my stomach wasn't up in arms about being in danger.

Hawke didn't speak, and I could feel his anger radiating. I also felt his guilt that he hadn't sensed them coming, his regret for not staying, and his fear that they would follow. It was best that I didn't speak, because what could I say?

"Bram will meet us in a secure location. Try to relax," his voice growled through my head.

My lower lip trembled, unsure of what emotion I should be feeling.

It was back to grumpy Hawke. The Hawke that tried to keep his emotions inside. I used to hate it, but with this new bond flowing between us, I could at least feel what he was feeling. I felt his love for me, and that was enough to keep my thoughts of abandonment away.

Now I was only fearful that Shane would somehow get between us. That he would take me away, or worse, hurt Hawke. Once we went back to the Iron Fang, we would both be protected. Or would we bring danger back with us?

My arms and legs ached from how hard I was holding on to Hawke as we rode until sunrise a few hours later. I should feel tired, but my adrenaline was at an all-time high. I didn't want to sleep. I wanted to watch and wait for Shane to drive up with his men and find them trailing behind us.

"Talk to me, Sunshine," Hawke interrupted my worries. His hand landed on my thigh, giving me a squeeze. *"I know I've been quiet, but I'm trying to calm my wolf so he doesn't... Well, go back and murder the bastard now."*

"I'm just scared he'll come back," I yelled over the roar of the engine.

His shoulders moved as if he was laughing. *"You can talk through our minds. Our bond is solidified now. I can hear your thoughts; you can hear mine. I can hide mine a bit more than yours though–"*

"Wait," I said inside my head. *"Have you been reading my mind all this time?"*

He sighed. *"Just since we left the apartment. But yes. You are a very loud thinker, Dede. But I am glad to know you think my cock is delicious."*

I groaned and lightly pounded my forehead against his back.

"And, I want to know more about this, Chad." He growled. *"I want to know all of what you went through because it seems you've left a lot of information out."*

"I don't like to talk about it. Besides, I feel like a lot of it's being erased."

Hawke tapped his thumb on the handlebars. *"What do you mean?"*

"The painful memories, they don't seem as painful anymore. Like, they're fading away."

Hawke hummed, scratching his beard. *"I believe Journey has gone through something similar. But I want to know. I want to know every bastard that has made you feel uncomfortable, so I have a nice long list to take out my anger on."*

I shook my head, laying it on his back. *"Whatever you say, my big, bad wolf."*

CHAPTER THIRTY-TWO

Hawke

All throughout the journey north, my wolf paced incessantly. The dust continued to fly behind us as we pushed the distance between us and the city as we traveled further and further away. No amount of distance would be enough to get my mate away from the danger I had put her in.

How the fuck did they find us?

I was so elated to be with my mate, I was unable to recognize the peril due to my overwhelming lust. For a week, I kept her hidden in the town where her stepbrother waited and watched for who knew how damn long.

And I trusted Bram to be on the lookout when I shouldn't have. I should have taken more responsibility and not relied on him so heavily.

But hell, without his warning, we would have been screwed.

He was a warlock, a powerful one at that, but he was only half the warlock he once was since his rejection. I trusted him too much. I should have—

"Just shut the hell up and concentrate on getting her somewhere safe," my

wolf snarled. *"We did the best we could do. We claimed her, we got her to trust us, we completed our mission."*

"But now she thinks of us as weak." My lip curled in disgust. *"I should have killed them all in front of her. Show her how powerful we really are."*

"And have half the town show up? What if you were shot, and you continued to fight? That would be hard to explain. And if another supernatural caught wind? We would have been reported to the Council for killing humans."

I let out an exasperated sigh of annoyance.

"She hasn't seen me yet, either. When am I gonna come out? I haven't stretched my legs in who knows how long. Let me out."

"You whine too much. Why were you gifted to me?"

"Beats me. Why are you such a wet blanket?" my wolf huffed.

"Hawke?" Delilah sighed into the link.

I adjusted my posture, extending my arm behind me to place my hand on her thigh.

I had ignored her much of the trip. I didn't intend to do so, but old habits died hard. I didn't want her to feel my anger; I had to keep it bottled up and away from her. I was angry with myself. I never wanted her to see his face again, and I let it happen far too quickly when she was under my care.

"What is it? Are you getting tired?" I could feel her head gently pushing against my back in a sign of agreement.

We'd traveled late into the afternoon and covered a lot of ground. During our journey, we only stopped for gas, to quickly use the restroom, and grab something to eat. We were close to our destination, and then we would rest for several days. We were going to be so deep in the redwood forest, no one could find us there. Especially once Bram caught up with us. Then no human could track us.

"Her body is changing," my wolf mumbled.

"What?" I snapped.

"Her body temperature is rising. In the next few days, maybe?"

"Is that normal?"

"The fuck if I know. I've never seen a human shift. Just our kind."

Right.

I huffed in annoyance, accelerating as we drove deeper into the redwood forest.

Where we were going was off the path, away from the main road. We would have to kill the engine and walk the bike deeper into the forest.

There were many places all over earth where a supernatural could hide. Tiny veils, almost bubble-like areas that kept supernaturals hidden. No one knew who created these bubbles. Bram seemed to know where these bubbles were, the map he pulled from his curious box the night I told him about Grim and Journey showed me where the bubbles were located as we plotted our drive back to the Iron Fang.

If Bram was to risk his life to keep us safe, it was the least I could do to offer refuge at the Iron Fang. That is, if Locke was alright with it in the end.

As we reached the second curve, just past the drive under one large tree, I dismounted my bike and watched a car go around us. Delilah unbuckled her helmet and sat it between her legs and slumped her shoulders.

Her eyes were drooping, her hair dripping with sweat. "Come on, Sunshine." I wiped away the sweat from her forehead. "Let's get you safe, alright?"

I picked her up in my arms, her head automatically leaning against my chest. My cut was rough against her forehead, but that didn't keep her from purring against it.

Shit, she was purring.

"I told you."

I rolled my eyes at my wolf, walking through the sparse underbrush and further away from the road.

"Where are we going, Hawke?" she muttered, her eyes closing.

"A safe place. Just beyond those trees over there." I nodded forward.

At least, I hoped we were going in the right direction. I was going off memory.

"It's okay, little mate. Hawke's scrawny body will take care of you. Once we are safe, I will warm you," my wolf purred.

"Is that your wolf?" Delilah leaned her head back, her eyes still closed.

I hummed in reply, trying not to curse the damned thing.

"Puppy, is that you?" she cooed, leaning her head back on my shoulder.

"It is I, your big Puppy. Is that my name?"

"You are not calling him Puppy, Delilah," I ground out.

"Then what is his name?" she asked.

"He doesn't have a name." I felt myself push through a barrier, as if stepping through a three-foot wall of water. Once we passed through, a cabin appeared.

It was a small, redwood cabin with a chimney puffing out small wisps of smoke. Bushes decorated the outside, and flowers bloomed, but as I approached, they closed up as if I was the predator.

The area inside this magical bubble was quiet. There was no sound, no birds, no small creatures skittering across the forest floor. It was calm, but the weather reflected that of what it was on the outside of this veil.

"That's so sad, Hawke. Didn't you give your wolf a name?" Delilah asked.

"No, the bastard didn't give me a name!" my wolf wailed, milking the attention. *"I've been with him since birth, fifty-four long years, and he hasn't given me a name!"*

"You're old!" Delilah perked up. "Oh, my gosh, what an age gap. We can check that off my bucket list."

"Old? Bucket list?" I snapped, walking up the steps of the cabin and pushing in the door.

The cabin was cool. It was very basic, with a fireplace, a wood-burning stove, a large basin that had a pump for a sink and a bed on the other side of the cabin. There was no bathroom, I would have to see if there was an outhouse out back.

"Yeah, a bucket list of all my favorite kinks to read. I'm living several of them. One is doing a werewolf." She grinned. "One is doing a biker, one is doing it on a motorcycle, one is doing it in the woods, one is doing it in front of people, one of them is an age gap. You don't look anywhere near fifty, though." She tried to smile, but her spark of energy was already fading.

I groaned, adjusting myself. This woman was going to be the death of me. Most of those kinks I could accommodate, but like hell were we going to have a damned audience. I would let no one see what was mine.

I led her to the bed. It was clean despite the rare use of the cabin, and I laid her down. She protested and tried to get up, but I shook my head.

"Wolves live to be almost four hundred years old. I will age much slower now that we are bonded. Now be still."

I went to the kitchen, grabbing a rag from a pile of fresh laundry. We would need to be sure to leave this cabin clean when we left. It would be common courtesy since we found it.

Once I returned, Delilah was already lightly snoring.

"She gave me a name," my wolf snorted, prancing happily inside my head.

"She did not, you idiot. It was just a nickname. It isn't normal to give out names, you know that."

"Grim's mate gave his wolf a name."

"How do you know that?" I growled.

"Just because I was silent in your head doesn't mean I couldn't talk to another wolf," he grumbled.

I took the cool cloth and ran it over my mate's forehead. She was burning up, and I didn't know if it was because of a human fever or because of her body changing.

I sighed heavily, my worries becoming too much to bear. I didn't want to mess up, not again. I couldn't after that stunt with her fucking ex-husband showing up.

My claws extended. I observed, with fascination, as the black nails glimmered in the fading light of the setting sun. I couldn't wait to sink them into the bastard's throat. I just hoped it was sooner rather than later.

"I think we should call our brothers," my wolf mentioned. *"Find out if Journey is alright."*

I responded with a nod, my nostrils flaring as I exhaled.

It was time. My mate was claimed. We were going home.

But I needed to know what to expect during her shift.

Because I knew she would not die.

I wouldn't allow it.

Delilah

"This was just ingenious. I don't know why I didn't do this before."

There was clicking on the floor, which must have been the wooden planks of the cabin. The morning sun was rising higher in the sky, brightening the cabin's interior. But I wasn't ready to open my eyes.

"Leif, that big cave-wolf was right. Taking over when the human is sleeping was a good call. Who knows when Hawke would have let me out?"

My head pounded, my heart racing and my body trembling from the adrenaline coursing through me. I felt like I could lift a car and toss it a hundred yards.

It was making my stomach roll.

"I get to touch my mate with my own body. I can't wait, can't wait."

I felt the air on my cheek. And then a gentle breeze from an open window brought cool relief over my sweaty skin.

Ahh, it felt nice.

I relaxed into the sheets. It smelled of Hawke, the forest, and those giant redwoods just outside the cabin. It was comforting being out in nature. I always preferred it more than the big city. In the small town where the Iron Fang was, I got a little of both. It was the best of both worlds.

A cold tap touched my nose.

"Oh shit! I touched her!" The sound of clicking and tapping on the floor echoed until it slowly dissipated. I felt the intensity of the sun's rays as they hit my face.

I was taken aback when I opened my eyes and felt the full force of the bright rays. I realized it must be much later than I had originally thought.

So, something was hovering over me, blocking the sun?

And there was something speaking earlier? It wasn't a dream.

Get it together, Delilah, you could have been in real danger here.

I rubbed my hand down my face and felt my nose. It was wet.

What the?

"I hope she likes a wet nose near her hot cunt. Because I would be happy to slip my long tongue right in to that slick, narrow—"

"Who's there!?" I shouted out in shock and instinctively grabbed the pillow to create a barrier.

My heart thumped rapidly, my breath coming in short, panicked gasps.

"Please do not be frightened, my mate. It is only me, your Puppy. I am just

now in my more handsome, less wet blanket, less constipated looking form."

"What?" I whispered, half giggling.

A massive wolf slowly traversed the circumference of the bed. He placed himself in the shadows behind various pieces of furniture, and when he stood at his full height, he was significantly bigger than any wolf or dog that I had ever seen. His body was coal black, and the top of his head had a generous amount of hair, which resembled the mohawk Hawke had.

He moved with a certain grace and dignity that was undeniably regal. The beast maintained a strong posture, its head held high, and its eyes narrowed as it faced me directly.

My heart raced as my eyes followed his graceful strides toward me, and my mouth went dry. He was massive and had fangs longer than the typical wolf you would see in the wild. I reached out my hand, and he leaned forward. As I felt the muscles beneath the fur of this beast, I was filled with awe at its sheer power.

But then I swore I saw a smile. It was small, a hint of white teeth showing. When I finally recognized who this was, I felt a sense of familiarity and warmth. It really was Puppy, but it was also Hawke.

I grinned, reaching out my hand to pet the fur on his head, but instead Puppy spread his front legs and leaned to the floor and raised his butt high in the air. His tail waved wildly to and fro like a puppy waiting on a treat.

I cocked my head, my hand still hovering in the air waiting to see what he was going to do next.

He was acting so proper, so tame just a minute ago, and now he looked like he was ready to fetch an imaginary ball.

"*He's a silly one,*" the voice snorted inside me. "*Have you not figured that out yet?*"

"*Of course I have,*" I replied. "*His beauty caught me off guard.*"

"*Ha! She thinks I'm beautiful!*" Puppy threw his head back, yowling in a Husky whine and wagged his tail excitedly. He rolled on his back, then got back to his feet and hopped around the room, doing zoomies until he ran into the kitchen oven.

"Fuck! Who put that there?" He shook his head, tripping over his legs until he fell over.

I let go of the pillow as I laughed, falling over into the mess of blankets.

CHAPTER THIRTY-THREE

Hawke

He made a fool of himself, rolling on the floor and making her scratch our belly like we were a common house dog on the floor.

Our leg thumped the floor, when she found *that* spot that felt too damn good to resist.

"Such a good boy you are, yes you are!" Delilah cooed as she ran her fingers through our fur.

"Yes, I'm a good boy, such a good boy." His tongue lolled out of his mouth, his sharp teeth not in the slightest ferocious looking. *"Pet me more, pet me more."*

She threw her head back, laughing and smiling like the Delilah I had always known. Carefree, happy to be alive, but this time there was a sparkle in her eye that shone brighter.

"She's happy, truly happy now," my wolf said to me. *"All because she has us now."* Delilah curled up next to our large wolf body on the bed, snuggling closer.

Her head nuzzled into our neck, taking big, deep breaths.

"She will be even happier when we destroy her past. Killing Shane will only be part of it. We will take down his entire empire. You've seen the glimpses into her mind. She has suffered much more than she has let on."

Delilah had hidden her pain well. The guards tormented her; she watched drug trafficking, orgies, and murders take place in the mansion she'd called home. I wouldn't be surprised if there was sex trafficking in there, but her blatant request that there be none of that in their home was made clear to Shane.

He seemed to honor that request, but he was a twisted fucker from her memories. He was a grade-A psycho. I wouldn't be surprised if he kept it away from his wife and had it going in secret. The Iron Fang would get their hands in it somehow, I would make sure of that. The entire empire would burn.

Delilah stilled until her head popped up.

"I gotta pee!" she squeaked, looking around the room.

She hopped over our massive form with ease, landing on the balls of her feet.

"Damn, she can move."

Delilah had always been clumsy. There were too many times she knocked over trays of drinks when she first started working as a server. She stood up, looking for a door for a restroom, but panicked when she didn't find one.

"Bathroom?" She nibbled her lip, pulling down her shirt to cover herself.

"My mate, I will take you outside," my wolf said to her, jumping from the bed. *"This is a basic cabin, I'm afraid."*

Delilah smiled, grabbing his tail and following him outside. But when we walked down the steps, Bram appeared through the veil.

He was wearing a dark sweatshirt and dark washed jeans with two bags on either side of his shoulders. His handlebar mustache was gone, his ozone scent heavy to wash away his scent, but his peppered beard was there as were his dark brown eyes.

He sighed, his shoulders slumped, and a small grin graced his face. "I see you both made it. That is good." Bram set his bags on the forest floor.

"I'm so glad you made it," Delilah said happily. "But if you will excuse me!" She pranced around to run around the house, but my wolf gripped her shirt by the teeth and pulled on it so she wouldn't run away without us.

He wouldn't let her out of his sight, not when we were unsure of the veil around us.

"What's wrong?" Bram approached us, a limp in his step.

"I've got to use the ladies' room, and there isn't one inside, and I just gotta–" She hooked her finger around the cabin, and Bram let out a laugh.

"Darling, this is a magical cabin. It will give you what you need; all you have to do is ask."

My wolf tilted his head, and my curiosity was heightened when Bram walked up the steps and knocked on the door three times. "We need two bedrooms, two full bathrooms please, fully stocked."

Bram stepped away, and the cabin shook for ten seconds and settled. The outward appearance didn't change, and my wolf scoffed.

"Ye, of little faith," Bram tutted. "Come Delilah, open the door."

Delilah hesitantly walked up the stairs to the porch, and Bram put his hand on the small of her back to encourage her. My wolf snarled, jumping up the steps and snapping at Bram. He ripped his hand back, chuckling and holding his hands away in surrender.

"Right, right, that was my fault." Bram winked with his smirk.

The bastard.

"Puppy, not nice," Delilah scolded as she opened the door.

She gasped, not taking a second glance at us, and ran inside. "Ah! A toilet! Yay!"

Bram chuckled; my wolf's teeth were still bared at Bram.

"Puppy, huh? What does Hawke think about that?"

My wolf snorted, not caring for the warlock. Animals didn't seem to care for warlocks and witches, anyway. Animals didn't understand the magical properties, they understood what they could see and feel while magic couldn't be seen. Their feelings could be manipulated, the ground, the water, and the air could all be altered, making their reality non-existent.

"He'll come around. I promise." He rubbed his leg and stepped forward, but instead of taking a firm step, he dropped to his knee, letting out a painful cry.

"Oh my god, Bram, are you okay?" Delilah rushed to his side and tried to pull him up.

My wolf relinquished his form, letting me take control, and I shifted into my body to help Bram. I didn't need my mate touching another male, and I pulled him to my side and brought him into the cabin.

"Gods, you pierced it. Is that a biker or an animal thing?" Bram chuckled while I sat him on the couch.

The cabin had transformed into a different floor plan. It had an actual living room with couches, rocking chairs, and a roaring fireplace. The kitchen was stocked with food, and it had a fridge and an actual stove.

"You used your magic, you stupid old man," I grumbled.

Bram scoffed, grabbing his leg. He rubbed it tenderly, wincing as he hit a certain spot.

"I only needed to use a bit of magic; the cabin *is* enchanted. I just boosted it a bit. If I'm staying here a few days with you recently mated wolves, I need my own space. Now go put on some pants. We need to talk."

Delilah giggled, staring at my crotch, which was already hardening. Anytime she looked at it, she looked like she was ready to devour it.

Damnit.

"Let me get you some water, Bram. Are you hungry? Can I get you some pancakes?" She smiled.

"Sweetheart, I would love some."

I held my mate in my lap as Bram ate his pancakes. My mate wanted to cut them up and feed them to him but the possessive bastard in me wouldn't let her.

That was a mate tradition. We fed each other, and I wasn't going to let her feed him, no matter how exhausted he was.

Bram traveled as soon as he could after we left. We established our escape plan the night he told me who he was. We both had our own demons, and old habits died hard. Men like us always had to have escape plans. Bram said he would protect me and what was mine until the day he died, and I was to leave him, and he would make sure we got a head start if anything ever came for us.

And so, he stayed to make sure we had a head start and so he could tie up loose ends.

Once Delilah and I rode off into the night, Bram blasted them all with a chaos spell that caused mass confusion within a two-block radius. The humans were dazed and confused for at least three hours, but as he was casting it, someone shot him in the leg.

Bram repaired his leg the best he could with a tourniquet. His body would heal faster than a human with any sort of cut or wound. A bullet wouldn't necessarily kill him if he stopped the bleeding. But if it hit the heart, well, that was a different story. Magical beings also couldn't conduct healing magic on themselves. There had to be a balance.

Before the spell was cast, Bram said Shane had lost his shit when Delilah and I left. Shane's cold demeanor dissipated once we rode off into the night, and he said that all of his men would die horrible deaths if they didn't bring his wife back to him within the hour. He also wanted me dead and if I was seen, I was to be shot on sight.

I scoffed at that. Little did he know what I was going to do to him the next time I saw him.

The Chaos Spell gave Bram time to repair the shop and reanimate the shop owner. Bram didn't mention if the human did in fact, reanimate, and I didn't ask. That was tricky business reanimating humans. Delilah wouldn't know to ask if he actually survived the reanimation process, and thank the gods for that.

It was probably best the old male didn't wake up. Because if he woke with Shane staring at him in the face, he most likely would have wished he was dead.

Delilah sighed, wrapping her arms around her legs. She nuzzled under my neck, taking long deep breaths. She purred, and my heart pounded heavily in my chest.

We were safe, she was safe, and soon we would be back home where our family was.

Bram wasn't sure how Delilah's stepbrother knew where Delilah was hidden. It could have been straight-up coincidence, and they were knocking on every door in the city. Or Simon's memory spell wore off early, and he immediately reported to Shane. It wouldn't be a far-fetched idea, because Bram's powers were half as potent, and Simon would recall the caster of the spell.

Delilah watched as Bram took another bite, humming in appreciation. Her fingers pulled on the oversized shirt she wore. She ached to go help him, to wipe his mouth or grab his drink to put to his lips.

But once again, I was a selfish bastard.

Bram smirked, knowing exactly what was happening. I didn't know the extent of his powers, if he could read minds or could understand the body language between my mate and, I but he was reveling in my discomfort.

"Delilah, It's alright. Your mate will maul me to death if you keep trying to help me. I'm a big strong male; I can handle myself."

Delilah's mouth dropped open, her gorgeous hair flung into my face. "Wha–"

"You cannot help me right now; you are freshly marked. Puppy and Hawke would have a field day if you touched me." Bram wiped his lips with the napkin.

He shakily put the plate on the table and let out a sigh, leaning back in the rocking chair. "Now I need to let you both know that this Shane fellow is dead set on getting Delilah back. I wouldn't be surprised if he is scouring cameras to find out what direction you took off to. I did my best to scramble as many of them as I could, but I am no Switch."

I nodded in agreement, rubbing the phone in my pocket. "I've contacted him. He's already taken care of it."

And found out I've missed a ton of shit from home. Journey forced a shift, which was damn dangerous and Duke Idris, a dark fae who practiced necromancy, thought to be dead was very much alive and was part of sex trafficking ring that held Journey captive for years.

He'd been killed thanks to Journey and Grim, thank fuck, but the damage had been done. Many in the brotherhood were still healing, including Journey but she was on the road to recovery faster than the rest of them.

"You have? You called him?" Delilah's eyes lit up. "We are going home?"

I smiled down at her, watching her eyes sparkle. "Yes, Sunshine, we are going home. Right now, we are staying here for a few days. We will head back after Christmas. I'm sorry we won't have a tree. Some humans are putting one up at the bar."

"Really?" Delilah asked incredulously. "You guys never allowed that before."

I scoffed. "I guess Locke is becoming some sort of softy since Journey has shifted and survived, because he is also throwing a big party for all the single ladies in town."

Delilah's mouth dropped further.

Bram leaned his head back and smiled.

"I'm so glad I found you, Hawke." He closed his eyes and used his good leg to rock himself back and forth in the chair.

We all sat in silence, listening to the popping of the fire until Bram's soft snores grew loud enough for us to laugh at.

"I'll take him to his room." I untangled myself from Delilah and scooped up Bram from the chair. Delilah followed.

I took Bram to the furthest room in the back of the cabin and pulled back the covers of the bed.

"Thanks, Gunnar," Bram mumbled sleepily before he fell asleep again.

Delilah tucked him in like he was a child and tried to place a kiss on his forehead, but I pulled her away before she could.

"Sorry, mate, can't let you do that," I grumbled.

"You are such a fuddy-duddy. I bet Puppy would let me," she whispered.

"*Like fuck I would,*" my wolf huffed.

"And you can't call him Puppy. Give him another name," I said as I walked her out the door with my hand on the small of her back.

"But Puppy is such a good name, it matches his personality. He's big, fluffy, and he has such a big happy personality."

I shook my head.

Her fingers intertwined with mine as we entered the living room. She squeezed my hand, prompting me to stop, and her blue eyes captured me, causing my breath to hitch.

"Why did Bram call you Gunnar?" She tilted her head in curiosity.

I sighed, running my hand through my hair.

"It's my real name, my birth name. My name before I came to Earth." I squeezed her hands and brought them to my lips. "It was a life I didn't want to remember anymore. None of the other rejected males want to think about their pasts either. We all changed our names."

"That's so sad." Delilah's thumbs ran across my cheeks as my lips continued to press against her knuckles. "But I understand; you want to forget the bad parts of your past. Just like I do."

"My hurtful memories are fading fast, too though, Sunshine, just like yours are."

"Really?" She blinked. "You are forgetting about that princess?"

I nodded, stepping closer to my mate. "Yeah," I chuckled. "I don't even remember her name."

"I don't even remember sleeping with Shane anymore." She gave a sad smile. "Maybe soon I won't even remember his name."

Little did she know I would see his head hanging on the basement wall every day.

"And I'll taste his heart on my lips," my wolf hummed.

"I'm sure with time, it will certainly happen, Sunshine."

CHAPTER
THIRTY-FOUR

Hawke

Every morning, we made sure Bram was healing, and Delilah and I cooked breakfast together like a truly domestic couple. The sounds of sizzling bacon, cracking eggs, and the rustling of papers that Bram read each morning made it feel, well, normal. And normal is what my mate needed right now. I needed her at peace.

Along with that peace, Bram told us strange tales of his extremely long life. About how the realm of Elysian was once peaceful eons ago. That there was once love and happily ever afters, which put Delilah in a much better mood after seeing her ex-husband.

Her mind was a jumbled mess as I rummaged through the bond we shared, which I believe Bram had picked up on as well. Bram recounted stories of our home realm, his voice filled with nostalgia. He recounted different varieties of shifters, of bewitched hamlets and the animals that called them home. Delilah was entranced by the tales of undiscovered magical lands, exquisite palaces, and powerful kings and queens late into the nights as we gathered around the fire.

It kept her mind away from the darkness and her worry, but it also brought up questions the next morning.

However, Delilah surprised us when she asked if the veil between Elysian was near a turquoise lake. Bram and I both sat across from each other at the kitchen table in shock for the longest time until Delilah turned from the kitchen stove with a pile of bacon.

The veil was indeed over the infamous turquoise lake, Cracker Lake in Glacier National Park in Montana. Supernaturals could only cross during the winter months since the veil was situated mid-air over its waters.

We urged her to continue with what else she knew, and how she knew, and she shook her head.

"They're just dreams," she laughed. "Like fuzzy dreams of watching the pretty colored lake turn to ice and walking over the ice. Then when we went to the other side, it was...purple. Lots of purple leaves and when they fell to the ground, they turned to gold." She took the piece of bacon and popped it in her mouth. "Then I remember feeling hot, and I wake up." She shrugged and ate as if it was no big deal.

But it was a big deal. The trees of Elysian were a royal purple, and in the fall, the leaves transformed into a brilliant gold and silver when they scattered across the forest floor.

How would she know such a fact? Elysian was not known by any other human, and if she had dreams of this world, then there must have been a significance to it. Had she been there before and just forgotten? Was she truly part wolf? Had she been brought to the human realm and suppressed her wolf?

Thousands of thoughts ran through my head, and Bram's, I'm sure, was doing the same.

Bram stared at her, not in longing but in curiosity. He thought of her as a riddle he wanted to decipher. I could see the gears turning in his head.

It was both the warlock and the scientist in him. All warlocks had their own ticks for figuring out problems, and I could see him wanting to run experiments on her.

But that would not happen, not on my watch.

My possessiveness would never wane, and the thought of even a godfather-like male family member wouldn't impede that. We would just have to live with the mystery of why my mate had memories or dreams of a place we used to call home.

Christmas came and went, but with no snow, and no other humans to declare it a holiday. I did not feel like Delilah felt like she missed anything. But next year, when the Iron Fang was decorated, I would be sure she had the best Christmas ever. Our home would be filled with Christmas trees, presents, family, and, most of all, no more worries about her past coming for her.

But each day we spent in this retreat, my mate worried more about her safety. She worried about Bram and my life, that somehow Shane would find us like he had before, that he would torture and murder us in front of her and find the Iron Fang. None of these things would come true. It would never happen.

Delilah believed Shane had unlimited resources. He was a part of the East Coast Mafia and had so much at his disposal. It was a miracle she'd escaped when she had. She'd made a mistake handing over her driver's license when she'd tried to build a new life away from me.

Anxiety gnawed at her as she fretted over the situation.

But my mate's expression never changed, and her body language was devoid of any indication of worry. She maintained a facade of cheerfulness, but my wolf and I knew the truth.

How long had she pretended to be happy at the Iron Fang while I blatantly ignored her?

I'm such an ass.

Thoughts of running away popped into her mind frequently, which I quickly redirected with a firm swat to her ass. With a good fucking, I redirected that shit. We would not have any martyrs. Delilah was mine, and Bram and I both would protect her from her human stepbrother.

When we'd jumped over the barricade of cars with my bike, I'd gotten a good sniff of all those assholes. They were all human, without any remarkable features—their faces as plain and forgettable as the yells of annoyances they made. They would all be quick deaths for sure, but Shane, I wanted his torture to last. And maybe Chad too, because he popped up in my mate's fading memories far too much for my liking.

They both fixated on her; they couldn't take their eyes off her. My mate's terrible memories were fading faster than I could dig through them. I would destroy them both. They were both obsessed with her, I knew that much. But my obsession with Delilah far outweighed both of theirs combined. Did that make me worse than them?

My jaw ticked.

No, because my compulsion required it. A greater power had declared it to be right.

And if my touch was unwanted, I would damn well stop because I wasn't a fucking monster.

She liked it when I held her, touched her, rutted her.

My mate was a pure gift from the heavens. She was the most capable and talented human to have ever graced the realm. With her generous and caring heart, she always put others first. Despite feeling welcomed, she still feared she was an intrusion and a nuisance. She wanted to do the right thing and not seek help from anyone. She felt like this was her fight, that she needed to go it alone.

But she damn well wouldn't. Because she had a whole family at home ready to go on a mission and kick some New York mafia ass when it was time.

Once we returned to the Iron Fang, where she would be safe, our family would kill the bastard brother. She would never have to worry again. I had hoped we would be able to leave by now. But my wolf, who had now been given a proper name, a more masculine name, Tyr, said Delilah's wolf was far too close to the surface now.

It would be dangerous for her to travel. Delilah's fevers were becoming more frequent. Her claws, patches of fur were sporadically coming and going, and her heat liked to appear at the drop of a hat.

However, I had no problem with taking care of her heats. I smiled.

It all would have been one hell of a problem traveling on a bike trying to get home, though.

I sighed, my claws raking the kitchen table as my mate shoveled in her tenth sausage patty. Bram stared in astonishment as she devoured the bacon with relish. I smiled as I felt the texture of her hair between my fingers.

Soon my little mate would shift. It would be painful. But with all the things she had been through in her life, she would have the strength to do it so gracefully. I'm sure she would have no problem accepting her wolf.

I believe I was more worried than her. She was far more prepared than I ever was.

I was not prepared to see my mate suffer a shift. Pups were just becoming adults when they went through their shift. They could bounce back after a shift fairly fast. But for my mate, being just slightly older and her body still more human than wolf, it would be difficult.

I sighed, rubbing both hands down my face, watching her wash the dishes I told her I would take care of.

She was a stubborn female.

I would be there for her every step of the way. But I couldn't promise my heart wouldn't break into pieces. To watch her scream in agony as her body learns to rearrange her bones and innards for the first time.

To worry now when I had no control over the future was fruitless. Especially while my mate laughed and joked with Bram as he handed her a bundle of clothes.

It was time for our game. Originally, it was to give Delilah some fun, to keep her mind fresh and at ease, but now I believed it was more for me.

I licked my lips, watching her run to the bedroom with a squeal of excitement to change. An interesting game it certainly would be.

The winter brown leaves crunched under our feet as we moved through the forest. The ferns rustled and brushed against our furry legs as we hiked the perimeter of the veil.

Delilah had become familiar with the perimeter of our safe zone in the days we lingered here. We had become accustomed to the same monotonous pattern each day. We took walks and enjoyed being surrounded by the tall trees, the soft rustle of the needles above us providing a comforting blanket of protection.

I inhaled the sweet, fragrant aroma of the forest with deep, heavy breaths. After what seemed like ages, I closed my eyes and reveled in the sensation of the wet soil and the dampness on my fur. How long had it been since I had cleared my head from the nonsense of the world around me?

"Too damn long," Tyr rolled his eyes so far I could see him looking at me. *"I swore your inner monologue might never stop. I thought about rolling in the mud to shake you from your worries, but that would deter our mate from the pets."*

"Yeah, we wouldn't want to deprive you of those, now would we?" I laughed, watching him scan the area.

He squinted into the distance, but Delilah had vanished, leaving only a faint trace of her sunshine scent vanishing in the air. His heart thudded in his chest, and the panic built in his throat.

"What is this game again? I am not familiar with it." Tyr's eyes scanned a full three-sixty. *"This,* Little Red Riding Hood *sounds like a child's game, but our mate's smile was much more mischievous for something so innocent,"* Tyr mumbled.

"It isn't necessarily a game. It's a children's story. About a little girl that goes to her grandmother's home in the woods to deliver cookies. A great gigantic wolf wants to eat her and decides to meet her at her grandmother's cabin and pretend to be the grandmother so he can eat her."

At least, that was my interpretation when Delilah told me all those fables one stormy night.

Tyr cocked his head to the side. *"That sounds ridiculous. Why would one want to eat a child? Why not take the cookies?"*

If I could slap myself in the forehead I would, but—

"That isn't the point. We are the hunter. Our mate is the prey." I licked my lips, rubbing my hands together, and Tyr sat on his backside, wagging his tail.

"And that is when we get the cookies?"

With a bit of annoyance, I replied, *"Yeah, we get cookies."*

"Yesss!" Tyr jumped over a log.

Again, I questioned why I was paired with him.

Tyr trotted to another tree. He took a deep breath of the damp moss that grew around the other side, causing him to snort. He raised his brow, burying his nose deeper inside the unusual sponge-like plant, and shook his head.

"I can't smell her," he said irritated. *"I should be able to smell her."*

And we should, but we didn't.

Then we heard the snap of a twig above us. Darkness fell around us, and the musky smell of our mate surrounded us as the red cape draped over us.

Tyr closed his eyes, savoring the scent of the sunshine and warmth that filled his lungs, forgetting all about the game.

We were the hunters, and she was the prey.

We were to seek her out and gobble her up like the wolf in the story. Tyr was so overjoyed to have her back, he could hardly contain his love-struck emotions.

We were losing, and I didn't really care either.

Tyr shook the cloak, so it draped on our shoulders, enveloping our body in a thick layer of fabric.

In front of us stood our mate, dressed in a brown leather corset, tight enough to press her breasts together until they almost spilled over her top. The plain ivory skirt with a brown smock swished in the non-existent wind as she approached. With her one hand on her hip, her blonde hair messily skewed over her face, she smirked, brushing the fallen bark from the tree from her shoulder.

Her scent had changed. It was musky and sweet, and a realization dawned on me faster than Tyr because all he did was stand there in awe. His claws sunk into the damn soil, his nose flickering and his eyes widening at her appearance.

She took off out of the cabin earlier than we intended after she changed into proper attire. Bram gave her the clothing, and I was going to kick his ass or thank him for it later.

A flash of gold flickered in her eyes and her sunshine scent radiated once more.

"Her wolf is present," Tyr rasped. *"She is emitting her heat."*

"Glad you noticed."

Delilah's usual cheerful voice turned low and downright seductive as she parted her lips, her fingers trailing over her bottom puffy lip. "Shift."

I'm not one to take orders, but with a heat beckoning me, and a feral look in her eye, I was curious about what she would do.

Tyr gave me control. My body retracted its fur, my bones popping, and I found myself on my knees as my hip adjusted.

Once my head lifted, Delilah pinned me to the tree so fast, I wasn't able to stand. My knees were parted, and my back pinned against the wide base of the tree. She pushed my feet back, splaying my legs wide. My rock hard cock bounced while Delilah kept her hand pinned on my chest.

Her eyes were not set on mine, but on my cock.

"Looks like the hunter has become the hunted." She licked her lips, and when she did, I saw her canines had dropped. They were sharp, and the thrill and excitement of her biting me caused my cock to twitch and my knot to fill with seed.

Delilah's chest heaved, her heavy breasts begging to break free from their confines.

Before I could reach the strings and pull the tight corset loose to let her breasts hang freely so I could fondle them, her head descended, and she took my cock into her mouth.

I groaned, the sound of my voice breaking the eerie silence of the surrounding forest. Then her nails elongated and dug into my thighs. The sudden pain along with her mouth flicking my piercing made me feel the tingle of pleasure at the base of my spine.

"Fuck, Delilah, you are going to kill me," I muttered, my fingers running through her hair.

She mumbled incoherently, her throat widening and relaxing until it opened and welcomed my cock.

Goddess.

How in Hades did I deserve this?

CHAPTER THIRTY-FIVE

Delilah

Some women may think being on your knees and taking a cock in your mouth would be considered weak, maybe even degrading to our gender.

Well, I had something to tell them.

It was not.

It was power.

His hands trembled. His legs quaked, and his breaths came in uneven, heavy pants.

I was the one giving him his pleasure, and I could take it all away.

"I didn't know you could be so sadistic," the voice purred in my ear. *"We will get along just fine."*

I lifted an eyebrow in surprise. I had to concentrate hard to make sense of what she was trying to tell me. Before I could think further, I pulled my skirt above my thighs and rubbed my throbbing clit furiously.

Lost in my thoughts, reveling in my selfish pleasure, I felt his hand rest upon my head. He caressed it lovingly, like he was afraid to push me any farther down.

I mean, there isn't much more my mouth can take. I was stuck at the top of his knot.

His other hand braced against the tree the deeper I sucked. His claws dug into the wood. His sharpened nails buried themselves deeper, digging into the fibers of the bark. As I hummed he ripped and shattered the remaining log-like root with his claws.

He scattered pieces of the root as he groaned. "Fuck yes, Sunshine, just like that!"

Hawke's groans, his sighs of pleasure urged me to continue my vicious assault on his cock. The smoothness of his skin, along with the ridges of his veins as I slid my tongue upward, made my thighs tighten, and my arousal drip down my leg.

Going without any underwear was a good choice, because wet underwear wasn't the best feeling.

But now I had another problem. My poor breasts were about to pop out of this dang corset. How women wore them in the old days, I would never know. The leather was rough against my aching, sensitive nipples. From the combined sweat and my constant movement, it rubbed my skin in all the wrong places. The constant bending over, bouncing my head, becoming far too much.

"Please, Sunshine, let me see those glorious tits," Hawke moaned, the sweat on his brow gleamed as the stray rays of sunlight hit his forehead. "Give those babies some air."

"He would like that, wouldn't he?" she mocked.

Her words weren't just words anymore. She was the one doing the actions now, and since we started this game, she was in control. From climbing the tree, from pushing Hawke on his back, to taking him into our mouth, she was the one fulfilling a fantasy I would have never conjured on my own.

"I suppose we could listen to him, just this once. Besides, you don't know how to wear or lace a corset correctly." She led our fingers in between our breasts, untangling the laces.

I felt my fingers slipping over the string as flashes of light and dark filled my vision.

The fuzzy picture came into view and my mind was filled with the vivid image of a blue periwinkle corset adorned with white flowers. A traditional, old-fashioned dress that you would see from a historical film laid before me. The dress swayed as the woman rocked back and forth in front of the mirror as she admired herself.

The woman's long, blonde, hair laid over one shoulder in a braid and a raised bite mark sat on the other. It was fresh, red, and she traced it with her finger. She smiled and when she turned; it was my face staring back.

Oh, my god.

Suddenly, the image was no more, and my back bent as I allowed the corset to slide off my body.

Instead of Hawke snarling and lunging at me like a predator, he merely stared at me as if he was looking at me for the first time.

"Fuck, Sunshine, you are beautiful. How did I get so lucky?" His lips were curved in a gentle smile as his hand stretched out toward me, drawing me closer until my chest was pressed against his.

His fingers moved through my hair, and I purred in satisfaction as I kept my cheek against his. His scent was so intoxicating; I couldn't get enough, and I wanted to be consumed by it.

He pulled my skirt off my body. It had a plain elastic band and slid off my hips with ease. He took his time, trailing his hand over my smooth skin, leaving no piece untouched as it reached my ankles.

"Such pretty skin my mate has," he mumbled in my ear while his hands traced back up my body. "Can you tell me why my mate was so good to me and gifted me with that wonderful mouth?"

My purr strengthened, my hands running over the sparse curls of his chest. He felt so good, to feel the heat of his body on mine, to feel safe in his arms.

I never thought it would be this way, to have him all to myself. The dull ache in my heart of never feeling complete was long gone.

My heart had swollen with so much love for this wolf, I couldn't stand it.

And the more feral I felt, feeling an animalist quality underneath my skin, the more I wanted to bury myself in his soul. It felt familiar. From the rhythm of his heartbeat, from his passion, from his love.

I felt a deep connection with him that felt as if I'd loved him for a lifetime before.

"Now, you're getting it."

I pressed further into his neck, nipping his skin as I hummed contentedly. "I was tired of waiting," I finally replied.

He chuckled, and his hand groped my breast. Hawke caressed it, kneaded it until his thumb traced the nipple. My hips jerked, and I felt his muscular thigh beneath my clit.

"You poor thing; you are so wet," he rasped. "Is it for me?"

"Mmhmm," I hummed.

My clit throbbed, my body growing needier by the second. I was always so needy for him, and as the seconds passed, it only made me more so.

Who knew all this thinking was such hard work.

"Then let me take care of you, Sunshine. Because I always want to take care of you."

Hawke dipped his fingers into my pussy, stroking a very special spot inside. It didn't take me long to shatter, moaning his name until I finished riding his fingers.

"You ready for me?" he whispered into my ear.

Starstruck, I nodded, ready for him to make love to me out in the open. It didn't seem so daunting anymore. I wasn't worried that Bram or someone else would see us. Because no one could, not in this veil that shrouded us from the outside world.

This all felt too natural, too perfect, and all so animalistic that I felt like this was where I belonged.

"Please," I begged, rubbing my needy pussy along his leg.

Hawke rose from his sitting position, placing kisses up my neck until he found a small clearing. As he laid me gently onto the ground, I felt the ferns swaying against our bodies and tasted his sweet, gentle kisses on my puffy lips.

This was a new side to the Hawke I'd come to know and love. He was being gentle, caressing me like I was fragile. He wasn't rough, or playful, his touches were soft, feather-like as they traced over my skin. It was a tease, giving me just a taste of the norm.

"I love you, Delilah," he whispered. "You know that, right?"

The big, scary biker caressed my face. His heart was filled with a great deal of worry, and his eyebrows were furrowed in a state of apprehension. It was the sweetest thing I had ever seen.

"And I love you. I don't know why you are acting like that." I shook my head. "Don't you feel it?" I placed my hand over his heart. "In here, don't you feel I love you?"

He swallowed, his cock laid thick against my inner thigh.

I reached between our legs, stroking his dick with my hand, and he let out a whine of gratitude.

"I have this unexplainable fear of your shift. I've been trying to keep your mind off it, but I think it's me. I'm trying to keep *my* mind off your shift."

He shook his head. "It's like you've done this before and you didn't make it. What if you don't make it? I can't live without you, I'll die without you. My heart can't take–"

I wrapped my free hand around the back of Hawke's neck and pulled him into a kiss. "I'm going to make it," I whispered. "The voice told me so."

"How are you so sure of this voice?" he replied pitifully. "How can you trust her so much?"

I rolled my lips together in thought.

"Because she's always been with me. Be kind of silly if I didn't trust her now." I smiled up at him, twirling my fingers in his hair.

Because, I'm like, 99.9% sure she's my wolf.

"Now make love to me before your knot explodes and wastes your precious seed."

Hawke let out a groan that was a mixture of content sigh and gratefulness. He pushed the head of his cock in slowly, like it was the first time we'd ever made love.

And heavens, he took his time, letting me feel all of him, letting me savor his piercing, the enormous head of his cock, the veins of his shaft. I felt all of him while he slowly made love to me.

The wrinkle between his eyebrows creased while his body shook as he held onto his resolve. This man would be the death of me, watching him try to take me slow.

"How are you so tight, after all the times you have taken my knot?" He arched his back, sliding his knot deeper.

He stretched me, pushed me while I lifted my hips higher, begging for more. "My mate loves my knot, doesn't she?"

"Yes, I love your knot," I panted, watching him pull himself from me.

His cock glistened with my arousal. There was so much, I couldn't believe it was mostly me dripping from him.

Hawke smirked, obviously happy with himself.

He reached down and stroked my lower lips with his fingers and placed them into his mouth.

Dear. Lord.

"Let me make you feel even more full, Sunshine. Roll on your stomach."

Without hesitation, I rolled over, and Hawke lifted my hips. He massaged them, planting kisses up and down my back while he spread my legs and pushed me down onto my elbows.

"I've never felt pain like this before," he murmured, stroking himself. "But it will be worth it when I'm locked inside you for the longest time yet."

Oh, my.

Without warning, he pushed inside me, his strokes coming in short, shallow thrusts. My cries couldn't be contained, feeling the overwhelming pleasure after an orgasm rushed over me in an instant.

Then he inserted his knot, slowly sinking it inside me while bursts of his come filled me. If Bram didn't hear us before, he certainly could now because Hawke's roar shook the needles from the trees.

He tenderly rocked his cock inside me and placed his wet thumb at my back entrance. My head perked up at the weird sensation. But then he distracted me by stroking faster, pushing his knot against my clit. I arched my back meeting his thrusts. He continued to seep his knot further inside me.

"That's it, take it like the suitable mate you are," he snarled. "Take my knot and let me take your whole body."

His thumb dipped inside my ass, and I threw my head back at the feeling. I felt so utterly full, and it was just his thumb. The sharp sting to my back side faded, and he pushed his digit in and out of my body while his knot pulsed inside my pussy. My orgasm didn't build, it hit me like a freight train coming out of nowhere. I saw stars behind my eyes, and I let out a silent scream. Hawke continued to rock while he grunted into me as my pussy milked him from his release.

"My good little mate," Hawke breathed, kissing down my back.

I purred, the vibration making Hawke swear under his breath.

"Fucking. Death. Of. Me. Dede."

I snickered, fingers tracing patterns in the leaves, as his rough, calloused hands kneaded my hip.

By the time Hawke's knot released, the sun was high. He was still mumbling grumpy curses, pushing his come back into my body *where it belonged* and kissing down my neck. He didn't have a care in the world right now.

I shouldn't either.

I should laugh at his incessant ramblings, his usual grumpy tone I first fell in love with, but something was wrong. The inkling in my stomach had returned, and I would not ignore it.

"Hawke," I sat up, pushing him away.

The flash of disappointment looked just like Tyr's puppy face, and I repressed the urge to smile. "Something is wrong. I think we need to check on Bram." I wrung my hands together with worry.

Deep dark claws emerged from my fingers, and I pricked myself on my palm. I pulled in a breath through my teeth, and Hawke grabbed the wounded hand. He licked it, slowly, not meaning for it to be sensual in the slightest, but it made me squeeze my thighs together.

"I hear nothing, but this veil can dull the senses." Hawke licked his lips. "We will go check on him."

Hawke pulled me to standing, and when he released my hand, the cut was already gone.

Nifty.

Hawke had no clothes, and I was too much in a hurry to put any on, but Hawke insisted I at least put on the base of the skirt and the red hood and cover myself. He walked naked beside me, keeping me close with one arm around me as we walked into the dead silence of the veil.

As calm as the veil was, it was almost too quiet. I missed the birds chirping, animals running in the bushes, the swaying of the trees, and the wind. I was ready to leave, to go home. I missed my roommates, the bar, Anaki, Bear, Bones, and the rest of the gang.

When would my wolf come?

"Did you hear that, voice? When are you coming?" I called out to her.

Of course, she didn't reply.

As we approached the cabin, Hawke's body stiffened. His nails clicked together, and his grip on my body tightened.

"I need you to be quiet as possible," he commanded through our link.

"What's going on?"

"Don't question, don't worry, and do not go in the cabin no matter what, do you understand me, Delilah?" Hawke growled.

The intensity in his eyes was so overwhelming that I chose not to challenge him.

"Now hide and don't come out until I call for you."

Without hesitation, I spun on my heel and immediately sprinted back to the tree line. I continually looked back over my shoulder while I was running, and Hawke never took his eyes off me until I was safely out of sight behind a tree.

"You aren't really going to stand back here, are you?" she chided.

"Nope, definitely not."

CHAPTER THIRTY-SIX

Hawke

My hands curled into tight fists. As I approached the cabin, I could feel the sensation of my claws piercing through my palms. I moved forward but didn't hear any yelling, however I could feel the static in the atmosphere as the hair on my neck rose.

Delilah was right. There was something amiss. Her ability to pick up that something was wrong from such a distance was uncanny.

"You know she will not stay away, right?" my wolf whispered, as if the world could hear him speaking.

In a hurry, I crouched down into the bushes, my hand situated underneath the window as I worked to maintain my balance.

"That's why we are going to assess the situation and shut it down fast, because we do not need to be stressing her out before her shift."

The slightest bit of stress could force her over the edge. She was close. I could taste her wolf just on the other side of the climaxes we'd shared just an hour before. I thought she would shift then, hell I hoped she was going to.

But no, that would have been too easy for her to shift out in the open in nature. Luck was never on our side since going rabid. And if stress was the major factor for humans to shift, then today was going to be the day Delilah would shift. Because I was staring at the back of Shane's head.

How the fuck did he get in here?

Shane's suit fit him snugly across the back, presumably due to him crossing his arms and standing up in a very tall and imposing manner in front of Bram. His men surrounded Bram, hands sitting on either of Bram's shoulders, pushing him down into a chair. Bram's fingers pulsed on either side of the seat, spouts of electricity pulsing through his fingertips.

"They aren't here, Shane. Now get the fuck out." Bram's tone was flat, unamused while staring up into the human's eyes.

I couldn't imagine what Bram was thinking. A warlock, one of the most powerful in his prime, and now he was sitting beneath a human.

Bram's eyes glowed red, the lightning beneath his finger tips growing with each passing moment.

Did he want to get caught using his powers now?

"I think we both know I'm not going anywhere. And your little firework show has died out. Now tell me, when will they be returning?" Shane pulled his sleeve over his watch and tapped it several times. "I've got a private jet waiting close by, and I need her back in New York for the infusion."

"And what makes you think she will go willingly? Delilah is free from you. She's got Hawke. She's got a family now. She isn't alone anymore, and her family won't put up with your shit any–"

Shane pulled his arm back, his black leather glove tightening before he punched Bram straight in the face. Bram didn't flinch when he saw the fist coming. He took the brunt force to the cheek.

Despite Bram being a Warlock and still stronger than a human, his head slumped to the left at the impact. The men that held him in the chair let go, letting Bram fall to the floor. Shane chuckled, nursing his hand with the other as his henchmen pulled Bram from the floor.

Bram was thrown back into the chair. His cheek was obviously broken, a bruise already forming and blood streaming from a cut.

"Not right," Tyr snarled.

It wasn't, none of it was. Shane was a human. A punch to the face could not cause that much damage even to a broken soul of a warlock.

What was so damn different?

I took large, deep breaths through the cracked window. No unfamiliar smells, no hints of any other supernaturals inside the room. Shane smelled human. The rest of the men searching the cabin smelled human as well.

I moved cautiously, ducking low as I rounded the cabin. Men surrounded the front, no vehicles or quick getaways were in sight. Just hordes of men lining the walkways and coming in and out of the veil. At this rate, civilians and tourists could see men disappearing and reappearing from a random spot in the forest.

I had to shut this down, fast.

"While you're naked?" Tyr snorted.

I rolled my eyes, hunching my back, and let Tyr contort our body into our wolf form. We were larger than the average wolf, but this was the great redwood forest. Everything was fucking huge here.

As I took steady steps around the cabin, I counted how many I needed to take down. They all held weapons, including machine guns Beretta would be jealous of. They were recently cleaned, shining black and glistening in the sunlight as they talked amongst themselves.

"Don't know why he still wants her. He could have anyone he wants," one of the suited monkeys said.

Another pushed him in the shoulder, grunting. "Don't fucking say that.

You don't talk about the boss's woman."

"Unless you want to get drained." Another elbowed his companion.

"Yeah, she's gorgeous and actually nice. He practically raised her to be the woman he wanted. I can see why he's hunted for her, it's hard to break in a new woman. She's a marvelous piece of ass, and once he does that fancy infusion with her"—he whistled—"you know, frozen in time and all that?"

They all agreed, holding their guns closer to their bodies.

"Vampire?" Tyr asked.

I internally shook my head. "He didn't smell like a vamp."

Vamps had that recently dead smell that a lot of wolves couldn't stand. With my tracker nose, It stuck out horribly. I would have smelled vampire blood in him if Shane had been bitten and turned.

I lifted one paw, ready to step forward and take out the small group in front of me and bring them around the cabin away from the sight of the larger group.

Shane did something to his body, and only to himself. It wasn't done to his men, they smelled human. They lacked the confidence and the arrogance that Shane did. They knew their superior could kill them not with a word, but with either a swipe of his hand or...something else.

"Boss wants us to spread out." A larger male interrupted my thoughts and approached the smaller group in front of me. "They are in this fucking bubble shit and think they're safe. They won't leave. The male is to be shot on sight; bring Delilah back unharmed. She is not to be touched, just threatened." He glared.

The men nodded, agreeing in unison as they backed away to join the larger group. The entire group did not radiate fear as they reached into their suit coats.

A vial was brought from their pockets. They all snickered, removing the caps, and dropped them to the ground, not afraid of the contents inside.

The clear container was opaque in appearance, with flecks of silver inside.

"Could be liquidized silver," Tye said. *"If Shane knows Bram's a warlock, he could know we are wolves."*

It was plausible, not that it mattered.

Liquid silver could hurt an unmated wolf shifter, but it wouldn't touch a mated one. That would be nothing but a slight sting to my skin now. Not that a human would know that.

Tyr licked his maw, his heart racing, ready to rip into the forty-some-odd men that were lined up ready to enter the forest. Only two were in the cabin, while five more stayed outside as guards.

Once the men entered the forest, they were in our domain.

"Delilah, where are you?" I snapped.

Delilah sighed heavily through the link. *"I'm hiding in a tree."*

I followed the bond, like I should have from the beginning, and traced the string that connected us to high into the tree. The trace of red cloth could be seen between the branches, high in the tree, no human would think to look so high.

"Good girl, now stay up there."

"You won't always be the boss, you know?" I could hear the amusement in her voice, but all I could taste was the hunger for blood.

"Stay," I growled and watched the men in suits grip their vials and hold their guns at their side.

They were trained well. Moving is a human military strategic manner. A herringbone style, fanning themselves in twos, so they were covered on either side. If only they had done it as a coil, with at least two men walking backwards to cover their rear.

Because that was where I was going to strike.

I was going to take them two at a time, silently picking them off.

"We fan out the deeper we go into the forest," the head male called before reaching the tree line.

I scoffed, slinking to the other side of the forest.

Bram was hurt in the cabin and rescuing him was a priority, but I couldn't have Shane calling on his men. I was one wolf and if Shane had an ability, I was unsure of what strengthened him. I couldn't fight them all.

Unaware of where Delilah was, the humans spread out in different directions. Her scent hovered above us, far above the trees, as I trotted past her. She winked at me from the trees from across the clearing and waved while her feet dangled happily.

Like she wasn't in any danger.

She either trusted us, or she was going to do something completely stupid.

"Or both," Tyr mentioned as our claws dug into the damp soil.

We counted the breaths of the two men in front of us. Their fingers tightened on their automatic assault rifles. Their hair stood on their necks, their bodies feeling the impending danger, but they were too stupid to understand their body language.

"Then that is why we must make this quick," I replied, skin rippling and causing my fur to stand in anticipation for the lunge.

"'Tis a shame. I was looking forward to feeling the blood rush between my teeth."

"Another time. I'm sure we will have fun with Shane later."

Tyr hummed approvingly.

To maintain equilibrium, our toes cautiously stretched out, attempting to find a footing on the unpredictable terrain. The jump was flawless, our teeth wrapped around the back of the first human's neck. Our teeth sunk into the collar, the skin, the bone, and the resounding crack echoed into our jaw.

There was no time to scream, no time to pull the trigger. The male fell before I jumped onto the second and did the same to him. It was boring. There was no clawing at the skin, listening to the tears of skin or ripping of clothes. There were too many men to go through, and my mate was up in a tree thinking of ways to get down quickly and run to the cabin to check on the commotion.

I had to be swift, quiet, agile, which I was more than capable of doing since our bond had strengthened me tenfold, but damn it was going to be boring.

The first two fell within seconds. The soft thud in a normal forest beyond the veil wouldn't have caused others to turn back to look at the sound. It would have sounded like leaves, small animals prancing through the forest, but not here. They sounded like boulders falling from the mountain tops.

Four males turned with their guns drawn or vials held into position. One male sprayed the air, grinning maliciously as the squirt of silver liquid flew onto my fur.

I peeled back my lips and snarled, licking the useless liquid silver droplets into my mouth. His smile faded quickly after that, and he sprayed more, as if he hadn't used enough.

Tyr found the situation humorous, letting out a snort of laughter and shaking his head, his laughter indicating that the real fun was about to start.

The others were too far ahead, and I would not give them the chance to call for backup. I could most likely take them, but what sort of bragging rights would I have if I had no one to watch me? No one at the Iron Fang would fucking believe me, why should I give myself that much work when I didn't need to?

With a lunge forward, my teeth found their way into the body of the first male. The others grunted, the butt of one gun hitting my side. I ripped out his throat with my teeth, blood gushing and covering the male at his side.

"Fucking shoot the damn thing!"

I clawed his face, my teeth sinking into another throat. It was a jumbled mess to them, but it all flowed flawlessly to me as each one fell to the ground in a heap.

A gun went off as the last male fell into the ferns. It missed by a hair, grazing my tail.

"Oh, my god! He tried to shoot me!" Tyr squealed.

An additional five men stumbled out of the trees, their chests heaving, and their collars undone, their weapons pointed in the air.

"Think that's the point. Do you think they are silver?"

Tyr sniffed his tail. Not that it would matter if it was silver or not, but one to the heart would hurt like hell and Delilah wouldn't know to dig it out to reanimate our body.

"Laced with it, not completely silver. If that hits our balls, oh god, I don't want to think about it."

"Let's not let that happen then." I smirked.

Tyr puffed out his chest, letting out a roar that blew enough wind that pushed the fern's fronds toward Shane's men. Some of these males were large for humans, but even they smelled of fear.

They held their shaking guns, and they shot without warning. We leapt from the ground, using the large tree as a springboard to avoid the shots.

A string of curses flew, and we collided with the group. Our claws, teeth, and weight bared down on the men as we ripped flesh from bone, eyes from sockets, and tongues from their mouths. We took more time with these males as they begged for us to stop.

Another shot rang out, hitting us in the side. We paused the assault of the nearly lifeless men who were bleeding out onto the forest floor. We now glared at male that dared to interrupt our torture.

Blood dripped from our maw, and our face was covered in blood, flesh, and brains. I'm sure we looked terrifying, but we were far from done.

Another shot rang out. But again, we stood still, taking the shot and not moving.

We snarled.

"It isn't moving," the male said, his eyes widening with horror.

Another shot ripped into my back. Blood spattered on the ferns beside us.

It was painful, but we knew pain. It wasn't nearly as painful as when our soul was ripped from our bodies.

The two males dropped their guns to the ground, their legs shaking, faces paling.

We took one step to their two, and then two steps to their four until they turned and did a full on sprint into the forest.

The chase made our heart leap for joy, the animalistic part of ourselves screaming to be released. Overcome with anger, Tyr rushed forward and with both of his front paws, he pushed the two men down onto their stomachs. Instead of burying our teeth into the back of their necks, he let the humans squirm. Their nails sank into the dirt, digging, pulling into the stones until their nails were ripped from their fingers.

They tried to get away from the magnificent beast that stood atop of their bodies, but to no avail.

They were nothing to the wolf.

They were weak fools who took orders from a male that harmed the innocent. They all knew what Shane did to Delilah, and... They. Let. Him.

Tyr curled our claws deep into their backs.

And they would all pay.

CHAPTER THIRTY-SEVEN

Delilah

These claws were pretty nifty.

I snapped them together with a satisfying click. They were black as onyx and hard as stone. They shimmered in the light and not a flicker of a scratch shone on them from climbing the tree. Claw marks showed brightly against the bark; it couldn't be helped. It was my first time climbing a tree with no branches close to the base.

"You will get better," the voice assured me. *"We'll practice more back home."*

Home.

If we ever got there.

The pit in my stomach was a raging inferno of butterflies trying to escape. Staying in this tree was only making them worse. Not to mention the ridiculous amount of peach fuzz that was spreading out over my body at the moment.

"I guess that laser hair removal was a complete waste," I muttered, rubbing the hair down my legs as it continued to grow. "Be helpful if you would just let me shift, and I could help him."

She giggled in my head.

"Go on, just hurry and admit it." I petted the fur on my arms.

This time, instead of hearing silence, my world went black, and I saw a head appear from the darkness. A blonde wolf tilted her head and winked long, beckoning eyelashes. Then the world all came back to light, and I leaned on the branch to regain my balance.

"What was that?" I whispered.

"*Well, you seem to know it all. What do you think?*" she asked.

"You are my wolf?"

"Delilah! Where are you?" Hawke called out sharply, demanding my attention.

My breath hitched, and I moved my head in his direction. I knew exactly where to turn, like intuition, where to look.

Hawke had transformed into his wolf and was standing tall, facing the other side of the open clearing. There was a swarm of men in suits that were holding guns, marching toward the forest, fanning out to delve deeper into the woods.

They looked familiar and as I took deep breaths, narrowing my eyes, I realized who they were in an instant. Shane's men. The guards I'd known for years who'd watched me as I grew, as well as some new men sprinkled in.

My hands shook as I grasped the branches, my heart pounding in my chest.

Shane had managed to track us down, and there was a high chance that he was in the cabin with Bram.

With Hawke and Tyr looming on the other side of the clearing, heading into the woods, which meant he was going to take down all of Shane's security. But what of Bram?

He would be left alone with a psychopath.

"Answer him already, be calm," my wolf spoke. "Be calm when you answer."

"I'm hiding in the tree!" I replied to him. I swung my feet excitedly as I watched him.

Tyr bowed his head, his paws moving almost in a dance as they touched the ground. With his head held high, he trotted off into the depths of the forest. "Good girl, now stay up there."

"You won't always be the boss, you know?" I replied, trying to keep a playful demeanor.

"Stay," he growled.

I went to snap at him, but my wolf intervened, pulling my—our hand over my lips. "That's enough, or we won't be able to help Bram."

I felt a sudden jolt in my chest as my heart skipped a beat.

Right, we were going to be sneaky and get Bram out of there.

But first, we had to get out of this tree.

"Now, you can't just jump out of the tree, we aren't a feline–"

"What? A feline?" I scratched my head.

My feet continued to dangle over the thick branch, my hand grazing over my now un-furred legs. It was quite confusing how it came and went more frequently. I was really beginning to have an identity crisis.

"There are more than just wolf shifters, Delilah, there are also felines such as panthers. Beretta is a panther."

I blinked, staring off into space.

That made so much more sense. She was so graceful—how her eyes reflected the light, catching things before they fell, her reflexes, her beauty.

I mean, of course there would be more shifters other than wolves. There were wolves, warlocks, witches, vampires and—

My wolf yipped in my ear. "You will have more time to gawk at your new world later. For now, you need to climb down."

I waited for Hawke to pass us, giving him a pretty little wave as he went deeper into the forest. Most likely to kill the squad.

I climbed down as quickly as I could and raced across the clearing, avoiding the guards. I wasn't out of breath as I approached the back side of the cabin. My feet were unmarked by any scratches from sticks or stones.

I tried to concentrate on everything else. Being stealthy, being hidden, and not being caught by—*him*.

Over the past several days, I'd noticed my senses had heightened dramatically, but now my skin had taken a dramatic new turn. I really hoped I was close.

I looked at my fingers, placing them on the splintered log window. No splinters pierced my skin, and it didn't even feel rough to the touch. I raised my head to peek inside. Of course, there he was, but still my heart sank to my stomach when I saw the back of his head.

Shane.

And after just two years of being away from him, I was still afraid of him.

He had never yelled at me. But his voice would be cold and heartless when he was disappointed with me. It was worse than being yelled at. And with my, well, obvious praise kink, I now understood why it hurt me worse than the yelling. I hated to feel like I was a disappointment to anyone. I hated to feel less than with anyone.

He knew it and used it against me.

I tapped my finger on the wood, just enough to prick away the nervousness.

How was I going to get inside? How was I going to get Bram away?

There was a knock at the door, ripping Shane's attention away from Bram. The clicking of his expensive Italian leather shoes echoed off the wood floor.

And that was when I saw the kind-hearted warlock.

Bram was tied to the chair, his head hung in a defeated position. How was he tied, just sitting there? Could he not let himself out?

As I moved the unlocked window up, it gave off a small squeaking noise. I looked in either direction to see if anyone was coming around the cabin, but no one came. I grabbed the red cape, wrapping it around me so it didn't catch on the bushes, and jumped through the window, feet first.

As I touched down softly. All was still, and I slowly and carefully made my way inside. The cabin wasn't in its glamorous two-bedroom style any longer, returned to the basic cabin when Hawke and I first arrived.

Bram must have used his powers to make us comfortable for days.

I moved my head from side to side in disbelief. This cabin was nothing out of the ordinary, but the warlock inside was someone who had a heart full of kindness and generosity.

Gosh, he was a stubborn warlock.

I pulled one of Hawke's old shirts from a bag on the floor and threw aside the red hood. I didn't need to go topless during a rescue.

Once covered, I rushed over to Bram, shaking his shoulder.

"Bram? Bram? Wake up?" I whispered.

I carefully placed my hand on his cheek, feeling the warmth of his blood as it ran down my fingers.

"No, Bram? Please wake up!" I panicked.

I gave a light shake to his shoulder, slowly pushing his head back. His heart beat rhythmically, echoing in his chest like a metronome. His eyes brimmed with salty tears, threatening to spill over.

His throat bobbed, eyes tightening. "Is it over? Is it done now?"

I shook my head, wiping a tear away from my cheek. "No, it isn't over. We need to leave. We need to get out of here before he comes back. Can you walk? Can you–"

"Ah, I'm afraid he can't walk out of here, Delilah." His smooth voice boomed from the open doorway.

A sudden jolt of electricity zapped through my body as I spun away from Bram. I used my body to protect my friend. I was small, and I couldn't shield him from much, but I would do my best.

Shane walked into the room. He was stealthy, more so than when he had left the room. Now I wondered if he left the room on purpose to lure me inside. Stupid on my part, I should have known, but coming in here was inevitable.

I couldn't leave Bram alone.

"Bram's life is almost over, I'm afraid, and my patience has run thin. Now..." Shane stepped forward, and his nostrils flared. "You need to wash the filth from your skin. You smell like an animal."

His nose turned in disgust, and he waved two fingers, looking behind him. Chad's hulking form stepped into the room.

"Watch the warlock while I take her to the ladies' room. I believe that's the last magical room left in this god forsaken cabin. Come, Delilah."

I felt my heart beating quickly inside my chest, the wolf within me no longer making a sound. And there was no way I was calling for Hawke. Not when he was in the middle of a bloodbath of his own.

My gaze turned to Bram. He was unconscious, his head hanging over his body once again.

I helplessly followed Shane to the bathroom just a few steps away.

"I've missed you, my wife. I understand that you never had a rebellious period in your lifetime. I hope you enjoyed it because it will not happen again."

I ground my teeth together, determined not to utter a single word. Hawke would be back, I knew he would. I just had to bide my time.

Shane spun around as I followed behind him. "Will it, Delilah?" Shane grabbed my chin, forcing me to look into his cold eyes.

"No, it won't." My voice shook.

I hated that it shook.

He pinched my chin harder. "Good."

Shane leaned closer, staring at my lips, but his breath deepened, and his eyes dilated.

"He's smelling you," my wolf said. *"He isn't human anymore."*

I shivered as an icy breeze washed over me. How could he not be human? And what could that mean, not anymore?

"Then what is he?" I asked her.

"He has no smell, not even a human marker in his blood."

"You are certainly no help. What does that even mean?"

My wolf shook her head, as if she couldn't tell me at the moment. She lowered her head, still accessing.

All the while, Shane accessed me, looking my body over. "God, Delilah. What are you wearing? Have you worn rags since you left me? Are you that stubborn?" His lip curled into a smile. "Here, I brought you a gift, despite your leave of absence."

He pulled a Dior and Chanel bag from behind his back that happened to magically appear. "Chad brought these from the car. Inside, you will find things for a shower, undergarments, clothing. Be quick, Delilah, you have eight minutes. You are lucky I am not coming in there with you, but I have more information to beat out of your friend."

I took the bags reluctantly. And when Shane smiled, a fang appeared from his mouth.

I gasped, falling into the door jamb of the bathroom.

This made him straighten his back even more. It must have lit a fire in his ego, because he chuckled darkly. His eyes sparkled with mirth as he leaned his forearm over my head. Shane smiled down at me, now exposing both sharp fangs.

"Yes, my little wife, I have been busy while you've been away. But don't worry, you will join me soon and be bonded to me instead of that dog."

Shane took off his black leather glove, exposing a long, grey fingernail. He wrapped it around my blonde hair and pulled it toward him. He smelled it and frowned, dropping it to my shoulder.

"But first we will get rid of this wet dog smell and…" He pushed the loose t-shirt away from my shoulder bearing the mark on my skin and hissed.

He grabbed my neck, pulling me off the ground to meet him in the eyes. "You fucked that wolf, didn't you? Let that mutt fuck the pussy that was always mine, huh?"

I grabbed around his wrists, nails digging into his skin. I tried to will my claws, the black ones I'd used just minutes ago to scale the tree.

But they never came. I couldn't break into the cold barrier of his skin.

"*Where are you when I need you!?*" I screamed at my wolf.

When the world looked bleak, when my vision was going dark, he let go, setting me down on my feet and pulled me to his chest. He no longer smelled of rich, expensive cologne. He smelled of—nothing.

No shampoo, no natural or artificial smell. He smelled empty.

My wolf was warily tilting her head. Her lip curled, showing her fang. "*He does not smell like a vampire, but he shows signs of one,*" she snarled. "*I do not understand.*"

"*There you are, great timing,*" I snapped at her.

Shane petted my hair, his nose delving into the roots of my hair as if trying to smell my original scent.

He patted me gently on my back, his claws detangling my hair.

"I'm sorry, Delilah. I shouldn't have done that–I just, well." He patted my back again, pulling me away. "You had some wild oats to sew. No matter. We will get this taken care of. You have not shifted, I'm assuming?"

He raised an eyebrow.

I shook my head quickly, not wanting to be strangled again.

Why did I feel so small around him? After two years away from him? It wasn't like I remembered a lot of what he'd done, but just his presence was so suffocating.

He turned his back, the deep, heavy cloud retreated, and the air returned to my lungs.

"S-Shane?" I weaved my fingers together, my head hanging lower than I intended.

God, I hated this.

He turned his head, his eyebrow raising.

"Yes, my wife?"

My wolf snarled, snapping her teeth.

I swallowed, feeling my confidence returning. "How do you know, about–" I waved my hand weakly around the short cabin hallway that used to be the elaborate one that led to a master bedroom. "This? The warlock, the wolf, the bite, the–"

"The supernaturals? The world hiding beneath all the human world's noses?" His smile widened, showing both his fangs.

His normal crisp suit looked cleaner and even more intimidating than ever. His features were sharper, stone-like. Almost as if I could prick my finger on both his jaw and cheekbones. Maybe that was why I feared him more; he wasn't human. He was unpredictable, and even my wolf couldn't figure out what he was.

"The conference I went to before you shamelessly left"—he frowned, picking at his nails—"was the beginning of a beautiful partnership with a businessman by the name of Duke Idris."

Holy Cheez-its.

CHAPTER THIRTY-EIGHT

Delilah

My mouth dropped, along with every other organ in my body.

"I see you know him. I guess the dog educated you in some ways."

Shane's thought he'd won. I could see the smugness in the lines on his face building with each passing breath. Or was he breathing at all?

Can vampires breathe?

He tapped his long fingernail on the door frame, taking a real breath? A fake one? Either way, he sighed and pushed away while Chad approached from behind.

"Make sure she doesn't do anything stupid, like run away," Shane said as adjusted his vest underneath his suit. "Not that she would, unless she wants to see her friend in the chair suffer a worse death than he is already experiencing."

I tightened my hold on the bag, my claws now making their untimely appearance. Shane noticed, taking a deep breath and expelling it through his teeth in a hiss.

Okay, so breathing to smell the air, he does do.

Noted.

"We need to leave sooner rather than later. Seven minutes Delilah." He took one longing glance toward me.

Chad gestured for me to enter the bathroom, and I heard a low murmuring as I walked in. I knew not to waste time, not when Bram was sitting helplessly in the chair. But I would not waste the few minutes I had alone.

"You better have a good fucking explanation why your heart is racing out of your chest right now." Hawke's snarl blasted through my head while the hot water ran down my body.

His come ran down my leg, and I bit my lip not to snort.

If Shane could smell my blood on my hand, I prayed to the goddess he smelled that other part of me, too. Not that he would mention *that*. He was too proper to mention another male's come.

"Oh, how are you, honey? Did you get all the bad guys?" I cooed.

"Delilah, where the hell are you? Did you go to–"

"The cabin? Yeah, I did, Bram needed help."

I rubbed my chest, an unexplainable pain radiating from it. I leaned on the shower wall, while using the unscented soap on my body.

Shane was in a mood. A mood that was a precursor to another mood that would be bad news for everyone, including his own men. And now that he was, what? A vampire with unexplainable powers meant hell for all of us, maybe even Hawke.

"I swear to the gods, Delilah, when this is all over, I'm going to spank your ass so red, and fuck you into oblivion. You don't listen to a damn word I say. I'm trying to protect you and you go walking in there without a care, do you have any idea–"

"Hawke, he knows Duke Idris. Shane knows him."

Yup, I was deflecting. But anything to get him off my butt right now.

There was a long pause. The only sound between us was the rushing of the shower beating down on my body, and his panting breath. His heart raced, his paws pounding on the ground. It was a strange feeling this bond we shared. I knew when he was far, yet I knew what direction he was going. Now, I felt the bond not as stretched, the distance between us now shorter.

He was coming back to me.

Part of me was selfish to run to this cabin and think I could save Bram. But I couldn't just sit there. After all that man had done for us. He had used magic to make us feel safe and comfortable, when obviously it was hurting him and keeping him weak all this time.

Or he was just a stubborn man that thought he would use his magic like he could in the past.

But that was beside the point. All of this was.

Duke Idris was evil. And my soon to be dead husband, ex-husband, used to work for him.

A few nights ago, Hawke explained to Bram and me how Grim and Journey fought the Dark Fae that started a sex trafficking ring that involved shifters just weeks ago. But now they were involving humans as well. Journey was one of the first humans. They were slowly working on the west coast, but how Idris got into the human sector and pulled the strings to make it happen was a mystery.

Now that didn't seem so far-fetched anymore.

Shane had his fingers in everything. Shane must be the first connection Idris made in the human world to get him started.

But Idris was gone now. He was dead.

Or so said Switch when I had brief contact with him several days ago.

Journey ripped into him like butter. Her bite was venomous because the goddess made her into a priestess. His body turned to ashes weeks ago, along with most of his followers.

Switch couldn't be mistaken, could he?

So, was Shane running the show now? He wasn't normal now. He was different.

"Hawke, Shane is—"

"Different, yeah," he interrupted while his bones popped. *"He has no smell. I saw he punched Bram in the face."*

"He has fangs, claws," I whispered into the shower.

Banging on the door shook me out of my trance, and Chad shouted into the door. "Get out of the shower, get dressed!"

Butthead.

"Who the fuck is that?" Hawke snapped.

"Chad being a bossy butt. Where are you?" I turned off the running water, then reached for the towel sitting on the toilet.

It was fresh cloth; it didn't smell of any fragrances just like the shampoo, conditioners, and soaps. There were no scent on anything, even the clothing inside the bags. Normally, Shane would have some sort of expensive fragrance inside.

Hmm, sensitive nose maybe?

"At the edge of the tree line. I see five men outside. I can take them out. How many are inside?"

I shimmied, putting on the lace thong. Shane loved lavender and maybe that was why I hated the color so much. I rolled my eyes as I put them on. I wouldn't give him the satisfaction of going thongless. He'd like that just as much.

"Chad, Shane, and Bram are the only ones here. I haven't seen or heard anyone else. My wolf has been less than cooperative since I've been in the cabin."

I could hear Hawke's amusement. *"Your wolf? How?"*

I chuckled, putting on the cream cardigan. *"Yeah, that voice I've heard all this time? It's her. She admitted it. I guess I'm not crazy after all."*

I felt his pride swell inside him. *"Sunshine, that's amazing. Wolves don't talk to us until weeks after they shift. That's an amazing feat!"*

I bit my lip, fumbling with the buttons until the bathroom door flew open. The abruptness startled me, and I fell backward, landing on the toilet. The momentum made me fall on the other side of the porcelain throne until I hit the decorative table's corner.

I whimpered, hitting my head. Blood trickled down my temple.

A roar outside the cabin shook the bottles of glass that decorated the shelves lining the bathroom. Chad's sneer turned to curiosity, and he stomped to the window. He pulled back the curtain and smirked.

"I've been waiting to see this dog of yours. Get up." He motioned for me to stand.

Chad knew better than to touch me, and I took my sweet time standing up. When I finally stood, Shane was at the doorway. His eyes narrowed at Chad but then flickered to me when he saw blood trickling down my cheek.

"Did you touch her?" Shane hissed.

Chad shook his head, bowing his head. "No, sir, you know she's skittish. She's always like this."

Chad waved his hand in my direction and, not wanting him to know how I felt, I rolled my eyes discreetly behind him. Sure, he'd never touched me, but I'd seen what the human wrecking ball could do. I'd seen him sit on some guy for no reason and suffocate him to death.

I wasn't about to test him.

Shane let out a scoff and gripped my upper arm, taking me out of the bathroom in a hurry. He screamed out orders for Chad to get outside and take care of whatever was causing the commotion.

I guessed he didn't get the memo that most likely the men who went frolicking in the forest were dead. Because my mate was a freaking badass.

Good luck to you, Chad, I bet your innards are going to be dog food in a minute.

Shane directed me to the kitchen table, and I felt the worn texture of the wood under my fingers as I settled in. He had a plate of fruit and cheese on the table. It was the rich people's cheese. Not the cheddar and Swiss that we had at the bar. This was stinky cheese.

I snubbed my nose at it. I didn't even want *this* cheese. What I wanted was a burger.

"Here, Delilah. Why don't you eat something?" Shane asked, pulling out his silk handkerchief.

Shane dabbed the spot on my temple, wiping away the blood. He dabbed it once more, then stared at it. "Well, at least it's healed, I guess. That's the only good thing about this predicament right now." He inhaled the blood on the cloth, his eyes closing as he did so.

"Mmm, you smell good."

I leaned away, crossing my arms.

"Now, please eat and let me prepare for our transportation. I won't have you walking everywhere anymore like some peasant." He shoved the cloth into his pocket, like it was painful for him to do.

Shane walked to the window, his phone going to his ear, and pulled back the curtain to watch the carnage like he was watching television. He didn't even flinch as he gazed outside. He shook his head, put his hand in his pocket, and fumbled with the keys.

My gaze went back to the fruit and cheese, and I immediately snubbed my nose at the food again.

Bram chuckled in the corner, his finger doing a funny little wave. His head was lulling to the side, as if he could barely hold it up.

"Bram, are you okay?" I whispered, glancing back at Shane.

He was oblivious to the both of us.

Bram pointed to the small icebox that stood in the tiny kitchen.

Did he want something?

I hunched over and crawled silently to the icebox. When I opened it, I found a piece of steak inside.

I hung my head, shaking it.

This. Old. Man.

"Stop using magic," I mouthed to him.

He curled his lip into a smile. Blood dribbled from the corner of his mouth until it fell into his beard.

The smile was convincing, but I knew it was fake when I saw the sorrow in his eyes. His pale skin and shallow breathing were a reminder of his condition, yet he still found it within himself to give to others.

"We are going to get out of this," I whispered as I crawled to him.

His eyes closed as I ran my hand across his face, the bristles of his whiskers tickling my palm. "Hawke's coming, and everything is going to be fine."

Because there wasn't anything I could do. I couldn't even will the claws to come out of my fingers because my wolf wasn't letting me do anything.

She would help me climb a tree, she let me run barefoot across the forest without it hurting, yet I stood in front of a man I wanted to hurt the most and nothing happened.

I gritted my teeth to the point of almost breaking my jaw.

"And yet you still have nothing to say," I yelled at her.

"E-eat," Bram barely whispered.

I shuffled closer, just to feel what little warmth he had left.

I had no knife to cut, no utensil to use for what little meat I had. It barely fit in my palm, but I picked it up and tore off pieces of the medium rare steak with my sharp teeth and ate it as quickly as I could, like a starving woman.

And it was the best steak I had ever eaten.

As I finished my meal, Shane finished up on the phone. I shoved the plate under the kitchen table, so Shane didn't see it. I didn't need a lecture about eating half-cooked steak on the floor conjured by magic.

Who knows what his expectations were by now with his whole vampire vibe he had going on.

As he turned, I was now sitting on the chair, cleaned, proper, back straight, hair drying somewhat satisfactorily. He smiled, approaching with even tapping steps.

"Delilah, I've missed you. I can't wait to bring you home." He kissed me on both cheeks, startling me.

I remained impassive and unresponsive despite the absolute repulsion running down my spine as he pulled away. I could see my wolf curling a lip as well.

"You will love what I've done to the place. More curtains, but not dark and dreary. They are cream and lavender but are thick enough to not let in as much light. Your skin will be sensitive to light for a few months."

Uhhh, I do not like purple.

"It will be better as you transition."

"T-transition?"

"Yes, the first year is the hardest. But after that, it's much better. The scientists I've hired have actually improved on the formula, so you won't have as much difficulty as I had. In fact, you may feel no adverse side effects."

"Effects of what?" I tilted my head.

"To the vampire venom. You are going to change, like me." He put his hand over his chest, like it was an honor to become a part of a prestigious institution or religion.

I felt the scrape of the chair legs against the floor as I pushed it away from him. "I don't want to be a vampire. Why would I want to do that?"

"Delilah," he said condescendingly. "I would have chosen fae, but Idris said that vampire venom is easier manipulated than fae. He already had scientists working on the vampire venom and by the time the fae venom was safe for humans, we would have already aged too much. So, this would be the safer route so we can freeze our youth."

He laid a hand on mine. "This venom is very safe. No other supernaturals can detect that we have been changed to vampires. We do not have to drink only blood. We can also enjoy food and its tastes. We will no longer age, and we can have chosen mates. That means we can mate and not have to worry about some goddess choosing for us and still be powerful. It really is the best of both human and supernatural worlds, Delilah. Isn't that wonderful?"

I shook my head, but his hand firmly gripped mine as I tried to tug it away.

"All this, eternal youth, physical powers, all to just help him step into the human world. We've become partners, he and I. It's a win-win. He will work with part of the business you never wanted me to take on, and I will do the rest."

"The sex trafficking?" I muttered.

He nodded, squeezing my hand. "Yes, I've kept my promise. I've done none of that."

"But you've done so many other things that are illegal. You kill, smuggle drugs, and weapons. I don't want to be a part of any of it!" I screamed.

With a slight tilt of his head, he looked down on me condescendingly. "But I need to give you all the pretty things. There are still crooked cops and politicians. There are no good people left in the world. It's all about staying on top. With me, you are safe, Delilah. I will keep you safe, pampered, free. You will never have to worry."

My wolf stepped forward from the darkness. Pushing forward.

"But it's you I need to be rescued from," I whispered.

Shane's eyes narrowed.

"I have a mate." I said louder. "I have a fated mate. The goddess paired me with Hawke."

Shane frowned. "No, Delilah. You are human. Humans are not paired with supernaturals. He is lying to you. He is a rogue. He was rejected because he is a criminal, too."

"No, he isn't," I yelled, pulling away from the chair, ripping my hand away from his. "He is my mate! He is my soulmate. I will not go home with you."

"You will!" Shane grabbed my wrist, standing, his chair landing on the floor with a bang.

Shane took my wrist, bending it until the pain became too much to bear. My knees hit the floor, tears pricking my eyes. "You will come home, meet Duke Idris, and be blessed with the transfusion to rid you of this *dog's*—venom," he spat. "Then I will bond us together!"

The tears that welled into my eyes disappeared. The pain in my wrist no longer ached, but amusement filled me.

A snort of amusement filled the air, followed by loud, hysterical laughter. Outside, wails and screams of pain filtered into the open windows and quickly died.

Hawke was coming. Just a little longer.

"What's so funny?" Shane asked with no amusement.

The laughter died in my throat as I locked eyes with his cold, lifeless gaze. "Duke Idris is dead. How is your little plan going to work now?"

Shane leaned in, his cold vampire breath on my face.

"You think you have it figured out, don't you, my little wife?"

I wiped away the last few tears that clung to my lashes.

"You think he's dead, don't you? From that little fire a few weeks ago?"

My excitement faded, my heart sinking. *What?*

"Oh, little dove, how weak you look when your wings are clipped." He traced his finger over my cheek. "Duke Idris is a dark fae that practices necromancy. Don't you think he would have created a fail-safe if his life was in danger?"

I took a sharp breath, feeling the chill of the air on my skin.

Shane's cheek brushed mine, lips trailing to my ear. "Duke Idris is very much alive."

CHAPTER THIRTY-NINE

Hawke

The sharp pain we felt at our temple through the bond was enough to cause Tyr to viciously tear the skin from our body. In turn, the fur replicated, claws and fangs lengthened. We secured our paws into the earth and unleashed a thunderous roar that caused the branches of the nearby trees to tremble.

There was no longer an element of surprise. Our position was given away and maybe it was better this way. It could give us a hint of a challenge.

Men rushed from the front, guns in hand, magazines on their belts clinking together as they rounded the cabin. Having never seen our capabilities, these men did not know what to expect.

I almost felt sorry for them as they approached in their shined shoes and their three-piece suits.

Key word was, *almost*.

We charged, abandoning the haven of the lifeless forest, our fur recently cleaned from our previous transformation. It was matted with blood and the innards from our previous fight, but now we just looked like a rabid wolf looking for a fight or a meal.

We shoved the first male onto his back, and our claws entered his chest cavity. We ended his screams by piercing his throat with our fangs, the blood oozing into his voice box.

The loud bangs of gunshots rang through the air, zipping by our ears. A number of them found their way onto my hindquarters, with some even making their way through my rib cage. My body jolted as I felt the graze of hot metal on the bone, and I winced in response.

Shit.

Chad, the male that was impressively large for a human, came into sight. It fueled my adrenaline to see the smug bastard. He thought he was going to win this, but he was sorely mistaken.

Chad shifted the tailored fabric of his fitted jacket, the material clinging to his toned biceps. He pulled his gun from his leather holster, and it made a slight squeak as it came free. He felt the smooth handle of his Glock beneath his fingers as his lip curled into a smirk.

His face was a mask of calm, and there was no sign of fear emanating from his body.

He was ready for this, and so was I.

Chad's face flashed through my head. He was the one that caused fear in my mate. He caused her pain. He didn't touch her; I knew that much, but he'd startled her and that was enough for me to bring him death.

As each male before me fell, my skin stiffened, my fur bristled. The bullets no longer penetrated my skin because my mate was so close. The bond was too strong now, too powerful for a bullet to penetrate.

My body was indestructible, impervious to anything except supernatural claws, fangs, or a magical or cursed device.

I licked my maw. We were ready to test our strength after ripping the pathetic humans apart like shreds of paper. Chad's neck was thick, filled with veins and steroids pumping through the tough meat. Our teeth would take more than just a millisecond to rip through that.

Might take... I don't know, a full five seconds.

We could already feel the resistance of the tough meat under our teeth. Maybe we could slice into his gut a little deeper with our claws. But Tyr's snarls broke my concentration, as he nudged me to listen to the thoughts of my mate's conversation with Shane.

Shane wanted to remove my venom from my mate.

Remove my mark.

That alone infuriated me until he stated Idris was alive.

I felt a deep, raw howl emanating from within me, rising until it erupted from my throat. My legs pushed me forward, bounding further into the tunnel vision I had created.

I couldn't worry about anything else.

I dug my claws into the fabric of Chad's suit, but he remained standing, his back pushed against the rough, splintering wood of the cabin. He smiled, his gun pointed upward, not even aimed toward me, but tapping the camera in his other hand.

It was a picture of a woman who was tucked away in the corner of a small room. A mess of wild curls and round glasses.

"I know you fuckers got a soft spot for saving women. Put a scratch on me and she dies."

My breathing was ragged as I exhaled, droplets of blood fanning across his neck. He cringed as the substance clung to his tight, white collar, creating a messy stain.

"I'll do it. Just got to say the word."

I felt my throat vibrate as I released an intimidating growl.

"Hawke!" Delilah screamed, and I lowered back down to all fours, huffing in frustration and darted inside without looking back.

As I entered, I saw Shane's long, opaque fingernails wrapped around Delilah's neck. His fingers softly caressed her jawline with such tenderness, his eyes full of a yearning that made me feel sick.

I snarled, my nails scraping against the floor as I inched closer.

He tsked, looking me up and down. "Shift, mutt, or the woman on the phone won't last much longer."

Chad entered and sat in the chair like he was the one that had done all the fighting outside. He wiped his forehead with a handkerchief and stuck it back into his pocket.

I let out a deep, growling noise, unable to decide my next move.

"Please, Hawke," Delilah whispered. "She helped me escape from Shane."

Shane let out a chuckle that echoed in the room. "That she did. Tiny thing she is. Took me a while to find the culprit who kept sneaking away all the good help, but when I did, off to solitary confinement she went. Now, shift." Shane's hand tightened on Delilah's throat.

She didn't show any fear, instead her lip curled, her nose twitched and her nails that laid delicately at her side grew into claws.

"She wants to shift," Tyr said, as he retracted our fur. *"But her wolf is scared."*

"Why would she be? It's a shift. She shouldn't be nervous. If she is that connected to Delilah already, then this shift should be a walk in the park."

"She's shifted before. She failed her first shift. This is her second attempt."

"How is that possible?"

"You are even more disgusting in your human form." Shane sneered. "Now, you are going to stay here while I take Delilah back to New York. If you behave, I'll keep Delilah's friend alive and let you have a swift death once this unholy bond between you is eradicated. The warlock will die in peace."

Bram remained frozen in place, the only sign of life, the slow and steady drops of his blood falling onto the floor.

Like hell, he was taking my mate anywhere.

"No, I don't think so." I stepped forward, letting the fucker get a good look at my cock.

I cracked my neck, reaching for my mate until Delilah told me to stop.

"I'm going with Shane," she stated.

We both stared at her in disbelief until it quickly turned to anger, and I clenched my hands into tight fists.

"I don't want her to die. I don't even know her name." She glanced at the phone on the other side of the room. *"She said she was going to leave right after me. After all this time—"* She swallowed. Guilt filled her. I felt it drowning inside her.

Delilah turned to Shane. "I need your promise that you will let her go."

Shane petted her hair, smiling down at her. "I've never broken a promise, have I?"

Delila pursed her lips.

She can't possibly think about doing this.

"Delilah, I can't let you do this. You can't do this. You ran away from me once, and I won't let you do it again," I pleaded.

My mate stared at me with understanding, her head nodding, but her heart was unyielding. I could feel it in the bond we shared. She was selfless to a fault; I knew that.

"I can't let someone innocent suffer, Hawke. You saw her. For all I know, she has spent two years in a room while I've been free. She sacrificed herself for me. I can't live my life knowing she's there."

Her claws pierced the palms of her hands. *"Get our family. Come get us both?"*

Tyr howled, crying for anyone to hear us. If we had a pack to connect us, they would have heard us all the way back home and come to find us, to save us. Because shit, we needed a pack.

"Fuck, Delilah." I ran my hand through my hair, pulling until I swore I was ripping my scalp.

A thick fog of uncertainty surrounded me.

The Iron Fang was built on the foundation of helping those who were helpless. Delilah was close to shifting. She could protect herself from Shane once she shifted, but who knew when that would be? Her wolf was frightened.

I've never heard of such a thing.

I was losing hope, fast. I was out of options. I had no one to turn to. I didn't have an alpha. I didn't have my family with me. My wolf only wanted to rip the entire cabin apart, but not when there were innocent lives at stake.

I'd never prayed, not even before I was rejected. I knew to pay my respect to the gods. I knew to pay my dues, to make sacrifices, to show respect, but I never prayed wanting anything for myself. I took what I was given and was thankful for it.

But now?

I needed help.

I didn't know what the fuck to do.

And when I closed my damn eyes, I wasn't greeted with blackness. It was a scene that caught my breath because it looked all too familiar.

It was a cabin, much more basic than the one we were staying in currently.

The cabin was built with minimal resources. The beds were fashioned from sturdy tables covered with dry straw for cushioning and draped with tan cloth. The bowls were handcrafted from clay, carved wood, and old, dented metal. The walls were decorated with half-made ropes of twine and straw, hanging like cobwebs. The fire crackled and was placed strategically in the center of the hut, with a hole in the rooftop to let the smoke escape.

Where was I?

As I finished scanning my surroundings, the twisted scent of copper rose to my nostrils, and I stepped further inside. And when I did so, a body lay on the floor.

A blonde-haired woman whose hair covered her face laid on the dirt floor. She lay there motionless, her once-blue clothes now tattered and stained with blood. The sight of her torn body was enough to make anyone's stomach turn. Her skin was peeled away in patches, revealing the muscles and bones underneath. The strands of her hair were matted with blood and dirt. The stench of death hung heavily in the air.

Blonde fur was spread around the room, in the pools of her blood and on the ripped clothes and bed. She was curled in the fetal position, or what was left of her, her hand reaching toward the door.

My heart ached for this woman.

Who was she to me?

I could feel the hairs on my arms standing on end, my body aching to be close to her.

I fell to the ground, my knees taking the brunt of the fall, but it was nothing compared to the breaking of my heart. I crawled to the body, wondering how I was related to this woman. This wasn't Delilah, it couldn't be. This wasn't my home, this wasn't the time frame I belonged in.

The agony I experienced made my heart race and my body quake. The pain was like a searing heat that reached into my soul, penetrating the depths of my innermost being. There was something missing, something vital that was keeping me from connecting me to this woman on a deeper level.

I swayed above her, my hands already covered in her blood from touching her. I traced my finger over her face to move her hair. As I did so, a faded spark ignited over the skin. I looked at the woman's face and felt a deep chill that seemed to still the air around me.

Delilah.

The silence was broken by a sharp gasp as all the air rushed out of my lungs.

No, no, no.

I pushed the hair away from her shoulder, finding a mark on her skin.

My mark.

I felt my shoulder, rubbing to feel her teeth in my skin, but there was none.

There was no completed bond.

The scene faded, my eyes flew open like the vision never happened. I was back in the same cabin with Delilah alive and right in front of me.

The fucking hell was that?

Delilah stared at me with pleading eyes to save the woman that had rescued her a couple years ago—a woman I didn't even know. Delilah wanted to be the sacrificial lamb to save another?

She wanted me to let her go?

Inside, Tyr howled, roaring into a frenzy. He would not have it. He wasn't going to let Delilah out of our sight. We would not let her go, no matter how much she begged, no matter how much she wanted to save this human.

She was ours.

If I lost her once before, in some fucking previous life, some damned alternate universe. She was fucking ours now.

Hell would freeze over before I let her out of my sight again.

My mouth twisted into an angry snarl as my body coiled with tension.

Shane let out a curse, pulling Delilah to his side.

I wasn't worried about him hurting her, and she wasn't either.

Delilah's eyes widened, knowing exactly what I was going to do before I executed my attack.

"Mine." I bared my fangs.

I heard a deep, guttural growl rumble from her chest, and her lips curled back into a feral snarl as her long nails dug into Shane's wrist where it lay on her throat. Shane hissed when Delilah slit four claws through his skin.

Using my speed, I spun around to see the bastard Chad, who was caught by surprise staring at my cock, swinging his way. I ran forward, laughing to myself, and punched him square in the face before he could open his mouth. His gun went off, barely missing Bram, who was still tied to the chair.

Chad had somehow regained his footing, knocking me in the side of the head with the butt of the gun, which only pissed me off further. It barely knocked me off my balance, and I took three claws and slit his throat.

He dropped the phone so he could grab his throat to stop the bleeding. The gurgles were now just background noise. The blood dripped down his expensive suit and splashed onto the screen.

I twisted my body to help my mate, and a sudden and deafening crack echoed through the room. It filled my ears with a powerful roar that made my blood boil instantly. My mate could be hurt, and I wasn't going to let the fucker get away with it.

In just three large strides, I arrived at my mate's side, the cry of mercy that followed sent an icy thrill down my spine. It wasn't from my mate's lips but from our enemy, and I smiled wickedly, my eyes widening in both shock and awe.

My mate was hovering over Shane, a worthless half-breed vampire who lay sprawled on the floor, staring up at his now ex-wife. The air around us was thick with death, and the floor was covered with an infinite sea of black blood.

Shane's hand was outstretched, struggling to reach Delilah's cheek, who kept her body at arm's length, besides the one arm that was deep within his chest. The smell of his rancid blood made me gag, and I wanted nothing more than to finish off the bastard myself.

His life force waned, the faint thud of his heart barely audible in his chest.

Delilah didn't move her face, giving me a side eye, waiting for me to watch.

Blood trickled down her cheek as she waited.

I wasn't sure why she wanted me to watch. This was her kill, this was her closure. But in a sick twisted way, I fucking enjoyed it. It would be a big damned lie if I said it didn't turn me on to see my mate elbow deep in the fucker's chest. To watch my little ray of sunshine extinguishing the light of some asshole was hot as hell.

"But I wanted to kill him," Tyr pouted, sitting on his hind legs. *"All these were so quick. I wanted to try some of Grim's sweet torture moves."*

I crossed my arms, feeling a sense of pride and admiration as I watched my mate. *"That is what is so great about being in the supernatural world. She can pull out his heart, but...we can put it back inside and reanimate him later."*

Tyr salivated, nodding eagerly, forgetting that little notion as she ripped the remaining veins and arteries that connected his heart to his body.

CHAPTER FORTY

Delilah

His skin yielded easily to the sharpness of my claws, slicing through it like butter. With a single motion, they effortlessly slid through the meat and tendon. My senses were heightened. I could smell the marrow buried deep inside his body, the metallic scent singed my nose, and his screams pierced my ears.

My wolf toned down my senses, almost knowing it was all too much to bear. She muted his screams, filtering out the metallic smells that made me sick. Unfortunately, the sight could not be taken away.

The blood and gore would haunt my dreams until the end of my life.

Blood pooled beneath Shane as I overpowered him with my strength. I'd never been able to push him off me. Not on our wedding night, not in my youth. He was a lean, muscular male that could easily overpower the non-athletic me. But now?

A powerful rush of adrenaline flowed through my veins, providing me with an energy and strength I had never known. The wolf within me was eager to break free, and I could feel its strength as the fur sprouted over my arms—the unmistakable sign I'd been waiting for.

I curled back my lip, revealing my fang, and with a menacing snarl, I pinned Shane in one swift movement before he had time to react. His eyes widened in surprise.

"Delilah?" His voice came in a shaking stutter.

His bloodied hand gripped my upper arm weakly.

His fingers could barely hold on to my shoulder.

I shook off his hand and watched as it dropped to the ground with a thud. I refused to submit to him in defeat and instead of looking away in a sign of submission, I gazed at him directly.

"Destroy him," my wolf demanded. *"Take back what he took from you."*

What did he take from me?

He took everything.

My innocence, my youth, my happiness, my mother, and at one point, my will to live.

How many times had I thought about ending it all in the confines of that hell?

I trailed my tongue across my lips, remembering the blades I had stolen from one of the coffee tables where it was used to divide a white powdery substance. Party after party each night, more and more cocaine was brought into the house.

More drugs, weapons, endless parties. When was it going to stop? When was I going to get my escape?

So, I collected the sharp objects like candies, put them in my pockets and took them to my room. I could still see the remnants of powder that made the men forget their worries for a time. It wasn't enough for me to forget mine, however.

Not that I wanted a moment of forgetfulness, I wanted something more.

I wanted something permanent.

My collection of blades sat in that bathroom drawer, ready to be used when I was ready to make my own escape. But in the end, I was too chicken to watch my blood run down that pasty arm.

But really, it was that silly voice that told me not to. The voice that I now knew to be my wolf telling me to hang on a little longer.

I tilted my chin, assessing the bastard that tried to ruined me. At one point I thought he broke me, but in the end, I came out far better than I ever dreamed.

I learned to love life, have friends and hell, even learned how to fall in love.

And I almost missed it all, because Shane pushed me to where I wanted to kill myself.

And that was enough reason to kill him.

I didn't have the stomach to do it alone, but my wolf certainly did.

My wolf's warmth gradually spread throughout my body, enveloping me and taking charge bit by bit. Hair thickened around each limb, claws strengthened as she ran them slowly and deeply down each limb, savoring each agonizing tear of his skin.

Shane's screams were nothing but pitiful cries. The sticky wetness between the pads of our fingers painted his pale, grey skin as we filleted his arms and legs, letting the skin flaps fall to the floor.

Shane tried to sit up until my wolf straddled him with a heavy pounce. She sliced his suit to shreds, along with his muscular torso. Blood seeped through the shredded material, and bone emerged through the mangled muscle.

He didn't even try to put up a fight, or it didn't seem that way. Every time he tried to sit up or move his arm, my wolf pinned him with our claws or a heavy push of our forearm to his neck.

Our faces were filled with an evil and vindictive joy, our cheeks stretched in a malicious grin. Fangs descended longer than ever before, reaching our chin.

He was now lying in a pool of his own dark blood.

Shane's breaths were shallow, his body weak he wasn't able to lift his arms.. There was no more blood for him to pump through his body. The only possible thing left to do was to rip his heart from his chest.

The bare bones of his chest, the hunks of meat that hung to them like a terrible horror movie hack job, made my stomach roll. My wolf quieted that part of my body, not wanting us to look weak in front of our mate.

But boy, was I sick.

"Delilah, why?" Shane whispered.

Did he really not get it? Was he that oblivious?

He didn't deserve an answer, didn't deserve an explanation of it all.

My wolf didn't think so either and with a quick glance at our mate watching on in pride, she plunged our sticky, long claws into the chest cavity.

Once the tendons, the arteries, and whatever else was stuck to his blackened heart were pulled away, we tossed the muscle to the other side of the room.

I panted, watching as it thumped across the floorboard, leaving sticky, bloody heart patterns in its wake. It thumped against the wall, and I closed my eyes in gratefulness that it was over.

As my golden peach fuzz fur receded, I collapsed onto the floor. My breathing became heavier as I shut my eyes, unable to bear the sight of the destruction.

I couldn't stand to see or smell anymore blood.

"Delilah!" Hawke ran forward, landing on his knees to pick me up.

He cradled my head to his chest. Blood was everywhere, and it was even on his body.

Ick.

"I love you, but you stink," I groaned.

He chuckled, pulling me into his arms, and took long strides to the bathroom.

Before I knew it, the hot steam of the shower filled the small bathroom, and he put us both under the highest jet setting and let the red liquid fall from our bodies.

The heat felt good, and his large hands steadied me as he pulled off the wet clothing and threw it on the bathroom floor without a care.

"Are you okay, Sunshine?" His thumbs rubbed over my cheeks, and his eyes searched mine, looking for signs of any life in them.

"I killed someone." I swallowed. "I didn't enjoy doing that, even if they deserved it."

Hawke pulled me toward his chest, rubbing the shampoo into my hair. He bathed me, running the soap along my body as I stared into the stark white bathroom tile.

"If it makes you feel better, he isn't dead yet." He winced.

I squeezed my eyes shut. "What?"

Are you freaking kidding? After all that dramatic pulling out his heart, throwing it across the room, clawing his body into freaking Swiss cheese... He isn't dead yet?

My wolf shrugged inside me, shaking her head.

Dear. Lord.

Hawke pulled a fluffy towel from the nearby railing, wrapping it around me, and pulled me out of the shower with care. He fastened it around my chest, making sure it was secure.

"We burn the heart, or stake it, along with his body. And let's be honest. He got off too easy. Grim and I are going to have some fun with him later. Give him what he really deserves. But you did great for the first time, and if you want to do it again—"

I groaned, very unlady-like.

"I don't have to be a part of that, right? Please say no." I tapped my forehead repeatedly against his chest.

Hawke tilted my head back with both of his large hands, cupping my face. His smile grew wide, and his nose traced mine as if to beckon me to open my eyes. "Of course not, my sweet mate. He's the Iron's Fang's problem now."

"Good, they can have at it." I laid my head on his chest and wrapped my arms around him. I was a little disappointed that he had wrapped a towel around his waist. I was becoming accustomed to him being naked all the time.

A repeated knocking and shuffling from the other room made Hawke tighten his grip around my body. I stiffened, wondering if Chad or some other guard managed to get inside the cabin.

"Hey, is it over?" Bram's raspy voice radiated from the other room.

Whoops, forgot about the warlock.

"Bram!" I had almost forgotten the poor man and wiggled my way out of Hawke's powerful arms.

With a loud, deep grunt, Hawke marched out of the room, his footsteps clattering and shaking the floor with each step.

"Delilah!" Hawke abruptly took my hand and yanked me in his direction. He wrapped his hand around my waist and had me tucked under his arm. "You stay with me, you don't leave my sight, do you understand?" He tapped my nose with his finger. "You don't listen well, and you will be punished later for your blatant disregard for my orders."

His eyes narrowed, and the vein in his forehead throbbed.

"Yes, Daddy," I rolled my eyes.

Hawke's eyes widened, and his cock responded with a flick to my thigh. *Oh, he liked that, didn't he?*

He squeezed my hip, and a lustful purr radiated from his chest. "You know, finishing the day with blood on my claws and rutting my mate sounds like a good plan."

Hawke kept me pinned with one hand on my hip and the other next to my head while he leaned up against the wall. "And I think you just opened yourself to a new kink I might like."

My cheeks blazed red, and I felt it running down my neck and to the tops of my breasts.

"Hmm, how far does this blush go?"

"Guys!" Bram shouted more forcefully this time, and Hawke groaned. "Such a buzzkill."

"He is hurt." I playfully tapped his shoulder.

Hawke didn't let me go. He held onto my hand as we entered the room and found Bram still sitting in the chair where we left him.

What kind of selfish friends were we?

Dried blood was crusted around his mouth, and he had adjusted his head to a more upright position. "You guys put on a good show. Didn't know you had it in you, Delilah." He winced when he moved his shoulders.

"Are you okay? You are such a stubborn thing using your magic. This cabin isn't magic at all is it?" I asked, looking him over.

I went to the sink, which was no longer as luxurious as it used to be and grabbed a rag. Then I wetted it with some clean, refreshing water from the pump and used it to gently dab his forehead with it. He groaned, feeling the cool water on his forehead, even daring to lick at the dirty, bloody water droplets rolling down his face.

Hawke worked with great haste in order to undo the tightly tied bindings, which were emitting an unpleasant odor.

I coughed.

"Delilah, step back." Hawke ripped the bindings and raced to the other side of the room to throw them out the door.

"Valerian," Bram said, as I helped him straighten himself in the chair. "Not normally poisonous for my species, but in my weakened state, it certainly kept me tired and weak. Over time, I could have slipped into a coma."

Bram's hooded eyes were becoming more alert, and his heart was gradually getting stronger.

"I'm going to be just fine. I'm not that old." He waved his hand as I tried to help him from the chair.

I raised an eyebrow, putting my hands on my hips.

"How about we check the phone?" He jutted his chin out with his bloodied beard. "Make sure that woman is alright?"

Cheese and crackers, I almost forgot.

I patted Bram's shoulder before racing over and tripping over Shane's leather shoes. I must have tripped wrong because then my body was jolted with an electrical searing pain. It was like thousands of tiny fire ants under my skin trying to poke through every little pore.

Hawke, making his way back from the open door, rushed to me and caught me in a gentle embrace before I could fall to the floor. His hand softly cupped my head, and I heard the steady beat of his heart as he drew me to his chest. His loud purring was like a lullaby, calming the pain to a manageable level, but I still felt uneasy.

The muscles were pulsing with the pain radiating to each ligament of my body. I felt the bones in my body bending. Bones can't bend!

They aren't supposed to bend right?

"You're hurt. When did you get hurt? And why are you running?" Hawke's panic came hard and fast through our bond.

My wolf whimpered, unable to manage the force of his emotions.

"The maid? I need to see if she's okay?" Hawke's arms caught me as my knees gave out, and I felt myself being carried across the room and laid down on the lone couch. Luckily, there was no blood, just the soft cushion and Hawke's firm body keeping me close.

The pain was subsiding, but I felt like exploding. Like my skin was too small for my body.

My wolf—she was just mingling at the surface. I could feel her.

"Come out," I whispered. "I want her to come out. I think that's what she needs to do."

Hawke patted my hair. I felt the nervousness on his side of the bond. "She's scared, Sunshine. She's scared to shift."

Hawke's eyes followed Bram's movements as he trudged through the pools of blood to our side of the room.

Please tell me having bodies all over shifter's homes wasn't the norm?

"Do wolves get scared to shift their first time?" I asked.

My body contorted into the fetal position, and I gripped Hawke's arm, piercing his skin, but he let me.

I needed to feel close to him.

Bram stood closer, sitting on the other side of the couch. He grabbed my ankle, and Hawke let out a growl in warning.

"Easy, now," Bram said. "Let me see what's going on here. Why don't you find out about the maid?"

Hawke cleared his throat and reached over to the phone that laid on the floor. He wiped the screen that was splattered with blood.

"Dede, it's just a picture." He tapped the phone several more times with his thumb. "It isn't a live feed. It looks like a picture from a security feed."

My lip quivered. She couldn't be dead.

"Shane isn't a liar. I know that. She's alive. We have to go get her," I demanded.

Hawke nodded, petting my sweaty forehead.

"We will get her, Sunshine. I believe you. Switch will hack the phone. We will get a team up there. I don't know how, but we will."

"W-what do you mean?" Another shock of warping bones made me gasp. My fingers dug into Hawke's leg, and his purr grew heavier.

I kept the sounds of pain inside me, not wanting to upset him but I believe he felt it. He was whispering harshly to Bram, but he shook his head, unable to give him any encouragement about what to do.

As the pain waned, Bram continued to rub his thumb over my ankle until he sighed audibly.

"I hate to admit failure, and I've been doing a lot of that lately, failing," Bram said, rubbing his forehead.

I reached my hand out to grab his, rubbing it over his still bloodied knuckles. He placed his other hand in mine, patting it.

"Delilah, you are–"

Roars of motorcycle engines blasted through the veil. It was an onslaught of noise, no gentle rumblings like they were approaching from far away. They came straight through. It was powerful, thunderous, like it came out of nowhere.

"What the fuck, no way!" Hawke leaned back, letting out a bark of laughter. "How the hell did they find us?"

Bram chuckled, running his hand through his bloodied hair. "The Goddess has blessed your crew. The Iron Fang is now the earth's soldiers." His hand slapped down on his leg.

"Go get our family," I nudged Hawke.

He looked out the door, the shiny bikes beckoning him as they continued revving, calling out to him. "Go on, I'm right here, and Bram is with me." I pushed him again. "No pain right now. See if Journey can come in, please?"

If Journey was there, the priestess, she could help, couldn't she?

My wolf nodded tiredly inside me.

Hawke gently laid me on a pillow, stroking my hair and placing a kiss on my forehead. "Are you sure? I don't like leaving you," he whispered softly.

"I promise this time." I closed my eyes. "Just get them in here."

Hawke pecked my lips and stared at Bram. "Touch her, you die."

And there he was, my big grumpy biker.

Bram tilted his head, still rubbing my feet and staring at me like my mate had lost his mind. "It's okay, you can keep going with the feet," I said giggling.

The further Hawke ventured away, the more the ache in my chest intensified, and my wolf's pitiful whines echoed in my head.

CHAPTER FORTY-ONE

Hawke

I had little time once I left the room. Her pain would return tenfold, and I did not want to subject her to that for very long. But my mission wasn't to welcome my brothers, but to retrieve someone who I knew could help my mate—Journey.

If it was true, that Journey was this newly appointed priestess that the goddess had given to the Iron Fang, then she would be the only one that could help her.

Switch had been in frequent contact. Giving me updates each night, and that piece of information, had been the most shocking. Almost too unbelievable. But after all this, with Delilah being my mate, my second chance. I believed it all.

Because dammit, I did not know how to help my mate.

Her wolf was too frightened to shift. Her bones should crack, break, and shift into her beast-like form, but she wouldn't. She was hesitating, forcing the bones to remain in the human frame. I had seen nothing like it in all the years I'd seen pups transform.

Tyr was pacing, prancing, urging me to return to Delilah. With Bram by her side, he could coax her to remain calm, but only our bond could soothe her.

The roars of the multitude of bikes were cut off, fifteen in all. All of them were kicking out their stands, trying to get them to stay upright in the soil was cumbersome.

The members that stood out the most, the closest of my brothers, were Locke, Bear, Bones, Anaki, Sizzle, Karma, Surkash, Switch, Hammer, Morpheus, Beretta, her witch mate Tajah, and Grim and his mate Journey.

Thank fuck.

I ran toward the middle, bypassing them all. They gave me strange hurt looks. My tunnel vision only had one wolf in mind, and that was Journey.

Journey sat up straight, with more confidence than the last time I saw her. Her long brown hair tumbled out of her helmet, and the bright crescent moon shone bright on her forehead. She smiled, waving once she saw me.

As I stepped forward, about to reach for her, Grim grabbed my arm, ripping me away from her.

His deep, menacing snarl reverberated through the group, causing them all to tense up as they watched the scene unfold.

It was stupid on my part. To run toward any claimed female, but I was desperate to save my mate from any more pain. The sound of her gentle sobs pierced my ears, and I felt my heart breaking as I realized how long we had been apart.

Journey let out a huff in frustration, her eyes darting to the cabin and back to me.

"Grim, stop, he's desperate for help." The gentleness in her touch soothed his grip on my arm.

Grim let go reluctantly. His snarl and forceful nudge was enough for me to step back a good three feet. He delicately helped her off the bike like she was a princess, hell, she sort of was to the pack now that she was a priestess. He wrapped his arm around her waist and pulled her close.

"Please," I asked with urgency. "Something is wrong with her. She won't shift."

Journey's eyes softened. She grabbed her bag and pulled it over her shoulder, only for Grim to take it away from her and shake his head.

"Then let's go check on my new best friend, huh?" She tilted her head in amusement, her feet crunching the fallen leaves as she took gentle strides to the cabin.

The first few nights that Journey came to the Iron Fang, Delilah knew Journey had it rough. My mate made her feel welcome while the other girls stayed away; only because Grim made it known Journey was off limits to all. Delilah was never afraid of any male at the Iron Fang and ignored him. Delilah knew Grim wouldn't hurt any female.

And now, Journey wanted to return that kindness.

Locke slapped his hand on my shoulder and pulled me away from Grim, who was stewing for even looking at his mate with pleading eyes. "He's still pretty territorial. I don't think it goes away." Locke frowned, squeezing my shoulder and took me further away from Grim.

Locke stopped when a body stood in our path. More bodies were sprinkled around us, a total of maybe five or six spread around the area.

Locke looked at the forest, taking in a large breath. "Now, I know my nose isn't what it used to be, but it really stinks around here."

"There's forty more out there," I muttered, rubbing my neck.

Locke nodded, stepping over the body.

"And we missed it all?" He nodded his head to the bodies on the ground and rummaged through his pocket to pull out a cigarette.

"Yup."

"Well, shit. The boys will be upset. I promised them a fight." He put the neatly self-wrapped cigarette in his mouth and rolled it along his lips. "Damn. You did all of that, huh?"

I chuckled, nodding. "Her ex is in there." I jerked my head toward the cabin. "It's a long story, but we can put his heart back in his body and play with him a little."

Locke looked at me, then returned his attention to the open door. He nodded and puffed out a thick cloud of smoke.

"How the hell did you find us through this bubble shit?" I looked over our heads for emphasis.

Locke threw his cigarette on the ground and put it out. "Journey. Don't think we will get many more of those letters. She's the direct line to the goddess now, I guess. She said we were needed, so we hopped on our bikes." He slumped his shoulders. "And like good little mutts, we took her lead."

A squeal came from the open door of the cabin. Anaki pranced like a dragon hatchling and screamed, "My Sunshine! Oh, how I've missed my Sunshine!"

I growled.

"Ah, let him have his fun. He isn't doing so well." Locke tapped my shoulder, leading us up the steps. "None of us are doing well."

Once we entered, Journey was already sitting on her knees next to Delilah. She was brushing the wet strands of hair away from Delilah's forehead, whispering encouragement in her ear.

My heart constricted in my chest, seeing my mate in such pain. I never wanted my mate to feel this. She shouldn't have to. I always wanted to see her smile, watch her prance around the bar she had come to know and love.

I stepped forward, adjusting the towel and headed toward Journey until Grim stepped in front of me.

"Let my mate work." He crossed his arms, staring down at me.

"My mate needs help," I snapped back. "I will touch mine."

Grim and I were different heights. He may be taller and bulkier, but I had more combat training. I could kick his ass if I wanted.

"Wolves, that's enough." Locke puffed out another puff of smoke from a new cigarette and stepped between us. "Don't care if you both have mates, but there won't be any fighting in this cabin on my watch. We have enough dead bodies here. Now let Journey figure out what's wrong."

Even if Locke wasn't technically alpha status, we treated him as such. A broken soul couldn't carry an alpha title, especially with no luna beside him.

"I know what's wrong," I whispered to them both. "Her wolf is refusing to release herself. I think her wolf failed a previous shift in another life." I tugged on my beard.

Grim's face fell. He no longer stood in a defensive position. He turned to his mate, who stared up at him with a solemn nod.

I heard Delilah's cry and felt my heart leap into my throat as I rushed to her, lifting her into my arms.

We all sat in silence for a time while Journey continued to mutter to herself. She touched various points on Delilah's body. Journey's eyes glowed, and her lips moved in a sequence of patterns that no one understood.

As time passed, people moved around the room, carrying in bags from their bikes, most likely filled with clothes, weapons, and food. Locke muttered to Sizzle and Bear, pointing to various areas in the room, then circling his finger in the air around the cabin and pointing to other men to take the bodies outside.

My lip curled into a smile, and nodded to Locke, who gazed at me for approval.

Me. He looked at me for approval.

Fuck, he was going to make me get damned emotional.

"*Fuck you,*" I mouthed to him.

He threw me the bird and smirked, leaning up against the door frame of the cabin.

I don't know what the fuck I'd do without the bastard.

Tajah broke me out of my thoughts. Thank the fucking goddess, when she stepped out of the dark corner of the room and walked toward Bram.

Tajah couldn't take her eyes off of Bram for a long time. And it seemed she found her confidence. She took slow, calculating steps toward him. He could barely keep his eyes open, until he lifted his head and looked up at the captivating witch before him.

"Master Bram, is that you?" Tajah mumbled. She bent over, her long hair brushing against his exposed arm.

As she moved, the leather pants she wore made a soft groan, and the dark trench cloak she wore kept her beloved purple corset out of sight.

Bram peered up at her, his eyes narrowing in concentration until they widened in shock.

"No, really? Tajah, is that you?" He nudged Journey's foot. She nodded for him to leave, and he followed Tajah into the kitchen to give them privacy and let Journey concentrate.

"Can you tell me the spell to change the cabin, and I will make it accommodating to fit all of us? I just can't recall it. That way we can get you resting again? You look like you need it." Tajah's hand rested on Bram's.

He clenched his jaw, his fingers coming away from his face stained with his own blood. "Ah, Tajah, that's a lot of magic."

"It's my turn to take care of you, Master Bram," Tajah whispered. "Let me take over, now. It seems *you* are the one in need of a little care."

Bram's eyes glistened, the salty wetness of unshed tears coating his lashes.

Delilah held her breath, watching the scene unfold; I could feel her warmth in her gentle grip on my hand. It was such an intimate moment, one we shouldn't watch.

Bram had so many secrets. He was one of the most complicated warlocks I'd ever known. But he wasn't alone anymore. Whatever connections he had with my family, my father, made him permanently tied to us. We would not get rid of him so easily.

Not that I wanted to.

"Is Bram like your godfather or fun uncle, or wait, a funcle or something now?" Delilah asked over our mind-link, with a wobbly smile. It didn't reach her eyes, but she was trying so damned hard.

Her exhaustion was evident, and the tiny ways she tried to hide it were futile. I knew better. I knew how the bond worked. Besides, her skin was pale, sweat dotted her nose, and her breathing was labored. I could scold her for trying to lie, but I let her get away with it so she could try to forget the pain.

"A funcle?" I asked playfully.

"Yeah, a fun uncle that gets you into trouble? Like he spikes the drinks at parties? Holds out his finger and asks you to pull it?" she giggled.

I didn't understand that one. But I smiled anyway.

"Please, Master," Tajah pleaded.

"I don't deserve that title anymore, sweet Tajah." Bram shook his head.

Tajah pressed her forehead to his and kissed it. Beretta who stood in the corner with her silver claws extended growled lowly. But a stern look from Tajah to Beretta made it clear it was a brotherly and sisterly exchange. Beretta didn't let her guard down, however, and she stayed in her corner watching them both warily.

If it was Delilah doing that to any male, or female, I believe I would have already ripped out their throats.

But perhaps female bonds were different.

Bram looked defeated but nodded. He whispered a language I couldn't understand to Tajah, and she stepped to the open door of the cabin wistfully.

"Grab the heart and the body you wish to save for later and take it outside." Tajah urged quietly as she gazed at Journey, who was still speaking in strange tongues.

Tajah took off her trench coat and laid it in the dusty chair. Her purple corset inlaid with gold and silver patterns on the bodice reflected in the setting sun.

"Shh, it's alright," I soothed Delilah, who had become restless in my arms. "She's going to make us more comfortable." My purr grew louder in my chest, and I used my arm to pull Delilah's face away from Chad and Shane's bodies.

Unfortunately, their bodies being dragged out of the cabin couldn't be unheard. *"Just think about sucking my cock later, eh?"*

I could feel the warmth of Delilah's breath against my chest as she giggled, shaking her head.

Once the body was removed, Tajah tapped the door with one knuckle three times, whispering the spell uttered to her earlier. The inside of the cabin moved around us, even with everyone inside.

Furniture rose above the floorboards as if from another dimension. Doors slid downward from the ceilings and settled on the walls that would lead to other rooms. The living room doubled as well, couches and chairs able to hold strong sturdy men and women appearing along with decorative blankets and throws.

Large widows, a fireplace, wardrobes, and closets all appeared faster than even the supernatural trained eye could keep up with. Decorated walls, blankets, and a large kitchen all appeared around us.

If you blinked one too many times, you could have missed it.

"Woah," Delilah breathed.

"There, fifteen bedrooms, fourteen bathrooms, clothing, food, drinks, and a medical room. I think that covers it," Tajah said, patting her hands.

"My, your power has grown," Bram said with pride in his voice. "I never thought you would have grown so much since–"

Tajah smirked. "Yes, well. Things change when you find your second chance, now don't they?"

Beretta stepped from the shadows, her hand interlacing with Tajah's, and licked Tajah right up the cheek. Her tail had also wrapped around her waist, and Locke rolled his eyes.

"You felines and that tail. It's rather disgusting."

"You just wish you had an appendage long enough to do anything with," Beretta purred.

Sizzle snorted, covering his mouth with a balled fist. "Oh shit, she got you!" He pointed to Locke in laughter.

Delilah smiled, her fingers rubbing my skin as she watched everyone laugh and speak with one another. "It's nice to see everyone back together. Like one big family," Delilah said.

I released a contented hum to show my agreement. I pressed my cheek against her forehead, feeling the warmth of her skin.

Bram chuckled, rubbing his hand up and down his leg. "Thank the goddess for that, Tajah. And I believe you have surpassed the master now. We should hold a ceremony. Like back at the academy."

"No way." Tajah waved her hand in dismissal. "Those were so lame. Like 'here is your cloak, don't go set anything on fire now!'" The room laughed while Tajah made jokes about Bram being a professor until Delilah let out a whimper.

Her body jerked, her claws descended into my thigh, and she let an ear-piercing scream that had the entire room grabbing their ears.

"Make it stop!" Delilah's forearm snapped, piercing the skin. Instead of it rearranging into a longer version of itself, it stayed broken, so she felt the pain for that much longer.

Journey grabbed Delilah by both wrists. My heart pounded hard in my chest seeing her grab the broken one. Journey's eyes glowed bright blue, almost white, and Delilah's screams stopped, her eyes closed, and a delightful sigh escaped her lips.

The pain was gone, and Delilah's body fell limp in my arms.

"What did you do to her?" I panicked, cupping my mate's cheek. "Is she okay?"

Delilah laid still, her lips parting. The soft pants of her sweet smelling breath brushed against my cheek. Her eyes fluttered open and sparkled, and I swore she could smile with them.

"Shit, Sunshine, don't do that to me," I pleaded.

Journey backed away, her hands still raised in surrender. Grim wasn't far, standing behind his mate, with both hands on his mate's shoulders.

"I just put her wolf to sleep, at least, I think that's what I did." She wiggled her nose as she gazed at Delilah. "I did what the Moon Goddess told me to do. Selene wants her wolf to rest before she forces her to shift. Her wolf is suffering from PTSD, but Delilah's body needs to shift."

The room muttered amongst themselves.

Anaki and Bones stood behind the couch. Out of all the brothers here, Delilah was closest to them. Anaki was gripping the couch cushions with his claws, the stuffing almost pouring from the brand new couch. He tried to touch Delilah, but I pulled her away.

Delilah snorted, her body too weak. Her broken arm slapped my shoulder, and she screamed in agony.

"I'm okay," she whispered to Anaki.

Anaki shook his head. His hair was a mess. I knew I was being a bastard, but fuck she was hurting, and she was mine. I had to take care of her the best way I could and that was not by having some other male intervene. It's not like anyone could do anything for her besides Journey.

I growled at him again.

"I know man, I'm sorry." Anaki backed away, holding his hands up. "As long as you let me dance with her later."

Delilah smiled, nodding her head.

I think fucking not.

Bones examined my mate's protruding bone but dared not to touch it, for both my sake and Delilah's. It was trying to heal, the shards rounding, bending inwards, only to revert back to its previous broken form.. He ached to examine it further, but at least he was smart about what the mating bond could cause.

"There isn't much I can do," he muttered to Delilah. "We can just make you comfortable. If I try and push it back together, it's going to break again, you're in the middle of a shift. Its best to leave it alone." Bones nodded to Delilah, and I held onto her a little tighter.

But, they all loved her, not as much as me. They cared for her. Saw her as family. Just like Journey. I couldn't tell them to just leave.

"There is a reason your wolf doesn't want to shift," Journey whispered to the both of us.

Journey and I looked at each other.

"It involves the both of you, of your past lives. With each other."

Delilah's lips parted.

"It isn't a happy ending, your past life. And if you want everyone to leave, so I can share it with you both alone, we can do that." Journey reached out to Delilah's hand, taking it softly in hers. She rubbed it tenderly.

Immediately, Delilah shook her head.

"I'm okay to share it with everyone," Delilah said. "I think I would want to share it with my whole family." She sniffed, looking around the room. "If that is okay with you, Hawke?"

She rolled her head backwards, her big blue eyes staring up at me so innocently like she hadn't pulled a heart out of her ex-husband's chest earlier.

I blew a puff of air out of my lips, blowing away the hair from her forehead.

"Why are you so okay with sharing something that might be so sad?" I asked.

"Because I know what happened. You saw me lying dead on the floor in that cabin," she whispered. *"That's why you snapped earlier. Why you wouldn't let me leave with Shane."*

I gritted my teeth, pulling Delilah into the crook of my arm, and gave her a searing kiss. Yips of laughter and "get a room" took over the cabin.

Delilah snorted, wincing when I accidentally moved her arm. I gently pulled away, holding her arm delicately and making sure not to harm it again.

"How do you see that?" I shook my head. "How did you know—"

"It's like, I saw what you saw. A dream, but not. And when you opened your eyes, I knew my idea was really stupid. And I couldn't leave you. But I still want to save that girl that saved me," she added. *"I also need to know more. More of this story. Why I died, why we didn't make it. And will we make it now?"*

A tear fell down her cheek.

I held her tighter, my own emotions bursting forth from my soul.

She would fucking make it because this was our second damn chance.

Journey continued to sit on the floor, on her knees, waiting patiently. The rest of the room waited as well. Anaki was like a damned golden retriever. He should have been a damned wolf, but I guess a golden dragon would have to do for him. He blinked repeatedly, shuffling closer until Tyr snarled loudly for him to back away.

"I have an idea of what our story may be." I patted my leg. "But I would like to understand it from the priestess herself. And I think we would all benefit from it, don't you all think?" I looked around the room.

Everyone nodded, taking places in various spots to get comfortable. Even Bram, who had taken it upon himself to wash the dried blood with the help of Beretta and Tajah.

Locke leaned by the doorway, speaking to Bear about packing away Shane's body. Sizzle and a few others were ordered to gather the other bodies and ready them for burning.

The room was now smaller, more intimate, and the story would be passed along later during a debriefing meeting. It would be held when this whole damned ordeal was over so the rest of the brothers of the Iron Fang would understand the history of how second chances came to be.

Journey smiled and clapped her hands excitedly and then placed them prettily like a child on her lap. She looked toward her mate for his nod of approval, like she needed it.

He ate out of the palm of her hand.

"Okay, just know the joyous part of the story doesn't come until the end of tonight," Journey explained.

CHAPTER FORTY-TWO

Delilah

"You got this." I squeezed Journey's hand, which suddenly began shaking.

She was so sure of herself just moments ago, but now she reverted to the night I first met her when I entered Grim's apartment. So unsure of herself, frightened and wary.

"Just talk to me and Hawke. Forget they are even here."

Journey smiled gratefully, her hand resting on mine. I tried to ignore the bone protruding from my skin. My stomach churned at the sight of it, but I kept my gaze glued to Journey.

Hawke's fingers lightly glided over my skin, as if afraid of the pain that might burst forth from beneath if he stopped. But the nerves were fragmented, broken by another, stronger force. I only felt the soft touches of warmth and tingles of the bond we shared.

"I don't have a lot of detail, just what needs to be told," Journey said. "But, the attempt to give shifters, all supernaturals, a second chance"—Journey looked to Tajah and Bram—"at mates had been tried a long time ago. But it ultimately failed." Journey licked her lips and broke her gaze with me to find Grim's.

Grim knelt beside her, the sound of his hand running along her back providing a soft, soothing rhythm.

"There was a wolf of the lower warrior class. You, Hawke. Your soul, anyway. He was rejected after a female alpha saw him hunting. You never met her. She chose another, but you felt the bond break and left the realm. You took refuge in a human village and felt a bond with a human woman and fell in love."

I smiled at her words and squeezed Hawke's hand.

My mind was weaving a tapestry of colors, sounds, and textures that I never could have dreamed up. The market was filled with the sound of merchants haggling and the chill of the fog as it descended over the area.

The horses cautiously made their way around a stranger in strange clothing, their hooves squelching in the mud with each step. He wore no tunic, his hair wasn't tied back like most of the men in the marketplace, and his beard was unkempt.

Women stayed away, and the men stared at him in disgust. The bags he carried were large, but it did not deter his gate as he walked through the market. The village people stayed away, not even offering him food for money or trade.

Yet there was one woman with blonde hair that walked up to him with no fear and stood in front of him with such confidence. The stranger stared at her in confusion until he looked around him to be sure that it was in fact him the woman was speaking to.

Journey laughed, patting her leg. "Hawke, I think you really tried not to get involved with Delilah then, too, but you could not deny the connection. The pull, the longing you had for her was just as strong as it is now. She was your little ray of sunshine then, as she is now." Journey leaned back into Grim's arms. "And Delilah, you obviously had a pull toward him back then."

"But of course." I rubbed my hand up and down Hawke's arm.

"There was a bond for them, even back then?" Bram asked.

Journey nodded. "There was."

Everyone except Journey, Grim, Hawke and I stared at one another in confusion.

"And then one night, Hawke bit her and claimed her. It was his instinct to do so. Delilah's soul didn't mind, obviously. They were in love."

A flash of the past awakened another memory. Hawke was biting me on my shoulder. I felt a rush of heat between my legs and pressed my thighs together to muffle my desire.

Hawke's rumble in his chest could be felt on my back, his hand tightening on my thigh.

"I can see it all, too," he said. *"I'm down for a reenactment later."*

I clamped my teeth down on my lip, trying to muffle the sound of my burning desire.

I am all down for some role play.

"But then, eventually, she got sick," Journey continued. "Her body got warm. She couldn't keep her food down. The town's doctor couldn't help her, they even banished her for fear of spreading disease. Hawke was outraged her own kind wouldn't help her, so he did the only thing he could do—take her through the veil and back to his own kind."

Journey's words filled the hushed room, creating an uneasy atmosphere.

"As they traveled, her smell changed. She was turning, like him."

Locke uncrossed his arms, pushed away from the doorframe, and came closer to the group. He had always been more distant, more stand-offish than the rest, but now, he seemed more interested than anyone.

"When they arrived, the pack seemed to understand what was happening. First, they were angry that Hawke bit her, they were afraid they would bring the Council's wrath, but with the change of her smell, they hoped they would keep the secret."

"They took them both in, put them in an empty cabin. The pack doctors told them she was shifting but immediately knew that the shift wouldn't be completed because her bones were not healing fast enough."

There were no more visions coming to me. I did not see myself breaking, dying in a cabin. And thanked the goddess for that.

Anaki's icy hand sent a chill through my body as he tenderly rubbed my ankle with his thumb. He held my gaze with eyes that brimmed with tears, as if he could sense the suffering of my past life. But honestly, I was doing okay.

I felt sad for her, but she was another person, another path that my soul had taken. I was here on another journey, in another time and space. If I had not died, if I had bonded, then my soul would not have gained the family that I had standing around me.

My soul had undertaken many lives, maybe more than this one that Journey told me about, but it was now that I knew my journey would end in happiness.

Maybe that was why I wasn't crying.

Hawke held me tighter, his fingers intertwining in the back of my hair and pulling my head back.

Such softness in his eyes, I'd never seen; he was almost unrecognizable from the big baddy I first met.

"The woman died shortly after," Journey concluded. "Along with the wolf of a broken heart."

"But why?" Locke snapped, breaking the solemn atmosphere. "Why the fuck did she, Delilah, have to die and suffer? They were following a bond, they were–"

Locke's face grew red with anger. As his chest moved with his wide arm movements, his satchel opened and the contents inside spilled out onto the floor with a thud.

Journey winced as Locke's voice grew louder.

I managed to get myself partly up, my body tense as I tried to protect Journey, but the men in the room had already sprung up to contain Locke.

"Let's calm down." Bones grabbed Locke by the forearm. "We aren't quite done with the story. Let's hear her out, alright. You're scaring Journey."

Journey curled into a ball, the sound of Grim's purring vibrating against her chest.

Journey had enough trauma from her past to last ten lifetimes, and my own anger rose in my chest.

My lip curled into a snarl. It was painful, and I felt my wolf wake from a deep slumber.

"It's okay," Journey's voice shook. "I'm alright."

"Fucking shit, sorry." Locke backed away, turning to walk out the door. "I need to leave. I... I don't need to be here. Just tell me about it later. I'm sorry Journey, I–"

Journey stood, tripping over Grim's large boot, but Grim held her to his chest and let Locke step out the door. "Let him go," he growled. "He needs to cool off."

Journey whimpered, shaking her head. "But he needs to hear." She looked up at him.

"At the briefing. He's got some things to sort out," Bones said, moving a cushioned chair next to Journey. "Now, sweet thing, come sit and tell us why things didn't work out for our couple so long ago."

Grim rolled his eyes at Bones, pulling Journey into his lap in the nearby chair.

Journey again looked to Grim for guidance and waited for the room to go silent again.

Hawke pulled me close to his chest, his musky scent surrounding me. He made sure not to move my arm, carefully cradling it.

Bones draped some gauze wrapping over it, nodding to Hawke as if to let him know it was to settle my unease. Hawke still shuffled me away once it was laid upon my arm, like he was perturbed that someone else was trying to take care of me.

Silly wolf.

Hawke and I were in our own world while Journey explained to the others how our lives ended. I hadn't returned the bite and completed the bond. It was incomplete. I was still human, and I didn't understand how to complete the one-sided bond. And Hawke, well, he was too angry to speak or pray to the goddess to complete it. Why would he do such a thing and seek help from a deity who he thought betrayed him?

But all along, she was trying. The goddess was trying to fix all the broken souls, to give them another chance—but she failed. She couldn't get through to Hawke, and it all ended in a bloody mess.

Hawke and I were the first human and wolf bonding. And the goddess was so saddened by the result, she didn't try again until one day a human came to her.

Journey started a chain reaction that led us all together again.

As a child, she prayed to that *big giant rock* for a better life, for someone to love her, and now here we all are.

All of us getting second chances.

Who would have thought?

Anaki nudged Bones, who muttered, "See three of them got their shot. I'm going to pray every night now. What about you?"

Bones rubbed the back of his neck. "Don't see how it couldn't hurt. That moon on her head"—Bones pointed between Journey's eyes—"was enough for me."

Anaki scampered up to Bear, who had his arms crossed and a stern expression on his face as he surveyed the room. His black tee was tight against his body, and his chest hair was visible through it, with a beaten human's skull laying on his shirt.

It was kind of morbid the more I looked at it. I mean, shouldn't it be a bear skull now that I knew he was a bear shifter?

"What about you?" Anaki pointed his long slender finger into Bear's chest. "You gonna ask for help now?"

Bear scoffed, pushing Anaki away. "I'll do it when I'm damned ready. Get your scaly hands off, dragon."

I barked out in laughter, but instead of feeling numb like I had been, a shot of pain went down my arm.

Hawke yelped in pain as my claws dug back into his leg.

"We should probably take her outside." Journey gazed out the window.

Despite the darkness of night, it was still illuminated by the moonlight that shone through the gaps between the large redwoods.

"Shouldn't she eat first?" Hawke muttered, putting one arm gently under my legs and the other behind my back.

He cradled me to his chest, and Anaki helped move my arm, so it laid on my stomach.

"That steak will hold her over," Bram said, grabbing bags from the closet. "I'll bring some clothing for when she shifts back."

"She won't last long with her shift, not as long as Journey," Tajah said, opening the door to lead us out. "Not with that pup in there, she'll be too tired after the events today."

I raised my good hand and delivered a sharp slap to Hawke's chest in surprise. A crack sounded in the room, leaving a sharp feeling in the air.

There was no breathing, the silence deafening in the room, and the grip that Hawke had on my body grew tighter.

She did not say what I think she did, did she?

That just couldn't be possible. There was no way that could happen! Each day I took preventatives during my heat, during all the times we had sex. I did everything I was told to do to prevent a pregnancy.

A baby? We were going to have a baby? A pup?

Hawke's heart reanimated, his heart thundering louder in his chest. Everyone in the room took slow and steady steps away from him, taking their places amongst the walls of the room.

"What..." Hawke whispered. "Did you say?"

Tajah audibly gulped and looked at Journey. "Did he not know?"

Journey shook her head. "Guess not?"

Grim pulled Journey behind him, a growl radiating from him for Hawke to stand down.

With a slight pivot, Hawke pointed himself and me toward Bram, who was stumbling backwards.

Bram licked his lips, his hands shaking in front of him. I don't know if he looked frightened before he got the crap beaten out of him by Shane, but I bet I had a feeling it wasn't like this.

Hawke's face was contorted in rage. His face was red, and there was a visible throbbing in his neck veins.

But was he really mad? Or was he just worried?

I ran my good hand gently over my stomach in a soothing gesture.

I never thought about having a child. I never thought about having a family. I always made sure not to get pregnant with Shane. The thought of having his baby was downright disgusting.

But Hawke's?

A muscular, tattooed, completely out-of-place man cradling a tiny bundle with a baby inside sounded so perfect. Feeding them a bottle, changing a diaper, pushing them in a stroller.

In all honesty, it sounded sexy as hell and turned me on a little.

I couldn't wait to watch our son or daughter grow up. I wanted to watch Hawke teach them how to ride a bike. Color funny pictures for all of their uncles and aunts and be loved not just by their mommy and daddy, but their whole family at the club.

Tears flooded my eyes at the thought of having a little baby. Hawke's baby.

Hawke kept me in his arms, walking slowly toward Bram. His growling echoed through my body, vibrating, shaking me down to my soul. It was so loud, I worried my wolf would wake too soon.

Bram continued to back away until his body hit the back of the couch. He had nowhere else to go. He braced himself—waiting.

Hawke's hands were full, yet Bram was downright terrified.

Surely, Bram didn't think Hawke would hurt him, would he?

Moving my fingers cautiously up Hawke's chest, I trailed them over his piercings and up his neck, feeling the bumps of the metal along the way. We were still in the same white terrycloth towels, and lucky me, I got to feel all of his skin until I finally cupped his cheek.

Once we were just a step away from Bram, I whispered in his ear, "Daddy."

Hawke paused, his eyes widening.

I tried to hold back laughter. I amused not only myself but also everyone in the room. The tension had disappeared. They all watched, and I waited for the rest of the room to laugh along with me, but maybe they knew better.

"Can you believe you're going to be a daddy?" I asked.

Hawke broke his gaze from Bram. Tajah reached for him and pulled him out of the line of fire.

Hawke shook his head, his forehead resting on me, letting out a breath.

"No, I never have. I didn't think I would have a mate." He swallowed heavily, sitting down in the chair next to the sofa.

He placed his hand on my stomach, rubbing it tenderly.

"How did this happen? I gave you the preventatives. This... How?"

"Mistakes happen, and you know Bram has been weak. Plus, when should women ever really trust a male to use contraceptives, I mean really?" I smiled, placing my hand on top of Hawke's, who was still rubbing my stomach tenderly.

He scoffed. "Yeah, I should have known."

I nuzzled into his neck. "It will be great. This little pup will have the biggest family to love him, too. I bet he will ride his first bike by three, huh?"

Hawke let out a bark of laughter. "If you think we are raising our pup around a bar, you are insane."

I raised an eyebrow at him. "The Iron Fang bar is the safest place. You said so yourself."

Hawke nodded. "I said that, didn't I?" He paused for a moment. "Are you okay with it this soon? I feel like I just got you to myself."

His thumb continued to rub circles around my stomach.

"In case you haven't noticed, I think we have a large pool of babysitters to pull from."

Anaki waved excitedly in the corner.

Hawke rolled his eyes and sighed loudly.

He used his finger to push back a strand of hair away from my cheek and trailed his fingers down to the curve of my breast.

"I hope our baby enjoys sharing because I cannot give these up. Maybe they will let me have a snack, too."

My face reddened, and I snorted a giggle.

"Everything okay now?" Journey whispered from across the room. "Because the goddess says you need to come out now. Your wolf is all convinced to come out!"

Hawke sighed heavily, kissing my cheek once more and rubbing my belly one last time. "It won't hurt the baby?"

Journey shook her head. "No, the only time it is unsafe is when she is in the later part of her pregnancy like normal shifters, she says. Just the last month would be uncomfortable for her to shift."

Hawke, as well as the rest of the crew, took me outside. Everyone was in higher spirits except for Bram. He looked utterly defeated, but Tajah and Beretta stood by him, giving him words of encouragement, but even that did not bring him any more happiness.

I would have to speak with him later, but Journey was too busy trying to explain the process of how a shift feels and what I should expect turning from a human into a wolf.

Pain. Basically, more pain than I could ever imagine.

And Hawke wasn't happy about it. He was groaning, moaning on and on about how I had to do this twice. Which, technically, my soul was doing this twice, but this body was doing it once. I didn't remember the first time.

And now that our souls were bonded, I would never have to do it again. Our souls were completed, and that meant in the afterlife, we were to be together forever.

I purred in contentment, and my colossal beast of a biker sighed, dare I say, wistfully as he led me to the small clearing behind the cabin. It was encircled by our family of big burly bikers with their leather vests, hands on either their weapons or arms crossed over their chests.

They might look like they're tough, but I could see the faintest of smiles on their faces.

"I've got the camera." Anaki waved the camera in front of Bones.

Okay, except Anaki. Anaki did not look like a scary biker.

"Do you think Hawke will shift too so I can get a picture of them both?" Anaki asked.

Bones shook his head, rubbing his hand down his face. "They won't be able to run together. Not this time. First shifts are hard. Journey was the exception."

Anaki pouted. "Still want my picture."

Hawke settled me on his lap, his towel unraveled. Luckily, mine stayed in place, so my body didn't go on display like his already was. But I guess it wouldn't matter much longer.

"I think you are going to have to let me go, Daddy." I petted his cheek. "I don't think I can shift in your lap."

Hawke grunted, placing his hand on my face. The warmth of his hand started a purring competition between us, and the rest of the circle chuckled.

"Aw, fuck off," he snapped at them.

"It will be fine. Journey said it will be, and then we can go home," I smiled.

Hawke nodded. "Home would be nice."

I hummed and patted his shoulder with my good hand. "Now, why don't you go pry Locke away from behind that tree so he can join us, huh? We don't want to leave the big alpha man out."

Because if Hawke doesn't go now, I'm going to freak the fudge out.

Hawke sighed, giving me one quick kiss. He unfolded the towel, holding it up high so no one would see me naked, just yet, and kissed my stomach.

"I love you both, Sunshine. See you on the other side."

EPILOGUE

Hawke

"I can't!" she cried out, voice echoing into the empty bar.

I gripped her ass, my claws piercing the skin. Drops of blood dripped onto the bar while my other hand pushed her one leg closer to her head.

Fuck, I loved her like this, so exposed. Her pussy was open so damned wide, I could get my cock so fucking deep I swore was tickling her belly button.

Or hell, maybe I was rocking the pup to sleep.

Tyr shook his head. *"Ew, don't think about him right now."*

"You can too, Sunshine, fifth time's the charm."

I grunted. My sweat dripped between her breasts. Her beautiful tits were fuller, the pinkness around her tits darker. I dipped my head, trying to drink in as much as I could of her skin.

The sweetness of her body, along with the salt of her sweat, brought my senses roaring to life with happiness.

Shit, I didn't think it was possible to get any harder, but I think I just might.

"Hawke!"

Delilah, in a fit of confusion, waved her arm, trying to get a better grip. She grabbed the bar tap, pulling it until a cool stream of liquid poured on the floor.

"Shhhhhhit!" she hissed.

I pounded harder, moving her down the bar while her other leg wrapped around my waist. Her heel pressed into my back, urging me to continue and hell, I obliged. She looked so damn hot, so sultry with her flushed cheeks, damp hair sticking to her forehead.

Our bodies were covered with sweat, arousal, and alcohol. Taking body shots off your mate was the hottest damned thing I'd ever done, and I planned to do more of that later.

The idea popped in my head when my mate was sitting on the bar in front of me, eating whipped cream from a can. When she missed her mouth, I got to lick the corners, and fuck, licking other things off her sounded better, too.

So now the bar has been claimed. I'd licked her and fucked her right here on the bar, where everyone had their drinks at the end of every day.

I ripped my lips from her sweet tits. "Do you have any idea how much I've wanted to fuck you on this bar?"

"Not," she panted, "sanitary."

Didn't really fucking care. We paid off the sanitation grade inspector anyway.

More of her slick coated my shaft. I gritted my teeth in anticipation.

"Hold on, Sunshine, you're so close, I can feel you already milking my shaft, damn it."

She closed her eyes.

"No, no, look at me so I can see your eyes roll into the back of your head," I snapped.

Her eyes snapped open, and she sat on me and exposed her mark.

She knew what she was doing, showing my claim on her body. It made Tyr snarl, his pride radiating through both of us.

Delilah was ours.

The pup was ours.

Our mate's hand let go of the tap, and I grabbed her wrist, setting it above her head. The curve of her breast, the bend of her body. I wanted to savor it.

But right now, I was a greedy bastard.

My cock twitched, my knot expanding as I forced the base of my dick inside her with one large thrust, making us both gasp at the tight squeeze. She came undone, her one hand raking the sides of the bar.

I silenced both of our roars with a kiss, thrusting my tongue into her mouth as spurts of my come jetted into her body, coating her already seeded womb.

Fuck, if this wasn't the happily ever after I had always wanted, I didn't know what else I could have asked for.

Delilah's back rested on the bar. The fans blew a cool gust of air over us, evaporating the sweat and sending shudders of relief down our bodies. Our breaths were heavy and labored. Our foreheads met, and I could feel the drop of sweat trickling down my temple.

We said nothing as we enjoyed the afterglow. Well, as much as we could laying on the cold wood of the bar.

"I also used to daydream about you taking me on this bar." She let out a giggle. Her arms wrapped around my head, fingers running through my hair.

"I thought the same. After closing, I would go back to my room and think about ripping your clothes off and bending you over every table and showing everyone you belonged to me." I lifted my head and trailed kisses down her neck.

Her pussy pulsed. My cock felt the fluttering of her walls. Our bodies melded together in a passionate embrace that sent sparks of pleasure through us both, and we gasped in unison.

"I thought you sat outside my window after work," she whispered, using her claws to tickle my back.

I licked down her neck to her collarbone. "I may have done that, too."

My cock was on a damn mission to get another pup in there. I knew it was. Not that I would complain, but that was damned near impossible.

We'd been back for nearly a week. Her shift was flawless, painful, but flawless. It damn near killed me to watch from afar, but she shifted well.

She was in her wolf form for only ten minutes, enough for Tyr to shift and for Anaki to get his damn fucking picture. It was now framed and hung up at the back of the bar, just like Grim and Journey's picture.

Delilah's wolf was a sight to behold, with her golden locks and mesmerizing blue eyes. Her fur was thicker than the average wolf, the front of her body resembled that of a golden retriever. It did not reduce the intensity of her glare when Anaki attempted to pet her as if she were a domesticated animal.

Our wolves got to know each other. Tyr was ecstatic he could get a good whiff, and Delilah's wolf was equally happy. Delilah had yet to name her and suggested that I name her, but that was a tradition that was uncommon for shifters.

Shifters had never named our animals until humans came into the picture.

Journey started this new tradition of naming the animal part of us, and Delilah wanted to continue it. But me naming my mate's wolf? It seemed like a task too difficult to handle. I found it more stressful than picking a name for our pup.

Delilah's body relaxed as my knot slipped from her body. Come slid from her but the urge to shove it back inside her was gone. She was already with a pup, and the wastefulness Tyr used to see was no longer there.

"I need to clean you up," I muttered.

Delilah's eyes were fluttering shut as I lifted myself from her body.

Her leg was still pushed close to her head. She was fucking flexible as hell, and I loved it.

I wonder if she did gymnastics as a teenager.

I lowered her leg and motioned for her to stay as I hopped off the bar and warmed a rag with some water. I watched her, like a damned treat as she laid there. Her stomach was still mostly flat, but you could see it was already changing.

It was slightly rounded, and her breasts were faintly fuller. If I hadn't known she was pregnant, I would have thought my rough lovemaking would have been the culprit, but no.

I put a damn baby in her.

I was angry at first when I found out my mate was pregnant. She didn't consent to it, neither did I. I didn't think we were ready for something like that. I hadn't fully gained her trust back about not leaving again. She was thrust into our world, forced into a bond because of a sickness, and now she was also tied to me with a baby.

But she...accepted it.

And damn, it made me happy.

Because we made a *baby.*

Two parts of us made a baby.

I wrung out the warm towel, still staring at her body on the bar like a meal to be eaten. She giggled, covering her face with her hands. "Stop looking at me!"

I cleared my throat, trying my best not to look at her sexually. I had another mission, and that was to take care of my mate and not sport another raging boner.

I wiped between her legs, her folds, looking at every bruise, every bite and mark before it faded. Her healing abilities were just as strong as mine now and as much as I loved her being human and seeing my marks on her body after a good fuck, seeing her heal was satisfying, too.

I rinsed the rag, adding soap to it as well. She had her own soap she kept under the bar when she worked. Some girly smelling shit, it would get most of the sweat and sticky shit off of her. I wouldn't be able to wash her hair, but I would take care of that in the morning.

I hummed, washing between her toes, and she giggled, trying to pull away.

"How long is a pregnancy for a shifter?" Delilah asked as I helped her sit up.

"Four months." I pulled her up to sitting and handed her my shirt.

Her eyes widened. "Four months?" she squeaked. "That's it?"

"How long does a human pregnancy last?" I picked her up from the bar and cradled her in my arms and headed to the stairs.

"Wait, where are we going!" Her head peaking over my shoulder. "We gotta clean the bar. People eat there!"

"I know," I winked at her.

"Hawke! I'm serious!"

"I am too. I had my best meal yet there."

"Oh my god, you are terrible!"

I silenced her with a kiss as we came to the dormitories.

Obviously, the dormitory rules had been lifted if you were mated or you were pursuing your mate. There would be no casual dating, Locke was fervently clear on that. He didn't want a bunch of males or females coming back here and risking knowledge of supernaturals and the club.

"I'll take care of it. I'm just getting you to bed. You worked too much tonight."

Delilah remained quiet as we entered my room. Over the week since we had been home, I took her to her apartment, brought her things, and made my little apartment more like a home. It wasn't ideal to have just a room and have to share a communal bathroom shower with the others, but we would have to make do. We were both shifters and staying in an area with humans was out of the question.

Schedules had been made for the showers, and Locke even hired Bear's old clan members to come in and do some renovations. We were going to see if we could get a small bathroom set up in our already small room.

But the closeness didn't bother Delilah. In fact, despite her overly elaborate upbringing, she was perfectly content with sharing a tiny room with a shared shower and space with her new family.

Thank fuck, because that was all we had right now. Until the land that Locke and Grim had set up was ready to go. One day we hoped that everyone would have their own cabin with their mates and their own families.

"Sunshine, I will get you settled and clean up the bar." I opened the door to our room.

It held a light blue comforter, better than the single sheet that used to lie in on the bed. Two pictures were gifted to us by Anaki. One of our wolves sitting together after her first shift and the other of our welcome home party the night we arrived back home. Flowers sat on the desk we'd brought over from her apartment. Her clothes hung on one side of the closet, while mine were on the other side.

Fully fucking domesticated.

It looked all homey and shit.

I loved it.

"But four months. Why four months?"

"How long do humans gestate?" I asked again, pulling the blanket to her chin.

"Nine full months." Delilah groaned.

"Fucking shit, that sounds awful. Good thing you don't have to do that."

"Because the hormones, that would suck for all of us," Tyr whined.

Delilah bobbed her head. "I guess if you put it that way. But, but... We don't even have a crib!"

I scoffed, laying her naked body on the bed. "The pup will sleep in my arms. Why humans have cribs is beyond my understanding."

She opened her mouth to speak, but I closed it with two fingers.

"We have many things to discuss later. My mate needs to sleep, and I need to go clean up our mess, and I have a meeting."

Delilah sat up, messing up the covers I used to tuck her in. I growled, straddling her waist, and pushed her back into the bed. She laughed, trying to wiggle away.

"A meeting about what? Can I come?"

I pinned her with a kiss, wrapping her again in the covers. "It is about the woman who saved you. Switch was able to break into Shane's phone, as well as the security system at the mansion."

Delilah's eye brightened. "Is she alive?"

I nodded. "She is, and we are sending men first thing in the morning. But I need you to sleep."

"But I wanna go to the meeting!" she argued, trying to wiggle out of the cocoon.

I growled, pinning her with my body.

"No, you will stay. I feel how exhausted you are, the pup, and you need rest. I don't want stress put on either of you. I promise to tell you everything in the morning."

With that, she yawned, and I tilted my head in triumph.

Her nostrils flared as a low growl escaped her, her eyes narrowing in anger.

"Trust me, Sunshine. I'll get her out of there and whoever else needs help."

"If I wasn't so tired, I'd argue some more. But I know you guys will do your best." Her eyes slowly blinked.

"Good thinking on orgasming her out," Tyr snorted.

"It was a hardship."

"I heard that," Delilah said with a yawn.

Damnit. She was getting good at that.

I gave Locke an affectionate pat on the back. The cigarette flew from his mouth, but the malicious grin on his face never left. The ground was covered in blood, and yips and yowls of laughter echoed in the basement.

Locke, the sadistic fucker, he would be sporting a hard-on right now, if he could. But right now, he just stared at the drain while the sprays of water pushed the dark blood down the pipes.

The pieces of Shane were thrown into a wheel barrow that would be taken to be burned. Except for his head, which was being kicked around on the tiled floor, of course, because I meant what I said. His head was going to hang on our wall where I could stare at the fucker every day.

"Get anything?" I leaned over Switch's makeshift desk. He looked up at me with his thick glasses, pushing them up with his finger.

"Yeah, Shane's technology was laced with magic. I couldn't get past a firewall because of it. Once Grim tortured Shane enough, he squealed that the technology was under control of magic. Tajah and Bram looked at it and broke the connection so I could get in."

Grim stepped out of the shadows in the corner and grinned smugly while wiping his hands with a dirty rag. His mate was sitting nearby with headphones on, reading a book. He never let her out of his sight, but he also made sure she never saw or heard anything he ever did.

"And the girl is indeed alive?" Locke asked, coming out of his trance. He crossed his arms and stood beside me.

Locke's outburst from the other day hadn't been brought up again. We could only assume it was part of one of his psychotic break episodes. A word, a phrase, bringing up any sort of pain dealing with the Moon Goddess, innocent people, pups, or humans always got him going.

Switch dramatically pushed the enter button with his finger and brought up a live feed of a woman in a room meant for a criminal. A single toilet, sink, and cot with the bare minimum for a blanket and pillow.

Concrete walls surrounded her. There was only a single door leading into the room. One way in, one way out, with a small slot on the bottom of the door to insert food.

She was sitting up, rocking back and forth on the cot, her lips moving, but we didn't have any sound. Poor thing looked half-starved and was so damn small with a head full of wild curls and glasses too big for her face. She may as well pass as a child.

"Is she a child?" Switch asked, turning to all of us.

I scratched my beard. "Nah, don't think so. Delilah said it was a woman. Maybe she's short, and the picture is grainy. But we need to get in there. But I worry about Idris being there. We need to do a simple extraction. We can't send a whole team in right now."

A lot of members were weak now. Traveling wasn't advised by Bones. We needed to stay together as a pack, especially after the fight with Idris had left a lot of them wounded. They were still healing.

And I wasn't leaving Delilah, not with my pup inside her.

"Agreed," Locke grunted, pulling out his phone. He tapped out a message. "I've got a few ideas. We can send a small stealth crew in the morning and—"

"Hey, Pres, where do you want me to put the head?" Bear was holding Shane's head by the scalp, trying not to get any more blood on his clothes.

Bear's expression showed his conflicting feelings of pride and disgust as he gazed upon the severed head. And when he turned, his gaze hit Switch's screen, Bear's heart stopped in an instant.

Literally stopped because we could no longer hear his heart.

The screen was paused and zoomed-in on the woman's freckled face. Bear dropped the head, pushed Switch out of the chair, and banged his fist on the computer table. The screen flickered, losing the image, and Bear growled.

"Who is she?" Bear asked.

We all stood back from the table, and Journey perked her head up from her book and took off her headphones. She pushed her chair away from the table, and Grim followed behind her and came to watch the growing heated scene.

"Well?!" Bear's voice reverberated, filling the room with its intensity as he glared at us.

"She's our next target," Locke said, fumbling with a new cigarette. "Gonna send a squad in to extract her."

"I want in." Bear turned his massive body away from us and headed up the stairs.

"The fuck was that?" Tyr muttered, perking up his ears.

Journey tilted her head and peeked at the computer screen which flashed the girl's sad face back on the screen. She blinked a few times and looked back up at the stairs where the grumpy Bear was disappearing.

Tyr snorted. *"Grumpy bear."*

For fuck's sake.

"Oh," Journey said. Her fingers playing with her lips. She turned to Grim, who shook his head and grabbed her by the waist and led her to the stairs.

"Wait, what happened?" Switch rose from the floor, fixing his glasses. "Grim, wait, where are you going?"

Grim looked back, nodding us all off. "Home." He wrapped his arm around his mate and trudged up the stairs, leaving us to clean up the mess.

After I helped clean up the mess, packed the head, and cleaned up the bar like I promised Delilah, it was nearly sunrise.

I closed the door, seeing my mate still wrapped up in our new nest of blankets—a permanent nest. It gave Tyr a sense of calm, knowing we would not have to remake a new nest for some time.

It was stressful recreating a third nest in just a month's time, but well worth it for a longer term stay.

The quick shower I took to clean my body from the splatters of Shane's blood would hold me over so we could bathe later. I had come to enjoy our time in the showers, touching but unable to fuck.

Stupid damn rules, but it was the greatest foreplay.

Cleaning her, taking care of her. I never thought we would have these moments together. And soon, her belly would grow. I would watch her body change, grow round with our pup, and then we could clean our pup together.

My heart warmed to that, sliding into the covers. She rolled over to me, seeking my warmth, and nuzzled into my neck.

My hand grazed down to her ass, pulling her hips close to my cock. I was already hard, and I needed her warmth to just to tease me.

She hummed, and I felt a smile on her lips. "I need you," she sleepily said.

She wasn't coherent. She could be dreaming right now, but we're mates, right?

It's fine.

I gripped my cock, easing the head near her slit. The piercing tickled her clit. She raised her leg over my hip, and I groaned at the willingness of her body, even in sleep.

Shit, she felt amazing, and was already wet for me.

She hummed, her hips pushing toward my dick, and I slipped inside her. I didn't want to fuck her. I only wanted to be close. I wanted to fall asleep inside her.

I slowly rocked my hips, cupping her ass, letting my cock take long, deep loving movements inside her tight cunt. And then I stilled, letting my teeth sink into her mark.

So. Fucking. Good.

Her head rested into my neck, her breath evened, and I heard a soft snore while I let my cock rest inside her pussy.

She was mine.

Delilah was all fucking *mine.*

"Celeste," I whispered into her ear, licking at her wound. Delilah didn't move, too deep in her slumber.

Her wolf name fit her perfectly, as she resembled a star from the heavens amidst the hellish realm of earth.

MORE BOOKS BY VERA

Iron Fang MC Series

Grim

Hawke

Bear

Coming soon

More to Come

Under the Moon Series

Under the Moon

Clara and Kane's Story

The Alpha's Kitten

Charlotte and Wesley's Story

Finding Love with the Fae King

Osirus and Melina's Story

The Exiled Dragon
Creed and Odessa's Story

Under the Moon: The Dark War
Clara, Kane, Jasper and Taliyah's story

His True Beloved: A Vampire's Second Chance
Sebastian and Christine's Story

Alpha of her Dreams
Evelyn and Kit's Story

The Broken Alpha's Princess
Melody and Marcus' Story

Twinning and Sinning From Mutts to Mates
Dax, Dimitri, and Seraphina's Story

<u>Under the Moon: God Series</u>

Seeking Hades' Ember
Hades and Ember's Story

Lucifer's Redemption
Lucifer and Uriel's Story

Poseidon's Island Flower

Poseidon and Lani's Story

Under the Moon: The Promised Mates of Monktona Wood Orcs

Thorn

Coming Soon

Valpar

Coming Soon

Sugha

Coming Soon

Visit authorverafoxx.com for updates and future books!

Vera Foxx | Facebook